I0818323

"Kowvis, control yourself," Eilwyn ordered. "There will be no bloodshed."

"Don't be so sure," Hasefi's father growled. "Next time I come, it might be with the full force of the Tribe."

The wolves that had surrounded him and Hasefi stepped closer, forcing her to shuffle towards her father.

"Do not threaten us in our own home, *lynx,*" Eilwyn growled, her lips drawing back to show the tips of her fangs. "If I were not already preoccupied with a more pressing matter, I'd have my wolves throw you into our cage-den."

"Why not do it anyway?" Kowvis asked. "See what that abomination would do with this excuse for a creature."

Anger snapped Hasefi out of her shock.

"He's *not* an abomination," she growled at him. "He's a better wolf than you or any others here!"

"No wonder lynxes fail to show formality," Kowvis mocked. "They don't even teach their kits manners!"

"How about I teach you some manners, you cowardly mutt!" Hasefi hissed.

Kowvis lunged towards her and she was prepared to meet him, but a flash of black darted between them, sending Kowvis stumbling with blood trailing from his muzzle. Hasefi blinked in surprise as another lynx stood before her, this one fitted in black armor so complete even his eyes were hidden.

Barks and snarls broke out in the ravine, but before it could escalate further, Eilwyn's voice rang with sharp clarity.

"Enough!"

Silence enveloped the bristling group. Eilwyn aimed a glare at Kowvis until he slunk back a pace away.

"Emperor," the white wolf growled, turning her icy stare on him. The black-clad lynx had moved protectively to his side. "Leave now and do not return. Your false accusations will no longer be tolerated and any lynx on our side of the River will be chased off or taken prisoner."

"Don't think this is over," the Emperor snarled, unfazed by the warning note in her tone. "We know what you've done and we will have justice."

Eilwyn offered no response, instead turning to a wolf in tough black armor and murmuring into their ear. When the white wolf padded away, the black-clad wolf advanced. Hasefi noticed that there was a black paw on her chest, like Kowvis's, only visible when the moonlight hit it a certain way.

"We will escort you and your kind off our land, Emperor," she said shortly.

"We have more honor than you," the Emperor hissed back. "But, if an escort makes you feel better, then so be it."

The black-clad wolf proved to have more self-control than Kowvis and said nothing as she led the way out of the ravine. Hasefi didn't move, bound by her purpose to save her friend.

Just as another black-clad wolf started to usher her forward, a series of barks and angry howls broke out farther in the ravine. Before Hasefi could figure out what was happening, she was nose-to-nose with the black-furred face of her beloved companion.

"Kolahn," she gasped.

He responded with a whimper, his jaws bound by a glowing yellow tendril.

"I'm going to get you out of here," she promised.

His amber eyes looked back with deep misery as if he'd accepted his fate to end with the Clan he so foolishly tried to protect.

"A black wolf?" Hasefi heard her father gasp to no one in particular. "I thought you said they were gone!"

"This is none of your concern," Kowvis intervened before turning towards Kolahn. "Back!" he snapped, giving Hasefi's friend a hard shove. Anger rose within her and she was prepared to draw upon a strength that lay deep within, but a voice stopped her.

Don't, it said. *There's nothing you could do now that you wouldn't regret.*

But I can't leave him here! she protested.

TERENMORO

The wolves will keep him alive for now. He has raised suspicion; they will try to get more information from him.

Hasefi hesitated, staring after Kolahn as he was shoved back into the ravine.

Follow my brother, Hasefi.

It took all the willpower Hasefi could muster to obey. Every part of her screamed in protest as she tore her gaze away from where Kolahn had disappeared so she could join the two lynxes and the group of six wolves that flanked them. She hardly noticed as the wolves surrounded them so tightly she was forced to walk with her fur brushing her father's armor.

Kolahn, you sunblind, selfless, stupid furball! I swear I'm going to cuff your ears until they're numb when I get you back!

Hasefi felt physically ill. She wanted nothing more than to explain the situation to her father and his companion, hoping desperately that they might offer a way to help, but she figured trying to speak to them with the wolves around would only make things more difficult. So, she followed in silence, trying to conjure a plan she could put before her father as they moved along the recently dried up stream leading out of the ravine.

He was angry with them, she thought. *Hopefully it won't be hard to convince him to help me. But I'm not sure if I liked his reaction when he saw Kolahn.*

Hasefi replayed the events in her head, trying to experience them in a calmer mindset. But she was still torn two ways. Though every fiber of her being urged her to rescue her friend, her head whirled with the shock she had accidentally stumbled upon one of her parents.

Could he really be my father?

The dried streambed led to a vast river that cut the forest into two. Hasefi guessed the stream had once fed the river, but it held nothing more than the odd, opaque puddle and a path of stones and pebbles that reflected the faint moonlight.

Just a quarter moon ago, a landslide had destroyed the place Hasefi had been staying with Kolahn. It hadn't been a random act of nature, though, and the thought that its destruction followed her even here added unease to the myriad emotions she was struggling with.

The escort led Hasefi and the other two lynxes upriver for a time. Wherever they were being led seemed to lie moons away and each paw step that took Hasefi further from Kolahn added more and more to her rising panic. So, she withdrew further into herself, diverting her attention to the presence that had urged her out of the ravine.

He generally spoke for the eight others that resided within her since listening to nine different opinions at once had proved utterly disorienting. But every now and then, one of the other voices came through, providing some useful tips or knowledge that the first couldn't offer.

Hasefi had lost her tribe nine moons ago, but they had found a way to return to her, even if only in spirit. They had guided her and given her strength since almost immediately after they had been killed, but she'd only recently helped unlock the full potential of their aid, allowing her to communicate directly with them, tap into their knowledge and skills, and summon strength beyond any lynx or even any black wolf.

Not even Kolahn knew about them, but not because she had decided to keep them secret. A lot had happened in the last moon involving near-death experiences that left both of them with visible evidence of their struggles. Alongside her permanently crippled foreleg, Hasefi bore fresh wounds that were the results of a wolven ambush preceding the devastating landslide. Now that the adrenaline of her situation was slowly passing, she was beginning to feel the effects of her injuries.

Sefonis, Hasefi said silently, summoning her uncle's presence to the forefront of her mind. *How can you be sure they'll keep Kolahn alive?*

I can't, he admitted. *But if Kolahn can prove he can be of aid, I believe that will be reason enough for the Lady to stall an execution.*

What if they don't believe him? What if they choose not to trust him?

If he can gain your trust, he can gain anyone's.

His words comforted her, lessening her urge to turn and charge back into the ravine. Knowing, as her uncle had warned, it would only result in a series of regretful actions helped, too.

Do you think my father will help? Hasefi asked him.

To her dismay, her uncle was silent.

The claw-shape of the moon had nearly hit its peak when the group broke away from the forest and came across the biggest waterfall Hasefi had ever seen. Its roar had increased with every step they'd taken towards it and now the sound was deafening. If she hadn't been so riddled with worry and confusion, she would have gazed at the spectacle in wonder, marveling as the water transformed into a mist that sparkled in the moonlight and soaked the luscious green clearing surrounding it.

The wolves continued to usher the lynxes towards the waterfall. A brief flash of fear jolted Hasefi from her mind as she wondered if they intended to drop them into the gushing water. Then, to her surprise, she glimpsed an opening behind the cascading waterfall that carved a space into the huge cliff-wall, allowing access to the forest on the other side of the river.

"Off you go," the black-clad wolf that had led the escort ordered curtly. "And remember the Lady's warning."

The Emperor and his companion offered no words in return and Hasefi did the same. In silence, she followed her father and the other lynx behind the waterfall, trying not to flinch as her fur was thoroughly soaked by the direct spray. By the time they left the slick rock and emerged onto the other side, she was drenched.

After giving her pelt a good shake, Hasefi glanced back at the wolves. They disappeared one by one into the shadows of the trees, with the lead wolf last to go. Her gaze bore into Hasefi's fur. Then she, too, turned and disappeared into the dark shadows of the forest.

"Hasefi."

She turned as her father spoke, forgetting for a moment about the troubles that had unintentionally led her to him. He had opened his helmet again, revealing eyes alight with affection and wonder. Without the pressure of wolves around, Hasefi was able to get a better look at him, seeing the subtle differences between him and her uncle. He certainly had Sefonis's sandy fur, but his eyes were green, not yellow, and his face was broader. Her instincts told her that he was bigger than Sefonis, but for some reason he and the black-clad lynx felt a lot smaller to her than they should be.

This is my father, she thought. *My* father. *It's really him.* He looked as awe-struck as she felt and she thought they might just stand there, staring in wonder, until the sun came up. But Hasefi noticed his delight was fading into concern as he took her in, his gaze lingering on her twisted foreleg. Not wanting to waste precious time explaining her disability, Hasefi recovered, reminding herself of her purpose. After a moment to ask Sefonis what her father's name was, she spoke.

"Garfonis," she began. "They have my friend."

Her father's expression shifted with confusion as he tried to make sense of her words. "The wolves have a lynx prisoner? Who?"

Hasefi shook her head. "No. It's Kolahn, the wolf that came to us."

Garfonis's confusion deepened, making the whiskers on his brow tremble as he frowned. "A wolf?"

Hasefi nodded eagerly. "I have to go back and help him. But I can't do it on my own."

Garfonis merely stared at her uncomprehendingly. Hasefi worked her jaw, not knowing what else to say.

"Knight Emperor." The other lynx spoke for the first time, his voice smooth. "Our land is not as secure as it once was."

"Yes, of course," Garfonis agreed, recovering from his bewilderment. "And the Highchief will want to hear of your arrival immediately," he added to Hasefi. "Come, let us return to the Tribe."

"But, Kolahn—"

"The Highchief will decide what to do," her father assured her, but his tone implied that he merely wanted to hush her.

Hasefi's mouth hung open as a protest rose within her, but she pushed it down and followed. *Having the support of a Highchief and their*

Chapter One

"My father?"

Questions swept through Hasefi's mind in a whirlwind of utter confusion. In front of her was a lynx in heavy silver plate, turned ghostly by the sliver of a moon above, with a tuft of black fur on the helmet that ran down to his neck and two more tufts on the ears. Wisps of black curled and stretched along his helmet, flowing over his shoulders, and down his back in beautiful, twisting shapes, like the patterns of the stars in the sky.

The armor resembled that of her uncle's. He had been killed nine moons ago, along with the rest of Hasefi's tribe. In a brief moment of bewilderment, she had mistaken this lynx to actually be her beloved uncle. Instead, he was someone she had thought she'd never meet.

My father.

There were so many things she wanted to say and ask, but she was conflicted with the reason she was there at all. She and this lynx stood in the entrance to a ravine which was home to what Hasefi knew was called the Clan of the Gray Wolf. Close behind her father stood one of their leaders, a wolf armored in pelts as pure white as her fur, her unusual blue eyes blazing with impatience and what seemed to be the same sense of overload Hasefi was experiencing. With the white wolf stood a bulkier wolf in silver plate with a black wolf's print on his chest. His face was twisted in a vicious snarl as he glared at Hasefi and her father as if eager for the command to sink his fangs into their hides.

Hasefi wasn't afraid of him or the other wolves that were beginning to surround them. She'd spent her life running from a version of their kind that was bigger and much scarier—until she managed to kill some of them, including the one that had taken her uncle's life right before her eyes.

Yet, neither her father nor these strange wolves that were so very different from her shadowy hunters were the reason Hasefi had ended up there in the first place. Deeper in the ravine, a wolf bearing resemblance to the monsters that had pursued her had been restrained by the Clan and moved out of sight. He, however, was not like the ones she had been running from. Instead, he was her friend and savior countless times over. And he was a stupid furball, so she'd come to save him from his own foolishness.

"Emperor," the white wolf, Eilwyn, spoke, her tone sharpened by irritation. "I advise you deliver your message quickly and remove yourself and this kit from our land."

"It can wait," the Emperor responded, his wide green eyes still on Hasefi. He was mirroring her shock and had raised the front of his helmet—revealing a sandy brown face so heartbreakingly similar to her uncle's—to get a better look at her. "Something else has come to my attention."

"Typical lynxes," the silver-armored wolf Hasefi knew was called Kowvis, spat.

Now her father moved his gaze to glare at the growling wolf. His face twisted with a kind of hate she'd never seen before, one fueled by something deeper than anger, making her uneasy.

"I'll be back," he warned, his voice low. "You will not get away with what you've done."

"Just because prey is running short on your side of the River doesn't mean you have to take it out on us," Eilwyn growled softly, stepping in front of the other wolf before he could retort.

"We do when your kind's scent is all over our land," the Emperor returned. Hasefi detected unsaid words and it seemed the silver-armored wolf did, too.

"You want a fight, is that it?" Kowvis snapped, moving out from behind his leader. "Come on, I'll give you a fight. I've been itching—"

Terenmoro

Wolfcat: Fading Light

Sam Ritchie

To Jael, my compassionate and stubborn friend, who is always by my side even during my most dumbfounding moments. You've been a sturdy support during these tumultuous times and, without you, I would not have become the man I am today.

tribe would be better, she pointed out to herself. *I didn't get to see much of the Clan, but there sure were a lot of wolves in there—more than the Pack had. I'll need a lot more help if I'm going to save Kolahn.*

Convinced that it wouldn't be long before she was back on her way to Kolahn, Hasefi allowed her mind to follow a different path as the three of them moved deeper into the forest and away from the cliff-face.

So, this is where we came from, right? Hasefi asked the presences in her mind. *The place our ancestors were trying to keep us from finding?*

Not exactly, Sefonis admitted. *We were leaving the Tribe.*

Surprise rippled through Hasefi. *Really? Why?*

Now is not the time, wee lass. You need to focus on what's at your paws. This tribe is not like our own.

I don't understand, Hasefi replied, confused by her uncle's sudden wariness.

They are numerous, many times bigger than us. And they have strict rules here. You will have to tread carefully.

Uneasiness spread through Hasefi. *Am I in danger?*

No. Just...don't assume anything.

Still confused by her uncle's warning, Hasefi tried to ask for further explanation, but he receded, leaving a sense of his own disquiet behind that added to hers. She realized her entire tribe had taken on a troubled silence which none were willing to break. Wanting answers, Hasefi tried a different path.

"Garfonis?"

"What is it?" he responded, turning an eager gaze on her.

"How come we were sent away?"

Her father hesitated, stopping for a moment as he searched the ground for an answer.

"The Highchief will be better able to answer any questions you have," he finally said, continuing ahead. Hasefi hesitated, unsatisfied by his answer but helpless to improve it. Stifling a sigh, she decided it would be best to just wait until she met the Highchief.

The forest they walked through grew denser. Towards the cliff, Hasefi could barely make anything out between the trees, but to her left, the trees opened welcomingly. There was a time Hasefi hadn't known what a forest was. It had taken her time getting used to it after spending moons surviving in the harsh conditions of the snowy mountains, but she'd eventually learned to love the trees. She found it strange to think she had actually lived among these trees, once.

Hasefi looked to the lynx that walked a pace behind them like a shadow. His armor prevented her from seeing his expression or even determining what color his fur was. If the armor didn't hug his body so tightly, he could have been a wolf in disguise for all she knew.

But he's just a keeper, she thought. *Like you were.* Her words brought forth one of her tribemates who had once donned the same armor as Garfonis's companion did. However, he'd recently taken on the title of Keeper Overlord when Hykalof, the previous title holder, had been 'killed' in an undead battle her tribe fought in so that they could escape the hold of their ancestors and return to Hasefi. She still didn't totally understand what had happened during the time after her tribe's death, but she knew that their struggle for survival had been as great as her own—perhaps even greater.

Gelinaf, her new Overlord, acknowledged her words, but said nothing. Even if her tribe hadn't fallen into the same apprehensive hush her uncle had, she suspected the Overlord would have little to say, as was his nature.

The rest of the forest began to thicken around them until, suddenly, they emerged into a small clearing. Hasefi stepped into it with surprise, having thought it was dense forest ahead. To her further surprise, another keeper stepped in front of them, materializing from the shadows of the trees.

"Knight Emperor," the keeper greeted with a deep bow.

"Keeper," Hasefi's father returned with a nod.

"Your arrival is earlier than anticipated. Would you like me to inform the Highchief?"

"No, Mirahlin can do that." On Garfonis's nod, the keeper that had accompanied him to the Clan's territory hurried away, disappearing through a clump of closely-growing ferns.

The new keeper crouched into another bow and, without further words, slunk back into the shadows.

"Come," Garfonis said to Hasefi and she followed him through the same ferns that had swallowed Mirahlin.

A gasp left Hasefi's jaws as they emerged into a huge open space that stretched all the way to the cliff-face. Despite the night growing old, there were lynxes about—more lynxes than Hasefi had ever seen before.

By the stars, you were right! she thought to her uncle. *This is huge!*

A few of the lynxes appeared to be fulfilling some duty or another, while others had settled around the clearing, some of which were fast asleep. There was a time when sleeping beneath the night sky was potentially lethal for Hasefi, but now she thought of the nights her and Kolahn had spent chatting beneath the moon and stars.

Maybe if things go well, we'll be doing just that tomorrow night.

The lynxes that were moving about wore all sorts of armor; hard and soft, black, silver, purple, white, brown—but the colors had all been changed to ethereal whites and grays by the sliver of moonlight shining down on them, making these lynxes look more like ghosts, sort of like Hasefi's tribe when they revealed themselves to her.

Hasefi's gaze moved to her left where a chunk of the clearing was taken over by smooth stone that glowed in the pale light. It was bare now, but Hasefi suspected it would be a favored spot late in the day when the sun had cast its rays upon it for some time. The large patch stretched almost all the way back to the cliff-wall which was dotted with caves at different heights. Ones above ground had convenient stone paths leading to the entrances. One cave in particular stood out; it was highest, set in the middle, and its path led to a large ledge that jutted from the cliff. Each cave also had white, star-like light emanating from it, though the source was unknown to Hasefi.

Those caves are sort of like the ones at Kolahn's home, she thought wistfully. *Except for that strange light.*

On the right, the farthest cave over was at ground level. To its side, along the edge of the clearing, were rows of different plants, some with such strong smells that Hasefi could taste them from where she stood, determining they were herbs of all kinds. Lynxes in white robes tended to them, some of their eyes glowing as they used their magic.

Ahead of the plants and closer to Hasefi and her father was a tree stump and its fallen trunk. Both were marked with countless scratches, stripped entirely of bark. During her time alone, Hasefi had used rocks or, later, tree trunks to sharpen her claws and practice fighting moves, so she thought this fallen tree might serve the same purpose. It seemed peculiar, though, that the tree had broken in such a way, as if it had been deliberately split at the base. In fact, a lot of the clearing looked like it had somehow been deliberately made.

This is so strange, she thought as she swept her gaze over the clearing again.

"Hasefi?" Garfonis's voice brought her out of her amazement. He had stopped a pace ahead and Hasefi realized she had halted as soon as they had entered the massive clearing. She resumed following him, absorbing every sight, every scent as she went. They passed a hollow in the middle of the clearing where prey was kept. The enticing aroma of fresh meat reminded her that she hadn't eaten since the night before.

This is home, she thought. *This is where I was born.*

She could feel Garfonis's gaze hot on her fur, but, as much as she wanted to ask the questions that were beginning to fill her head, she restrained herself, trying to keep herself focused on her goal.

Every heartbeat counts, she told herself. *We need to get to Kolahn before it's too late. Questions can wait.*

Garfonis headed to the big ledge over the clearing which Hasefi figured was where the Highchief would address their lynxes. As they got closer to it, she realized the lynxes in the clearing were stopping to glance over at them. Or, more accurately, at her. Some of their gazes were curious, but she was astonished when she saw recognition in some of them.

They remember me, she thought. *But...I don't recognize anyone.*

Her father led the way up the stone path that brought them onto the ledge. At the top, Hasefi looked briefly out, but was too far from the edge of the ledge to see the lynxes below. She followed her father into the yawning cave in the cliff-face.

She was further bewildered when the white light glowing at the entrance to the cave continued inside as if the ceiling itself had been touched by moon and starlight, allowing her and Garfonis to walk deep into the rock without losing the ability to see.

A part of Hasefi was lost in awe at everything she had witnessed from merely walking into the Tribe's home. But another part, a stronger part, continued to remind her why she was there at all.

I need to save Kolahn. Surely I could convince this Highchief to help me.

She hardened her mind against the wonders of this place, muting her amazement and ignoring the intriguing nature of the light filling the cave until it no longer dazzled her.

Little more came to surprise her, though. The tunnel they followed led to a wide, empty cavern, which then split two ways. Garfonis led her through the right path which, after a curve, opened into another cavern.

A lynx bearing the black Keeper Overlord's armor sat guard just outside the cavern, as still as stone. They were slim and shorter than Hykalof had been, but the curved spikes along the shoulders and horns sprouting from the helmet were no less intimidating. Glancing at the lynx's wrapped paws, Hasefi could see the tips of armored claws peeking out. She knew how devastating such weapons could be in battle.

"Emperor," the lynx greeted with a nod. "We were surprised to hear of your return so soon." Her voice was friendly with a hint of concern, contradicting her terrifying presence.

"Something has come up," was all Hasefi's father said.

"The Highchief is inside waiting." With another nod, the Overlord moved slightly, letting him and Hasefi pass. Hasefi glanced towards the Overlord, but the lynx seemed to have no interest in her as she passed. *Unless her eyes are still following me and I can't tell.* Fighting a shiver, she entered the cave with her father.

Inside was surprisingly warm, despite the stone interior. Unlike the other cavern they had passed through, this one was not empty. Four hollows were near the middle as if a giant paw had scooped them out. Three of them were filled with leaves and feathers, one bigger than the others and more recently used.

Near them was a lynx bearing armor that was startlingly familiar to Hasefi. It was black with silver trim, with a sparkling white stone on the forehead and spikes protruding from the head, down between the shoulders, and along the back. It was the same armor Hasefi had worn until about a moon after her tribe had been killed and she'd grown too big to wear it. However, this lynx's armor bore a silver star on the chest, identical to the one Hasefi knew gifted lynxes had naturally in their fur.

Is the Highchief gifted?

"Emperor," the lynx spoke as Garfonis and Hasefi entered, her voice thick with authority.

"Highchief," Garfonis responded, sinking into a low bow with his right paw outstretched.

Should I be doing that? Hasefi wondered.

As far as she's concerned, Sefonis responded, nearly making Hasefi jump, *you're her equal. She'll expect nothing more than a nod.*

When the Highchief looked to Hasefi, she did what her uncle said. The other lynx appeared satisfied.

"Were you able to deliver the warning to the Clan?" the Highchief asked.

"Not in full," Garfonis admitted as he rose. "I was interrupted the moment I entered their home."

The Highchief's gaze moved to Hasefi. "By you, I presume," she said. "Why have you returned to the Great River? And why were you in Clan territory?"

Hasefi's mouth opened, but she wasn't able to get any words out. The Highchief didn't notice.

"Why have you come alone? Where is your armor?"

"I left my armor in the high mountains," Hasefi finally managed to answer the last and simplest question. But her answer only displeased the Highchief.

"Where?"

"The...high mountains. Erm, where the snow is."

"Why would you leave your armor there?"

"It didn't fit."

"Didn't fit? Why didn't your gifted resize it for you?"

"Um..." Hasefi trailed off, overwhelmed by the Highchief's rapid, demanding questions. *I don't have time to be interrogated, I need to get help to save Kolahn!*

"Perhaps Hasefi can answer our questions by telling us why she's come to us," Garfonis suggested quietly. The Highchief studied him where he had moved to sit a couple pawsteps from her before returning her gaze to Hasefi. When she didn't say anything, Hasefi took it as a sign to speak.

"The Clan—"

Start at the beginning, Kilarsa, one of her gifted lynxes, filled her head. *It'll help them make sense of your situation.*

Hasefi bit back her frustration, knowing she was probably right. She forced herself to take a breath, then started again.

"We were following the rising sun like we were told." She could hear the bitter note that entered her voice and struggled to keep it neutral. "We were looking for home. But we were attacked and...I was the only one who survived." Her gaze flicked between both of the lynxes before her as she tried to read their expressions. Garfonis had removed his helmet while the Higchief's was open-faced.

"So you came here," the Highchief assumed.

"That was nine moons ago."

Shock rippled through both lynx's eyes.

"That was only a couple moons after we'd sent you out," Garfonis gasped, getting to his paws. "How...?"

"What attacked you?" the Highchief demanded as if Garfonis hadn't spoken.

Hasefi swallowed, trying to remain calm despite their intensity. "Do you know the wolf Resahn?" she asked.

The Highchief's gaze twisted with hatred. "I'm surprised *you* know of him," she admitted.

"Wolves like him attacked us. They killed everyone and would have killed me, too, if I hadn't escaped." Hasefi's mind flashed back to that brutal day. Her tribe had sacrificed everything to protect her and, even bloodied and broken, they had saved her life by luring the deadliest predator of the mountains into the clearing just in time to chase off her would-be killers.

After meeting Kolahn, she hadn't thought about that day quite as often, but, when she did, it was always as if she was seeing it for the first time. She blinked, clawing her way back into the present before she was overwhelmed with fear and grief. Her gaze met her father's, who was watching her with grief and sorrow bright in his eyes, while the Highchief's expression remained contorted with loathing.

"Black wolves?" she snarled. "The Clan said they were gone."

"I saw one," Garfonis admitted with a wary glance at Hasefi. "When I found Hasefi. He was being held prisoner by the wolves."

Surprise entered the Highchief's expression, but Hasefi jumped in before she could say anything.

"That was Kolahn," she explained quickly. "He helped me when I broke my leg. He saved my life."

The Highchief let out a snort. "So even before they've been stealing our prey and taking our kits, they've been lying to us about their tainted kind?"

Stealing prey...taking kits? Hasefi hesitated, caught off guard by the accusations. But she pushed aside her surprise, knowing she had to convince the Highchief that Kolahn wasn't like the others.

"Kolahn isn't evil," she told the Highchief. "Like I said, he saved me and we attacked the Pack together and killed one of their leaders."

"The Pack. You mean the black wolves that attacked you? There's an organized group of them?" the Highchief demanded.

Hasefi nodded, trying to figure out if it was fear that had entered the older lynx's seething glare.

"They were hunting me, but when they caught up again, we were able to scatter some of them." She remembered then that the Pack's ultimate goal had been to take over the Clan that had cast them out. "But they're still dangerous, especially if their other leader is still alive."

The Highchief sank into thought, her darkening expression making Hasefi uneasy.

"I need to save Kolahn," she reminded her.

"Who?" the Highchief asked, her tone indicating she wasn't really listening.

"The wolf back at the Clan."

"The black one?"

"Yes," Hasefi said, her ears twitching with irritation.

"Why? What danger is *he* in?"

"The Clan will kill him. They exiled black wolves," Hasefi explained, struggling to keep her impatience at bay.

"So what?" the Highchief asked.

Hasefi's ears flattened this time. "He saved my life! And he's my friend! I *have* to help him!"

The Highchief merely snorted again.

She won't help me, Hasefi realized. *I'm wasting my time here. I need to figure out how to help Kolahn.*

"Don't waste your energy on a wolf, much less a black one," the Highchief said, still distracted.

"It's not Kolahn my energy's being wasted on," Hasefi growled, standing. "If you don't want to help me, then there's no more reason for me to be here." In the corner of her eye, she saw Garfonis recoil.

"Help you?" the Highchief blurted. "Is that what you want? I have more important things to worry about than the well-being of *wolves.* Much less black ones."

"So I'll get out of your way." Hasefi turned away.

"But I can't let you leave, either."

Hasefi halted. The Highchief's tone had become cold, sending a chill through her. *What?*

"And why would that be?" Hasefi tried to sound annoyed, but her words shook with the dread building up in her, especially when she looked to the white star on the Highchief's chest-plate.

"The moment you leave our home, you'll walk right back to the Clan." The Highchief's tone had become abruptly casual as she lifted a paw and inspected the black and silver armor reinforcing her claws. "We are on the brink of a war and I cannot afford to give the Clan any reason to strike first. So you will remain here."

Despite the Highchief's words, Hasefi took another step forwards, but the Keeper Overlord was suddenly in front of her, towering menacingly with the void-holes of her helmet glaring down at her. Hasefi turned back to the Highchief, her mouth dry, unable to form any words.

What do I do? I can't stay here. She waited, but there was no response. *I could probably get out, even if she is gifted.*

You would hurt a lot of lynxes in the process, Sefonis pointed out.

"So I'm your prisoner, now?" she murmured quietly to the Highchief.

"Only if you make it that way," she responded.

Hasefi looked to her father, but his expression had become impassive. A part of her raged, urging her to barge past the Overlord and claw her way out of this tribe's territory until she was back over the River, but something she hadn't felt before quenched that flame almost entirely. She didn't want to show weakness, but she had little control when her head hung limp with defeat. Kolahn entered her mind and she saw him trapped and alone in the Clan's prison-cave. He had the same look on his face that he'd had when he came to her before he was shoved back into the ravine and it tore her heart now just as it had then.

I can't stay here. The voice of her mind insisted, but it was hardly louder than a whisper. *I have to find a way out. I* won't *let the Clan or this tribe keep Kolahn from me!*

"I will name you High Heir," the Highchief continued, bringing Hasefi from her thoughts. "As is your rightful position."

Hasefi lifted her head and stared at the Highchief, taken aback by her words. Her own tribe reeled with the same shock.

"You are not long from twelve moons, so you will start your training tomorrow. I suspect my tribe has become curious of your arrival, so I will call the other champions so I can announce your arrival to the rest of the tribe." The Highchief's eyes hardened. "But you mustn't speak to any of the lynxes about the Pack. Or about black wolves at all."

"What?" Hasefi blurted. "But...they have the right to know!" She looked to Garfonis. "Your brother died by their jaws—along with nine other lynxes. Their kin have the right to know!"

Garfonis was silent, his impassive mask breaking as his gaze flickered between her and the Highchief.

"You will say nothing," the Highchief ordered.

"Or what?" Hasefi challenged.

"I will have no choice but to detain you."

Anger bubbled up within Hasefi and this time it wasn't extinguished so easily. Her tribe's strength responded instinctively, but she knew enhanced abilities couldn't help her here.

"You have no right to keep anything from them!" Hasefi snarled. "Maybe if you had kin in my tribe you'd understand!"

"I do," the Highchief replied, causing Hasefi to hesitate. "She's standing in front of me."

Surprise briefly swept over Hasefi before realization took over, making her fur hot with embarrassment.

Of course, she thought. *It's in that stupid prophecy. How did it go? 'The first Heir to the Highchief will lead a destiny beyond the river'. I'm the first Heir. And she's the Highchief. Of course she's my mother.*

"Take her to my brother to heal her wounds and fix her leg," the Highchief said to Garfonis. "I would like her to be presentable when I announce her presence to the Tribe in the morning."

Hasefi was already shocked into silence and, even though her mother's comment sent another flash of anger through her, she was unable to act upon it. All she could do was fume in silence while she trailed after her father.

In the tunnel, they passed the Keeper Overlord again, who had resumed her position outside the Highchief's cavern. Hasefi flashed her a glare, but she showed the same amount of interest as when they had arrived, only making Hasefi angrier.

I dreamt of this, she thought as she and her father moved through the strangely lit tunnel. *I dreamt of meeting my parents, of finding home. But I never imagined* this.

She tried to hold onto her ire as it was the only thing fueling her against the complexities that had arisen, but helplessness took over, sweeping through her like a giant wave and bringing with it a pang of grief.

How in the world am I going to save him now?

Chapter Two

Hasefi emerged from the cliff behind Garfonis, following him along the base of the ledge and back down the moonlit path to the ground below.

I can't stay here, she thought once again. *Kolahn needs me.*

The wisest thing to do now is follow the Highchief's orders.

Another flare of anger swept through Hasefi at her uncle's words. *Why? Kolahn could be killed at any moment!*

But there's nothing you can do just yet, Sefonis pointed out. *Acting in a way that forces your mother to restrain you will only make things more difficult.*

'My mother.' *What do you expect me to do in the meantime?* At first, there was no response and Hasefi's anger rose until, finally, someone spoke.

Tension is high between this tribe and the Clan, Kilarsa told Hasefi. *Action will be taken soon and opportunity will arise. Opportunity where no one needs to get hurt.*

Bloody images entered Hasefi's head and she let out a slow breath, her rage cooling. Her paws still itched to run to the ferns leading out of the clearing, but she knew the last thing Kolahn wanted was a repeat of his last rescue. Especially when his former Clan was the target.

Okay, she conceded. *But if nothing happens soon, I'm going after him. Whatever it takes. And if I find a way to escape, then I'm taking it.*

There was no response to her words. The unease that had fallen over her tribe since she had found her father rendered them silent once more. It didn't help her own agitation, especially since they were much better at hiding their thoughts from her than she was from them.

Hoping to distract herself from the dread churning in her gut, Hasefi's attention moved outwards. Curious lynxes still hovered around, but they kept a respectful distance as Garfonis led her towards the array of plants being tended to by the few white-clad lynxes working through the night. One of them halted in their duties and hurried over to meet her and Garfonis.

"Knight Emperor," the lynx said as he bowed.

"Healer," Hasefi's father responded. "Would you be able to inform the Sage we have need of him?"

"He's actually awake in the mainchamber," the healer responded. "He's working with the new novice."

Garfonis looked a little surprised, but he dipped his head in acknowledgement. "Thank you."

The healer bowed again before returning to the herbs. Hasefi watched him for a moment, seeing how he sat back on his haunches and lifted his forepaws, sending whirls of yellow light around the stems and leaves, before following her father to the nearby cave-mouth.

They entered, stepping into a short tunnel that opened up into a massive cavern. Five entrances lined the back and one opened to Hasefi's left, this one with a sweet smell that made her think of her mother, though the image was of the one she had imagined while she was trying to survive on her own rather than that of the Highchief she had met. She tried to merge the two, but it made her lips draw back in a silent snarl.

She shoved the images away and continued to inspect the spacious cavern. In the walls to the right were various holes holding all kinds of plants with myriad smells. Some of these crevices also held other items like pieces of armor, random bits of plants, claws, teeth, scraps of fur. She was a little put off by the strange collection, but her befuddlement was forgotten when she noticed another lynx clad in white. This one was a little different as he bore a hood with the rest of his garments and had twice the amount of pouches along his flanks and shoulders, the entirety decorated with silver in the same starry pattern as Garfonis's and the Highchief's armor. His chest was open, revealing a collar of white with a small white star akin to the Highchief's. Below that was the true star in the Sage's fur that marked him as gifted.

He's the Healer Sage, Hasefi thought.

And your uncle, Sefonis added.

Hasefi tilted her head slightly before looking to the other lynx crouched in front of the Sage.

This lynx was younger, barely bigger than Hasefi, and bearing only the white collar and star. In the strange light of the cave, his fur was silver and his pale spots gray, but she guessed, in the sunlight, his fur would shine a brilliant orange-gold. The same white star the Sage had on his chest was on the novice's, too. His attention was directed to the ground where he hovered a paw over various dried plants, speaking in a soft voice.

"Emperor." The hooded lynx looked up and gave Hasefi's father a welcoming smile. "And Highchief Hasefi." He stood and gave a deep bow. The young lynx with him started in surprise, then scrambled to do the same. "What brings you here so late in the night?" the Sage asked Garfonis.

"Our Highchief wants her wounds tended," Garfonis explained, nodding to Hasefi. "And...Hasefi is now our High Heir."

Surprise sparked through the Sage's expression, nearly masking the darker look that entered his eyes, but he made no comment. "Of course. Come on over." The Sage brushed aside the herbs. The young lynx started to move away, but the hooded lynx beckoned him back over. "If you don't mind, I'd like to use this as an opportunity to train my newest novice here."

"It's past moonpeak," Garfonis pointed out. "Shouldn't he be resting?"

"Gifteds never sleep," the Sage said with a wink. "But he's welcome to go whenever he'd like." He looked at the novice expectantly.

He didn't seem to hear the Sage at first. He blinked, acknowledging the silence that followed, confusion seeping into his eyes. Then they widened and he shot to his paws.

"Oh!" he blurted. "I'm great. I mean, I don't mind." His ears flattened with embarrassment and he sat back down.

"If you'd allow it, I'd like to show him what it looks like to heal another creature," the Sage said.

"I'm not sure if..." Garfonis spoke, but the Sage was looking at Hasefi.

"Is that alright with you, High Heir?"

"Sure," Hasefi answered, not entirely sure what was about to happen.

"My name is Hesilar, by the way," the Sage continued as he motioned for Hasefi to sit in front of him.

"You're my mother's brother. My uncle."

"Yes," he said, pleased. Hesilar, like the Highchief, had a brownish gold pelt. His spots, however, were smaller and more prominent where his robes didn't conceal his fur, and his eyes were a pale green.

Hesilar walked once around Hasefi, clicking his teeth. "Looks like you've been through quite a bit."

Hasefi waited for him to ask, but he merely sat in front of her and looked to the younger lynx.

"This here is Salifen. He's been a novice healer for just three days now."

Hasefi gave the novice a nod. Salifen's eyes darted around nervously before he jerked his head sharply as if he hadn't immediately noticed her gesture right away.

"Do you remember what I told you about handling injured lynxes?" Hesilar asked the novice. Salifen's eyes flickered nervously.

"We have to find out what's wrong?"

"Right. Can you tell me what's ailing her?"

Salifen's ears twitched timidly, but he kept his gaze on Hasefi this time as he studied her. "She has bruises and cuts," he murmured. "And a broken leg. But...I think it's been that way for a while." His eyes moved to hers for a moment before quickly looking away.

"Right," Hesilar praised. "So, now what?"

Salifen hesitated before raising his paw. "We heal her?"

"With what?"

Salifen hesitated again and made no response.

Hesilar chuckled softly. "Our powers are mighty," he said. "But they are a gift and to be used wisely. If we can keep from depending directly on them, it is required that we do. And looking to the world around us can even help enhance them."

Salifen nodded, not meeting the Sage's eyes.

"We'll need some goldenrod and comfrey," Hesilar encouraged gently.

Salifen immediately stood and moved to where various herbs were stored in the wall.

"Is there anything that hurts inside that we can't see?" Hesilar asked Hasefi.

"I don't think so," she responded.

"Good. We'll have you back in shape in no time," he assured her. Salifen returned, carrying herbs which he placed on the ground.

"Wait, are you going to chew them up and spit them onto me? Because I can do that myself," Hasefi said, wrinkling her nose.

Hesilar laughed. "No, High Heir, you needn't worry about that. One of the great things about being gifted is we get to skip some of the undesirable aspects of life."

Hasefi was a bit relieved, but now she was confused.

"We will use these herbs to heal you, but with our abilities," he continued, reading her expression. "It will not hurt at all, but you may feel a bit uncomfortable if you're not used to this." Hesilar's eyes gradually brightened until they emanated a pale green glow. Then, the herbs at his paws began doing the same. They swirled into the air, dissolving as they went, and followed Hesilar's paws as he sat back on his haunches.

The Sage lightly touched the wounds along Hasefi's flank. The pain faded into itchiness, making her want to twitch, but it soon vanished entirely. The soreness of her bruises eased and her muscles relaxed. She let out an audible sigh as he moved around, healing each wound.

"How do you feel?" he asked when he returned to stand in front of her.

"Much better," she told him. "Thank you." Hasefi went to stand, but Hesilar lifted a paw.

"We have yet to fix that leg of yours."

Excitement rippled through Hasefi, but she did her best to stifle it, knowing how painful false hope was.

"Fix it?" she asked, looking down at her twisted limb. "But it's been this way for a long while."

"Then I imagine it'll take some time to get used to having four legs again," he chuckled.

This time, Hasefi struggled to keep her excitement in check.

"You can really fix it?" she asked and the Sage nodded.

"If you would allow it, I'd like to give Salifen a chance to try."

"Is he capable?" Garfonis interjected, but Hasefi nodded without second thought, overwhelmed by the idea that she might have her leg back.

"It'll be his first time," Hesilar admitted with a glance at Hasefi's father. "So, the moment there's any pain, let us know."

Hasefi nodded again, this time more controlled. She looked to Salifen who seemed to have found the courage to meet her gaze for a few heartbeats more than before. When he looked away, he came to sit directly in front of her.

"May I?" he asked quietly, holding out a paw. Hasefi lifted her broken one and laid it gently on his paw. He lifted his other foreleg and carefully ran it over her fur. "Does it hurt?"

"Only when I use it," she admitted. Salifen nodded. His eyes narrowed and Hasefi watched the green in them start to glow.

"It's been this way for moons," he murmured. "How did this happen?"

"It is not our place to ask questions outside what is necessary," Hesilar warned, causing the novice to flatten his ears in embarrassment.

"It's okay," Hasefi said. "I don't mind."

The novice lifted his gaze and their eyes met.

"I fell into a pit," she explained. "It was hidden in snow and I slipped into it."

The novice's eyes widened. "That must have been scary," he breathed.

Hasefi shrugged. She wasn't sure 'scary' was the right word. If it hadn't been for Kolahn showing up then, she would have died, one way or another.

Salifen held her gaze for another heartbeat. His expression had changed, his nervousness suddenly gone, replaced by a strange determination she didn't understand. Before she could make sense of it, he turned to the remaining herbs beside him. Like with Hesilar, they began to glow and moved to Salifen's paws. Then Salifen began to run his paw along her leg, this time applying a bit of pressure.

Hasefi tensed, waiting for her leg to protest against the light weight applied to it, but instead she merely felt it shift. She watched in wonder as her leg started to turn and the part that stuck out unnaturally straightened. A tiny sting made her stiffen.

"Sorry," Salifen said quickly and the pain vanished. Hasefi's attention moved to him as she watched with awe. *I never realized how amazing your powers could be,* she said to her tribe.

They truly are a gift, Kilarsa agreed.

And this novice has been given a generous one, Dahsefer, Hasefi's own Healer Sage, added. *A broken bone is no easy fix. Especially for a novice. And he's barely out of kithood.* His tone held an echo of the same apprehension her father's had.

"There," Salifen gasped, his light fading. He let go of her and stumbled slightly.

"Are you alright?" Hasefi asked, standing to support him if he fell.

"He's just drained," Hesilar explained. "A young lynx's gift takes time to strengthen." Despite his words, the Sage's eyes shone as he helped steady the novice. Hasefi hesitated before letting her attention move to her newly healed leg.

She had already put weight on it when she stood, but now she relished the ability to do so. She leaned on it, half expecting it to collapse. But all it did was shake under the pressure.

"It'll take some time to strengthen it again," the Sage told her.

Hasefi nodded, speechless. Though her leg had remained crippled, the despair that had followed had healed with Kolahn's help and she had learned to accept it.

But now I can stand. I can run. *And I can fight.*

Hesilar was stepping towards her again, taking her out of her mind. "Broken bones can be difficult to heal," he began. "Especially when they heal incorrectly. But scars are a little easier." Hesilar lifted his paws towards Hasefi's face and she ducked.

"Wait," she said quickly. The Sage withdrew and she straightened, eying him warily. When he made no other move, she lifted her newly healed foreleg and touched her paw to her face. From her right brow down to her left cheek were three rough lines. She lowered her paw and met the Sage's eyes. "I'd like to keep my scars."

"The Highchief may not approve," Garfonis said, moving from where he had been hovering a pace away to stand beside her. "She wants you to look your best when she presents you to the Tribe."

"The *Highchief* doesn't get to choose how I look. If she has a problem with that, then she can let me leave."

Garfonis frowned. "Hasefi—"

"Let the young fighter keep the memory of her battles," Hesilar interrupted Hasefi's father. "They're hers to wear, not Esafi's."

"But—"

"My duty as a healer is to help lynxes with their struggles," Hesilar continued. "If Hasefi wants to keep her scars, there's nothing I can do about it without going against the rules of a healer. Much less those of a Sage."

Garfonis's eyes flicked between him and Hasefi until he finally let out a defeated sigh. "Very well. Thank you for your help, Healer Sage."

"Of course." Hesilar dipped his head to the Emperor, then bowed to Hasefi. Salifen moved to do the same, but Hesilar put a paw on his shoulder. "You did well, Salifen. I will bring you some prey and then you can rest for the night. Or what's left of it," he added with a chuckle.

Salifen nodded, his gaze flickering to Hasefi's. Hasefi tried giving him another nod and this time he responded more confidently.

"Come, Hasefi," Garfonis said, easily losing the disappointed look he'd had when Hesilar had rejected him. "You'd better rest, too."

Hasefi turned to follow her father out of the cavern. Each step she took was like a breath of fresh air, sending a brilliant thrill through her that she was worried was the stuff of dreams.

Maybe this would be better as a dream, she thought. *Then I wouldn't have to be so worried about Kolahn.*

Her thoughts on her newly healed leg changed to how much easier it would make escaping this tribe. But those thoughts were pushed aside when she and her father returned to the clearing and she was met again with many curious gazes failing miserably at being discreet.

They won't approach me, she thought. *Even though some of them seem to know who I am.* She recalled Hesilar's words to Salifen about asking questions. *Is that a universal rule?*

It is rude to intrude in the business of other lynxes, Sefonis spoke.

Even if it affects them? she asked. *I'm supposed to be their High Heir, right? They'll have to know, otherwise they might all be calling me a Highchief like Hesilar did.*

The Highchief will announce the news, Sefonis said distractedly, his tone not unlike the one Garfonis used every time he had deferred to the Highchief to avoid answering a question.

With Sefonis, however, Hasefi knew that her uncle was holding something back, but he withdrew before she got the chance to understand what might be bothering him. She let go of the thought for now as Garfonis led her back onto the ledge and into the cliff-face.

This time the Highchief—Esafi, as Hesilar had called her—met them in the first chamber. The Overlord was with her. Hasefi frowned at her before looking to the Highchief.

"I thought I asked you to bring her to Hesilar to be fixed," Esafi said to Garfonis.

"My apologies," Hasefi's father said quickly with a bow. "Hesilar insisted that he wouldn't remove her scars as long as she intended to keep them."

The Highchief's eyes moved to Hasefi. "Then you will return to him and ask him to remove them."

"No," Hasefi told her. "You may be able to keep me prisoner, but I will not let you alter my pelt."

Esafi frowned deeply.

"If you want them removed so badly," Hasefi continued. "You'll have to drag me down in front of all the lynxes out there and bring me to Hesilar yourself."

Garfonis ducked his head and the Overlord's helmet twitched towards Esafi.

"As High Heir, you are expected to present your best self," the Highchief spoke slowly. Then she tilted her nose up. "But if you insist on flaunting your flaws, then I will leave it to the other lynxes to prove why you should fix them." She turned her gaze on the Overlord. "Sifara, my daughter will need a keeper assigned to her, ready at dawn tomorrow." The Highchief started to turn towards Garfonis, but she hesitated. "Give Arsolin the task."

Hasefi heard a soft intake of breath as if the Overlord meant to respond, but she merely nodded and sank into a deep bow before she left the cavern.

"Garfonis, I've spoken briefly with Myafos and Lisefi about this new turn of events. After tomorrow's announcement, I will have you and the other champions meet me here to discuss how this will affect our current plans."

"Yes, Highchief," Garfonis responded with a bow.

"Get what rest you can for the night," Esafi added, her tone softening just a little. "I will see you in the morning."

Garfonis sank into a parting bow. He snuck a glance at Hasefi that was too quick to read, then hurried out of the tunnel, his clinking armor fading into the night.

"I will show you your sleeping hollow," Esafi said to Hasefi.

Hasefi didn't think she'd be able to get any sleep; too many questions, too many new things, and too much worry for her imprisoned friend kept her mind racing. But there was nothing else she could think to do if she were to keep from hurting innocent lynxes in her goal to return to the Clan. So, without a word, she followed Esafi back to the chamber she had met her in.

Tomorrow I'll be able to think more clearly, she assured herself. *And then I can start thinking of a way to escape this place.* She also hoped her tribe wouldn't be as elusive.

Now that she wasn't focused solely on getting the Highchief's aid in rescuing Kolahn, she was able to get a better look at the cavern where the sleeping hollows were.

The largest hollow was in the middle, with the other three loosely surrounding it. The one that had been empty before now had fresh bedding, while the other two had been cleaned out.

Across from the hollows, the wall had holes like the Healer's Cave, though not quite as many. They were filled with odd bits and pieces. Pinecones, tufts of grass, dandelion fluffs, a tiny claw. It was as if a kit had gone around and picked up everything they thought was interesting.

Some of the crevices were empty, but one was neater than the others. It had a couple pretty-colored rocks, the wing of an orange and black butterfly, and, in the middle, was a beautiful golden flower with speckles of black. Somehow, it hadn't wilted and remained as lively as if it were still in the ground.

"You will use this hollow," Esafi said, bringing Hasefi's attention back. The Highchief patted the hollow that had been made. It was closest to the entrance which made Hasefi instinctively nervous until she remembered there were plenty of lynxes between her and whatever lay outside the clearing.

This is the safest I've been, she thought as she padded over to the hollow. *And here I am wanting nothing more than to leave.* She had to stifle the snort that followed her thought.

"Tomorrow," Esafi continued, moving away. "You will be taken to get new armor." The Highchief stopped at one of the empty crevices in the wall which was closest to Hasefi's hollow. "This is where you will put your helmet for the night."

Hasefi remained silent and sat down in her hollow. The lining was comfortable, made with feathers and a few kinds of plants she didn't know the names of, but some were sturdy and kept the mesh from falling apart when she moved, while others were soft, and some sent a pleasant smell into her fur as she settled into it.

This is the most comfortable hollow I've ever laid in.

Hasefi looked to the other hollows. She guessed Esafi's was the large one, then sniffed discreetly at the two newly emptied ones, but her nose was too full of new scents to offer anything useful.

I've never had so many lynx scents to decipher, she realized. *They all smell like the river.*

"You said you left your armor behind."

Hasefi lifted her head to look at Esafi. She had hoped to settle for the night without conversation, but she realized it was a futile wish.

"Yes," Hasefi replied.

"Pity." Esafi frowned. "A Highchief's armor is adorned with a highstone—an invaluable item." Esafi lifted her paw and touched the white stone on the middle of her forehead.

"What is a highstone?" Hasefi asked, unable to supress her curiosity.

"A highstone is a soulstone created from the energies of a previously deceased Highchief. Highchiefs wear those of their predecessors. This stone was made from my mother, Narafi."

"What stone was on my armor?" Hasefi asked.

"My mother's predecessor and father, Lakilom."

Hasefi felt a sliver of guilt for having lost such an important item, but she knew there was nothing she could've done about it.

"Will I be getting a new highstone?" she queried.

"No. The High Heir's armor does not carry such an item."

Hasefi nodded, figuring it was for the best.

"Now, I advise you rest," Esafi said, moving to leave.

"Where are you going?" Hasefi asked.

"I have other matters to attend to. I will be close."

Hasefi knew her mother's parting words were meant as a warning in case she felt like trying to sneak away. But, despite her earlier thoughts and though her wounds had been healed, Hasefi was feeling the effects of travelling all the way from the Great Valley where she had been with Kolahn. She had climbed down a sheer cliff-face to get him, only to leave him behind and make her way across the giant river into this tribe's home. She hadn't eaten since last night, but her exhaustion was greater than her hunger and she curled easily into her nest.

She buried her nose into the lining, inhaling the muskiness of the feathers mingling with the sweet scent of young plants. Before she could close her eyes, a thought nagged at her mind like a fly buzzing circles around her ears. She lifted her head and looked to the other two hollows again. Unable to suppress the curiosity that made her fur twitch, she spoke to her tribe.

Why are there two extra beds?

She didn't think they would respond, but then her Sage stirred, coming to the forefront of her mind.

Lynxes can typically have up three kits. Dahsefer's tone was matter-of-fact. *They would be occupied by the Highchief's kits until they are about your age and would move to the other sleeping caverns in the five Paths, with the exception of the High Heir.*

The five Paths being the different roles of the tribe?

Aye.

Could Esafi have had more kits?

Dahsefer was silent.

Did she?

It might do well for you to get some rest, Sefonis suggested, taking Dahsefer's place. *You've had a long day.*

Hasefi's ears flattened with annoyance, but a part of her did want to heed her uncle's words. However, she forced herself out of her hollow and went around, scrutinizing every inch of the cave and giving the little items in each crevice a quick inspection. Their purpose remained unclear to her, but she wasn't particularly concerned about them.

Whatever they were, though, she was sure each item had their own history, just as her tribe had one here.

So this was your home, Hasefi thought, returning to her hollow. *This is where you grew up. Why would you ever leave this place?*

We volunteered, Kilarsa explained.

Most *of us, anyways,* Sefonis added. *There were some who were chosen.*

Hasefi knew they were dodging around her question, but she was determined to get at least *one* straight answer from them. *But* why *leave? Because of the stupid prophecy the ancestors gave me?*

Aye, Kilarsa said. *Your mother interpreted it as the tribe's next divide. That you were to lead us to a new home for lynxes.*

'Next' divide? What does that mean? she asked.

Another divide took place during your grandmother's time, Kilarsa explained. *It was the first time the Tribe split and, back then, it had been due to a home too small to support the Tribe's size.*

I wonder if they found home, Hasefi thought. *I hope so.*

They followed the Great River into the hills beyond, Sefonis told her. *I'm sure they found a better place to be.*

Hasefi lowered her head onto her paws, relishing for a moment the ability to curl up without her lame leg getting in the way.

I miss Kolahn, she admitted.

I know, wee lass.

I don't want to be here. Her words sent a pang of sadness through her. Loneliness ached in her heart and she could feel her tribe reacting to it with their own grief. *This was everything I wanted, once. But now...I don't want it. I don't even* like *it. There are so many lynxes, so many things—too many. And my parents.... Esafi seems...displeased.*

I'm sorry it isn't what you wanted, Sefonis told her.

It's alright. Maybe it's for the best. I never had a clue what I would do if I found other lynxes because I didn't want to leave Kolahn. But now...it's hardly a decision at all.

A lot has happened today, Kilarsa pointed out. *You may yet learn to enjoy your kind.*

Maybe. But I still have to help Kolahn. Esafi talked about being close to war with the wolves. Like you said, there may be an opportunity for me to get to him. But...if nothing happens soon, I'm going to him.

We will follow, Kilarsa assured her.

Hasefi expressed her gratitude, then let her eyes close.

Chapter Three

A sharp jab to her ribs woke Hasefi up immediately. She sprang to her paws and prepared to defend herself until she recognized the golden face glowering down at her.

"As High Heir, you will be expected to rise before dawn to prepare for your training," Esafi told her.

Hasefi's alarm immediately dissipated, letting her still lingering exhaustion return. She hung her head. *Did I actually get any sleep? I was up nearly all night.*

"Do not sulk—it will offer an ill impression to your fellow tribemates."

Hasefi's ears went back and she lifted her head. She held Esafi's gaze until the Highchief turned away and moved towards the entrance.

"Training?" Hasefi asked, registering the Highchief's words. "What training?"

Esafi turned back, her ears twitching with annoyance. "Every lynx at twelve moons begins training. Your first moon will consist of the same basic training every lynx is taught." Esafi's gaze flicked to something near Hasefi. "I have more pressing matters to attend to, so I have shifted that responsibility to your assigned keeper."

"You want me to do that now?" Hasefi sighed.

"First, I must announce your presence to the Tribe and the losses yours suffered. I will also require a detailed account of your time outside the Great River, but I must speak with my champions first." The Highchief's eyes narrowed until her gaze was piercing. "I will remind you to say nothing of the black wolves to anyone you may encounter."

Anger boiled within her chest, but Hasefi did nothing more than flatten her ears and grit her teeth.

"You act like an ill-mannered kit," Esafi observed. "I cannot fault you as you did not have anyone to teach you otherwise, but I hope you will learn quickly not to glare at every lynx that speaks to you."

I still don't want to be here, she thought, averting her gaze lest the Highchief give her yet another reprimand.

"The Tribe is waking. I expect you on the Highledge shortly."

To Hasefi's relief, the Highchief padded out of the chamber, leaving her alone. Hasefi sat back down, her jaws stretching in a huge yawn.

I like your Highchief advice better, she thought to Sefonis.

His chuckle filled her head, spreading a warmth through her. Feeling a bit better, Hasefi pushed herself onto her paws and padded out into the cavern before the exit.

Esafi wasn't there, but Garfonis was. He was deep in thought, not reacting to Hasefi until she was in front of him.

"Hasefi," he blurted, getting to his paws. "How'd you sleep?"

"I think I got a few heartbeats in," she tried to joke, but her tone just sounded bitter. She cleared her throat and tried again. "What about you?"

"I didn't sleep," he admitted after a moment.

"A lot on your mind?" she asked, sitting in front of him.

He studied her for a moment before nodding. He had on his Emperor's armor, but his helmet sat beside him, glinting in the strange cave-light. Hasefi noticed the white was gradually changing to purple, mimicking the light of dawn.

"I'm sorry for how things were when you came," Garfonis began. "Your unexpected arrival is just one of the many things that have happened in the last half moon." His gaze was on the floor between their paws.

"Esafi is the one keeping me here," she reminded him. "If my presence is a bother, blame her."

"That's not what I meant," her father replied, his expression hurt and disappointed. "This isn't easy for you, either, I see that." An attempt at a smile made his whiskers twitch. "But maybe it'll help to speak more kindly to your mother."

"I'll do that when she does the same," Hasefi told him shortly.

Disappointment dulled his expression again and he sighed, sitting back down. A twinge of guilt tightened Hasefi's chest, but she had nothing else to say, so she was silent.

"We should meet the Highchief on the Ledge," Garfonis suggested, leaning back on his haunches so he could lift his helmet over his head.

Without a word, Hasefi followed him into the tunnel leading out.

She thought there had been lots of lynxes last night, but now, there was more than twice as many. Dozens of them filled the dawn-cast clearing, their gazes lifted to watch Esafi where she sat at the very end of the ledge.

Garfonis put a paw out to stop Hasefi before she could go over to the Highchief. Instead, he motioned for her to sit beside him at the back of the ledge. The Keeper Overlord, Sifara, was there, too, on the other side of the cave entrance, sitting as still as stone. Hasefi narrowed her eyes at the black-clad lynx until she remembered Esafi's comment about glaring.

"Good morning, my tribe!" Esafi's voice filled the air, bringing the hum of voices below to a gradual silence. "I have several announcements to make." She swept her gaze across the crowd below her. "First, I suspect most—if not all—of you are aware by now of our unexpected guest." The Highchief went silent and flicked her ears. Garfonis nudged Hasefi and, reluctantly, she moved to her mother's side.

At the edge, she was able to see more of the lynxes and was amazed and more than a little uncomfortable when countless gazes turned to look at her. It was like looking out at a lake, only the lake was made of fur and eyes.

Most of them didn't have armor on, but Hasefi still had a hard time reading their expressions, leaving her to guess at what they might be thinking.

"While I am delighted to have my daughter, Highchief of the Second Divide, return to us, I am afraid to announce that her arrival comes with unfortunate news." Easfi lowered her head a little, sweeping her gaze over the lynxes below. "The Tribe of the Second Divide has perished."

Shock and grief twisted the faces below. One lynx let out a wail before he was hushed by someone sitting beside him.

Hasefi's heart clenched painfully. *You have kin here,* she thought to her tribe. *These lynxes knew you. Much better than they ever knew me.*

Her tribe was silent, but their grief was as strong as if they were among the shocked lynxes below.

"Without her own followers and without a home," Esafi continued after letting the lynxes recover a little from the heart-breaking news. "I have decided to welcome Hasefi back into our tribe. Her timing couldn't have been better—our need for a High Heir is greater now than ever. So, I ask that you welcome Hasefi as our newest High Heir."

Hasefi jumped as the crowd began to cheer for her. It was strange to hear such a joyous reaction after what had just been announced but, this time, as she looked upon the faces peering up, she could see the reaction was done more out of necessity than excitement.

Guilt twisted her chest as she thought of the lynxes that could've—*should've*—returned with her.

You have no reason to feel guilty, Sefonis said, his tone gentle but firm.

I know, Hasefi replied with an inward sigh. *But that doesn't make it hurt less.*

"Return to your father," Esafi murmured under her breath, her words nearly lost in the loud cheers from below.

Hasefi obeyed. She knew Esafi wanted to keep the Pack a secret, but she hoped the Highchief would at least provide some sort of consolation, especially to those that lost friends and family.

"With all that said," Esafi continued to the crowd when they had hushed again. "Our warning to the Clan was interrupted and could not be delivered."

Hasefi felt the air change. The expectant silence became charged and her fur prickled uneasily.

"They will not get away with what they've done," Easfi growled, her fur bristling and her shoulders tensing as her armored claws gripped the edge of the stone ledge. "They have gone too far and must be punished for their actions. Be assured, we will have retribution."

Eager growls and vicious yowls sounded below. Once again, Hasefi was taken aback by how quickly the lynxes shifted from one feeling to another.

"I will discuss with my champions on our next move. For now, you will continue with your regular duties."

Esafi rose to her paws and turned away from the crowd. A surge of shock and anger rushed through Hasefi when she realized her mother had no intention of elaborating on the deaths of Hasefi's tribe. She shot to her paws, following the Highchief back into the cave.

"Wait," she hissed at Esafi. Garfonis and the Overlord came in behind Hasefi and had to squeeze around her when she came to a halt at the entrance of the cavern. "That's it?" Hasefi snapped.

Esafi stopped in the middle of the cavern, turning slowly to face her. Her eyes narrowed when she met Hasefi's gaze.

"Some of those lynxes down there lost family. Aren't you at least going to give them *some* consolation?"

"What would you suggest?" Esafi asked, her ears twitching with bored impatience.

"I—I don't know," Hasefi stammered. "I mean, maybe you could at least tell them that—that they were brave and that they were—they were—"

Esafi turned away.

"Why can't we tell them what happened?" Hasefi blurted before the Highchief could walk away.

"If you are right," Esafi began with a sigh, turning towards her again. "And the black wolves have united, telling the tribe will make already high tensions worse. Surely you saw how they were after I mentioned your arrival interrupted Garfonis's message to the Clan?"

Hasefi wrinkled her nose, refusing to feel guilty for something she hardly knew about, let alone cared for.

"Spirits are low as we teeter on the edge of another war with the Clan. Bringing in another enemy—one that still gives some of my lynxes nightmares—will only make things worse. Especially after what we've already lost."

"That doesn't mean you get to keep them in the dark!" Hasefi protested.

"What I get to do isn't up to you," Esafi said with a bemused expression. "A Highchief must make difficult decisions in order to protect her tribe. You will learn this once you are older."

Hasefi gritted her teeth, biting back an angry retort that would not help anyone.

"Sifara." Esafi turned an expectant gaze on the Overlord.

"Arsolin is ready," the dark-plated lynx announced. "He awaits the High Heir now."

"Good." There was something in Esafi's eye that Hasefi couldn't grasp. "You and Garfonis will fetch the other champions if they are not already on their way up."

Hasefi's father and the Overlord obeyed after bowing, leaving Hasefi alone with the Highchief.

"Your keeper is outside," Esafi told her dismissively before padding into the tunnel leading into the sleeping chamber.

Anger rooted Hasefi to the spot.

How can she just leave them like that? she thought. *Your parents, your siblings, they just learnt that you died. And what do they get for it?*

They knew our parting would likely be our last, Kilarsa pointed out, though her tone was dejected.

But they expected you to find a new place to live, to make a home and raise generations of new lynxes. Not to die in the first two moons!

Kilarsa didn't respond.

Hasefi let out a long breath, aware her anger was being wrongly directed.

If I'm going to be spending time here, maybe I can at least talk to some of your kin and help ease their pain, if only a little.

That would be very kind of you, Kilarsa said, a smile in her voice.

Hasefi looked to where Esafi had disappeared. She was a little surprised the Highchief didn't feel the need to keep an escort on her at all times, especially when there was a third tunnel connected to the cavern she stood in.

Where does it lead?

Not to an exit, Sefonis replied and that was all Hasefi needed. The tiny bit of curiosity she had to check it out was easily quashed and she padded into the tunnel leading out.

What would be the best way to get out of here? she asked her tribe.

It is difficult to say, Sefonis admitted. *The Tribe keeps a tight hold on the clearing.*

Oh, Sefonis, don't pretend you never used the bramble-path, Kilarsa said, her tone thick with amusement.

It was secured long ago, he replied with a defensive note that made Hasefi's whiskers twitch with her own amusement.

Aye, but kits and novices are clever, Kilarsa purred. *Especially if they've got a gifted with them. I'm sure they have another way out, by now.*

It'd be easy to find for a young lynx, too. Mersaka, the guardian under Kilarsa's command, was the one who spoke. *Hasefi, if you were to befriend some of the novices here, I'm sure they'd tell you.*

How long would it take? she asked. *I doubt they'd be willing to tell the daughter of the Highchief about a weak-spot in the Tribe's home.*

That's a good point, Mersaka admitted.

It's worth a try, Kilarsa insisted. *While you're here.*

Plus, Gelinaf added. *If you can befriend lynxes, they'll be more likely to trust you and will not suspect you of sneaking out. Especially if you can make a routine that allows for time to plan and execute an escape.*

Hasefi's head was beginning to throb with all the voices speaking to her and she gave it a shake.

I hope I'm not here for that long, she said, intending to quiet them. *So if you have any ideas that are a bit less complex, let me know.*

She was both relieved and disappointed when her tribe went quiet. She knew they were doing their best to help, but she couldn't help but feel like they were also trying to find a reason for her to stay as if she might change her mind.

But I won't. I have to save Kolahn.

She could hear activity outside the cave, along with a gentle breeze that whispered past the entrance. The light in the tunnel was a deep purple with a hint of orange that was strengthening with every heartbeat, changing the white fur of her paws to a gold not unlike Esafi's and Garfonis's.

I'll play along for a little while, she told herself, snapping her head back up. *Long enough for opportunity to rise. And if it doesn't, I'll make my own opportunity.*

With a deep breath, Hasefi stepped out onto the Ledge. Early morning sunlight matched the strange light glowing behind her, turning the clearing into a mixture of golden light and long shadows.

Her eyes went immediately to where the fern entrance was, but she was too far back on the Ledge to see it. She moved towards the edge and was surprised to find the clearing emptier than it had been when she'd first arrived. There were little movements around the clearing where keepers were keeping watch and a group of brown-clad hunters were making their way towards the entrance. Other than them, there was no sign any lynx had come to listen to the Highchief's announcements.

Do High Heirs actually get up this early, or does Esafi think she can keep me too busy to think of an escape plan?

Hasefi's thought was pushed aside when she noticed a keeper sitting below the Ledge. A strange bird-creature with soft red flesh around its neck lay beside them. It took Hasefi a moment before she recalled Kolahn had described something like it once and called it a turkey. The keeper's helmet was angled toward her and she suspected this was the keeper Esafi had assigned to her.

An extra measure to make sure I don't escape.

All highbloods are assigned a keeper, Gelinaf told her.

Highblood? Is that what I am? Hasefi asked, wrinkling her nose.

Her Overlord didn't respond. The distance he and the rest of her tribe were giving her was painfully wide, but she made an effort to rein in the helpless frustration hanging over her like an icicle ready to drop and shatter on the rocks below.

Hasefi descended the path from the Ledge and padded over to the keeper. Their armor was akin to Sifara's except it lacked the spikes and horns. This lynx was shorter than the Overlord, but their shoulders were broader and their limbs stockier.

"Good morning, High Heir," he greeted as she approached, sinking into a deep bow.

"Morning?" she echoed with a glance at the last few stars still in the sky. "Can we even call it that?" She turned her gaze in the direction of the river where the sun was hidden behind the mountains that surrounded the Great Valley she had come from with Kolahn.

"Almost," the keeper replied in a neutral tone as he sat back up again. "I hope you aren't too tired."

"Oh, I'm fine," Hasefi said quickly. Her words had been intended as a joke, but the keeper seemed to have taken them seriously. "I'm not too bothered, really." She glanced at the prey lying beside him.

"I was informed you might not have eaten in a while," he explained. "I brought this for you before we begin your training."

"Right. Uh, thanks." Hasefi twitched her ears, wondering who had told the keeper she hadn't eaten. It wouldn't be hard to guess, given the state she was in, she was sure, but she was surprised by the gesture, especially if it had been from Esafi or her looming Overlord.

"Erm, have you eaten?" Hasefi asked, hesitating.

"I have."

"Alright." She bent over the bird, giving it an awkward sniff. Her belly tightened immediately. If she hadn't been so hungry, she would have been uncomfortable eating while the keeper sat silently, but the pangs in her belly quelled any discomfort she felt.

Even still, she did her best to try and make conversation.

"You're Arsolin, right?"

"Aye." The reply, too, came in a neutral tone, but his head lowered a little. "Overlord Sifara said I was to be your keeper. But I understand if you would prefer to have someone else."

"Why would I want someone else?" Hasefi asked, confused by his words.

The keeper hesitated. "Has the Highchief told you of my previous charges?" His words were slow, carefully chosen.

"No." Hasefi frowned, noticing a stir of reaction from her tribe. "Why would she?"

"It is not my place to discuss," he told her quickly. "Perhaps you should speak with her before—"

"Don't worry about it." Hasefi wanted to keep her interactions with Esafi as scarce as she could before she left, so she gave her head a dismissive shake. "I'm sure it's not a big deal."

"But—"

"You'll be a fine keeper, I'm sure," Hasefi assured him before taking another bite of the turkey.

The keeper was silent. Hasefi's gaze flicked up to look at him, but his armor was just as complete as any other keeper's. There was no way for her to read his face or even his body language as he took on a stone-still posture.

A part of her felt bad for being dismissive, but she tried to console herself with the fact she wouldn't be here long and the poor keeper wouldn't have to deal with her once she was gone.

I should try and get on his good side, she thought, remembering Gelinaf's words. *If he's the lynx going to be by my side all the time, I don't want to give him reason to look for something to report about me.*

After a few moments of silent chewing, Hasefi made another attempt to talk to the keeper.

"What are we doing today?"

"I am leading your basic training," he said without moving. "Normally the Highchief trains their Heir, but with everything that has happened and continues to happen, I understand why she would pass it on."

That hardly answers my question, Hasefi thought irritably.

"Forgive me if my knowledge is insufficient," Arsolin added.

Hasefi stared at him incredulously before jerking her gaze back to the remains of the turkey at her paws.

"It'll be fine," she tried to assure him, but she was too caught up in her bewilderment. *I didn't think keepers could be so nervous. He doesn't sound young...he couldn't be a new keeper, could he?*

She thought her tribe would remain silent, but Gelinaf's presence stirred.

Something has rattled him, he replied slowly as if he, too, was choosing each word carefully. *I suspect it has something to do with his previous charges.*

Is that your way of telling me to ask Esafi about it?

It may help in understanding him.

"Training begins with getting your armor," Arsolin continued and Hasefi returned her attention to him. "But it is early, so we will tour the territory first. I will begin with the outer border today. Once we return and you've received your armor, I will bring you to the Cavern of History."

"That sounds great," Hasefi told him, hoping to give him a little bit of encouragement. "I think I'm done," she added with a glance at the bones at her paws. "Where do you bury these?"

"Actually, we leave bones in a hollow beneath the Guardian's Cave," he told her. "The guardians use them for their magic. I can take them for you."

"Erm, it's okay, I can do it. Could you just show me where?"

With a dip of his head, Arsolin got to his paws and led the way to one of the caves beside the ledge. It was the tallest, aside from the Highchief's cave, with a winding path that led to it.

At the base was an empty hollow. At Arsolin's direction, Hasefi dropped the bones into it. During her time with Kolahn, he had taught her to bury bones to keep predators from sniffing them out. Before then, however, if she'd been lucky enough to catch prey, she would leave its remains where they were. In the high mountains, there was little time to give to finish a meal, let alone hide it, before something just as hungry arrived.

But the idea of bones being used for something else was strange to her.

Hasefi looked up into the guardian's cave. It shone with the same light as the cave she had slept in, turning golden just as the sky above was. There were no guardians about, but her fur prickled as if someone was looking down at her.

She stifled a shiver and turned to Arsolin. "Shall we?"

With a dip of his head, he led her towards the fern entrance. Hasefi studied the walls around the clearing, wondering if she could see a weak spot in the barrier. To her disappointment, there was nothing but a barricade of thick foliage intertwined with brambles and branches that she guessed could only have been created by gifteds.

You see where the log lies along the wall? Kilarsa spoke up.

Hasefi looked to the bark-stripped log her Elder indicated and gave a mental nod.

Around its middle, a part of it had been removed by some of the gifted novices so they could open a path into the wall without any of the bigger lynxes knowing. Her tone had a mischievous note to it that made Hasefi's whiskers quiver.

Novices couldn't leave the clearing?

There's a curfew, she explained. *Plus, novices often had friends not yet old enough to leave the clearing.*

So they let kits out? Hasefi asked. *Did kits not like staying here?*

You know well enough the curiosity of a young lynx, Kilarsa said with an amused purr.

Yeah, I guess. I couldn't imagine being cooped up here, Kolahn or no Kolahn. A wistful twinge entered her chest at the thought of what it would be like to sneak away with friends so they could explore the territory on their own. *Is it safe out there?*

As safe as it can be. It was Sefonis who spoke. *The territory is guarded constantly by knights and keepers. I suspect even more so now.*

Why now?

Sefonis hesitated.

Tension is high between the Clan and Tribe, Gelinaf reminded Hasefi. *Extra patrols at the borders and keepers in the forest are a reaction to such.*

Hasefi was a little disappointed by the news, knowing it would make it harder for her to leave.

Unless Esafi does decide to attack the Clan, she said to herself. *Then I'll have a great distraction.*

She and Arsolin passed through the fern entrance. Hasefi looked behind but was surprised to find the forest looking quite thick even though she knew it was empty just a couple paces away.

That's weird.

Magic, Kilarsa explained. *You are right in assuming the walls were made by gifted lynxes. They also casted an illusion to make the clearing harder to find for attackers.*

Hasefi gave the illusion an impressed look. *That's quite useful. Is there a limit to what you can do?*

Magic is a conversion of energy, Kilarsa explained. *It doesn't just 'happen'. Look to your left. See the raspberry bush with the few shriveled leaves? It is the anchor of this magic. An illusion such as this does not require much, so this plant will suffice to keep it alive, but it sacrifices a part of itself in order to do so.*

I'm not sure I understand, Hasefi admitted. *But that sounds like it could be dangerous.*

Aye, if used recklessly. But there are many rules all gifted learn before they are allowed to use their abilities freely.

Hasefi's thoughts shifted. *The wolves have gifted, too, right? I didn't have any problems finding their ravine.*

Their home is easier to defend, Kilarsa pointed out. *Their walls are secured by long drops and there's only one way in.*

That makes it easy to get trapped in, too, Hasefi added.

Kilarsa's attention moved beyond Hasefi and she realized Arsolin had begun to speak as he led her into the territory.

"...while the River is the border between our land and the Clan's."

Hasefi looked in the direction of the River. A strong pull tugged at her paws and she wondered just how fast Arsolin was.

He's already noticed your twitching tail, if that's any indication, Gelinaf offered.

Hasefi swung her head around to Arsolin and realized the keeper had gone silent. She couldn't read his expression, but she could feel his eyes hot on her fur.

"Sorry," she mumbled.

"We will have time to explore the rest in other days," he told her, and she wondered if he had misread her intentions or if his words were a subtle warning.

He continued to lead her parallel to the cliff-face. Hasefi kept an ear angled toward him in case he decided to quiz her on anything he said, but her primary focus was the lay of the land and anything her assigned keeper said about the various paths leading to the borders.

I could try and cross this outer border he mentioned, she thought. *And then go around the territory and find a different way to cross the River.*

The only way across without gifted is behind the waterfall, Kilarsa admitted. *And it would take you a day to reach the River without crossing into the Tribe's territory again. Esafi's keepers would track you down by then.*

Fallen stars, Hasefi sighed inwardly.

The sheer cliff rising above them became more warped the farther they moved from the Tribe's home. Bulges of rock with stubborn trees dotted the cliff-face which slanted down until, eventually, it met the hilly ground they were walking upon. A little farther ahead, there was a large, square-ish boulder covered in a blanket of rich green moss so thick Hasefi wondered if it had been there since the beginning of the world.

"This is Greenrock." Arsolin said, stopping beside the boulder. "It marks the beginning of our border. We identify our borders with scent which is renewed by the guards that constantly watch it."

"What would happen if someone were to cross it? Like, during a hunt-chase," Hasefi added quickly when the keeper's helmet turned directly on her.

"There are no repercussions for full members of the Tribe if there is good reason for crossing. Chasing a hare over the border is acceptable. But beyond lies a territory free for other creatures. Some of which can be very dangerous. Younger lynxes are required to stay within the borders at all times."

"So the border is to keep novices inside?" Hasefi asked.

"It also warns unwanted creatures to stay out of our territory."

Hasefi nodded absently. It was another strange thing to do for her, as she had grown up trying to leave as little scent of herself as possible to avoid being tracked by anything that might hunt her, even without the Pack. But those kinds of hunters were scarce here and there was a whole army of lynxes just a little ways towards the rising sun they could call upon, should a situation arise.

Not that I can rely on Esafi to help me.

"How often do they mark these?" Hasefi had intended to ask her tribe the question, but she realized she had spoken aloud when Arsolin was the one to respond.

"There is always a patrol on each of our borders," he told her. "We have added extras since—." His words ended in a muffled cough.

"What about the border to the River?" Hasefi decided to ask, since they were on the topic.

Hasefi, do not be obvious, Gelinaf warned.

Arsolin was silent for a moment. "That is where our patrols are focused. You do not need to worry, High Heir, you are safe here." His words trailed off as if he weren't so confident in them, spiking Hasefi's curiosity.

"How often do lynxes visit the Clan?" she asked despite her Overlord's warning.

Arsolin didn't respond.

"That's where Garfonis found me," Hasefi explained. "Does he go there often?"

"No," the keeper replied hesitantly. "He had gone to...deliver a message."

There was more Hasefi wanted to ask, but she could sense the keeper's discomfort. *What kind of message? He was alone, apart from his keeper, but he seemed really upset. Eilwyn said the Tribe had accused them of stealing prey. Is that why there might be a war? There's lots of land around each territory; surely both sides have enough prey.*

There is a deep rift between the Tribe and the Clan that has lasted for seasons upon seasons, Sefonis told her. *Any little thing can be enough to push either side to violence.*

I suppose that's good for me, she thought, though it didn't sit well in her mind. *Do you think there's any way I could convince Garfonis to let me come next time he needs to deliver a message?*

Her uncle was silent.

Arsolin resumed padding along the border and Hasefi followed, using the time to scour her mind for a plan to get back to Kolahn.

It was simpler before, she thought, *when the Pack had him. Terrifying, but simple.* Blood flashed in her mind, along with the white of fangs, wolven and not. *I wasn't afraid of hurting anyone then. But, if something like that happened to Kolahn's clan, he'd never forgive me. I wouldn't forgive myself.*

A long sigh nearly left her jaws before she clamped them shut, glancing at Arsolin to make sure he hadn't noticed her broken attention. He had come to a sudden stop and she had just enough time to side-step awkwardly around the keeper before she crashed into him.

"Sorry," she mumbled.

He didn't respond, so she rounded him and found him sniffing the air. Hasefi did the same, then lowered her nose to the ground. A pungent scent permeated the earth, making her nose wrinkle.

"Bear," she choked. "I almost forgot how nasty they smell."

"You're right," Arsolin replied with a bit of surprise. "But there's no need to worry—it was probably just passing through."

"Did I look worried?" Hasefi asked, tilting her head.

"No, I suppose not." Arsolin swept his gaze quickly through the trees in the direction the scent led.

"Um, I've never seen a bear," Hasefi admitted, realizing her words may have come across as a little arrogant. "But I was told they were quite scary. Have you seen one before?"

"I have," he admitted.

"What are they like?"

"It depends," he said. "Bears with black fur tend to keep their distance. But brown bears are bigger and usually a lot angrier."

"You've seen both?"

"No," Arsolin told her. "I've been fortunate enough only to encounter a black bear. I was with a patrol and it hurried off."

Hasefi nodded. *Kolahn was quite afraid of them,* she thought. *I wonder if he saw a brown one.*

"This is a black bear," Arsolin continued. "Unfortunately, their scent is the more tolerable of the two."

It took Hasefi a moment to realize the keeper was trying to make a joke.

"Great," she moaned. "So, if you ever find me passed out in the woods here, it's probably because I smelt a brown bear."

A chuckle echoed within Arsolin's helmet, sending a ripple of delight through Hasefi.

"Even still," she continued, becoming serious again. "It would be a good idea to let someone know, right? In case it came back or something?"

"Aye, it would," he agreed. There was a note in his voice suggesting he was pleased by her words. "I intend to inform Keeper Overlord Sifara once we return to the clearing."

Hasefi jerked her head to the path before them. "How much longer do we have?"

"We're about halfway," he replied, looking up through the forest canopy. "We should keep going if we're to make it back before sunpeak."

They continued along the border, walking in silence for a bit. Arsolin would offer more information about the things they encountered and things she might encounter in the future. Some of these were things Kolahn had taught her, but she had spent most of her time with him in a forest called Edgewood. Where she was now, the Great Forest, was quite a bit different. There were so many more kinds of plants, all sorts of trees in place of the needle-covered ones she was used to, and even more bugs.

Once, she would have been eager to learn but, while curiosity still pricked her pelt, everything, new and not, made her think of her friend.

Eventually, they reached a part of the territory where the trees gave way to rolling hills of bright green grass. The sun had risen above the mountains, making the ground sparkle with the bits of dew still clinging to the blades.

Woah, she thought. She had seen this strange, open land from the edge of the Great Valley, but had forgotten about it until now. *Just when I think I've seen the whole world, it gets bigger. Does it go on forever?*

Before anyone could respond, Arsolin announced it was time they began their trek back to the clearing. As she turned to follow, Hasefi's newly fixed leg gave out.

"High Heir, are you alright?" Arsolin rushed to her side, but he seemed hesitant to help. Fortunately, she had a lot of practice using just three legs to support herself.

"Yeah," she told him, sitting so she could rest. "I think my leg is just a little tired. It was broken for moons and your healers fixed it last night, so I just need to build up a bit of strength, I think."

The keeper sat and bowed his head slightly. "My apologies, High Heir."

"What for?" Hasefi asked, confused.

"I should have been more aware of your state and shortened today's tour so your healed leg could strengthen," he explained.

"It's alright," Hasefi told him, bewildered by his guilt. "I didn't even think about it. I'm sure if we rest for a few heartbeats, I'll be good to go."

"Are you sure?"

"I've handled much worse than this, trust me," she assured him.

The keeper nodded and grew silent. Hasefi looked around, not sure what to say. She stole a glance at the keeper who was still facing her, but he sat straight and was still as stone.

"How long have you been a keeper?" she asked him.

"For more moons than I can count," he admitted.

Hasefi nodded. She tried to think of something else to talk about, but all she ended up saying was that her leg was fine and she was ready to continue.

I'll need to be careful with my leg if I'm going to escape, she thought to herself. *But, if I really need to, I can always use my tribe.*

The thought of using her tribe's strength for something trivial didn't make her happy. In their spirit forms, there was no way for them to regain strength, so, if she were to deplete what was left of them, she'd have no tribe left.

I can do this on my own, she thought. *I can't always depend on them.*

Arsolin quizzed her as they retraced their steps and, though Hasefi had tried to at least appear attentive, there was much she hadn't picked up. Her tribe was there to give her enough answers, however, to avoid arousing the keeper's suspicion.

When they returned to the clearing, Hasefi's left foreleg was sore and couldn't hold her weight without shaking. She enjoyed it, though, taking that pain over being crippled any day.

"Before we go to the Cavern of History," Arsolin began. "We will get your armor now that the guardians will be awake. We won't be moving quite as much, so you'll have time to rest your leg."

Hasefi followed him to the cave beside the one she had met Hesilar and Salifen and where she'd left her bones. The path to the Highledge was a simple ramp that curved away from the wall at the base, but the path to the Guardian's Cave wound back and forth until it reached the cave-mouth.

"How did this path get here?" she asked Arsolin as they ascended.

"Guardians made it," he explained.

"This, too?" she asked.

The keeper hesitated, glancing back at her.

"They concealed the clearing with magic, too, right?"

"Yes," he replied, sounding surprised.

"I figured," Hasefi said quickly, realizing it had been her tribe who had told her. "It seemed strange that the clearing disappeared the moment we left it. Um, what else did the guardians do?"

"They carved these caves," Arsolin continued, leading her up the path again. It was almost as high as the Highchief's ledge and she had to limp up on three legs lest her left leg give out again. "They created the light within. And it's said they even carved out the cliff-face."

"The entire cliff-face?" Hasefi gasped. "What about the part in the Clan's territory?"

"They weren't always here," the keeper explained. "But I can talk more about that in the Cavern of History," he added before she could ask more questions.

They entered the cave and Hasefi saw that it was quite similar to the healer's cave she'd been in. There were various tunnels, holes in the walls, though there were more miscellaneous items and fewer herbs.

Two lynxes in dark purple armor were in the chamber, one flitting about as if looking for something, and the second studying a stone about the size of Hasefi's paw that looked like a piece of the night sky.

"High Heir," the second lynx greeted, standing and bowing. The first lynx stopped in his tracks and offered a bow of his own, before snatching a branch and hurrying into one of the tunnels leading farther into the cliff.

"Um, hi," Hasefi greeted, feeling awkward. "What's your name?"

"I am Guardian Silvera," the lynx offered. "I've been expecting you," she said. "Though I had assumed the Highchief would be accompanying you," she added, lifting her head.

"I've been instructed to guide the High Heir's training," Arsolin admitted.

"Really?" Silvera asked. "Interesting. I suppose the Highchief would have her paws full."

Hasefi found she was already beginning to like this guardian. She was the first one to show any sort of curiosity.

Aside from that novice, she remembered. *Salifen, I think?*

It's how they're raised to be, her uncle spoke up, an unexpected hiss in his words. *Obedient and loyal, without question.*

But gifteds tend to have a harder time following that path, Kilarsa added.

Silvera was studying Arsolin and Hasefi wondered if the guardian could see through armor. But Silvera said nothing more to the keeper and returned her attention to Hasefi.

"Let's get you armored up, shall we? Sit with me."

Hasefi joined the guardian, sitting in front of the night-stone so she was facing the gifted lynx. "Is there something I need to do?" Hasefi asked her.

"Just stay as still as you can," Silvera said with a smile. "I will start by measuring your structure so I can form your armor to fit comfortably. Then I will begin to create it." Her head bobbed up and down as she rounded Hasefi, inspecting her.

"And you just...make it out of nothing?"

"Not nothing," Silvera corrected. "Everything comes from something. When you eat, food doesn't just disappear, it creates energy for your body. And everything is made of energy—living, unliving, or both."

"That sounds really complicated," Hasefi murmured.

"It can be," the guardian admitted, whiskers quivering with amusement. "Gifted lynxes have a sort of...awareness of both planes. But I won't bore you with lessons. I suspect that will be your afternoon," she added with a chuckle. "Now." Silvera sat back. "I'm going to start forming the armor around you. Each lynx's set has its source piece which will be how you put on and take off the armor. Yours will be your helmet. I will make that before I start with the rest."

Hasefi nodded.

Silvera's yellow eyes glowed beneath her hood. Hasefi did her best to sit still as the guardian moved her paws around her head. A weight formed and she saw something appear in the sides of her vision. When the guardian moved away, Hasefi dipped her head, testing the helmet. It fit securely and didn't slip when she gave her head a gentle shake.

"How is it?" Silvera asked.

"It feels good," Hasefi replied. "I just don't like how it shows in my vision."

"You'll get used to seeing the helmet in your peripheral," the guardian assured her. "Now, I'm going to begin making the armor along your body." She began, securely wrapping Hasefi's legs with a soft material that went all the way down to the joints at her paws. Then harder armor like her helmet formed along her chest, shoulders, flanks, and haunches, overlapping and folding easily so moving wasn't much more difficult than usual. It was black with silver trim, but it lacked the starry design she'd seen on the Highchief and champion armors, nor did the chest have the star Esafi's had. Reaching up her paw, Hasefi could feel the absence of the highstone and spikes.

"Good?" Silvera asked and Hasefi nodded. "Now, one last thing. I'll enchant the armor to respond to your thoughts. That way, when you want to take it off, all you have to do is slip your helmet off."

"What if I was in a battle and it got knocked off?" Hasefi asked.

"The enchantment will be designed to your thoughts, so the rest of your armor will remain. And you can even have the armor disappear without taking your helmet off, too. I'll let you try it out once it's on." The guardian placed a paw to Hasefi's helmet. Her eyes glowed for a moment before fading back to normal again. "Try it out."

Hasefi slowly slipped off her helmet, feeling the armor around her fold into itself until it was gone. She put the helmet back on and it returned. Taking it off a second time, the armor stayed.

"Nice! Sometimes it takes lynxes a couple tries to figure it out," the guardian said.

"I had armor before," Hasefi admitted.

"Ah, that would make sense." Silvera's eyes flickered towards Hasefi, but, despite the curiosity in them, she did not pursue the topic further. "Armor can be customized if you wanted to add anything like design, items, or what intrigues you, so don't be afraid to come to me or ask for any of the armor specialists to help you out."

"Armor specialists," Hasefi echoed. "It sounds like you're saying you're not one of them."

"I'm not," Silvera confirmed. "I serve as the Elder's right paw. Typically, he would help you with this, but he is a very busy lynx."

"Ah," Hasefi replied. "Well, thank you."

"My pleasure. Enjoy the rest of your day, High Heir." Silvera bowed, making Hasefi feel awkward again.

"Erm, you too."

As Arsolin led her back outside without a word, Hasefi tested the weight of her new armor. It wasn't very heavy and, now that her leg had been given a chance to rest, even it had no problem holding her up. She thought she would find it uncomfortable, but the new armor was unexpectedly easy to get used to.

Maybe it's because I used to have it before, she thought. *It's too bad I outgrew it. It could've helped a lot, even when I was with Kolahn. But even if I take this with me when I get Kolahn back, it'll probably end up the same way as my last set.* She shrugged. *At least I don't have to feel bad about losing another highstone.*

Her eyes went to the sky and she had to stifle a gasp. The sun was already past its peak, making its way back down to the horizon.

Kolahn has been with the Clan for half a day. Surely that white wolf wouldn't have him killed so soon, right? Her fur spiked with anxiety. She took a deep breath in and let it out slowly, urging her fur to lie flat before Arsolin noticed.

I have to stay calm. Panicking won't help anyone. Even if I can't find an idea for an escape plan today, Esafi wanted to talk more about what happened before I came here. At the very least, I might be able to find something out about what she intends to do about the Clan stealing prey. Maybe I could even suggest something to hurry things up....

Hasefi ducked her head a little as she descended the winding stone path leading from the Guardian's Cave, ashamed by her thoughts.

What choice do I have? she argued with herself, grateful her tribe had retreated to the far reaches of her mind. *If I don't act soon, Kolahn could be killed.*

I won't *let that happen.*

Chapter Four

"So, it's the Cave of History now, right?" Hasefi asked Arsolin when they were on the ground and the Guardian's Cave was behind them.

"The Cavern of History, yes," he replied and Hasefi thought she detected a note of excitement in his voice. "We'll go through the Keeper's Cave." He led her under the Highledge and to the cave beside it which was just a little lower than the Guardian's Cave. Inside the mainchamber, it was pretty much the same as the others she'd been in, only with less random items and not a lynx in sight. Arsolin led her down one of the tunnels leading further into the cliffside.

The path sloped down until Hasefi was sure they were below the ground level. Light akin to the sunlight outside shone from the walls and, after a while, she could see more light ahead where the tunnel gave way to what looked like a huge chamber. Voices travelled to them and Hasefi guessed there were quite a few lynxes ahead.

Arsolin was in front of her, so she wasn't able to see past him until they exited the tunnel. Her jaw dropped open as she gazed around in wonder.

Ahead, the wall had been transformed into a series of countless images, rising high above her and even a bit lower from where she stood, stretching the width of the cavern. Pictures of lynxes of all colors and armor covered the wall—even wolves made part of it. She could see the territory they lived in, too, and saw different versions of it across the wall.

"By the stars," she whispered. "How is this possible?"

"Magic," the keeper murmured, following her gaze. "This is our history. This is the Tribe's story."

With difficulty, Hasefi moved her attention from the spectacular sight to look at the rest of the cavern. Zigzagging pathways lined the adjacent walls of the decorated one, allowing for a closer look at the higher images. There were lynxes on these ledges, along with others on the ground. Some lynxes were alone, studying in silence, while others were grouped together. One group below where she stood had a couple hunters in tough, brown armor speaking to five novices with bracers on their left legs. Many voices filled the cavern, but they were hushed, like Arsolin's.

There's so much here, she thought. *I feel like I could spend a lifetime in here and still be learning.* There was an older knight sitting quietly half-way up the right wall of the cavern, gazing intently at the wall, and Hasefi wondered if he *had* spent a lifetime studying.

She returned her gaze to the decorated wall, tilting her head back until she could see the image at the very top. It was a lynx with golden fur and fierce yellow eyes.

"Is that the first lynx?" she asked.

"The first lynx like us," Arsolin explained. "Erina. And below her are her three kits."

Hasefi saw three different lynxes sitting proudly beneath their mother. They were all golden, like her, but one was tall with long ear tufts, another had a beautiful face and kind green eyes, and the third was built with broad shoulders and huge paws.

"What were their names?" she asked.

The keeper was silent for a moment before answering. "Talofin, Farena, and Nyosin."

"Talofin...Nyosin..." Hasefi's ears perked up and she looked at the keeper with surprise. "You're a descendant of the first lynx!"

Arsolin chuckled and lowered his head a little. "I am, yes. Do you see the dark-furred lynx there? A little farther down the line?"

Hasefi scanned the wall until she found a lynx with long ear tufts, an elegant form, and angular eyes.

"That is Shakofi," he told her.

"I'm related to her," Hasefi murmured.

"She is the first of your namesake," Arsolin explained and Hasefi's eyes widened. "And there, you see that gray lynx?"

Hasefi's gaze moved even farther down until she saw a lynx with a coat similar to her own.

"That's Halarik. He's the first of the gray lynxes."

"Gray lynxes," Hasefi echoed. "You mean there's different...kinds of lynxes?"

"Three," he told her. "Golden lynxes, like Erina and the Highchief. Dark lynxes, like Shakofi. And gray lynxes."

Hasefi's ears twitched and she looked to the wall again. "So what does all this mean?" she asked, nodding to images lower down.

"I will explain that in time," Arsolin told her. "Today, I'm just giving you a tour." His gaze flickered to something below, at the base of the wall.

A pair of novices with keeper helmets had turned their shadowy eyes on Hasefi while the keeper with them tried to regain their attention with a sharp word. Other lynxes in the cavern were glancing at her as they moved about, entering and exiting the various tunnels lining the walls beside her.

Why do I get the feeling I'm less than welcome?

Her tribe was ominously silent.

With a self-conscious shake of her fur, Hasefi moved her attention to the other tunnels, guessing they were all connected to each of the caves lining the cliff-side outside.

"Does that lead to the cave where I sleep?" Hasefi asked Arsolin quietly, nodding to the cave next to her.

"The Highcave, yes," Arsolin assured her. "Normally you would use that tunnel, but since I'm going to be mentoring you, we'll just use the keeper's entrance." He stood and led her to a nearby path. It curved along the wall, splitting off to create the zigzagging path up while the other half sloped down towards the brilliant wall ahead. They descended the latter and, when they reached the bottom, Hasefi saw that there were more caves beneath the ledge they had been standing on. Hushed voices drifted from them, their tones indicating they were teachers. Hasefi jumped when a ripple of laughter came from one of the caves, the sudden noise foreign in this quiet place.

Adding to the magical nature of the cavern, each of the six caves had a pair of stone lynxes sitting on either side, representing the respective armors of their champions and their followers. For the tunnel she suspected represented the Highchiefs, one stone lynx had armor akin to Esafi's, while the other had armor identical to her own.

What more could there possibly be? she wondered, unable to imagine what might lie in the caves before her. *How long did it take to make all this?*

She hadn't expected her tribe to answer, but Kilarsa spoke up.

It is a project guardians have been working on since the first gifted was given to us. Our abilities have helped preserve much of history, allowing us to learn and better ourselves.

It's incredible. I had no idea something like this could even exist. Is there something even more astonishing I should brace myself for?

This is about the extent of it, Kilarsa replied with amusement.

"These caves represent the History of the Paths," Arsolin explained, bringing Hasefi's attention outwards again. "There weren't always things like keepers and guardians, but when the tribe grew to a size that was difficult to maintain, it was necessary to separate it into smaller groups. At first, there were just two—knights and hunters. When the first gifted was offered to us, guardians came. Keepers came next. And, lastly, healers."

"What about Highchiefs?" Hasefi asked.

"There was always a leader," Arsolin explained. "The title of Highchief came later and so did the rules, but there was always a single leader."

Hasefi nodded.

"I will show you what it is like inside."

Hasefi followed Arsolin into the Highchief cave. This was the only cave that was quiet and, inside, it was empty of lynxes. The walls were decorated but weren't quite as big as the wall they had left behind, so the highest pictures were within reach. Instead, the walls spread lengthwise.

To her left, in the very top corner, she saw Erina again, but only one of her sons was with her—Talofin, the tall one. After him, other lynxes lined the wall until they began to wear various armors, eventually matching the kind Hasefi once wore; the kind Esafi wore. Their faces were exposed with their helmets at their paws.

"These were all Highchiefs?" she breathed. She saw under each was the same kind of stone Esafi had on her helmet. Hasefi lifted a paw and brushed it against one beneath a solemn-faced lynx. She leapt back with a cry as images filled her mind, images of battle and loss. The pictures vanished the moment her paw left the stone.

"What was that?" she gasped, her fear dissipating when Arsolin let out a quiet chuckle.

"The soulstones—these in particular being highstones—of every lynx that was recovered are in these caves, laced with their memories. Touching them grants access to those memories."

Hasefi looked up in utter wonder, further baffled by the abilities of magic.

I thought you said there wasn't anything else, she thought to Kilarsa.

I merely said it was 'about' the extent of it. Now you've reached the full extent. Her tone was laced with laughter. Hasefi had to swallow the amused purr that rose in her throat.

"So I could live the lives of every Highchief?" she asked Arsolin.

"If you wanted, sure. These are used for historical purposes, so most of their personal lives have been excluded for their own privacy. The more you use the stones, the easier it will be to understand them," he added when she eyed the stone she had touched.

Hasefi shook her head. "I don't think I'll ever understand magic," she admitted. A thought came to her and she frowned. "My armor in the high mountains had one of these," she remembered. "I'm sure I touched it, but nothing like that ever happened."

"Soulstones are enchanted so kits can't use them," Arsolin explained. "The experience can overwhelm them."

I'm still overwhelmed, she thought as she turned her attention to the right where more lynxes were. The armor of the later lynxes was like the set she wore now. "Who are these?"

"These were High Heirs that passed before their time to claim leadership of the Tribe."

Hasefi frowned and looked to the last lynx in the line. He was small with golden fur. But there was no stone beneath him.

"How come he doesn't have a soulstone?" she asked, studying the image. Arsolin didn't provide an answer, so Hasefi looked to the keeper and saw that his head was angled towards the lynx kit. "Arsolin?"

"Not all lynxes are recovered," he murmured quietly. "A stone will be made for him, but it will be from the memories of the guardians that create it and other lynxes he may have been with." The keeper fell into silence again.

Hasefi wondered who this lynx might have been. She wasn't sure just how old Arsolin was since she had yet to see his face, but he'd revealed he'd been a keeper for many moons. She wondered if this High Heir had been a friend of his when he was young. "Will you be one of those lynxes?" she dared ask the keeper.

"I will," he admitted.

He cared for this lynx, she observed as she watched him. *He said the body wasn't recovered. Could this have happened during Resahn's Reign? This couldn't have been his kit, right?*

"There is one more thing to show you," Arsolin spoke abruptly. He moved past her, padding through the chamber towards the far wall.

Hasefi hurried to follow.

"Each Path," he began, "has three qualities a novice or High Heir must learn before they become a full member of the Tribe." Arsolin stopped before the wall, his helmet angled up as he looked at it. Three images were portrayed there with a lynx in Highchief armor in all of them. The lynx didn't have a definite fur color or gender.

"The first is compassion," the keeper continued, nodding to the first image where the Highchief was touching their nose to another lynx's head. "Next is selflessness." The following image showed the Highchief watching other lynxes eat. "And finally, sacrifice." In the final picture, the Highchief was curled in the middle of a group of lynxes with their heads bowed. "These are the qualities of the Highchief, which you will learn by following in the Highchief's pawsteps.

I remember some of this, Hasefi thought with surprise. *These are things you told me about, Sefonis.*

Aye, wee lass. And you've certainly proved to possess each and more.

Hasefi didn't reply, overcome with something she couldn't identify. She turned to Arsolin. "Can I stay down here?" she asked without really meaning to.

The keeper was silent, but she couldn't tell if he was surprised or suspicious by her request.

"Unless there's something else you have to show me," she added. Escaping was her priority, but it was clear this cavern was one of the last places she'd be able to get out unnoticed.

"The other Paths are much of the same," Arsolin finally spoke. "You've had a lot of excitement, I suspect, so I will not go into detail today. Tomorrow we'll continue our tour of the borders and I will describe in detail the role a Highchief plays, though my knowledge is limited and you may have to learn some on your own. These high-stones will help with that and it may do you well to linger in these caves. There is a lot of knowledge here." He turned towards the tunnel leading out. "I am still your keeper, so I'll be just around the corner if you need me."

"Thank you," she told him and he bowed before leaving the cave. Hasefi returned her gaze to the three images, studying each one with more intensity.

Is this where you got the lessons you were teaching me in the high mountains? Hasefi asked her uncle.

Some of it. But there are things I believe every lynx should know. There was no hiss in his tone, but there was a note that reminded her of the tight grip he and the rest of her tribe were keeping on their thoughts.

She looked around, letting her gaze linger on each lynx before moving to the next.

This is beyond anything I've ever imagined. Anything I could *imagine! I never knew what magic could do.*

Lynxes have been able to do great things with these gifts, Kilarsa agreed, her tone wistful.

Did you used to spend a lot of time in here? Hasefi asked her.

Aye, every moment, though I tended to keep to the Guardian's Path. If you are to take anything from life, Hasefi, it is that one never stops learning.

Hasefi went back to the stone she had touched before. The Highchief above it had a somber expression on his face. Perhaps it was from the brief glimpse she caught, but she felt as if there was a great weight on his shoulders, too.

Hesitantly, she put her paw up and touched her pad to the stone.

The images returned and, for a moment, they threatened to overwhelm her. But Kilarsa stepped in, helping her organize the barrage of memories.

This is Highchief Kalirim, she spoke, narrating as the images played. Some were in his perspective, but some were outside, from someone else's eyes. *His is a sad tale.*

Hasefi watched Kalirim as a young lynx kit. He was the only kit of his litter and there were no other kits about.

Both of his parents passed before he reached his twelfth moon, making him one of the youngest Highchief's in Tribe history. Indeed, Hasefi watched the young kit get Highchief armor before he was her size.

At least he had champions to guide him, she thought as the young Highchief was surrounded by the representatives of each Path.

She released the stone and returned to the cave, blinking. This time, the memories lingered until she gave her head a good shake.

There are so many of them, Hasefi thought as she scanned the wall. Her eye went to the very last lynx who was positioned at the bottom near the middle. There was no stone beneath her and Hasefi suspected this was Narafi, her grandmother.

She looks a lot like Esafi, she thought, studying the star on the Highchief's armor. *Was she gifted, too?*

Narafi was, Kilarsa confirmed. *But Esafi isn't.*

She's not? Then why does she have the star on her chest?

Armor can be personalized, she explained. *I suspect it's in honor of her mother.*

It is also a good tactic to deter enemies, Sefonis added.

Hasefi gazed at the wall, wondering how long it would take to experience the lives of each lynx represented there.

It's probably a good thing I won't be on here, she thought, imagining what future lynxes might think when they saw her growing up with a black-furred wolf. *I wonder if the Clan has something like this.*

Another thought came to her and she darted back out into the spacious cavern. She passed by a puzzled Arsolin and scurried into the next cave over, this one with lynxes in Overlord and keeper armor. Two keepers were there with a trio of novices, each conducting their own lessons. They all passed Hasefi glances masked by their helmets, but she paid them little attention.

Hasefi looked to where Overlords lined the wall. The last one was a lynx she didn't recognize, so she looked across to where keepers were. Again, she couldn't recognize the final lynxes.

They haven't put you here yet, she thought to her tribe. Before they could respond, Arsolin entered the cave.

"My tribe isn't here," she said to him. "Hykalof and Gelinaf should be on these walls."

"They will be," Arsolin told her. "Since you've returned, I'm sure the guardians will add them."

Hasefi nodded, but a frown twisted her lips. *What am I doing?* she thought to herself. *These walls shouldn't worry me. This isn't my tribe. I should be working on a way to get out of here. This cavern is the last place for that.*

"Is everything alright, High Heir?" Arsolin asked.

Hasefi realized the other lynxes were still watching her and she shifted uncomfortably. "Yeah.... I think I'm done, now." She hurried out of the Keeper's Path and back into the cavern with the massive, decorated wall. With hardly a glance at it, she made her way back up towards the tunnels leading out to the clearing. Arsolin was close behind, but she didn't stop until she'd passed through the Keeper's Cave and was outside in the fresh air.

"High Heir." Arsolin rushed to get in front of her. "Are you sure you're okay?"

"Yeah," she lied. "It's just a lot to take in. I just need a moment to breathe."

Arsolin dipped his head and retreated a few paces, giving her space. Some of the lynxes about glanced curiously at her, but she ignored them, hoping Arsolin might stop any that tried to approach her.

Why was I thinking like that? she asked, deeply troubled. *Was it the highstone? Did it alter my thoughts? I know that I can't stay here. I don't even want to. But down there....*

A soulstone cannot alter your mind any more than a story can, Kilarsa assured her. *It is only natural for you to feel this way. This is where you were born—this was your home, once. You can't blame yourself for wanting to be with your own kind.*

But I want to be with Kolahn. Kolahn is my home, not this place.

I'm sorry, Kilarsa told her. *I wasn't trying to deny that.*

I know. But this was your home, too, and a lot longer than it was mine. It means a lot to you. She looked to Arsolin. *Is he kin to any of you? Or a friend?*

I've crossed paths with him, Gelinaf offered. *But he wasn't one of the lynxes I said farewell to when I departed for the Broken Peak.*

So who did you know?

I have a sister, he admitted. *Natahli. She's a keeper, too.*

"Arsolin?"

Her keeper hurried over. "Yes, High Heir?"

"Do you know a keeper named Natahli?"

"I've met her," he admitted.

"I'd like to speak with her, if that's okay." To her confusion, the keeper was still for a moment. Fear trickled into her and she could feel Gelinaf's own apprehension. "Unless she's...?"

"She's fine," Arsolin said quickly. "My apologies, High Heir. Of course. I can fetch her now, if you would like."

"Yes please."

"In the meantime, you may want to grab some prey. It could take some time for me to locate her."

Hasefi nodded, keen on the idea of finding a nice hare to tuck into. She turned as Arsolin started walking away, but stopped when she noticed him hesitate.

"Is everything alright?" she asked him.

"You...will remain here?" he asked after a few heartbeats. "In the clearing?"

"Of course. I don't have anywhere else to be." *Anywhere that won't get me in trouble, that is.*

"I will return to you with your keeper." Arsolin hurried off, leaving Hasefi frowning.

My keeper? Isn't he my keeper?

He may be thinking you'd like to replace him, Sefonis explained.

He keeps saying stuff like that. Why? Hasefi knew what her uncle was going to say before he said it. *Do I really have to talk to Esafi about whatever it is that's bothering him? Why can't he tell me? Why would Esafi even know, much less care? Why won't* you *tell me?*

It has been moons since we left, he told her. *Our information is outdated. Esafi is the best one to go to.*

Is it that *important?*

Sefonis was silent again. Hasefi could practically see his gaze darting around as if he were trying to avoid looking directly at her.

Learning what you can about your fellow lynxes may be wise, especially if you need to find a way around them to get to Kolahn, Gelinaf offered before Hasefi could say more.

You've already said that. She sighed, relenting. *Fine, I'll talk to her. But I'll wait until tonight—I don't really want to deal with Esafi more than I have to.*

Hasefi looked to the hollow in the middle of the clearing where the prey was kept. She padded over to it until she could peer down into the wide pit. A couple deer and a large bird Hasefi couldn't identify were there.

No hares.

Your taste for hares is not unique. Dahsefer, her Sage, chuckled.

Hasefi's ears flattened. *It's not?*

"Is everything alright, High Heir?"

Hasefi jumped and saw a brown and gold-furred lynx with yellow eyes padding up to her. His expression was friendly, but it shifted with embarrassment and he sank into a bow. "My apologies," he said to her. "I didn't mean to startle you."

"It's okay," Hasefi told him. "I was just in my head."

He straightened, a curious gleam in his eyes. Hasefi guessed he wasn't much older than her, but he didn't have any armor to indicate what his chosen Path might be. He nodded to the prey pile.

"You don't seem very pleased about the options here."

"Oh, no, it's fine. Really, anything to eat is great."

"Perhaps," he agreed with a shrug. "But you can never go wrong with some hare, though, right?"

Hasefi's ears twitched with annoyance when she could feel her Sage's amusement.

"I'm sorry," the lynx said. "I've overstepped."

"No, sorry, I didn't mean to glare at you like that. Apparently I do that to everyone." Hasefi exhaled slowly, trying to get a hold of herself. "Um...what's your name?"

"Nakilon," he offered with a grin.

"It's nice to meet you."

"And you, High Heir." He started to sink into a parting bow, but Hasefi spoke before he could say anything else.

"Would you like to share something with me?" she asked. Nakilon blinked in surprise. "I...don't really know anyone else. And I can't eat a whole deer on my own."

"I'd love to!" he replied, then cleared his throat and responded a bit more calmly. "It would be my pleasure."

Hasefi's whiskers twitched with amusement. Though he was polite like many of the other lynxes she'd encountered, he was a lot friendlier, and she already felt less like some untouchable creature and more like any other lynx around him. He also reminded her a bit of Kolahn with his goofy grin.

Nakilon slipped partway into the prey pile so he could start pulling out a deer. Hasefi helped, letting him choose where to bring it. He led her to a spot near the large flat stone at the edge of the clearing.

"I like to come here to eat that way I can move to the Warmrock and lay in the light before it disappears behind the trees," he explained.

"That sounds pleasant," Hasefi said.

"Oh, it is. Especially after a day of training." There was silence for a moment before he spoke again. "How's the armor?"

"It's alright," Hasefi told him. "But it's starting to feel heavy."

"Yeah, I know what you mean," Nakilon said. "But I've been told you get used to it."

"You have armor?" Hasefi asked.

"Just a helmet," he admitted. "I only became a novice knight a quarter moon ago." He lowered his head and tensed his shoulders, stretching his neck out. "It makes my neck sore."

Hasefi gave her head a shake, knowing exactly what he meant. Then she reached up and took off her helmet, letting the rest of her armor stay.

"Woah," Nakilon blurted before snapping his jaw shut.

"What?" Hasefi asked, wondering if she had gotten a leaf or something stuck in her fur.

"That scar," he murmured. "It's awesome." He flinched. "I mean, it probably wasn't at the time that you got it."

Hasefi snorted. "I'm glad *you* like it," she said, unable to keep some of the bitterness out of her voice.

"Did someone say otherwise?" His ears flattened. "Sorry, I'm not sure if that's being nosy."

Hasefi flicked her ears dismissively. "Don't worry. I didn't grow up with these kinds of rules, so you can ask me anything." She hesitated. "My mother wanted me to get rid of my scars because she thinks they look...flawed."

"Oh. Well, I don't think so. They're marks of experience, I think. Of battles won."

Hasefi responded with a purr, appreciative of how open Nakilon was with her.

"Would I be overstepping if I asked how you got it?"

"An eagle," she replied immediately, anticipating the question. "I was about three moons old."

"Three moons?!" he gasped, eyes wide. "I was scared of the sparrows that flit over our clearing at that age!"

Hasefi's whiskers quivered with amusement and her purr strengthened.

"You have to tell me more!" His ears flattened again and he ducked his head, but Hasefi continued before he could apologize.

"I was trying to find somewhere warm," she began. "I was scared and freezing; I was sure my paws would fall off. It was so cold I could hardly focus. So it wasn't until the snow beneath me was dark with shadow that I realized I was in danger."

Nakilon shifted, settling more comfortably in front of her, the deer between them forgotten.

"I looked up. It was one of the scariest things I'd ever seen. Strange, bunched fur on stiff sticks, huge piercing eyes, a curved, sharp face, and two sets of gleaming claws, bigger than my own paws!"

As she spoke, the memory of the event played in her mind. But, while it used to strike fear into her heart, she felt something different now, as she told it. Pride.

"I ducked and ran as hard as my legs could go. I was lucky; I was small and could fit into the narrowest of spaces. But it wasn't until after the eagle left its mark that I was able to escape its grasp."

"Wow," Nakilon breathed. "I would have frozen in terror!" He blinked, his eyes darting back and forth as he read her face. "There's more?"

Hasefi nodded.

Nakilon shuffled closer, watching her eagerly. Hasefi had to stifle a laugh before she continued with her story.

"The tiny crack I'd slipped through led to a cave. I stayed there for a long time, too scared and hurt to go out again. All I could think about was seeing that terrifying monster-bird waiting, ready to catch me again."

"Surely it moved on?" the novice knight blurted. "When prey is lost, the hunter knows to move on."

"Perhaps in a forest where prey is plentiful," Hasefi told him. "But in the high mountains, where you may go days without food, a hunter will do anything to take what prey it can." Hasefi paused, but he added nothing else, so she continued. "Sure enough, when I found the courage to peek out of my hiding place, it was there. It nearly got me again, when I poked my head out. But fear made me careful."

"So what did you do? If you couldn't wait it out...?"

Hasefi hesitated. When she was forced to deal with the eagle all those moons ago, it had been the first time her tribe had come to her, even though she hadn't been aware of it at the time. Now, she knew it had been her previous Overlord's voice, Hykalof, telling her that she would need to find the will to fend off this monster. And it was her uncle who had given her words of encouragement until she found the strength to form some sort of attack plan.

"Is it too much?" Nakilon asked, his excited expression suddenly worried. "You don't have to continue."

"It's alright," Hasefi assured him. "I realized then that, if I were to survive, I'd have to learn to defend myself." That much was true. She figured she probably shouldn't mention her tribe's involvement, but that didn't necessarily mean she had to lie. "It was kill or be killed. So, I found the courage and went back out."

"You *fought* the eagle?"

Hasefi shrugged. "I think I startled it more than I hurt it. I mean, if you saw a hare coming out at you with a blood-soaked face, claws and teeth flashing, wouldn't you be scared?"

Nakilon laughed and Hasefi purred.

"Wow," the novice murmured, calming down. His expression fell a little.

"Is something wrong?" she asked, wondering if she had somehow ruined the story for him.

"No. I just, it couldn't have been easy." He glanced diffidently at her. "You lost your tribe and...." There was grief in his yellow eyes.

"Did you know my tribemates?"

"No," he admitted, his gaze suddenly searching. Hasefi sensed there was something unspoken, but before she could ask, the novice's eyes darted past her. "Is that your keeper?"

Hasefi followed his gaze and saw two keepers hovering nearby. Even though she couldn't see past the armor, she recognized—or, rather, *sensed*—Arsolin.

"Yeah," she admitted.

"It looks like they need you." Nakilon got to his paws, then sank into a bow. "Thanks for letting me eat with you, High Heir." He gave the untouched deer a sheepish glance.

"Oh, please, call me Hasefi."

Nakilon's eyes brightened and he straightened.

"Yes, Hasefi."

Hasefi watched him go for a moment before turning her head to Arsolin and the other keeper. He approached with his companion at his side.

"I have brought Keeper Natahli as you've requested," he said with a bow.

Hasefi turned towards the second keeper. Like Arsolin, she couldn't see any part of Natahli, even her eyes. As much as she'd like to be able to meet this lynx's gaze as she spoke, she forced herself to proceed anyways.

"Hi," she started a bit awkwardly.

The keeper bowed. "Greetings, High Heir. What is it you need of me?"

"Um, well, I was...." Hasefi hesitated, realizing she had no idea what to say.

Just tell her what you feel, Sefonis offered. Behind his presence, Hasefi could feel Gelinaf's affection for his sister, which made her own heart ache. She gave a tiny nod and took a deep breath before looking into the shadowy holes of the keeper's helmet.

"Gelinaf is your brother," she began slowly.

The keeper made no reaction to her words.

"And I wanted to tell you that...that I'm sorry for what happened and if there was anything I could to do stop—"

"You have no reason to apologize to me, High Heir," the keeper said, her voice even.

"Don't I?" Hasefi protested as a rush of emotion surged through her. "He was out there because of *my* prophecy. Maybe I wasn't the one who came up with it, but if I—" Hasefi bit back her words, urging herself to calm down. "What I'm trying to say is, that, Gelinaf is a formidable keeper and...worthy of an Overlord." She went silent, waiting for the keeper's response. It was some heartbeats later when Natahli finally spoke.

"You said 'is'," the keeper murmured. "'*Is* my brother,' '*is* a formidable keeper.'"

Hasefi swallowed nervously. "*Was*, sorry. I meant *was*. I guess I'm still trying to get used to the whole...well, it's difficult to—"

"Thank you."

Hasefi looked up at the keeper again, puzzled.

"Gelinaf and I would give everything we have to being keepers," Natahli said. "I can only be glad he got the chance." The keeper bowed. "It may not have been something you could control, but you gave my brother a purpose. A reason. He would have gladly given himself to it."

Aye, Gelinaf agreed.

Hasefi bowed her head, not knowing what to say.

"And I appreciate you reaching out to me. I will sleep better knowing Gelinaf as a keeper to the end." The keeper rose from her bow. With a nod, she turned and walked away. Hasefi watched her, feeling both upset and glad at the same time.

Thank you, Gelinaf murmured, his voice gruff. *It is good to hear her voice once more.*

A pang tightened Hasefi's chest when she thought that, by leaving with Kolahn, her tribe would be leaving behind their former home yet again.

Our time has passed, Sefonis told her. *You needn't worry about us. Your needs are ours.*

I'm sorry, Hasefi told him. *You shouldn't have to stay trapped with me.*

We made a choice, Gelinaf said. *One Hykalof gave his life and more for. We will stand by it for as long as we have to.*

For him as well as you, wee lass, Sefonis added.

Despite their words, Hasefi couldn't help but feel guilty. *They're not the only ones who might be upset,* she thought to herself. *Garfonis seemed so happy when he saw me. Even Hesilar looked delighted.* She shook her head. *The longer I stay, the harder it'll get. I can't lose sight of Kolahn.*

Her gaze moved to where the novice knight had left to join another pair of novices. Even though every part of her continued to urge her back over the River, she couldn't stifle the little pang of longing that throbbed in her chest.

I'm just missing Kolahn. Once I have him, I won't think twice about this place.

Chapter Five

"Are you alright, High Heir?" Arsolin asked.

Hasefi blinked, realizing she was still standing over the untouched deer she and Nakilon had taken, staring off at where some of the novices had gathered.

"Yeah, I just..." Hasefi shook her head, trying to push aside the pain that had tightened her chest. "Do you want to share this deer with me?"

"My duty is to watch out for you," the keeper pointed out.

"We're in the heart of lynx territory. If something is threatening us, there are plenty of other keepers that will be looking out for us. I know you haven't eaten all day, so please, share."

The keeper continued to hesitate.

"What's stopping you?" Hasefi pressed.

"Keepers don't usually eat with their charges," Arsolin explained.

"Even if they ask?"

"Charges don't usually ask...."

"Well, I am. So are you going to sit down or are you going to make me drag the rest of this meal back to the prey pile?"

"I can bring—"

"Just sit your furry tail down and take a bite!" Hasefi cried with exasperation. The keeper obeyed immediately, sitting down before the deer. But it was a few moments before he raised his paws and drew his helmet off his head.

Arsolin was what he had called a gray lynx, like her. But his face was darker and speckled and his tufts were thick and spread out widely. When Hasefi met his eyes, she could see there was a sadness in their green depths that struck her with her own grief. But when he looked to her, they brightened a little. She gestured to the deer and, hesitantly, Arsolin lowered his head to take a bite.

"That wasn't so bad, was it?" Hasefi asked as he chewed.

"No," Arsolin admitted. "I'm sorry, High Heir. I don't mean to make things difficult."

"For the love of all the stars in the sky, can everyone please stop apologizing? And call me by my actual name?"

"It's how we are supposed to address highbloods," Arsolin explained. "Any possibility of inconveniencing you should be reconciled immediately and, if we called you by your name, it may be seen as rude."

"Really? So…I shouldn't call you Arsolin?"

"It doesn't apply to you," Arsolin pointed out. "Whatever you prefer is what goes."

Hasefi frowned. "What would *you* prefer? Keeper or Arsolin?"

"It doesn't matter—"

"It matters to me," Hasefi interrupted, trying not to get frustrated.

Arsolin was hesitant. "It may do well to call me by my name so it won't be confusing when we come across other keepers."

Hasefi stifled a sigh, knowing she wasn't going to get a better answer.

"What's going on here?"

Hasefi looked up to see her mother with Sifara and a lynx Hasefi identified as the Huntmaster. Like the hunters she'd come across, the Huntmaster had tough, brown armor, but it was decorated with green in the same starry pattern as the other champions. She also had a mask hiding her muzzle, which Hasefi thought was strange if they were meant to track and catch prey.

Arsolin had jumped to his paws the moment Esafi's voice reached them. "Highchief!" he gasped, sinking into a bow with his right leg outstretched.

"Why is your helmet off? And why are you eating with my daughter?"

"My apologies, I—"

"I asked him to," Hasefi interrupted.

"I am not talking to you," Esafi growled but Hasefi refused to be hushed.

"So, what, you're going to be mad at him for something I asked him to do?"

"He should know the rules."

"Your tribe has rules about who eats with who?"

"This is your tribe, too," Esafi snapped.

Hasefi clenched her teeth, forcing down a retort she knew she would regret.

"Go, take this elsewhere," Esafi said to the keeper. "I have need of my daughter."

Arsolin swiftly put his helmet on, bowed, and hurried off, dragging the deer back to the pile. Sifara's helmet twitched in the direction of the fleeing keeper.

I hope I didn't just give her a reason to scold him.

"Come, daughter," Esafi commanded. "We will go to the Highcave and meet with the champions."

Stifling a growl, Hasefi followed, trailing at the end of the group so she wouldn't have to talk to her or the other lynxes in the company.

But the Huntmaster fell back until she was by Hasefi's side. Hasefi made no reaction, feeling as if she would explode at any minute.

"I know chatting is probably the last thing on your mind, but I was hoping I could introduce myself before Esafi did."

Hasefi gave the Huntmaster a surprised look when she used the Highchief's name.

"I'm Lisefi."

Hasefi narrowed her eyes.

"I'm your aunt."

"Both of her siblings happen to be champions?" Hasefi asked, not caring to hide the bitterness in her tone.

"The Highchief gets to choose her champions when she rises to the title," Lisefi explained, not noticing or not bothered by Hasefi's tone.

Hasefi frowned, wondering what that meant for the previous champions.

"Don't let her mood get to you," the Huntmaster continued. "Times have been difficult."

"So that means she has the right to yell at any lynx that bothers her?"

"No, but every lynx is on edge. I'm sure you've heard talk about how things are with the Clan across the River?"

Hasefi nodded once.

"No creature wants war."

I know some that do, she thought darkly.

"Just give it some time and you'll settle in quite nicely."

Hasefi's frown deepened, but she remained silent.

They headed up the path leading to the Highcave. In the first chamber, three other lynxes waited, including her father and Hesilar, the Sage.

The third lynx with them was dressed like her Guardian Elder Kilarsa, with dark purple robes decorated in white stars and a hood that threw most of his face in shadows. All she could see was the white of his muzzle and dark gray nose.

Sifara and Lisefi lined up with them so they were all facing Hasefi and the Highchief.

"I have already discussed with you the nature of this new threat that has come with Hasefi's arrival," Esafi began, sweeping her gaze over the gathered champions. "Now that Hasefi has been settled, we will listen to her account of her experience beyond the Great River." Esafi turned to Hasefi. "Tell us everything you have on the black wolves and their pack."

Hasefi hesitated, thinking first of Kolahn.

I already know I won't be able to get her help. But the Pack is bigger than this. I can't just leave them with nothing, especially if the Pack does decide to continue with their plan.

For a moment, she imagined the same thing that happened to her tribe happening to this one.

"Well?" Esafi pressed.

"It cannot be easy to recall," Garfonis put in quietly.

"I know that as well as you do," Esafi returned. "But we do not have time to sit here and wait until she—"

"The Pack tore my tribe apart," Hasefi said, her voice flat. She met Esafi's eyes, unblinking. "Much like they did for those who didn't make it through Resahn's Reign, I'm sure." She looked to the other lynxes. "They had spotted me and didn't want to leave any loose ends. But a mountain lion scared them off, letting me get away."

The expressions she read were both similar and different. Grief, shock, sorrow, anger. Garfonis's was heartbreaking and she found she couldn't meet her father's distraught expression. Lisefi's eyes were narrowed with a fury barely restrained. Hesilar's face was twisted with dark memory, widening his eyes. Sifara and the Guardian Elder's expressions were masked by their armor, but the heat of their gazes burned into Hasefi's fur.

"I was in the high mountains for four moons." She paused, wondering if she should just let it all pour forth.

These lynxes take their ancestors very seriously, Sefonis warned. *Perhaps it would be best not to mention their involvement or ours.*

"I learnt to hunt," Hasefi continued. "I learnt how to cover my tracks. I learnt how to find shelter. But the Pack didn't give up. They continued to hunt, following me as I followed the rising sun like the ancestors told us."

"Pardon me," Hesilar said, glancing between Hasefi and the Highchief. "I thought you and the others were meant to go to the Broken Peak."

"We were," Hasefi replied. "And we did. Part of it fell and Kilarsa read it as the ancestors telling us to follow the rising sun." She let the fact that the ancestors had led her tribe to their doom hang in the air.

"You said four moons," Esafi observed. "There are five moons unaccounted for."

"That's when I met Kolahn." She may not offer the truth about her tribe, but she would be honest about Kolahn. Esafi and Garfonis already knew about him; the other champions probably did, too. But, if Esafi couldn't be sympathetic, perhaps her champions would. They were already showing more emotion than the Highchief had and, if it was knowledge on the black wolves they wanted, then most of what she had to offer was thanks to her friend.

"That's a wolven name," Lisefi spoke, her tone harsh.

"It is," Hasefi replied evenly. "Kolahn is a black wolf."

The expressions she could see became intense, urging her onward as if they were looking for a reason not to condemn her for announcing the existence of a black wolf, much less suggest he was a friend. But if they were determined to see Kolahn as only an enemy, Hasefi didn't care what any of them thought.

"Kolahn saved my life when I fell in a pit and broke my leg. He took care of me; I was permanently crippled—until I came here—so I couldn't hunt for myself. He brought me to a new part of the world, Edgewood, a pine forest stretching the length of the border between the Great Forest and the high mountains. He helped me follow the rising sun."

"You completed your mission?" Garfonis blurted before ducking his head in embarrassment.

"There was nothing," Hasefi told him. "Just ocean."

"Ocean?" Hesilar echoed.

"The end of the world," she explained. "When the land stopped, all that remained was water. As far as the horizon."

There was disbelief on Lisefi's and Esafi's faces, but Garfonis and Hesilar watched her with wide eyes, though she couldn't tell if they actually believed her. She didn't blame them; Kolahn had told her of such things and she didn't take him seriously until she'd seen them for herself.

"So, when you failed your mission, you came here?" Esafi asked.

"I didn't know this tribe was here," Hasefi admitted. "Kolahn lived in the Great Valley which is past the cliff above the Clan's home. But, on our way, there was a fire."

"Aye, there was," Hesilar said. "Could smell the smoke here, too. Never saw the flames, though, fortunately." Worry entered his gaze when he returned it to Hasefi.

"It never hurt Kolahn and me. We made it to the Valley, but the Pack was there. They had found traces of Kolahn and sought to recruit him. They were still after me, too." Hasefi remembered how she and her friend had found a place to hide and how Kolahn, who had walked heavily with the burden his fur color gave him, had suddenly found purpose. "Kolahn made a plan to infiltrate them, to figure out what they wanted and why they were after me." She hesitated. A lot of what happened involved her tribe. "He didn't come back when he was supposed to, so I went after him."

"By yourself?" Garfonis asked.

"Who else?" Hasefi looked to the Highchief, who continued to keep control of her own expression, hiding any thoughts she might be having. "When I went after him, I learnt some things. They had two leaders; Sal and Vek. Sal was the one who led the party that killed my tribe. And Vek, I think he's the mind of their Pack. He makes the plans and calls the orders."

"And what is their plan?" Esafi demanded.

"They want revenge on the Clan for casting them out."

"So the black wolves are returning?" Lisefi said, her growl mixed with both hate and fear.

"What about your friend?" Garfonis asked. "You escaped with him, didn't you?"

Hasefi hesitated, feeling all of their eyes on her.

"A mountain lion," she said. It was the truth, but she knew how flimsy it sounded without the rest of it. "It attacked. Kolahn and I escaped."

"Another mountain lion?" Hesilar asked. His expression was kind, but Hasefi could tell he was having a hard time accepting her words. "Luck has certainly played a role in your survival, but a second encounter like that seems extreme.

Then it's a good thing you don't know that's my fourth.

"What of the Pack, then?" Esafi asked, surprisingly eager to accept Hasefi's account. "Have they been decimated, then?"

"Not entirely," Hasefi replied. "Sal was killed, but I don't know about Vek. And wolves came to Kolahn and I not long before we came here —they were responsible for some of the wounds I carried here. They didn't really seem to care about Vek's plan, but if he's alive, then they are a threat."

"If I may," Sifara spoke with a glance at the Highchief. "You claim Kolahn befriended you?"

"He did," Hasefi said firmly. "He's not like the others. When he learnt what the Pack's plan was, he went straight to his clan to warn them, even though he knew he might be executed for showing up on their territory. I had gone after him and arrived at the ravine shortly before Garfonis did."

"Could there have been a purpose behind Kolahn's reason for befriending you?" Sifara asked.

"He was lonely," Hasefi replied evenly. "His kind shunned him for his fur and those that might understand wanted nothing but blood and violence. Kolahn is the opposite of that."

"Yet he never mentioned our existence," Esafi finished for the Overlord.

"There were a lot of things Kolahn didn't tell me," Hasefi pointed out with a growl at the Highchief. "And lots I didn't tell him." Hasefi never thought about Kolahn knowing the tribe was here. It made sense he would know and he'd said a few things that were contradictory, but she'd been too afraid of him turning on her to worry about what he knew. Now, however, she was almost certain he had kept this tribe's existence from her, but she could hardly blame him.

"There are too many variables," Sifara continued. "Why was Kolahn there when you slipped? Why didn't he tell you about us?"

"You're not thinking about him as a creature, but as something that serves only itself. I know Kolahn and I trust him with my life. I would be dead if it weren't for him."

"Maybe he's the Pack's spy. I mean, he is in the Clan now, right?" Lisefi asked.

"You're looking in the wrong place," Hasefi growled, trying to keep a hold of her frustration. "Kolahn is not the enemy."

"The Clan is," Esafi said.

"Surely the Pack is a bigger threat?" Hesilar pointed out.

"Their target is the Clan and, for all we know, it may take moons for them to recover from this mountain lion attack. Right now, our target is the present enemy."

Hasefi decided she was done with this conversation and stood. "I've told you everything I have on the Pack, so there's no reason to keep quiet about it anymore, right?"

"We still cannot risk alarming the rest of the Tribe," Esafi told her.

Hasefi gritted her teeth. She didn't want to argue anymore, but, even if she had no love for this tribe, they deserved to know the truth, especially if it became a threat.

"But what if the black wolves attack you here? No one will be prepared if they don't know what hit them."

"I will prepare them when it is time to be prepared. But instilling fear will do nothing but wear their spirits down. We're already about to face one enemy. They cannot worry about another."

"So you're officially declaring war on the Clan?" Hasefi asked, immediately thinking of Kolahn.

"They were the ones to declare it when they killed our kits."

Hasefi's eyes widened. "They actually killed kits?" She hadn't known about the gray wolves for long and, other than what Kolahn had told her about them, she didn't know much else. But she never imagined they'd be kit-killers.

Could it be so impossible? They have no problem banishing their own kind and it was clear they didn't care much for us. That wolf, Kowvis, called me a kit and was ready to fight.

"Hasefi, are you listening?"

"What?" she snapped, earning a stern glare from Esafi.

"We are not yet done, here," the Highchief growled. "It is part of your training for the champions to assist in your learning and, as we are gathered here, it is the best time for you to meet them."

Hasefi clenched her jaw against an exasperated groan.

"Arsolin will continue to mentor you in our territory and history, but my champions will teach you in combat, hunting, stealth, magic, and healing. It is your responsibility to understand each Path. Now more than ever with the Tribe on the brink of war." Esafi turned to the champions.

"Emperor Garfonis will teach you the ways of the knights. They are the armor of the tribe, protecting us from threats. Huntmaster Lisefi will teach you how to utilize your environment not only for hunting, but for battle, too."

"Will the hunters be fighting?" Hasefi asked with surprise.

"Every lynx has a part in battle," Esafi told her. "Overlord Sifara will show you the ways of the keeper, training you in stealth and observations. Sage Hesilar will teach you the ways of the healer and what it means to help those unable to help themselves, with a gift or not. And, if I am correct, Elder Myafos is the only lynx you have yet to meet."

Hasefi's gaze moved to the gifted lynx. He wasn't as fully armored as Sifara or Arsolin, but for some reason Hasefi had a hard time determining what he looked like. It was as if shadows were floating within his fur, making him difficult to truly see. She did, however, glimpse the strange golden eyes that glowed beneath his hood and looked directly at her.

Can he read my mind? she couldn't help wonder. Unnerved, she looked to Esafi again.

"It is unlikely he will be able to spare time for your training as his paws are nearly as full as mine, so a guardian of his choosing will show you the ways of magic and its role in battle and everyday life."

Hasefi narrowed her eyes. "Everything you said relates to battle. Are you saying you want me to fight?"

"Of course not," Esafi scoffed. "But times are unpredictable during a war. You should be ready for anything."

"If you're going to war, then I'm coming with you," Hasefi said firmly. "You said you're keeping me here because you don't want me to stir up trouble with the Clan," she added before Esafi could reply. "If you take war to them, then I'm coming so I can make sure you don't hurt Kolahn and the two of us can leave this place behind for good."

"You don't intend to stay?" Hesilar asked, disappointment clear on his face.

"We're your blood," Lisefi added, baffled.

"Maybe, but Kolahn is my home. After my tribe, he was the one who raised me." *Not you.* She had intended to say the words aloud, but between the disappointment and grief on Hesilar's and Garfonis's face, she found she couldn't.

"Kits don't fight wars," Esafi argued.

"But they can trek through the snow and cold because the stars said so?"

Esafi opened her jaws, an angry look on her face, but Hasefi didn't let her speak.

"I stopped being a kit when I watched my tribe get their throats torn out and their legs ripped off. I—"

"Fine!" Esafi snapped, shooting to her paws. "If you are so eager to leave, then so be it. I have tried to be patient with you, daughter, but I see you have no intention of doing the same." This time, Esafi didn't give Hasefi a chance to respond. "Normally your training with the champions wouldn't begin until after your thirteenth moon, but if you think yourself so skilled in battle, then Garfonis will test that."

Hasefi's father jerked his head up, looking about to protest, but he was silent.

Hasefi, however, was uneasy. Her own tribe shared that feeling. *I didn't have to fight very hard for that,* she thought. *Could Esafi truly want me to fight?*

It's hard to tell with her, Sefonis admitted.

It's quite possible she has her paws as full as she says and merely wants to keep you busy, Kilarsa offered.

Esafi is never so simple, Sefonis argued. *She always has another agenda.*

You're talking about her like she's the enemy, Hasefi pointed out with surprise.

"Daughter, for the love of the stars, would you quit making faces and listen?"

Hasefi jumped slightly at the sound of her mother's voice. "I'm not making faces," she protested.

"You will continue to remain silent about the presence of the Pack. My champions and I have yet to figure out the details of this war, so you will be quiet about that, too, until I can announce it to the Tribe."

Why bother telling me, then? She doesn't trust me. Does she have something else in mind? And why wait to tell the Tribe? Shouldn't they be preparing as soon as they can if they are going to war?

Deciding it wasn't worth trying to get answers, Hasefi shrugged. "Okay," she told the Highchief. "Is that everything?"

Anger flared in Esafi's narrowed eyes before she turned to the champions. "Dismissed," she forced through gritted teeth. "Daughter, come with me."

Hasefi watched all but Sifara leave. She avoided the Elder's gaze as he moved past her, feeling as if his glowing eyes were constantly on her, even when she was behind him. Lisefi hardly looked at her. Hesilar offered a sympathetic smile. And Garfonis lingered long enough to pass her a look too complicated for her to understand. She hesitated, watching her father pad into the tunnel leading outside, his armor clinking with each step.

An angry growl came from the Highchief and Hasefi bounced to where Esafi had moved into the sleeping chamber.

"You should show more respect to me and the champions," she growled, her lips raised in the beginning of a snarl.

"I don't want to be here anymore than I did yesterday," Hasefi reminded her and the Highchief went silent. Hasefi braced herself for yet another scolding, but, instead, Esafi let out a long sigh and sat down.

"You don't understand what's going on."

"Neither do you." Hasefi saw anger flash through her mother's eyes again, but the Highchief kept it in.

"A lot more is at stake. If what you say is true, you spent a lot of time without worrying about the lives of others. You don't know what it's like to have to care for an entire tribe."

Hasefi recoiled. "I know exactly what that's like," she hissed. "And I know what it's like to be helpless to keep from losing them. I may have been on my own, but I told you I had Kolahn—"

"A black wolf you claimed saved your life."

"He did! More than once! He was as much family as my tribe was! I have been through more than you know!"

"And yet you are still a kit!" Esafi snapped.

Hasefi flinched at the sudden outburst. Normally, such a statement would infuriate her, but there was a desperation in the Highchief's words that made her hesitate.

Esafi took in a breath and let it out before continuing. "When I was not much older than you, we were walking the first steps into war with the Clan. With Resahn. A lot of lynxes were lost in those days. Including my mother, the Highchief."

Hasefi relaxed a bit and perked her ears as Esafi spoke.

"When the war was over and I became the head of the Tribe, I vowed I wouldn't let anything of the kind happen again. Nothing would ever threaten the tribe again. And not a lynx died under my care. At least not until…." she trailed off, pain bright in her eyes.

"You said they took kits?" Hasefi ventured. "The Clan?"

When Esafi met her gaze, Hasefi was shocked by the angry grief that burned there.

"*My* kits. *Your* brothers."

Hasefi sat in silent shock. If it weren't for her tribe's collective apprehension and grief, she wouldn't have been able to believe Esafi's words. Accepting them, however, was something else entirely.

Brothers?

"They were part of your litter, but clearly you have no memory of them," Esafi growled softly. "We have been fighting over prey for moons now and they decided to retaliate by not only taking our kits, but the High Heir."

"I have brothers?" Hasefi asked quietly, still trying to overcome the shock that had seized her.

"*Had.* The Clan killed them."

"Killed?" Hasefi echoed, trying to grasp what Esafi was saying. "Why? Where?"

"Who knows why wolves do anything?" the Highchief snarled before the anger drained from her face, hardening into grief. "They were by the River, not far from the waterfall. What was left of them, anyway."

Esafi's words brought forth an image in Hasefi's mind, an image that showed her the last she had seen of her tribe. Realization jolted her from her shock.

"It wasn't the Clan," Hasefi whispered.

"Wolf scent was all over the area. Our guardians found traces of wolf signs."

"Black wolves," Hasefi told her. "This was the Pack. They're already here."

Esafi frowned deeply. "You implied it would take time for them to recover."

"There's no way I could know for sure. Vek might be dead, or he might not be. The Pack may have had other camps. Kolahn and I didn't have a lot of time to figure that out." Dread filled her. "It's…it's possible mine and Kolahn's interference pushed their plans into motion."

"None of my keepers have spotted black wolves," Esafi continued to resist.

"How long ago were my…?" Hasefi found she couldn't finish the sentence.

"Five sunrises ago."

She flinched. Her tribe's grief was as strong as her own, threatening to overwhelm her with emotion, but she forced herself to push it aside long enough to put her racing thoughts into words. "Black wolves heal fast. That may have been enough time for Vek to move forward with his...." Hasefi trailed off, wondering if she really had doomed the creatures around the Great River. But her growing guilt halted when Esafi shook her head.

"Your story doesn't make sense," the Highchief said, her ears half-flattened with confusion. "How does a lone wolf and a kit ambush an entire group of black wolves? And why suddenly make a move against us?"

"I don't know," Hasefi admitted to the latter. "And I know it might be hard to believe what I've said, but it's the truth. Which is why it's the Pack you need to blame, not the Clan. *They* did this."

Esafi only shook her head again. "You are young, daughter. A lot more is happening here than you know. The black wolves are a threat, but not now."

Hasefi stared at her, incredulous. "If they're not dealt with—"

"I know what they're capable of," the Highchief growled. "And I know what the Clan is capable of. We are going to have to take out one enemy at a time. We cannot fight two."

Hasefi's ears flattened with frustration.

The Pack will do more than the Clan ever could. Her mind hardened. *It doesn't matter,* she thought. *If Esafi doesn't want to listen, that's her choice. I'm not going to be here much longer. Once this starts to go down, I'll get Kolahn and we'll leave.*

"I'm curious as to what goes on in that head of yours," Esafi said, her words lacking their usual condescending note.

"Nothing you'd find important," Hasefi replied with a growl.

Esafi studied her for a moment. The cavelight was darkening, indicating the day was coming to an end. Hasefi yearned to retreat somewhere she could be alone and deal with the flurry of emotions raging within her. But it was clear the Highchief had no intention of leaving yet, so she decided to address some questions she might actually get answers to.

"What...what were their names?"

Affection glowed in Esafi's eyes, paired with a proud gleam, turning her into a different lynx.

"There was Mekonis," she murmured. "He was a handsome young lynx. And smart. He would have been a formidable Highchief." Her tone was thick with anguish and, this time, there was no anger to accompany her grief.

Hasefi saw the image of the latest High Heir in the Highchief's cave in the Cavern of History again. A tide of understanding flowed through her, bringing with it shame as she thought of how dismissive she'd been with her tribe and Arsolin about the topic.

"And Talonis," Esafi continued, gazing at something only she could see. "Clumsy, I'll admit, but I could see he would grow to be a strong, capable lynx."

"Will he get a spot in the Cavern of History?" Hasefi asked quietly.

"Of course—he's already there. But he shares the wall with other kits in the Healer's part of the Cavern, as he was not High Heir."

"What about my tribe?" she asked, wondering if they, too, might be somewhere else. To her dismay, however, Esafi shook her head.

"They pledged allegiance to a different tribe. They are not one of our own."

Anger cut off the desolate mood of her tribe.

Do you want to be on their walls? Hasefi asked them.

Our memories live with you, Kilarsa murmured.

But Esafi was quick to dismiss our roles, Sefonis growled.

Their anger was hers, but it was muted by the grief flowing into her from the knowledge she'd had brothers and never knew them.

"How come you didn't tell me about them? My brothers, I mean," she asked Esafi.

"You hardly gave me the chance," the Highchief replied, not unkindly.

Hasefi nodded, knowing she had a point.

Silence fell between them. A part of Hasefi wanted to hold onto this moment; it was terrible, filled with a kind of grief she hadn't experienced for moons, but it was the first time she felt in line with her mother.

She lifted her head to look at Esafi, seeing that the Highchief had sunk into her own thoughts. The pride that had shone in her eyes darkened back into grief, then swiftly altered to a deep fury.

"The Clan will not only regret their actions," she growled ominously. "They will regret ever having come here."

Hasefi's eyes widened when she recognized the rage in her mother's eyes as the kind that had resulted in the death of her tribe.

"Esafi, wait—"

"You will address me as your brothers did and as the mother I am to you," she snapped, reverting to her infuriatingly authoritative tone of voice. "You may be young, but you are in the first steps of your training—I expect you to act with maturity beyond that of a kit. You are here, now, Hasefi. If you do not accept that, it is not only yourself that will suffer." Before Hasefi could respond, the Highchief jerked her chin towards the sleeping hollows. "Go."

Esafi didn't stay to see if her command was obeyed, but Hasefi knew Sifara would be there to stop her if she tried to flee. So, she went to her hollow and curled up tight with her eyes squeezed shut and a paw over her face. She was still reeling at the knowledge of having brothers and the strangeness of this new place and new tribe only added to the chaos.

There's no way this is real, she thought despairingly. *How am I going to do this?*

A soft touch on her head made her look up. Sefonis stood over her, his Emperor's armor glittering with starlight.

Other starry figures sat nearby, surrounding Hasefi with their light.

"Sefonis," she whimpered.

Her uncle removed his helmet and armor and curled up beside her as well as he could in the little hollow. She pressed against his flank, grateful for the warmth of his fur, even if it was faint.

"I don't know what to do," she whispered, burying her face in his sandy brown fur. "I'm no closer to helping Kolahn, everyone I meet expects me to stay, and—and my brothers—I have—I had—"

"Hush, wee lass," Sefonis hummed. "You don't have to make sense of it now. Give yourself time to adjust."

Hasefi shivered against her uncle, feeling tiny in a place filled with so many lynxes. She wished Kolahn had never come here, that they were still in the Valley, living their days eating hares and sparring. She would even take her twisted leg back if it meant none of this ever happened.

But it did, a small voice inside her said. *Coming here or not wouldn't change that. It wouldn't change anything.*

Hasefi drew in a shuddering breath, then another, until the emotion raging through her began to settle. She withdrew her head from her uncle, meeting his pale yellow eyes.

"You knew," she murmured. She swept her gaze over her other tribemates. "You all knew."

"Aye," Sefonis admitted. "But we weren't sure of the facts."

"We're so sorry, Hasefi," Kilarsa added, stepping forth. The white starry design across her purple guardian's robes glittered brilliantly with their own light. "We wanted to tell you, but we didn't want to give you hope if..."

"If something happened to them," she finished for the Elder. "Which it did."

"It wouldn't have been right, coming from us," Sefonis agreed.

"I would have preferred to hear it from you," Hasefi sighed, bowing her head in misery.

"We're here now," Dahsefer assured her, his orange eyes round with grief.

"You...knew them?" she asked her tribe.

"A little," Sefonis replied. "They were my nephews, so I would often help watch over them when Esafi and Garfonis were busy."

Hasefi shook her head. "I don't remember them. Mekonis and Talonis; they don't even sound familiar."

"You didn't get a lot of time with them," Dahsefer explained. "Typically kits and their mothers stay in the Healer's Cave, but with your prophecy, Esafi was adamant about keeping you secure in the Highcave. Even your father had little time with you. Hasefi?"

Hasefi stared at the ground, her eyes wide with dread after a nasty thought entered her head.

"What if I'm right and the Pack came here because of me? What if—what if I killed my own brothers?"

"This is not your fault," Sefonis told her firmly. "No one is to blame except the Pack themselves."

Her uncle's words stirred an old anger in Hasefi's heart. "The Pack is *still* taking from us! But Esafi won't listen. She'd rather fight the Clan for some stupid reason than face the real danger!" Hasefi put her paws over her head, on the verge of being overwhelmed again. "I don't want to be here."

"I know," Sefonis murmured, giving her shoulder a comforting lick.

"I just want to see Kolahn again."

"Hasefi." Gelinaf spoke, urging Hasefi to lift her head. The Overlord's helmet was off, revealing his gray and white face and dark green eyes. "As your tribe, it is our duty to ensure your well-being," he said.

"I know," she told him. "But there's not much you can do about this, I understand that."

The keeper shook his head. "That's not what I mean. Kolahn, he...I suspect he knew the Tribe was here."

Hasefi was silent.

"He had kept that knowledge from you."

"Maybe he didn't," she argued. "We don't know what the Clan did to wolves like him before he was cast out. But, even if he did, I don't blame him. I would have done the same, I'm sure."

"Perhaps," Gelinaf replied in a tone that said he wasn't entirely convinced. "But you may want to—"

"I got it," she snapped. The keeper nodded, retreating, and she immediately felt guilty. "I'm sorry," she sighed. "I'm just..."

"We understand, Hasefi." Tenarli, her Huntmaster, had her head bowed, hiding her eyes.

"More than you realize," Sefonis added, not quite meeting Hasefi's gaze either.

Peering at the rest of her tribe, she saw that, while they all looked at something else, the same thing was written on their faces.

"What do you mean?" she asked.

"Not long before you were born," Sefonis began. "Your mother and Myafos shared your prophecy with the Tribe, announcing it as a sign from the Wanderers. They interpreted it as the Tribe's second divide. Volunteers were called for, but it was still up to the Highchief to choose which volunteers went."

Hasefi frowned, not sure what her uncle was trying to say.

"The lynxes you see standing before you are all lynxes that disagreed with Esafi's way of ruling."

Hasefi's eyes stretched wide. "Really?"

"That isn't saying she's not a good Highchief," Kilarsa pointed out. "She was being truthful when she said no lynx had died unnaturally under her reign. But..."

"No lynx has really lived, either," Dahsefer added.

Hasefi narrowed her eyes. "So she agreed to let you go so you'd be out of her fur. But what about me? Why is she making me stay?"

"For the very reason she told you," Kilarsa said.

"So I don't make trouble with the Clan? But now she's going to war anyways. Why not just let me go?"

"Because if the Clan got you, they could use you as leverage," Tenarli explained.

"What leverage?"

"Hasefi, she *is* your mother," Sefonis reminded her.

Hasefi lowered her gaze. "It doesn't feel like it."

For a moment, her tribe said nothing.

"You have to be strong, Hasefi," Sefonis told her quietly. "If we're going to save Kolahn without doing the same thing we did to the Pack, then this is the only path."

"Believe us we'd tell you if there was a better one," Dahsefer added.

"But until the opportunity rises, remaining with the Tribe is your best choice," Sefonis continued.

"And it hasn't all been bad, right?" Kilarsa pointed out.

Hasefi's ears twitched in reluctant agreement. "The Cavern of History is neat," she admitted.

"And how about the novice you met? Nakilon?" Sefonis tried.

"They're all the same." Even as she spoke it, she knew it wasn't totally true about the novice, but she refused to let herself get attached to him or any other lynx. "I want to talk to someone that doesn't treat me like I'm...like I'm wolfsbane." When she met her uncle's eyes, she saw the sadness in them. "You all treated me like family, not some untouchable creature."

"It is Esafi's way," Kilarsa admitted. "But...if you search a bit harder, I think you'll find that the lynxes here aren't so easily defined."

Hasefi narrowed her eyes only to find she was scrutinizing a feather in her bedding. She lifted her head and blinked, looking around the chamber in confusion.

I was dreaming?

It wouldn't do well to have Esafi's Overlord listening, Gelinaf replied. *But she has left.*

The cave-light had dimmed, indicating it was night, but Hasefi had no idea how long it had been since she'd fallen asleep. Esafi wasn't there, either.

Hasefi rose out of her hollow and peeked her head out of the cavern.

She was alone.

Where did she go? she wondered.

Likely to sleep, herself, or to attend other business, Gelinaf replied. *You were asleep, so there was no need to keep guard.*

If I step outside, will I be stopped? she thought.

There will be other keepers on duty through the night, her Overlord replied.

Hasefi padded out of the sleeping chamber and into the large one where she'd met all of Esafi's champions and where the other tunnel connected.

She hesitated for a moment, not entirely sure what she meant to do.

I wonder what Kolahn is doing right now, she thought. She imagined her friend in a dark cave, alone, his jaws still bound by magic.

'That's why you can't stay with me,' she heard Kolahn in her head. *'I'm evil. Bad things happen because of me.'*

'No. Kolahn,' she'd tried to argue. *'The last thing you are is evil.'*

'You don't understand—I am *evil. I* feel *it. Whenever I fight, whenever I hunt, I* feel *it. It's trying to get out. I'm scared I won't be able to keep it in. I...I could be like the wolves that took your tribe.'*

Not long before they came to the River, she'd promised she wouldn't let him turn into the thing he was so afraid of.

And yet, here I am, sitting in the Highcave while he suffers in a prison.

He believes in you, Hasefi, Sefonis spoke. *He knows you'll come for him.*

Does he? He was so worried I'd leave him. And he saw me with Garfonis. He might think I abandoned him, just like his clan did.

But you didn't. He knows how stubborn you are. Even if it's hard for him to believe, he'll know it's the truth.

"I hope so," she sighed. She started to turn back towards the sleeping chamber, but the other tunnel leading from this chamber made her hesitate. Then she altered her path and went down it.

As she suspected, it led down into the Cavern of History, depositing her right in the middle part of the wide-open area. A lone guardian was padding by on the ground below. They looked up at her before hurrying into one of the caves beneath the ledge she was on.

At least they didn't tell me to go back to the Highcave.

Hasefi looked up at the decorated wall, studying the pictures for a moment until dark figures caught her eye. These were closer to the bottom, so she trotted down one of the ramps connected to the ledge to get a better look at the shadowy images.

She'd known from the first glimpse they were pictures of the wolves she had grown up running from. One was in the lead, bigger than the others, making her think of Sal. The next scene was of battle, though it looked more one-sided as wolves were shown mauling and tearing through lynxes.

It's exactly like what happened to....

"Resahn thought to take our home." Sefonis's voice sounded to Hasefi's right and she was surprised to find him sitting beside her in all his ghostly light. She glanced nervously around the cavern. "Worry not, wee lass, no one will see me."

"You're sure?" she whispered, eyeing where she'd watched the guardian slip into the caverns behind her.

Sefonis nodded, confident.

"What about you?" she pressed. "Can't this drain you?"

"Because we're bound to you, it depletes your energy first. That's why you needed so much time to recover after we brought the mountain lion to the Pack."

"You know this for sure?"

"Kilarsa is the expert," he admitted. "I trust her. We're not going anywhere, Hasefi," he added with an amused twitch of his whiskers.

Convinced, Hasefi looked back to the wall before her, her mind changing the images of the dying lynxes into those of her dying tribe.

"You may think this tribe is different, but these are memories you both share," Sefonis told her.

"It doesn't make sense," Hasefi murmured. "If that's true, I'd expect Esafi to hate them like I do—maybe even more. Why is she so determined to fight with the Clan and not the actual wolves who did this?"

"I don't know," Sefonis admitted. "Esafi rarely explains her ways. Perhaps she blames the Clan for letting the black wolves live at all."

Hasefi frowned, then got to her paws. "That's not good enough." Sefonis followed her as she padded into the cave with all the previous Highchief's and High Heirs. Her gaze went immediately to the golden lynx at the end of the line of High Heirs.

"He was my brother," she murmured. "Mekonis."

Sefonis's eyes grew round with sadness as he gazed at the little image, causing anger to flare inside Hasefi.

"Maybe if Esafi decided to take this war to the Pack, I'd stay to fight!" she hissed.

"Perhaps you could convince her," Sefonis suggested.

"I've already tried," Hasefi sighed. "You know I have."

"You have to keep trying," her uncle insisted.

Hasefi gave him a questioning look, surprised by his sudden desperation.

"If they aren't stopped soon, they'll only keep taking," Sefonis continued.

"I know that," Hasefi pointed out. Before she could ask him what he meant, a voice sounded outside in the Cavern.

"High Heir?"

Hasefi's head jerked back just as a keeper entered the cave. Her eyes darted to where Sefonis had been, but he had vanished.

"Arsolin," she murmured, and the keeper bowed. "What are you doing here?"

"I, uh, was going to ask you that," he admitted. "Another keeper told me she heard you down here talking to another lynx."

"Oh, I, uh, I was just talking to myself," she told him, giving her chest an embarrassed lick. *So much for that,* she added to Sefonis.

Well, we weren't seen, he pointed out, a mischievous grin audible in his tone.

"Would you like privacy?" Arsolin continued, bringing Hasefi out of her head. "I can move to the shadows."

"No, that would just make things weird." Silence floated between them. Hasefi shuffled her paws awkwardly. "Erm, well, I'm sorry for getting you in trouble earlier."

"Why would you be sorry?" he asked, sounding genuinely puzzled.

"You warned me it was against the rules or whatever. If you hadn't listened to me, Esafi never would have yelled at you."

"There's no reason for you to blame yourself," he told her. "I don't."

"Really?"

The keeper nodded.

Hasefi glanced away and found herself looking at the image of her brother.

"Mekonis," she murmured.

Arsolin flinched and bowed his head.

"You were his keeper, weren't you?"

"I understand if you would prefer to have someone else," he said quietly.

"Why would I want that?"

"It was my duty to protect the High Heir!" he burst, then immediately recoiled and looked around as if expecting some lynx to scold him. "I should have prevented—"

"You're not the one who killed my brothers," Hasefi pointed out. "That wasn't your fault."

"But if I had been with them—"

"So why weren't you?"

He hesitated before responding. "They had snuck away from home." Arsolin's shoulders slumped and his head hung in utter defeat.

Hasefi stepped closer to him. When he didn't react, she lowered her own head until she could peer into the shadowy eyes of his helmet.

"How is that your fault?"

"I should have been more aware. I should have known that—"

"How could you have known?" she pointed out. "Kits will do anything to explore and take risks. You can't stop that."

"But I should've been better."

"But you weren't."

He flinched again.

"Arsolin, they would have found a way out one way or another. And even if you had managed to find them, do you really think you could've stopped what happened?"

Arsolin was silent.

"My entire tribe died," Hasefi continued, surprised how steady her voice was. "And I blamed myself for moons. If only I had been older and stronger. If only I hadn't been so scared."

"You couldn't control that."

"And you couldn't control them."

He was quiet again.

"Maybe others blame you for what happened," Hasefi said, thinking of Esafi's attitude towards him. "But I don't. And you shouldn't."

Arsolin remained silent for a few more heartbeats before letting out a long breath.

"Okay," he whispered. His armor shifted as if a weight had rolled off his back and he was able to sit more easily.

Without thought, Hasefi touched her nose to the keeper's armored forehead. He leaned towards her, a soft sound echoing from his helmet. They stayed like that for a few heartbeats before Hasefi drew away. This time, as she looked deep into his helmet's eyes, she caught the faintest gleam of his.

"Now, will you get it in your head that I won't ask for a different keeper?" she asked with a purr.

"Yes, High Heir."

Hasefi's purr strengthened when she heard a stifled yawn in his words. "I think it's time we both got some decent sleep."

Arsolin dipped his head in agreement.

"I'll see you tomorrow, Arsolin."

"Sleep well, Hasefi."

Chapter Six

The next morning, Hasefi found Garfonis waiting for her outside instead of Arsolin. She was a little disappointed; while her father was certainly friendlier than Esafi, it was clear he would do anything the Highchief told him. But a part of her was delighted, too, to actually interact with him.

"Good morning," she greeted through a large yawn. Her father blinked at her with amusement.

"How did you sleep?" he asked.

"Well enough, I suppose. I'm not exactly used to waking up before the sun," she admitted with a glance at the purple sky.

"It won't take long," Garfonis assured her. "You might even feel better after a quarter moon." Garfonis flinched at his own words, but Hasefi made no outward reaction to them. *Kolahn could be dead in a quarter moon. Or the Tribe could be marching towards the Clan. Or, maybe Kolahn and I will be days away from all this.*

"Are you ready?" her father asked, bringing her back to the present.

"What are we doing?"

"You and I will be joining the novice knights and their mentors in training and learning the way of our Path."

"Okay," Hasefi said. Her father seemed to be waiting for something else, but Hasefi didn't know what. Before she could ask, he quickly turned and led her to the cave on the opposite side of the clearing of the Healer's Cave.

"First, I'll give you a tour of our part of the clearing and the areas we use in our territory," Garfonis said.

Hasefi nodded, trying her best not to look bored, and followed her father through the Knight's Cave where he explained each area of expertise in the Tribe was called a Path and that each Path had their designated Caves.

Too bad Kolahn didn't name things here. It would have been a lot less boring, she thought.

Afterwards, just after the sun's golden light breached the sky, Garfonis brought her out of the clearing and into the forest.

"Our knights train in a large sandy hollow we call the Knight's Pit," her father explained. "Have you seen the open fields beyond our forest, yet?"

"I have."

"It's in that direction, near the heart of our territory."

"Is that where you and Sefonis trained together?"

"Aye," he replied, but he didn't elaborate liked she'd hoped. All morning, his tone had been matter-of-fact and any hope of getting to know her father was dwindling.

He was so eager before, but now it's like he just wants to get this over with.

The trees opened up before them, revealing a giant pit about five lynx-heights deep with roots protruding from the sides. Pale sand covered every inch of the pit, perfect for cushioning a fall.

There was a group of knights at the far end sparring with each other. Despite their bulky armor, they were fast and, though the plate they wore was difficult to penetrate, they found ways to fell their opponents and pin them in the sand.

A second group was closer to the side she and Garfonis stood above. A pawful of knights sat before a line of novices that outnumbered them only by a few. The latter had nothing but helmets, allowing Hasefi to see their fur.

Remembering Nakilon, she scanned the pelts until she recognized his golden brown one among the others.

"They wait for us," Garfonis said. "The sides can be difficult to climb. Will you be alright?" he added with a concerned glance at her newly healed leg.

"I'll be fine," she assured him with an encouraging smile. Her leg already felt much stronger since her tour with Arsolin yesterday and had yet to cause her any problems.

Though he still looked worried, her father turned away and skidded easily down the side of the pit to the group below. Hasefi did the same with little more difficulty and followed him to the other lynxes.

"Emperor!" One of the knights called and, as one, the novices immediately sank into bows while the other knights offered respectful nods.

"Good morning, fellow knights," Garfonis greeted them with warmth as he sat among the fully-armored mentors. "Today we will be adding the High Heir to your training."

"But isn't she just starting her training?" one of the novices asked before he was hushed.

"Aye," Garfonis admitted lightly. "But the Highchief has ordered her training of the Paths to begin immediately."

Some of the novices peered at Hasefi from under their helmets while others glanced respectfully away. Nakilon gave her a friendly wink. They were all sizes and she guessed some were nearing the end of their time as novices. But she could tell she was certainly the youngest and the smallest.

Don't let that intimidate you, Sefonis reminded her.

Were you thinking it was?

Her uncle's chuckle echoed in her head.

"Tell me why you've chosen the Path of knights," Garfonis asked the novices.

"To fight!"

"To protect the Tribe!"

"To show the wolves who owns the River!"

Garfonis's eyes were bright as he looked at each of the novices, revealing the part of him Hasefi had first glimpsed when they had met and he realized who she was.

He cares a lot about these lynxes, she thought, admiration spreading a warmth through her as she watched her father.

Garfonis stood, pacing slowly before the novices and meeting each of their gazes. "All great reasons," he told them. "But what about when there's no battle to fight? No enemy to pursue or protect against?"

The novices were quiet this time.

"What does it mean to be a knight during times of peace?" Garfonis paused again, but, still, no voices answered him. Even one of the mentors was scuffing the sand with an uncertain paw.

"A knight is not just armor and claws," Garfonis explained, clearly not upset by the lack of responses. "A knight is not just a fighter of beasts and a protector of lives. Our path teaches us to be strong and brave. But it also teaches us to be adaptable. Threats come in more forms than battle. When the Tribe is faced with illness or starvation, what is our role, then?"

"To bring prey to the weak," Nakilon answered confidently.

"To carry those who cannot carry themselves," another added quietly.

"Exactly," Garfonis said, looking pleased. "It's easy to resort to our claws, but it is important to use our minds and hearts, as well. We train to fight, but our true purpose is to ensure there's no reason to. We are the ones that not only keep threats at bay, but prevent them from ever becoming. We are the ones our tribe depends on to shield them from the dark realities of our world. We are the armor of the Tribe."

The novices nodded, some of them with proudly puffed chests and others not meeting the Emperor's gaze.

"I have no doubt that each of you will be necessary additions to my knights," Garfonis continued. "But, just like all the others before you, it takes time and experience. A knight can train their whole life to fight, but have no idea how to handle a bear or a moose. Or a wolf. If it weren't for the images the guardians provide, you wouldn't even know what any of those looked like."

Now none of the novices met his gaze.

"I'm assuming each of you has warmed up for the morning," Garfonis said, glancing at the mentors who gave him a confirming nod. "So I will let your mentors take over again before we insert the High Heir into your sparring." With a nod at the mentors, Garfonis returned to Hasefi while they took over and the novices starting splitting off into pairs and groups.

"You have fought before?" Garfonis asked Hasefi, looking doubtful.

"Yes," she replied. "But I did a lot of it with a broken leg," she added carefully. *And anything else with the help of nine other lynxes.*

"Would you be willing to face some of the younger novices to see where you're at?"

"Sure," she told him, genuinely excited at the chance to exercise her skill in combat. She had practiced a lot on her own and, later, with Kolahn, but she'd never had an official fighter to teach her, aside from the bits and pieces she'd gotten from her tribe.

This could help, too, when it's time to rescue Kolahn.

Garfonis brought her to a pair of novices sparring with each other. After a quick word from the Emperor, the mentors split the two younger lynxes, one joining another pair and one facing Hasefi. She was delighted to find it was Nakilon.

"Training usually starts off with a bit of free-sparring," Garfonis explained to Hasefi. "Just use your knowledge to pin the other, then go again."

Hasefi nodded, calling up her own experience with past adversaries.

Except you're fighting lynxes, now, Sefonis spoke.

What's the point of fighting lynxes if we're facing creatures bigger than us? Hasefi asked her uncle. *Didn't Garfonis say something about the guardians using images?*

Images aren't flesh and bone, as much as they may appear to be. Sparring with lynxes teaches you control, as you'll have to pull your blows, even more than you did with Kolahn. It also helps with building up strength, understanding patterns, techniques.

"Hasefi?"

"Hm?" she asked, looking to her father.

"Is everything alright?"

"Yeah, sorry." Hasefi focused on Nakilon. He was quiet, not at all how he'd been when she had first met him. He only had a helmet, like the other novices, while she had her full set of armor. Through the narrow space above the faceguard of his helmet, she could see his eyes glittering with nervousness.

Hoping it would dissipate once they began, Hasefi charged.

Nakilon flinched. He tried to recover and move away, but Hasefi swiped his forepaws from beneath him.

"Come on, you can do better than that," Nakilon's mentor said gently.

Hasefi caught his gaze again and saw that he was still looking nervous.

"You weren't afraid of me before," she said. "What's bothering you now?"

Nakilon didn't respond.

"Is it because your Emperor is here, watching? Or is it something to do with me?"

His gaze flickered.

"Why would I make you afraid to fight? Is it because I have armor?"

The novice gave a nervous glance at his mentor, then the Emperor.

Hasefi narrowed her eyes, thinking she might understand now. "Are you afraid of hurting me and getting in trouble?"

After a moment, Nakilon replied. "More of hurting you," he admitted.

"Don't be," she told him, allowing a challenging note to enter her tone. "Give me your best. Try and push me down."

His uncertainty sparked into excitement. Then he lowered into a crouch.

Hasefi did the same, watching the novice until he leapt at her. She moved out of the way, relishing the easy use of two healthy forelegs. Having been used to dead weight, her increased speed gave her even more time to bat the novice's helmet.

He turned to face her and rose onto his hind legs. Hasefi rolled away as he came down, then charged and head-butted the novice's flank, but he was bigger and only staggered at her attack. He swiped and she ducked. They were close together now and, since he had the weight advantage, Hasefi knew she had to take him by surprise before he pushed her into the sand.

With a surge of energy, she rose up and grabbed the part of his scruff sticking out of his helmet, using all her weight to pull him to the ground.

Nakilon let out a gasp, which turned to a grunt when he hit the ground. Before he could recover, Hasefi climbed onto him and was delighted to see the amazement and excitement in his eyes.

"Wow, I wasn't expecting that!" he gasped when she let him get up.

"That looked like a wolven move," Nalikon's mentor said suddenly, throwing a glance towards Garfonis.

"Well, I did train with one," Hasefi said before she could stop herself.

"Really?" Nalikon asked, his eyes wide with curiosity.

"Hasefi!" Garfonis stepped in, giving her an urgent look.

"I mean that I've faced one before," she offered, refusing to lie entirely. "You learn all kinds of things when you're on your own," she added to the novice.

"Maybe you could teach me," he said, eyes bright with an excitement that flowed over to Hasefi and made her paws twitch. "You should try fighting against the other novices!"

"I don't think—"

"Why not?" Nalikon's mentor interrupted Hasefi's father, to her surprise. "Obviously she has some experience in battle. We'll have to know her limits. Isn't that what you intended?"

The Emperor hesitated.

"I'd like to try," she told her father.

"But..." he trailed off, his intense gaze on her.

"Nothing will happen. I promise," she assured him.

"Come on, Garfonis, nothing will harm your kit here. And the novices would love a new challenge," the mentor insisted.

Hasefi's father sighed. "Fine. But if I think it's too much—"

"I'll be fine," Hasefi insisted even though she knew her well-being wasn't why he was reluctant. She gave him a knowing look and he let out another sigh.

"Very well."

Nakilon's mentor caught the attention of the others and they started forming a rough circle around Hasefi and Garfonis.

"There's been a change in plans," Garfonis told them. "It seems the High Heir's skill is beyond what I had initially anticipated. Her time outside the River has given her some skill in combat. So we will determine her level based on yours."

Some of the novices looked nervous while others were eager. One in particular met Hasefi's gaze without flinching and she thought she saw a flicker of contempt there.

"Nakilon has already fought her," Nakilon's mentor spoke. "Katrima, would your novice like to try?"

The mentor called upon looked to the novice at her side. "Well, what are you waiting for?" she encouraged.

The novice slunk into the circle, facing Hasefi. She didn't look much older than Nakilon, but she didn't seem quite as nervous as he had been initially.

Hasefi crouched, feeling her own uncertainty with all the eyes on her.

Don't be distracted. It was Gelinaf who whispered to her. *Be aware of your surroundings, but remember your target is her.*

Hasefi gave a tiny nod, heeding his words.

The novice charged towards Hasefi and she prepared to move, but she noticed the novice's gaze flicker for just a heartbeat in the same direction. Instead, Hasefi stayed where she was.

The novice feinted, then came to a clumsy halt when she realized Hasefi hadn't moved with her. Hasefi landed a blow to the cheek of her helmet, jarring the novice from her confusion. She reared up, like Nakilon had, but this novice was smaller than him, so Hasefi charged, taking out her hind legs, then sidestepping as the novice fell heavily to the ground.

Hasefi turned, ready for more, but the novice merely sneezed against the sand and gave Hasefi a bemused look.

"Well done," Garfonis praised and, though he still appeared a bit worried, Hasefi could see delight in his eyes, too.

"Let me try!" A lynx a couple moons older than Nakilon and the other novice stepped into the circle. He wiggled his haunches eagerly and Hasefi had to keep her own excitement from getting out of control.

This is fun, she admitted.

Don't underestimate your target, Sefonis warned. *He may be bouncy, but he'll be quick and hard to hit.*

This time, Hasefi lunged first, but instead of jumping away like she expected, the novice threw a paw at her. The blow hit her in the shoulder as she tried to avoid it, putting her off balance. Another paw flashed by, so she let herself fall to the ground and roll away in a less than graceful manner.

When she got up, the novice was in the air. She stumbled awkwardly to the side, barely catching herself with what used to be her broken leg, which was beginning to shake now. The novice landed beside her and shouldered her flank, making her stumble further. Then he was on top of her, but she slammed a paw into his chin beneath his helmet, dazing him.

Hasefi scrambled out from beneath him and, as quickly as she could muster, leaped onto his back and wrapped her paws around his neck. The novice tried to shake her off, but she held on, though it was difficult without the use of claws.

Trying another strategy, the novice fell to the ground in an attempt to dislodge her, but only managed to let her pin him down.

"Stars," he gasped as she withdrew. "I've never seen a move like that."

I wouldn't mention to him that you used it to take down prey, Tenarli chuckled. Hasefi laughed, too, and, not realizing her attention was directed elsewhere, the novice joined in the laughter.

"We might need the High Heir teaching our novices," one of the mentors laughed.

"Why not? I wouldn't mind the break."

"Come on." The lynx Hasefi had noticed giving her narrowed eyes before entered the circle. He seemed like one of the oldest of the novices and was almost as big as some of the knights that were there. "Just because she can take out a couple kits doesn't make her a fighter."

"Hey!"

"I'm not a kit!"

"Just wait until she takes you out, Firalos!" Nakilon called. He gave Hasefi a dutiful nod and she smiled.

"Alright," she said, turning to the older novice. "Why don't you show me what a fighter is, then?"

Firalos lowered into a crouch with a growl. Anger and determination burned in his eyes and Hasefi knew that he not only had more practical knowledge, but may have even used it against a real threat. Adding to his size, muscle rippled beneath his fur, flexing as he balanced his weight.

He lunged at her and she moved out of the way, but he stretched out a paw and bowled her over. Hasefi managed to recover before he could move on top of her and darted out of reach. She raised onto her hind legs and, as he came to meet her, quickly dropped to the ground and swiped out one of his forelegs. He didn't quite fall, but he let out a frustrated growl as he stumbled and she passed a teasing paw along his flank.

Firalos turned to face her, baring his teeth. Hasefi let him see her nose twitch with amusement, turning his growl into a snarl. He charged and she moved, this time farther away. However, he still managed to catch her, landing a hard blow to her cheek that sent her sprawling into the sand. She rolled away just before he could put a paw on her throat.

Upright, she cuffed his ears, making him duck, and slammed another paw hard into his helmet. Firalos grunted, his vision momentarily blocked as his helmet slid out of place. Hasefi moved around him, prepared to leap onto his back, but his hind legs suddenly kicked out. The blow hit her hard and she was sent rolling through the sand, her breath knocked from her.

For a moment, her vision blurred, and she could barely make out Firalos adjusting his helmet and looking to her.

"Just because you're suddenly High Heir doesn't mean you're invincible," he growled and one of the mentors snapped at him.

I think we should put this lynx into his place, Sefonis said.

How? I can barely land a blow and my leg is ready to give out.

Sefonis didn't respond with words, but she could see images in her head. Images of a scenario similar to hers. A tingle went through her and she got to her paws.

Let me do the move on my own, she ordered.

"What, is that all you've got?" Hasefi taunted. "I've taken harder hits from hares!"

Firalos turned on her and came to land a final blow. She rolled to the side, then head-butted the bigger lynx in the shoulder. It barely staggered him, but it allowed her the time to focus on the move her uncle had shared, using the novice's back to climb into the air, then come back down with a blow to the cheek. Firalos staggered while Hasefi circled back and charged into him, taking her paws off the ground as her whole weight slammed into the bigger lynx. He fell onto his flank and she quickly pressed both forepaws onto his throat.

"I've also hunted prey a lot bigger than you," she murmured into his ear.

Firalos let out a growl and jerked, but she didn't let go until he went limp.

As Firalos slunk back to his mentor's side, some of the novices cheered, with a bit of praise added by their mentors. But when Hasefi looked to her father, she could see uncertainty and even a bit of fear in his eyes.

"Well, Emperor, looks like your daughter is already one of our top students," one of the mentors chuckled to him, but he didn't seem to hear.

"Hasefi, can I talk to you?"

"Of course."

Garfonis jerked his head at the other mentors and they herded their novices back into sparring groups.

Hasefi's father moved to a secluded side of the Pit and she followed close behind.

"I'm sorry," she murmured when they were out of earshot. "I was showing off," she admitted. "I just thought a lynx like Firalos needed to be put in his place."

"That was Sefonis's move," her father blurted, turning around to face her.

"What?" Hasefi asked, caught off-guard.

"He came up with that in training moons ago. Using your opponent's back to get higher and land a harder blow, then circling back to finish."

"Well, any lynx could think of that," she pointed out with what she hoped looked like a nonchalant shrug.

"That was Sefonis."

"What?" she sputtered again. "I don't understand."

"He taught you to fight," Garfonis continued and she relaxed a little. "But you said he died nine moons ago."

Hasefi was quiet.

"Hasefi, what aren't you telling me?"

"Nothing," she insisted. "I guess I just picked it up when I watched him fight."

"When did he fight?"

She gave him a bemused look. "When the Pack came and slaughtered him and everyone else."

He flinched. "You were there when it happened?"

"Well yeah, I thought I had made that clear. What did you think I was talking about when I told you and the others what happened?"

"I don't know. I just thought—I didn't expect that you—I—" Garfonis's mouth hung open, a helpless look on his face. Then he sagged, grief widening his eyes. "I'm sorry."

"It wasn't your fault," she murmured, realizing the nature of his grief came from too many places a lynx should ever have to handle on their own.

He lost you, she thought to Sefonis. *And his sons. And here I am being prickly because he doesn't want me to leave.*

"Sefonis..." Garfonis continued as if reading her mind. "I knew I would probably never see him again, but I...we did not part on the best of terms."

My poor brother, Sefonis sighed, his grief washing through Hasefi. *You don't deserve to suffer for this.*

Hasefi was about to ask her uncle what Garfonis meant, but, instead, she spoke aloud.

"What happened between you two?"

Garfonis shook his head. "We were good brothers. But there were some things we couldn't agree on."

Hasefi sensed a lot more to those words, but she could also tell she wouldn't get a lot from her father on the topic without giving away the kind of knowledge she held.

Did it have to do with how Esafi ruled? she asked Sefonis.

It is a long story, he told her. *For another time, I think.*

Hasefi's father had a dull expression on, memories marching through his grim stare.

What if he could see you? Hasefi suggested. *Maybe that could help—*

No, Hasefi, Sefonis interrupted, his tone firm. *Believe me, I feel as you do, but this tribe is very close to their ancestors and Garfonis is unquestioningly loyal to Esafi. Revealing ourselves to him is too risky.*

Hasefi gave an inward sigh.

"You know he wouldn't want you to suffer, right?" Hasefi told her father. "For what happened to him? And to me?"

Garfonis let out a small, sad laugh. "That sounds exactly like something he would say," he admitted, blinking affectionately at Hasefi. "He didn't have much time with you, but I can see that he made an impression on you. More than I..."

This time Hasefi had no words to offer, having no idea how to ease what her father was feeling now. But there was one thing she wanted to address.

"Garfonis, I'm really sorry about—" She wasn't sure how to put it into words, but her father understood.

"Me too," he said. A sudden, hoarse purr rumbled in his throat. "You're a lot like Mekonis, you know."

"Really?" she asked.

"Aye. He was an exceptional young lad. Talonis, too. I could see them, Mekonis as the Highchief, and Talonis; he would have made an excellent knight once he grew into those giant paws of his. The two of them are unstoppable. They—they were, I mean."

Hasefi leaned towards her father and touched his cheek with her nose. His helmet was flipped open, allowing her to feel the warmth of his fur.

"I know how I've been since I came here," she said to him. "But I'm glad I was able to meet you." Her words were genuine.

"Me too," he told her, but his expression was crestfallen.

Knowing there was no more comfort she could offer without being untruthful, Hasefi diverted her attention to where the novices had split into several groups based on their ages and their mentors were demonstrating new moves.

"So what are we going to do?" she asked her father. "About training, I mean?"

"You still have a lot to learn," he told her and she nodded, agreeing. "But if the novices can't beat you, it may be discouraging for them to spar with you." Garfonis's nose wrinkled a little, as if he didn't like his own words.

"Shouldn't they welcome challenge?" Hasefi pointed out.

"Aye," he agreed keenly, but he was still hesitant.

"Besides," she continued. "The novices aren't less skilled than I am. You know why I beat them, right?"

He nodded and Hasefi knew she was speaking his mind. "You've dealt with things they haven't," he stated.

"I fought to stay alive. I fought to eat. Fighting was something I had to know so I wouldn't die. They don't know what that's like and, I hope this doesn't come across as insulting, but I don't think the mentors have a lot of experience, either."

"I agree with you," Garfonis admitted. "While I am grateful to the stars for this long period of peace we've had, it allows little chance for the Tribe to prepare for something like war." There was a shadow in his eyes as he spoke, reminding Hasefi he'd been present during Resahn's Reign.

"I'm sure you've tried to make them understand," she said. "But maybe I can help."

Garfonis eyed her doubtfully. "You know the Highchief doesn't want—"

"Esafi doesn't want me to talk about the Pack," Hasefi interrupted. "Talking about my life after my tribe died won't reveal something she doesn't want them to know. Besides, you know they're curious, what with the prophesized daughter mysteriously returning after everyone else she was with died." She had to make an effort to keep the bitterness out of her voice. "Esafi might want to prevent fear from spreading to her lynxes, but if they aren't given anything, they'll make their own conclusions. At least this way I can give them *something*."

Her father was silent, still looking undecided.

"Please, Garfonis. If you really are heading into a war, let me do something to help." She was surprised at the words coming from her mouth, but they were already out and she decided she would stand by them.

After a few more heartbeats, Garfonis let out a breath. "Okay," he agreed. "I suppose it couldn't do harm. Tomorrow I'll have you talk to the mentors."

"Thank you," Hasefi told him.

A twelve-moon old kit instructing mentors? Sefonis's voice entered her mind. *Refarmi, can you believe it?*

Well, she will have an Emperor and his knight at her back, Refarmi replied with amusement.

I have useful knowledge, too, Hasefi protested.

No one would argue that, Sefonis assured her. *I'm just curious as to how Esafi will react.*

Hasefi couldn't help but smirk.

It's not surprising, though, Kilarsa admitted. *While she has kept her tribe thriving, the Highchief's lynxes have little experience to use.*

Which isn't totally a bad thing, Dahsefer pointed out. *Especially when experience means battle and death and injuries—*

I wouldn't wish our fate upon any lynx, Hasefi agreed. *So if I can help them avoid it, then I have to try. At least while I'm here,* she added hastily.

Her tribe sent their agreement.

When Hasefi returned her attention to her father, she found him studying her intensely. *I think I need to learn a more discreet way of talking to you.*

"Did you say something and I didn't respond?" Hasefi asked him sheepishly. Garfonis shook his head.

"I was just wondering what you were thinking. You always seem to have a lot on your mind."

"Does that surprise you?"

"No. But…Hasefi." His tone was diffident as he leaned towards her. "If you ever want to talk or anything…you know you don't have to worry about staying quiet with me."

Hasefi tried not to flinch at her father's word choice. She nodded, glad when he seemed a bit happier.

"Now," he said, resuming his confident, Emperor's tone of voice. "Let's rejoin the others. The mentors have already split the novices off into their levels to train them in some new moves. We can join Nakilon and the younger novices for today."

Hasefi followed him back to the others. She felt lighter, as if a weight had slid from her back.

You've involved yourself, Gelinaf spoke up. *You've given your father and others a reason to trust you by offering to help.*

I will help, she assured, not entirely liking the implications of her Overlord's words. *But you're right. Maybe...maybe I can befriend Nakilon and ask about the Tribe without seeming suspicious.*

Gelinaf offered his approval, though Hasefi didn't feel great about her plan.

I'm not lying to anyone, she told herself. *What they assume about me is their own decision. I can make friends. I just have to keep them at a distance so it doesn't make leaving more difficult than it's already turned out to be.*

With a slow breath in, Hasefi hardened her mind, clearing it until only Kolahn was there.

I'm coming for you, furball. Just hold on a little longer.

Chapter Seven

For the rest of the morning, Hasefi joined Nakilon and two other novices at his level while their mentors demonstrated some new moves, then allowed the younger lynxes to practice them. She was delighted to learn and was pleased when the other novices, especially Nakilon, made a challenge of getting the moves down before she could. Since they had more technical training, they succeeded more often than not.

Garfonis was close by, overseeing the training. Every time Hasefi glanced at him, he offered her a smile, spreading a warmth through her. He'd also offer tips to her, the other novices, and to the mentors, but he let the last remain in charge throughout the morning.

There was little time to talk. The novices Hasefi trained with were clearly eager to ask her questions, but their mentors kept them focused and, when sunpeak came, they announced it was time to return to the clearing and the novices were herded off.

Garfonis moved off to talk to one of the mentors, so Hasefi climbed the rise on her own, using the roots to keep from slipping down the sandy sides. Arsolin met her at the top.

"I brought some food for you," the keeper offered, pawing a hare towards her.

Hasefi's stomach growled in response, but the sound of someone scrambling up behind her made her turn.

"Nakilon?" she asked with surprise as the novice shook out his fur, then came to stand beside her. "I thought you went with the others."

"Sunpeak is break time; the others are just going back to eat, but I thought I'd take the chance to hang out with you. If that's okay," he added, ducking his head in embarrassment.

"Of course," she purred with amusement.

He blinked happily, then glanced at the hare at her paws.

"Want some?" she asked.

"Oh, it's alright, I'm not hungry." He winced as he spoke.

"Right, and I'm not a lynx. Come."

Nakilon hesitated, giving Arsolin a wary look, before settling beside Hasefi.

"This is Arsolin," she told the novice.

"Nice to meet you," the novice said with an awkward nod.

"And you, novice knight." Arsolin turned to Hasefi. "I will walk the perimeter while you eat." He slunk into the shadows after Hasefi gave him a friendly nod.

"So," Hasefi began, hoping to ease the tension the novice clearly felt, even after Arsolin disappeared. "Now that battle training is done, what's next?"

"Well, Myrena usually takes me to the Cavern of History," he explained after swallowing a bite. "Then we do some studying in the Knight's Memories. Sometimes it's just us, sometimes we join the others." He turned an eager gaze at her. "Are you coming with us?"

"I'm not sure," she admitted. "Garfonis hasn't told me what we'll do next."

Nalikon nodded, bowing his head to take another bite.

"So you've only been a novice for a quarter moon?" Hasefi asked him.

"A knight novice," he replied. "But I completed a moon of basic training, just as every novice does. Er, most, I mean," he added with a glance at her. "But I can see why you didn't need yours."

"What normally happens in the first moon?" she asked before taking a mouthful of hare.

"You tour the borders, you learn about each Path. And you learn some of the history about the Tribe and the Clan across the River. We do some basic combat and hunting, too. And they tell us a bit about magic." His eyes flickered to the armor on her chest.

"I'm not gifted," she admitted and his eyes widened. "Did you think I was?"

"I'm not sure," he admitted. "But...I didn't think you'd tell me if I asked."

"Why not?"

"Well...it's not really my place to know," he admitted.

"I tend to be really good at getting other lynxes in trouble, so you might want to keep that a secret, then," Hasefi told him. "But not for me. I don't mind if you tell your friends. I just don't want Esafi to yell at anyone else because of me."

"Anyone else?" he asked.

"I got my keeper in trouble," she admitted.

"Yikes. I hear the Highchief is scary when she's mad." He narrowed his eyes. "She's kind of scary all the time." He flashed her a sheepish look.

Hasefi shrugged. "I'm not afraid of her."

Nakilon shifted his paws, his eyes on the grass. "Hey, after our lessons today...did you want to join me for another meal? We didn't really get the chance to finish that deer and use the Warmrock."

She blinked at him with surprise.

"If you want, I mean," he continued hastily. "Sorry, I'm not sure if I'm allowed to ask you that—"

"I would love that," she told him, making him blink with surprise.

"Really? I mean—great!" He ducked his head with an embarrassed smile. "Um..."

"What?"

"I know this isn't really my business either...but if you wanted, I'd like to hear more about your time before you returned to us."

"Sure," she purred.

He straightened, eyes glittering with delight. But before he could say anything else, Garfonis appeared with Arsolin a few steps behind.

"It's nearly time to head to the Cavern," the Emperor said, his friendly gaze on the novice. "You should get back to Myrena."

"Yes, Knight Emperor." Nakilon bowed, but before he hurried off into the trees, he hesitated, glancing at the remains of the hare and passing Hasefi an apologetic look.

"Don't worry about these," she told him.

With a nod, the novice ran off in the direction of the clearing.

"I can take these," Arsolin offered with a nod at the bones.

"Are they going to the gifted?" she asked.

"We're a ways from the clearing, so they can just get buried." He leaned in to take the bones, but Hasefi stretched a paw in front of his face to stop him.

"I'm capable of burying bones, thank you very much," she said with an incredulous look at the keeper.

"He can do that while you and I return to the clearing," Garfonis said.

Hasefi gave him a look, too. "I am *not* making another lynx bury my own meal," she told him firmly. "Maybe that's how you do things, but I'd like to think my paws aren't just for show."

Before either lynx could do anything, she found a soft patch of earth and quickly scraped a hole. She batted the bones and fur into it before stamping the earth. "There. *Now* we can go."

Garfonis blinked at her with bafflement before leading the way. Hasefi joined him while Arsolin followed a few paces back.

"I feel bad," she told her father as they headed towards the Tribe's home.

"Your keeper could have done it."

"Not for that," she groaned. "Arsolin has to follow me everywhere. Doesn't he have better things to do?"

"Protecting you is one of the most important things he could do," Garfonis pointed out. She noticed a strange note in his voice and saw him glancing back to where the keeper was slinking behind them. "But...I'm surprised the Highchief allowed him another chance."

Hasefi turned on her father, forcing him to stop. Though his words were quiet, Hasefi had a feeling Arsolin could hear them. "Why?" she demanded. "Because Mekonis and Talonis were taken by wolves? No keeper could have prevented that from happening."

Garfonis flinched, looking away.

A stab of guilt pierced Hasefi's chest at the hurt look in her father's eyes. "I'm sorry," she told him.

"No, you're right," he admitted. "I'm just...I just wish..."

"There's nothing you could've done, either," she pointed out.

"I know. I just want the Clan to pay."

Hasefi had to clench her jaw to keep from trying to explain it wasn't them who took her brothers. She knew she didn't have to hide that knowledge from her father, but she was confident he'd do little about it without Esafi's say.

"I don't want war," Garfonis continued. "But I will feel quite good sinking my claws into the pelts of those mangy dogs."

Hasefi sank her claws into the ground. She had no love for the Clan, but she didn't believe they should suffer for the wrong reasons.

"It wasn't them," she told her father. "The Clan didn't take Mekonis and Talonis. I don't even think they're the ones stealing prey."

Garfonis gave her a confused look.

"It's the Pack."

"You're sure?" he asked.

"Esafi told me how they were found; it was the same as my tribe. It has to be the Pack. Besides, what reason would the Clan have to kill them? What *real* reason?" she added when her father started to spit an insult. "The Pack wants the Clan's territory. I wouldn't be surprised if they wanted this side of the River, too."

"If this is true, then we have to tell the Highchief."

"She wouldn't listen to me. She's set on bringing war to the Clan."

Garfonis frowned thoughtfully.

"But maybe she'll listen to you," Hasefi continued, desperate not to lose his attention. "I mean, your two are still mates, right?"

"Of course," he blurted. "But if the Highchief doesn't think it was the Pack...then maybe it wasn't."

"What?"

"If Esafi believes the Clan took Mekonis and Talonis," Garfonis began, "then there must be something she knows that we don't."

"I really don't think—"

"Trust your mother, Hasefi," Garfonis told her. "She's never led us wrong."

"But that doesn't mean she can't."

Her father frowned. Not wanting to make him as unfriendly as her mother already was, Hasefi conceded. "Fine. Right. Let's just finish whatever else you have to teach me."

Garfonis gave her a sad look. "I hope," he began slowly. "That, before you leave, you get a chance to see your mother for what she truly is."

Hasefi didn't respond and he gave up, leading the rest of the way back to the clearing.

Garfonis brought her through the Knight's Cave, down a tunnel to the Cavern of History where some of the other novice knights were, along with various other lynxes performing their studies. She spotted Nakilon, but he was focused intently on what one of the mentors was describing as they waved a paw along the decorated wall.

Arsolin sat dutifully on the ledge while Garfonis took Hasefi into the cave with the stone Emperor and knight sitting on each side.

Nakilon called this the Knight's Memories, right? she thought. *Fitting, I suppose,* she added with a glance at the lines of soulstones.

It was empty in the cave, so she sat alone with Garfonis as he described when knights had first come to be and how their role had evolved over the generations.

Courage, strength, adaptability, she thought as she looked up at the images arcing near the ceiling of the cavern. *I feel like it would be good to have these qualities regardless of what you are.*

Aye, Sefonis agreed. *But these are what the knights focus on. We are the frontlines. We are the first into battle. Whether it be with the Clan, an angry bear, or a drought, we must be brave and strong and able to adapt to changing times if we are to fulfill our role in the tribe.*

Garfonis explained the current purpose of the knights, too, and what a Highchief expected of them. Sefonis and his knight, Refarmi, offered some words of their own, where appropriate, but they didn't overshadow Garfonis as he spoke.

Some of it was interesting to Hasefi, like learning about the first knight and seeing by the images on the wall how, when armor was available, it was shaped through history until it was akin to what lynxes wore today. But she didn't feel a need to hold on to the information and was looking forward to when Garfonis announced the lesson was over and she was free to go.

When that time came, she went in search of Nakilon.

He was no longer in the Cavern, so she went out into the clearing. She nearly bumped into him as she left the Knight's Cave.

"Hasefi!" Embarrassment crossed Nakilon's face and he dropped into a bow. "I mean, High Heir."

"Hasefi's fine," she purred. "Preferable, even."

A grin made his whiskers twitch as he straightened. "If we hurry, we might be able to find a hare to share."

"Share?" Hasefi echoed with amusement. "I think I got two bites of the last hare!"

Nakilon crouched, wriggling his haunches. "I'll race you."

Hasefi lowered herself into a crouch, but someone called out her title and she straightened.

Arsolin was on his way over.

"High Heir," he said again, stopping a few steps away. "The Highchief would like me to continue with some of your basic training," he told her.

Hasefi fought the urge to flatten her ears.

"Didn't you just spend the whole day training?" Nakilon asked as he sat upright.

"Yeah, but apparently stuff is being moved around because of th— of whatever reason." She blinked apologetically. "I guess we'll have to share that hare another time."

"You should at least eat," he protested, glancing at the keeper.

Hasefi followed his gaze, looking at Arsolin hopefully.

"There's a lot to do," he admitted. His voice was firm, but Hasefi thought she could detect a note of reluctance. "We're supposed to be done before dusk."

"It's alright," Hasefi sighed, turning to Nakilon. "I'll see you in training tomorrow."

Nakilon nodded and padded slowly towards the prey-hole.

"I'm sorry for interrupting," Arsolin told her as he led her towards the fern entrance.

"It's not your fault," she sighed. *I guess it's just easier for Esafi to keep me busy than to deal with me herself.*

She passed a glare over her shoulder at the Highledge, but it was empty. Her irritation dissipated, however, when she realized how little she'd done to find a way to help Kolahn.

And the moment I try to befriend someone, I'm dragged back into training, she thought as she stepped after Arsolin through the ferns and out into the forest. *I can't keep wasting time. But—but I don't know what to do!*

Time is not being wasted, Kilarsa assured her. *You know Esafi wants war. It will come.*

Arsolin was speaking as he led Hasefi in the direction of the river, but she hardly paid any attention to him. A mixture of self-loathing and longing writhed within her as her thoughts conflicted.

I know, she replied. *But we have no idea how long Eilwyn will keep Kolahn before—if I could just know he was okay....* She had to fight the urge to shake her head. *And I can't get the Pack out of my head.* They're *the real enemy. Even if Esafi wants to fight the Clan, she needs to understand the kind of threat the Pack poses.* She gritted her teeth. *But that won't get me closer to Kolahn.*

She stifled a sigh, wishing once again Kolahn had never come here and they were still in the Great Valley, figuring out what they would do about finding a new home.

I wonder if the Pack has been bothering the Clan, she thought with a new pang of fear. *If I'm right and they killed my brothers, then they must have an idea of what's going on in the Clan. Could they know Kolahn's there? They'd kill him before the Clan could.*

Her paws itched to run back the way they'd come so she could dart behind the waterfall and make her way to the Clan's ravine. But she knew her keeper would stop her before she even made it there.

Unless I didn't hold back.

Her tribe didn't respond to her prodding, but they didn't need to. Even before she got the chance to know her keeper, she refused to do anything that might lead to the same consequences that had resulted the last time she tried to save Kolahn.

What if it's the only way? she argued with herself. *What if others have to get hurt if I'm to save him before he's killed?* She looked over to the trees again. *If I could just know for sure he's okay, then maybe I wouldn't be so worried and I could find a way to stop Esafi.*

"Is everything alright, High Heir?" Arsolin asked.

Hasefi realized she had slowed down quite a bit and was barely moving alongside the River.

"Yeah, sorry." She hurried to Arsolin's side, but the keeper stopped. She gave him a questioning look.

"Are you afraid?" he asked.

"Afraid of what?"

"The Clan?"

Hasefi let out a sharp, bitter laugh. "You have no idea." She winced, trying to rein in the flurry of frustration and helplessness threatening to spill from her. "I mean, not really. They just seem like judgemental, whiny pups."

Arsolin was silent, the shadowy eye-holes of his helmet on her.

"Sorry," Hasefi murmured, trying not to glance towards the River again. "We should keep moving."

The keeper stirred, but hesitated. "Are you sure everything is alright?"

"Yeah. I'm just tired, is all."

After another heartbeat, Arsolin continued. Hasefi resisted the urge to look over the border and towards where she knew her companion was being held prisoner—assuming he was still alive.

He has to be, she thought.

He is, Sefonis assured her.

Can you know for sure? she pressed. *I know you're bound to me, but is there a way for you to see him?*

Not any differently than you could. It was Kilarsa who spoke. *Anchoring ourselves to you has its limits, but it was the only way to escape the ancestors. We only see and hear what you do.*

But you can leave me, right? Like you did? she added to Sefonis.

A starlit spirit would be quite noticeable, I think, even in daylight, her uncle pointed out with some amusement.

Hasefi stifled the urge to sigh as she trailed behind Arsolin. It was hard to believe it was only her second day in this new tribe; it felt like she had left Kolahn moons ago.

The sun was as reluctant to move as Hasefi was to stay and it felt like Arsolin was using every heartbeat to show her as much of the territory as he could. Despair dug cruel claws into Hasefi's fur until it became an effort to keep her head up lest Arsolin pause to see if she was okay again.

Eventually, when they did return to the clearing, the sun had released its grip and allowed the moon and stars to bring forth their softer light—dusk had come and gone.

Hasefi was afraid her keeper intended to bring her into the Cavern for another set of lessons, but, with a murmured word, he moved to the shadows, leaving her alone near the front of the clearing.

Most lynxes were returning to the caves for the night while some prepared for nightly duties. Hasefi looked around for Nakilon, but there was no sign of him.

There's not much I can do, she thought with a defeated sigh, glancing in the direction Arsolin was padding as he rounded the clearing. *And I'm exhausted.*

Hasefi was about to give up for the day and head to the Highcave when a particular lynx caught her eye. He had a white collar, marking a novice healer. He had come into the clearing behind her and was padding in the direction of the Healer's Cave with a mouthful of herbs.

"You."

The novice stopped and looked to Hasefi in surprise and uncertainty. As she trotted over, he dropped his mouthful and sank into a bow.

"High Heir!" he greeted.

"You're the one who healed my leg," she said, stopping in front of him. "Salifen, right?"

"Aye," he admitted.

Hasefi hesitated, realizing she wasn't entirely sure why she had approached him.

Uncertainty sparkled in the novice's eyes as he glanced from her, to the herbs at his paws, and the rest of the clearing behind her. "Was there something you needed?" he asked.

"Not really," she admitted. "Sorry."

"It's okay," he replied with an awkward shrug.

"I was just training all day and never really got the chance to just...*be*, I guess."

"I know what you mean," Salifen admitted. "Hesilar has had me working all day and I'm just exhausted."

"I should probably let you get some rest."

"It's alright," he told her. "I don't mind talking. I mean, you seem nice, so...well, I'm sure you have to be somewhere—"

"Not really," she told him. "Other than asleep, I guess."

They both chuckled, ears half-flat in discomfiture. Salifen looked again to the bundle at his paws.

"Um, what do you have?" Hasefi asked him.

"Oh, these are just some herbs I found outside the clearing." He pawed them towards her. "Hesilar wanted me to see which ones I could identify outside the garden and, well, this is what I found."

"That's…tansy, right?" Hasefi asked, pointing to a couple stems.

"Aye!" he said, looking delighted at her knowledge. "Have you been studying the Path of the Healer?"

"No," she admitted. "I just learnt some stuff when I was…." Hasefi shrugged.

Understanding lightened his gaze and he made no attempt to press. "This is parsley," he told her, pawing some strong-smelling herbs with little leaves. "And this is marigold."

Hasefi inspected each of them with a careful sniff. "What do they do?"

Salifen explained their purposes. He was passionate as he spoke and it made Hasefi think of Kolahn who had been excited about every new thing he could introduce to her. Longing ached in her heart as she replayed the memories she had with the wolf as they travelled through the mountains together. It wasn't until she realized Salifen had gone silent that she noticed him eyeing her. When she met his gaze, he looked away.

"Everything alright?" she asked him.

"I hope I'm not boring you," he said.

"Did I look bored?" she asked apologetically.

"No, I just…when I go on about this stuff to others, they usually get pretty bored. You're sure I'm not boring you?"

"You're not!" Hasefi assured him. "Honestly, anything to take my mind off of—" She cut herself off, but Salifen was already giving her a sympathetic look.

"I can't imagine what things have been like for you. And this must be such a strange place, with so many lynxes."

"Yeah," Hasefi breathed.

"Well, um…if you wanted someone to talk to, you could always hang out with me? I mean, healers are supposed to be good at helping with wounded minds—not that your mind is wounded! I just—if you want, I mean, I'm not saying you should, but…well, after training, I usually eat with my sister and Ivanus, one of the older kits. If you wanted…."

"Sure!" Hasefi laughed. Normally, she hated it when the other lynxes around her were nervous, but she got the feeling this novice healer would be nervous around anyone. "Well, I did promise someone else I would be with them, but maybe I could hang out with you one day, too."

"Great!" Salifen said. Their gazes met and the novice quickly looked away.

Hasefi's attention had moved inward. Her words to Salifen had bothered her.

I keep making promises to these lynxes, she thought. *Nakilon, and now him. I have to stop, before I make one I can't keep.*

"I think I'll head to my sleeping chamber, now," she stated.

"Yeah, me too," Salifen blurted. "My chamber, I mean, of course."

Hasefi had to swallow an amused purr as he hastily bowed, picked up his herbs, and hurried towards the Healer's Cave. She watched him duck inside, then padded wearily up the path to the Highledge. The Highcave was silver with its magical light, turning the stone a beautiful white. Hasefi passed Sifara just outside the sleeping chamber and, to her surprise, met Esafi inside.

"How was training?" Esafi asked.

"Fine," Hasefi said briskly, prepared to curl up in her sleeping hollow.

"Garfonis told me you overcame the other novice knights," the Highchief continued. She was nosing something in one of the crevices in the wall.

Hasefi stifled an irritated groan, gazing longingly at the hollow. "I suppose I did."

"Well done."

Hasefi jerked her gaze up in surprise.

"As High Heir, it is important you are a role model to your tribe."

Hasefi deflated somewhat, but Esafi turned to look at her, so she tried to sit up straight before the Highchief could find something to critique her on.

"You were out late," she observed.

"I thought you wanted Arsolin to continue my training," Hasefi pointed out.

"It was supposed to end at sundown."

Worried Arsolin could get in trouble again if she mentioned they had been out past dusk, she offered a nonchalant shrug. "I just...talked with another lynx after."

"Who?"

"A novice," Hasefi said dismissively.

"Good," Esafi said, padding towards the tunnel entrance. "It is important for a High Heir to find those she can rely on."

Hasefi frowned, pawing at a feather sticking out of her nest. *Why tell me this when you know I'm leaving?*

"I expect you are tired. You may rest." Esafi left the chamber.

As if I need your permission to sleep, Hasefi growled to herself as she curled into her hollow. She shoved her nose under her paw and squeezed her eyes shut.

Chapter Eight

"Hasefi?"

Hasefi let out a moan and tucked her nose farther under her paw.

"Hasefi, it's time to get up."

"I haven't even closed my eyes, Kolahn."

Silence followed. Hasefi's ears twitched as she wondered what the wolf was doing. Then her mind caught up and she jerked her head up.

"Garfonis," she gasped, seeing her father's puzzled expression. "I'm sorry." She scrambled out of her hollow, shaking out her fur.

Garfonis was silent for another heartbeat before turning towards the tunnel leading out. "I was thinking we could come up with a plan for you to talk to the mentors today," he said to the chamber wall.

"Sure." Hasefi gave her pelt a swift check to make sure no stubborn bits of bedding still clung to her fur, then followed her father out of the Highcave. While the moon was no longer visible in the sky, the sun had yet to lift the darkness. Exhaustion weighed Hasefi down; training yesterday had left her sore and her left leg was weak with strain. But she made an effort not to show it.

They descended from the Highledge and went to the Knight's Cave, moving into the mainchamber where a group of knights were assembled. Hasefi recognized some of them from yesterday and knew they were mentors.

"Like I showed you yesterday," Garfonis said to Hasefi. "This is where we do a lot of our planning." He wouldn't quite look at her as he spoke.

Is he upset with me?

She studied Garfonis as the mentors shuffled, giving the Emperor room in the middle so they were in a semi-circle facing her, but she couldn't guess what might be bothering him.

"Today, you can share some of your experience beyond the River, so that we may incorporate it into our training," Garfonis explained.

Hasefi cocked her head. A snicker sounded but it was muffled so quickly she couldn't tell where it came from. Garfonis hadn't seemed to notice so she dismissed it.

What should I say? Hasefi wondered, passing her gaze over each of the expectant mentors. Their helmets were flipped up so she could see their faces, but their expressions didn't feel as friendly as they had yesterday.

Tell them about how you taught yourself to hunt and fight, Sefonis offered.

A ripple of surprise passed through Hasefi. *You know about that?*

Even when we couldn't reach you we were watching over you, wee lass, Sefonis told her.

"Hasefi?"

"Sorry," she responded to her father and shook out her fur. "Well, most of what I learnt was self-taught," she admitted. She caught some surprised looks from the other knights and remembered they had no clue as to what happened to her tribe or when.

But I can tell them that, as long as I don't mention the Pack. Hasefi hesitated, wondering exactly what would happen if she told them anyways.

It is unwise, Kilarsa warned and Hasefi stifled a sigh.

"I was about three moons old when my tribe died," Hasefi said and the surprised looks turned into shocked ones. "So I had to learn to fight or I would die."

"You were hunting at three moons old?" one of the knights gasped.

"Not exactly," Hasefi admitted, glancing away. "I didn't really learn until about a moon after." She glanced up again and saw her father giving her a distraught look. Determined to change the mood around, she continued. "I learnt to fight things based on what they were. A lot of the time I learnt from experience." She winced, remembering some of her failures during hunting and the amount of times she had escaped death. "With bigger things, it's better to get on their backs where they can't reach you. And, if you can, bring them down as quickly as you can."

"That sounds like you're fighting to kill," one of the knights said with a frown.

"It was kill or be killed," Hasefi pointed out. "And most of my battles were with prey, not foes."

"We don't need help with hunting," one of the knights said to Garfonis.

"No, you don't," he growled, making Hasefi and most of the mentors start with surprise. "But when it comes to fighting, most of you weren't born until after Resahn's Reign and don't know what real battle looks like."

"What does that matter?" a bold knight asked. "Black wolves are gone."

"Black wolves weren't our first enemy and they won't be our last," Garfonis replied, his tone firm but not harsh like Hasefi would expect Esafi's to be after being questioned. "Peace is as strong as those who fight for it. As knights, we carry most of that weight; especially now. My sons were killed in our own territory. All of you here are smart enough to know there will be retaliation."

The mentors wouldn't meet the Emperor's eyes when he spoke of Mekonis and Talonis.

"All of you know how to train and how to spar—quite well, mind you. But none of you have ever actually faced a wolf before."

"The guardians give us images to fight," one of the knights pointed out.

Garfonis's green eyes flashed. "They are not real," he snapped, causing the knight to narrow their eyes in shame. The frustration in Garfonis's voice was just as clear on his face.

I don't think he likes being quiet about the Pack, either, Hasefi realized.

"So what are you asking of us, Emperor?" one of the knights questioned.

"To listen," he told them. "And to understand the reality of battle. Hasefi is young. But I wasn't much older than her when I joined the Tribe in defending our home against Resahn." He looked to Hasefi.

She blinked in surprise, caught off-guard by Garfonis's words. But she recovered quickly and gave her father a nod.

"The only reason I beat any of the novices yesterday was because I had experience," Hasefi explained. "I'm used to fighting for my life every heartbeat of the day. Being too tired or hungry wasn't an option. One little mistake could mean death." She eyed Garfonis briefly before continuing. "I was being hunted when I was in the high mountains."

"High mountains?" one of the knights echoed.

"Where the snow is."

"Hunted by what?" another asked.

Hasefi could feel Garfonis's gaze heating her fur but she continued smoothly. "Anything. Mountain lions, for instance."

"Mountain lions aren't real," one of the knights said, but there was a note of uncertainty in his tone.

"They are—I've faced them more than once."

"What do you mean by faced?" another knight asked.

Hasefi saw the doubt spreading through their gazes. She hesitated before responding, realizing both instances she actually fought with mountain lions involved wolves.

"I've seen them, is all," she said quickly, picturing the other two times she had merely glimpsed the monstrous creatures. "Once when my tribe was killed and once...not long before I came here, I guess." She had only mentioned two encounters to Esafi and her champions, including her father, so she figured she'd stick to the same details.

I hate being so secretive, she thought, looking away. *Even with Kolahn, before I knew him. It makes things so complicated.* Her longing for her friend swelled, making her heart ache.

"We're sorry, High Heir."

Hasefi perked up her ears and saw that all of the doubt in the knights' eyes had changed into sorrow.

The one who had spoken had taken a step towards her. "We can't imagine what you've been through," he said quietly.

Hasefi lifted her head, urging herself to be strong. "I hope you don't have to. Which is why I want to help."

"It's clear you have a lot of useful information," another knight—Hasefi thought her name might be Katrima—spoke up. She was a bit older than the others and had a look similar to the one in Garfonis's eyes. "Even if it's for hunting, clearly it was useful in sparring yesterday. Perhaps you could help with today's lesson by telling the novices what you told us?"

Hasefi looked to her father who nodded.

"Okay. I can do that."

The sun was just beginning to rise when they left the Knight's Cave. They waited outside for the novices to join them. Hasefi moved to sit with her father, but he busied himself murmuring to each of the mentors individually.

Rapid steps behind her caught Hasefi's attention. She turned, delighted when she saw Nakilon trotting over.

"Hasefi!" he greeted cheerfully, giving a quick bow before joining her at her side. "How did you sleep?"

"Pretty well," she said. "Until I had to get up before the sun."

Nakilon passed her a look mixed with concern and curiosity.

"Garfonis wanted me to talk to the mentors. It looks like I'll be talking to all of you, today."

"Really?" he asked, eyes wide. "Today's going to be so exciting!"

Hasefi's whiskers twitched with amusement.

Nakilon ducked his head slightly in embarrassment. "I mean, I'm looking forward to hearing what you have to say. You seem...really neat."

Hasefi's ears flicked with surprise. "Really?" she asked and the novice gave her a nod. "Wow. Er, thanks."

"Maybe we'll get a chance to spar with each other again, too," he said hopefully, lifting his head. "And maybe we can stick together in the Cavern of History!" Nakilon ducked his head again when Hasefi passed him another amused look. "If you want, I mean."

"Sure," she purred, giving his shoulder a friendly nudge. His tail tip twitched excitedly and he reared back.

"Race you to the pit!" He charged ahead and Hasefi raced after him.

Some of her weariness had worn off; Nakilon's energy proved to be contagious. Plus, she never tired of the ability to use four legs again, relishing even the stiffness of her muscles.

As she ran after Nakilon, her limbs warmed up and the ache in her body dulled. She welcomed the winds that tugged her fur, letting adrenaline rush through her like a gushing stream. Her paws hardly touched the ground and the trees blurred around her. She darted past Nakilon, gaining speed with every heartbeat.

Then she leaped over the edge into the Knight's Pit.

When she was in the air, realization of how far the drop was sent panic through her, but her tribe reacted immediately and she landed on four paws without injury.

She looked up and saw some of the knights already there giving her shocked and anxious looks.

"Hasefi!"

She turned just as her father appeared at the edge of the Pit, along with Nakilon and the other knights and novices.

"I'm okay," she called, padding over as they came down the side. She glanced again to the other knights, relieved to find they had returned to their activities.

"Are you sure?" Garfonis asked when he reached her. His helmet was up and his eyes darted to and fro as he scanned her over.

"You just jumped all the way from the top!" Nakilon gasped, his face lit up with wonder and worry.

"I'm fine, I promise," she said, ducking under their wide gazes. "I wasn't thinking, but I got lucky."

"Real lucky," one of the mentors commented. "That isn't an easy jump, especially for a young novice."

"Maybe we should take you to the Sage, just in case," Garfonis suggested.

"Seriously, I'm fine, see?" Hasefi lifted each of her legs and wiggled her paws. "Shouldn't we get on with the lesson?"

Her father eyed her for a few heartbeats before giving a relenting nod. Hasefi stifled a relieved breath and followed the group to the same spot they had been in yesterday.

That was close, she thought to her tribe when it was safe to do so. *What happened? I can't actually run like that, can I?*

That was us, Sefonis confirmed. *And though it's our strength, you can access it as freely as if it were your own. Intense emotion—anger, excitement, fear—can trigger it.*

Apparently so. I need to be more careful, then. Are you all okay?

Aye, we are, wee lass, her uncle assured her.

"That was incredible."

Hasefi's head jerked up and she met Nakilon's sparkling eyes.

"It was nothing," she murmured, ducking her head.

"Are you kidding? You were a blur ahead and all of a sudden you were *flying*! I thought you were going to break your legs, but when I reached the Pit, you were standing there, perfectly fine!" His eyes flickered back and forth as he studied her, clearly having something else he wanted to say.

"What is it?" she asked.

"I know you said you weren't gifted but...you...had a prophecy, didn't you?"

Hasefi couldn't stop her ears from going flat and he flinched.

"Sorry, I shouldn't—"

"No, it's alright," she told him, calming herself. "I just...think about what happened every time the prophecy comes up."

Nakilon blinked sympathetically. "I don't blame you. I can't imagine what that would be like. And living only because the ancestors willed it? It really doesn't sound that great."

"To be honest," she began slowly. "I don't think the ancestors are why I'm alive." She watched him closely, but Nakilon didn't recoil like her parents had. Instead, a curious gleam entered his eyes.

"I'd really like to hear your story," he murmured.

"Nakilon! Stop distracting the High Heir!"

"Another time," Hasefi said with a shrug. Nakilon gave her a sheepish look before racing over to his mentor.

Alright. Let's talk about fighting.

Hasefi spent the first part of the morning relaying what she had told the other knights, going into detail discussing various hunting techniques that she and the knights altered for use in battle. She was able to sneak in some moves that Kolahn had taught her to use against wolves, but she found, as the day went on, she was missing her friend more and more. When they were off to the Cavern of History, her heart was heavy with longing.

Her tribe was offering comforting words when Garfonis fell into step with her.

"Is everything alright?" he asked. "Did you want to see the Sage—?"

"I'm fine," she snapped and her father flinched. "I'm sorry," she sighed. "I just...." She glanced around before narrowing her eyes at the ground and going silent.

"You miss him?"

Hasefi's head jerked up in surprise. "Sefonis?" she asked, confused, but Garfonis shook his head.

"The...wolf."

Hasefi expected his expression to be uneasy like his tone, but instead she only saw sympathy there.

"Yeah," she admitted. "I...wish I could show him how fast I can run now with my leg. I wish I could...I wish I could be with him."

Her father watched her with sorrow in his eyes, but he said nothing. Hasefi knew there was nothing he could do to help, but she was comforted by the fact that he seemed to want to.

"Kolahn, right?" he asked.

"I'm surprised you remember," she admitted.

"You said his name when I woke you this morning," he explained, making Hasefi flinch. "You really care for him."

"He was like kin to me. After my tribe...he was all I had."

Garfonis nodded, his gaze on the ground they walked on. "I'm sorry," he whispered.

"It's alright. I know you can't help—"

"No." Garfonis moved in front of her, forcing her to stop. "I'm sorry I wasn't there for you. I should've...I should've went with you."

Hasefi shook her head in surprise. "But everyone—you could be dead."

"Maybe not. I don't know." Grief shone in her father's eyes. "I just...I should've been there for you. And Sefonis."

Hasefi felt a twinge in her chest, silencing her voice.

My dear brother, Sefonis sighed.

"You were," Hasefi told him, surprising both. "For me, through Sefonis, and him through me." She could see the emotion in her father's eyes and she instinctively pressed her nose to his cheek. Garfonis buried his face in her shoulder, sending through her an unexpected surge of emotion. She reached up with her paws and wrapped them around the armor on his shoulders.

"I thought about you every day," he whispered.

"I thought about you, too," she murmured.

Garfonis pulled away. "You remembered me?"

"Not quite," Hasefi admitted. "But I thought about what you might be like. What I would do when I saw you." For a moment, Hasefi felt like a kit again, yearning for her parents. She wanted to hug her father again, but she reminded herself that she couldn't get too attached.

"What did you imagine?" he asked.

Hasefi looked away. "Not what actually happened."

"I suppose that tends to be the way, isn't it?" he asked, sympathy clear on his face.

"Maybe. But it doesn't always have to be bad," she pointed out, her mind on Kolahn.

"Do you think being here is bad?" There was no reproach or disappointment in his voice. Only query.

"No," she replied after a moment. "But…it's not what I want anymore."

Garfonis nodded. There was hurt in his eyes, but she could also see he was trying to accept it, too.

She blinked warmly at him, appreciative. "I'm sorry. I know this isn't easy for you."

"You're your own lynx now," he said. "I can see that. But that won't stop me from worrying about you."

"I know," she said with a soft purr. She jerked her head in the direction of the clearing. "Why don't we catch up with the others?" she asked and he nodded, his eyes glowing with affection.

By the time they reached the other knights, they were already descending into the Cavern through the Knight's Cave. Hasefi and Garfonis followed and, to Hasefi's delight, joined Nakilon's group in the Knight's Memories. Nakilon shuffled over with a friendly smile. Despite his mentor's warning earlier, he distracted Hasefi while the older lynxes spoke, but she welcomed it, grateful to have someone help her pass the time.

When the lesson was over, they went outside together. Nakilon was offering his own, much more interesting version of his mentor's teachings when one of Hasefi's tribemates spoke up.

Hasefi, over there! It was Refarmi who spoke, her knight. *You see the guardian heading towards the Guardian's Cave?*

The one with the little leaf on her chest?

Yes! That's my sister, Denomi!

Almost forgetting she wasn't alone, Hasefi stopped herself before she ran towards the guardian so she could turn to Nakilon. "I have to do something." She didn't wait for a response and bounded over to the guardian that was hurrying up the path into the Guardian's Cave.

"Denomi!" she called before the guardian could duck out of sight. Denomi's head shot up and she looked around in alarm. When her gaze landed on Hasefi, her eyes widened and she bounded down, sinking into a bow.

"High Heir!" she greeted cheerily. "What may I do for you?"

"I, uh...would it be alright if I talked to you about Refarmi?" she asked hesitantly.

The guardian's eyes widened again. "Aye! Oh, but hold on! I need to get my sisters." Denomi closed her eyes.

Hasefi shifted, waiting, but the guardian didn't appear to do anything. Refarmi's amusement tickled her mind.

Denomi opened her eyes. "Alright, they're coming."

"Um...alright," Hasefi murmured.

"Oh, excuse me! That must have seemed quite strange," Denomi chuckled. "My sisters and I use our gifts to communicate," she explained. Denomi rifled through a pouch before pawing over a small silver stone. "Whenever one of us has need of the other, we send out our thought and this begins to vibrate and shine."

Hasefi studied the rock, but it just looked like a normal rock to her.

"It won't do so now," the gifted explained, making Hasefi wonder if Denomi had read her mind.

"Denomi!"

Hasefi looked up and saw another lynx clad in the dark purple of a guardian while another with the white of a healer followed close behind.

You have three sisters? Hasefi thought.

Aye, Refarmi responded.

And they are all gifted?

Aye, Refarmi repeated, this time with a chuckle. The knight's affection for them flowed from her, sending a warmth through Hasefi, and she returned her attention to the three lynxes standing before her.

"High Heir," the second guardian greeted, sinking into a bow.

"To what do we owe this pleasure?" the healer asked, copying the second guardian.

"What are your names?" Hasefi asked them.

"I am Mifami," the second guardian offered.

"And I, Lusemi," the healer spoke.

"It's nice to meet you," Hasefi told them. She hesitated, shuffling her paws.

"Is something wrong?" Lusemi asked.

"No. Or, well, I wanted to talk about Refarmi."

The three lynxes' expressions turned somber and they were silent, waiting.

"I just wanted to say how sorry I am and how brave she was against the—the dangers we faced." She watched as the sisters looked to each other, their gazes softening with grief. "I'm sorry, I don't mean to make you sad—"

"Refarmi was the bravest," Denomi murmured.

"And the strongest," Mifami added.

"She was more gifted than any of us," Lusemi sighed. The three looked to Hasefi and they blinked at her with gratitude.

"Refarmi had a hard time here," Denomi continued.

Hasefi cocked her head in surprise. "Why's that?"

"Well—"

"Sometimes," Mifami interrupted her sister with a meaningful look. "Lynxes have it a bit harder." She turned her yellow gaze on Hasefi. "Refarmi had a difficult time finding purpose. But, you gave her one."

"When your prophecy was announced, she was so sure of what she had to do," Lusemi agreed, but her expression faded into sadness. "It's a shame it was all for nothing...."

"Not for nothing, sister," Mifami said. "The former Highchief is with us now. Refarmi is with her."

Hasefi went rigid with alarm.

"In spirit," the guardian explained. "Like the rest of our ancestors."

Hasefi merely nodded, trying not to show her relief.

"The High Heir's purpose may yet play out," Denomi added with a distant gleam in her eye.

"If there's anything you need, High Heir, let us know," Lusemi told Hasefi.

"Thank you," she said to them.

The three bowed and went their separate ways.

They're right, Refarmi murmured quietly in Hasefi's head.

About what?

About you. You've given me purpose, Hasefi.

Hasefi's fur turned hot and she ducked her head in embarrassment. *But you're....*

Even in death I serve. If I had to choose life without you as my Highchief or this, I would take the latter without even the twitch of a whisker.

The rest of her tribe responded with their own agreement, filling Hasefi's heart with emotion.

"Hasefi?"

Hasefi lifted her head to see Nakilon approaching, a worried expression on his face.

"Are you alright? You look sad. Did those gifteds say something?"

"No," she told him, straightening and swallowing the lump in her throat. "I'm alright."

Nakilon held her gaze for a moment before nodding. "Did you want to see if we could find a hare to share?"

Hasefi opened her mouth to respond, but movement caught her eye. She recognized Arsolin as he appeared from the shadows, approaching her.

"High Heir," he greeted, then offered Nakilon a nod. "The Highchief would like me to continue your basic training."

Hasefi turned and gave Nakilon an apologetic look. "I promise we'll share that hare."

He shrugged, nudging her shoulder. "I'll see you tomorrow," he told her brightly. She gave him a friendly blink as he trotted away to the prey-pile.

"Alright," she said to Arsolin, trying to keep her disappointment in check since he wasn't to blame. "What now?"

"We've toured the borders and you've had a glimpse of each of the Paths, so we'll dive into the Tribe's history." He paused before continuing. "Your knight training is physically demanding, I expect, so I hope this allows for some rest."

"Is that why we spent so long in the forest yesterday?" she asked, whiskers twitching with amusement as she blinked warmly at her keeper.

"Aye," he admitted. "But I can see you are accustomed to hard work," he added, his tone indicating admiration.

"I prefer the physical stuff," she confessed. "The other stuff is a bit boring to me."

"We are the same in that," Arsolin told her with amusement. "I prefer the feel of working muscles and the taste of fresh air than the stuffiness of the Cavern."

"Really?" Hasefi asked, surprised both by his words and his openness.

The keeper nodded.

She was about to suggest doing something more exciting for training since it was more to keep her busy than to actually train her, but she remembered that Arsolin wasn't aware of her intention to leave.

"I suppose we better get the boring stuff out of the way then, huh?" she said, hoping her tone didn't reveal anything.

"Aye."

They went through the Keeper's Cave and into the Cavern of History. It was empty, save for a few lingering lynxes. Arsolin led her to sit in the middle of the ledge they stood on so they could gaze at the entirety of the decorated wall.

"Do you remember Erina?" the keeper asked her.

"The first lynx," Hasefi replied.

"Correct. As you can see, more lynxes like her arrived, coming together until they formed the Tribe of the Lynx."

Hasefi followed his gaze to the images of more golden lynxes appearing until a small group had been formed. As a whole, the wall was overwhelming to look at, but when she peered closer and studied each set images, they told many stories.

Her attention was caught by a sudden change in the images as they progressed towards the bottom. They were more plentiful and detailed below the invisible line that seemed to separate them as if recalling the stuff prior was more difficult.

"Is that when the gifteds came?" Hasefi asked, pointing to where the images changed.

"No, gifteds came seasons before," Arsolin said, indicating a lynx higher up with a star on his chest. "Safiris was the first lynx to be blessed by the ancestors." The keeper returned his attention to where Hasefi had pointed out. "This is where the Lost History is."

"The Lost History?" she echoed, her interest piquing.

"There is a gap in our knowledge of our past," he explained. "We don't know what caused it—some speculate there was a massive war that wiped out gifted lynxes for a time, or some other disaster, until the Wanderers gave us more. Which, in turn, would cause part of our history to be lost when the memories of those during that time faded without a gifted's ability to preserve them."

Hasefi stared at the wall with wide eyes, wondering what could possibly cause such a loss of time.

"Everything above this point was recorded by the guardians prior to the event. No lynx has any tangible memories between those moments."

"Starlight," Hasefi breathed. "I wonder what could have happened." Her thoughts brought her to the ancestors and she wondered if they had played some part in the missing memories like they had with her life.

Did they wipe them out like they tried to wipe me out?

It's difficult to say, Kilarsa responded. *Guardians have been trying to understand the Lost History for much longer than you or I have even existed.*

Hasefi shuddered. *The ancestors have a lot of power,* she thought. *What if they try something else to stop me?*

We will protect you, wee lass, Sefonis assured her, his tone confident.

When Hasefi looked to Arsolin again, he had continued speaking. She listened as he described some of the first events of the Tribe and how the first roles of knights and hunters came into play.

They finished earlier than yesterday and, judging by the golden cavelight, there was still some sunlight. Though exhaustion was beginning to numb her body, Hasefi wanted to do one thing before she retired for the day.

"Arsolin?" she asked her keeper.

"What is it?"

"Would you be able to show me where Talonis is? Esafi said he's in a different place than Mekonis."

Without a word, the keeper led her into the cave with two stone lynxes armored in the white garb of the Sage and a healer.

Like the other Memories, the cave walls running lengthwise had soulstones for the Sages and the healers. But there was a path at the end beneath the images representing the role of a healer that spiraled into the ground.

Arsolin took her down it and they stepped into a circular chamber with images of kits surrounding them.

A pang tightened Hasefi's chest at how many there were. Dozens upon dozens of kits stared back at her and, though their images gave no hint of whatever horror would end their lives so quickly, all she could think about was the image she'd created of her brothers' last moments.

"So many," she whispered.

"The Tribe has lived long," Arsolin reminded her. "These are the kits of generations upon generations." He lifted his paws and took off his helmet before looking to the latest addition.

He was big, even for a twelve-moon old kit. His fur was the same pale brown as her father's and Sefonis's, while his eyes were a green that made Hasefi think of the first time she'd seen her own reflection.

She put a paw in the spot where a soulstone should be.

"You were here this whole time," she whispered to the image. "And I had no idea."

"I am deeply sorry," Arsolin said, his eyes wide. "After your tribe, to learn this, it is too much for any lynx to deal with."

"But we do anyway, right?" she asked, studying his gray and white face.

"Aye, so we do." He hesitated, his green gaze studying her. "I am glad I got to meet you," he said.

Hasefi didn't respond, wary of the implication of his words.

Could Esafi or Sifara have told him I wasn't staying forever? she wondered.

Perhaps, Gelinaf responded to her thoughts. *But he is a keeper, trained in reading others, and may be making a guess. It is safest not to mention anything.*

Hasefi nodded agreement before meeting Arsolin's gaze again.

"I'm glad I got to meet you, too," she told him.

There was a light in his eyes that warmed Hasefi, like the warm sunlight after a long, cold night.

"There is still daylight left," the keeper said, swinging his head around to take in the dimming cavelight. "Perhaps some of the younger novices are still out."

"Thanks, Arsolin," she purred. With an affectionate touch of her nose to his cheek, she bounded up the spiral path and hurried out of the Cavern.

In the clearing, she scanned the open space, looking for a lynx she might recognize. Some of the older ones were about; Lisefi, the Huntmaster, was sitting with one of her hunters. Sifara was on her own, eating a hare. Her helmet was still on, but Hasefi caught a flash of white fur beneath it every time she lowered her head to take a bite. The Overlord looked up when she noticed Hasefi, then looked behind her to where Arsolin was emerging from the cliff-face.

She keeps a close eye on him, she thought as they both watched Arsolin pad past Hasefi towards the prey-pile. *Hopefully I haven't managed to get him into any more trouble.*

She continued to scan the clearing, moving her gaze to the spot Nakilon had showed her by the Warmrock. The large stone patch would be losing its warmth now as the sun hid behind the trees; few lynxes were there. However, she glimpsed a familiar pelt and straightened with delight when she met Nakilon's half-closed gaze.

The novice knight's eyes opened fully and he got to his paws and trotted over. Before he reached her, his jaw tightened with a stifled yawn.

"I thought you might be asleep," she said to him, narrowing her eyes playfully.

"I sort of was," he admitted. "Knight training always kicks me in the tail." He blinked. "Have you eaten?"

"Not yet," she admitted. "Have you?"

"I have," he told her with an apologetic glance. "And, unfortunately, I think all the good prey was taken."

"Food is food," Hasefi told him. "I'm just happy to have a full belly."

"Come on, then."

Nakilon helped her pick out a grouse, then led her to a spot where she could eat and he could stretch out in the cooling air.

"So," Hasefi began after swallowing a mouthful. "What would you like to ask?"

"Hm?" Nakilon responded, though the confusion on his face was flimsy.

"Come on, you've been insisting on hearing about how it was beyond the River. What would you like to hear?"

There was a sheepish gleam in his eyes as he shuffled towards her. "I wanted to give you a chance to eat, at least," he mumbled.

Hasefi waved a dismissive paw, saying nothing so he could ask what he wanted.

"Well," he began slowly. "One of the things you mentioned, the high mountains—you said that's where the snow is?"

"Yes."

"So what would you call here?"

"The green mountains."

Nakilon nodded.

"There's also different forests," she continued. "The one where I spent most of my time was Edgewood. You know the trees with all the needles and rough bark? That's pretty much all Edgewood is."

"Why 'Edgewood'?" he asked.

"Because it's the forest closest to the edge of the world."

Nakilon's gaze widened. "You've seen it? The edge?"

Hasefi nodded. "Ocean; water as far as you can see. The sun makes it sparkle and, I bet if you stayed long enough, you could watch the sun wake up."

"Wow," he breathed. "That sounds both incredible and terrifying at the same time."

"It was," Hasefi agreed, though, at the time she'd seen it, all she'd felt was despair. "There's another forest," she continued, jerking her head in the opposite direction of where she'd come with Kolahn. "Darkwood."

"Darkwood?" he echoed. "That doesn't sound pleasant."

"It lies lower in the ground and the trees there are dark. I never went into it," she admitted before he could ask what might be there. She realized, however, that the novice looked a little distracted as she spoke. "Was there something else you were curious about?"

He shrugged, licking his chest with sudden embarrassment. "Well." He cleared his throat. "To be honest, I just like being able to chat with you. Even if it's not about your time beyond the River."

Hasefi narrowed her eyes at him. "Did you think I'd only talk to you because you wanted to hear my story?"

He shrugged, a nervous grin making his whiskers quiver.

"Silly furball," she chuckled, nudging him in the shoulder. "We can talk about whatever you'd like and I'm happy, too."

"You are?" he asked, eyes sparkling.

A purr rumbled in Hasefi's throat. "I know how the Highchief is, but I'm not like that. I'm quite happy to talk and make friends and spend the day lying in the sunlight." A little voice sounded an alarm in her mind and Hasefi stopped herself before she could continue.

"I'm glad," Nakilon replied. "It seems like you're starting to settle in."

The novice's words were disconcerting to her, but she assured herself it was good, since she'd need lynxes to trust her in case she had to escape before Esafi decided to announce war.

"Yeah," she replied, doing her best to match his light tone. "It does."

Chapter Nine

"What happened here?"

Red filled Hasefi's vision. Her fur was spiked and damp. Her claws were clogged. A strong tang coated her tongue.

"Please tell me this wasn't you."

"Kolahn?" She could barely speak. The smell of death choked her. "Kolahn, is that you?"

"What have you done?"

She blinked and she could see, but everything was still red. All around her lynxes lay unmoving. Some were scattered in pieces, just like her tribe. Others lay in pools of blood.

"No," she whispered, horror tightening her throat. "No, I didn't do this." She whipped around, hoping to explain to her friend, but he was nowhere to be seen. "Kolahn, where are you?"

"What you did...what you've done here...."

"No, please!" She turned, trying to figure out where his voice was coming from. "I swear this wasn't me!"

"This is evil."

Hasefi jerked her head around, but the gaze she caught wasn't her wolven friend's. It was Arsolin's. His green eyes were blank. His helmet lay a pace away, black coated in scarlet.

A glint from above caught her eye and she saw the Highchief half dangling over the edge of the Highledge. One of her legs was on the ground below and her face was unrecognizable.

"No!" Hasefi gasped. "Please, stop this!"

She turned again and was met with two young lynxes that were scattered about like leaves. She knew instinctively these were her brothers.

"I can stop this," Hasefi said, though it sounded more like a whimpering plea. "I have to stop this."

She ran blindly, not too sure where to go. She passed more bodies; Hesilar and Salifen. Lisefi. Sifara. Nakilon. She tried to blind herself to them, but their empty eyes, the unnatural angles of the limbs still attached to their bodies filled her mind, threatening to send her into madness.

Her fur prickled with a gaze directed at her. She looked and saw the mysterious Guardian Elder standing at the mouth of the Guardian's Cave. Unlike the others, he was alive and untouched. He stared at her and she felt very small.

Sefonis! *Hasefi screamed inwardly.* Where are you? What's happening?

He was silent, as was the rest of her tribe.

Sefonis, please! I need you!

Hasefi turned again, wanting to run away from the Elder's piercing gaze, but she came face-to-face with the helmet of a Knight Emperor. For a fleeting, hopeful moment, she thought her uncle had heeded her call after all. But when the helmet flipped open, it was her father's gaze she met.

"Garfonis?" she breathed.

He didn't respond. His face was twisted with betrayal and he looked at her with disgust.

"No, I didn't do this," she told him. "You have to believe me, I never meant for this to happen!"

His mouth opened, but he choked on whatever he might have said. Blood flowed freely and his legs gave out. More red spread around her father's convulsing form.

"No!" she cried, slumping beside him. "Please, stop!"

"Hasefi."

"Leave me alone!" She clamped her paws over her ears, willing everything away.

"Hasefi."

Something prodded her flanks and she cried out, writhing away.

"Fallen stars, Hasefi, wake up!"

With a gasp, Hasefi shot to her paws. Esafi's worried face filled her vision and she stumbled back. Breaths heaved in her chest and her fur was spiked in terror. Her bedding was strewn about, torn to shreds.

"A dream?" she gasped.

"Hasefi, what happened?" Esafi pressed, looking nothing like the regal Highchief she was. For a moment, Hasefi saw her as her mother, but the next, she saw the mangled face and bloodied armor of her nightmare.

"No." Hasefi closed her eyes and shook her head. "No, I can't." She fled the chamber, ignoring the Highchief's protests.

Voices filled her head, but her thoughts were too scattered to make any sense of them. She ran, just like she had in the dream, flying down from the Highledge and passing by startled lynxes who narrowly avoided getting shoved aside.

At the entrance of the clearing, a keeper tried to stop her, but she shouldered them aside with a strength that sent the keeper sprawling. Then she was out in the forest, running until the trees were a blur and her paws barely touched the ground.

It felt like an eternity before she came to a stop, but it might have been mere heartbeats. She found a hollowed out tree and tucked herself inside, finding a little comfort in the confined space.

She wrapped her paws around her head, willing the horrific images to leave. It was as if she was back in the high mountains after her tribe had been killed and long before Kolahn had found her.

But this wasn't real. They're alive. I didn't hurt anyone.

You didn't. Her uncle's voice made it through the cacophony in her head. *And you won't.*

But the Pack will, she thought with growing terror. *They'll do it to the Clan. And then they'll come here. These lynxes won't stand a chance. And they can't fight the Clan. They didn't do anything.* Hasefi shook her head, overwhelmed. *I can't do this.*

Yes you can.

A gentle touch on her head made her look up. Sefonis's ethereal form sat before her, raising his head, and she shifted.

"You are strong, Hasefi," he told her. "You've been through a lot, which is why you will get through this. You always do."

"But last time...last time I tried to help, I decimated the Pack's camp."

"Which is exactly why you'll be able to stop that from happening to anyone else," he told her firmly. "And you're not alone."

More of her tribe appeared. Kilarsa, Dahsefer. Gelinaf, Tenarli. And the lynxes that followed in their pawsteps.

"We won't let something like this happen again," Kilarsa assured her.

"We promise," Gelinaf added.

"You trust us, right dear lass?" Dahsefer said, his gaze warm.

"I do," Hasefi said, calming down. "I trust you."

"Hasefi? Hasefi, where are you!"

Her tribe vanished just as Esafi broke through the brush onto the path leading to Hasefi's tree. Sifara was with her, a looming shadow in the darkness. The Highchief's scared expression relaxed when her gaze landed on Hasefi.

"Hasefi, thank the stars." She rushed over, her gaze scrutinizing every inch of Hasefi's pelt. "You ran like the wind in a storm. Are you hurt?"

"I'm fine," Hasefi mumbled. Now that her own panic was subsiding, she was feeling a torrent of other emotions and it took everything she had not to break down in front of Esafi. She felt like the kit the Highchief called her, unable to shoulder the things weighing her down.

"Esafi, is that you? Hasefi!" Garfonis appeared, followed by a gray-furred lynx Hasefi recognized as Arsolin. Only Sifara wore armor.

Her father came close while Arsolin hung back with Sifara.

"Hasefi are you alright?"

Hasefi went over to her father and buried her face in his shoulder. He leaned back, wrapping his paws around her.

"I want Kolahn," she mumbled into his fur.

"I know, wee lass."

Hasefi nearly let herself go in her father's embrace, but her uncle's words echoed in her head and she pushed down the helplessness she felt. With a steadying breath, she stepped back and turned on Esafi.

"The Pack," she said, aware Arsolin was within earshot. "They will destroy you just like the destroyed my tribe."

"Your tribe was a mere eleven," Esafi reminded her, half concerned mother, half relentless leader. "You underestimate these lynxes."

"No," Hasefi said. "You underestimate the Pack. Fighting the Clan won't help anyone."

"They're the reason this is happening," Esafi argued, assuming entirely her stubborn Highchief stance. "The Pack wouldn't exist if it weren't for them. Whatever blood is on their paws, is on the Clan's."

"No." Hasefi stepped forward, a decision forming in her head. "The only way we can fight the Pack is if we get the Clan's help."

A harsh sound of empty laughter left Esafi's mouth. Even Garfonis flinched at it.

"You know nothing, daughter. You were raised by a wolf. This war with the Clan is the only thing that will get your friend back. If you want him, I suggest you stop trying to thwart it."

A part of Hasefi wanted to argue, but, even after the nightmare, she hesitated. *Maybe she's right and this tribe is stronger than I think. Besides,* she added with a hint of self-loathing. *If I'm ever going to save Kolahn without hurting anyone myself, it'll be when the Tribe fights the Clan.*

These lynxes don't fight to kill, Sefonis told her. *When they do fight the Clan, it won't be like the kind of violence you've experienced.*

Maybe it won't be so bad, then, if this war happens. Maybe they won't need my help against the Pack. After all, they did fight Resahn. They probably have more experience than me. Despite her desire to believe her own words, the deep sense of foreboding that came with her nightmare continued to dig its claws into her.

She glanced at Arsolin who, despite wearing a mask of indifference, Hasefi knew was likely reeling at not only there still being black wolves out there, but Hasefi's own knowledge on the matter. But her thoughts were on what might happen to him, or Nakilon, or her father if—

No. I have to get Kolahn.

Without a word, Hasefi slipped between Esafi and Garfonis, then past Arsolin and Sifara. She ignored the gazes hot on her pelt, stalking back towards the clearing. The images of her nightmare were still in her head, but they were fading, making it easier to push them aside.

I'm not going to let Esafi hang this war over me like a piece of prey, she thought to her tribe. *I have to see Kolahn before then. If I failed him and he's...then I have no reason to stay here.*

Her tribe was silent. Unease emanated from them, but she didn't care. She hardened her heart against them, against her parents, against this tribe. All that mattered was Kolahn.

"Hasefi?"

"Hm?" Hasefi blinked, turning to look at Nakilon. They were in the Cavern of History together, listening as a pair of mentors described the actions of a heroic lynx who saved their tribe from a rampaging moose single-pawed. According to the mentors, a moose was sort of like a deer, only much bigger and, while they often kept to themselves, could prove to be very dangerous.

"Everything alright?" Nakilon asked. "You haven't said a word today."

Hasefi looked back to the images on the wall, but the mentors' voices were drowned out by her thoughts. She'd gotten little sleep after she returned to her hollow last night, especially after she learnt the keeper she'd barged past had suffered two broken ribs and star-vision, which was something a lynx got after hitting their head really hard. The keeper was fine, thanks to the healers, but it only made the images of her nightmare feel more real. And more like her fault.

Garfonis had insisted she take the day off, but the last thing she wanted was to sit and stew in the dark thoughts that had filled her head. So she insisted on continuing with training, even if she didn't see much point in it, while her father was off doing something else.

She hadn't seen Esafi since last night. A part of the Highchief had been revealed last night, the soft part that talked about her lost sons, but it had been directed at Hasefi. It was the part of her mother she had always dreamed of, but thought Esafi wouldn't be capable of.

But she won't listen, no matter what, she thought bitterly. *If she's wrong and I'm right, she could be dooming her tribe. And for no logical reason at all.*

"Hasefi?"

She snapped her head towards Nakilon, making him flinch.

"Sorry," she told him, trying to relax. "I had a difficult night." Exhaustion rolled over her and she hung her head.

"Nightmares?"

She jerked her head up and narrowed her eyes at him.

"I used to get them as a kit," he offered.

"Really?" she asked.

He shrugged. "I used to have this fear of losing my parents and my sisters, so I had nightmares about it all the time. But they went away after a while."

"Mine did, too," she admitted. "I had nightmares about what happened to my tribe."

Nakilon's expression softened and he shuffled a little closer so his fur touched her armor.

The touch was comforting, but it made her think of Kolahn. "They went away when I met—well, when I got older," she told the novice knight. "But they sort of came back, I guess."

"You're under a lot of stress," he observed.

She narrowed her eyes again, wondering how he could possibly know so much.

"You've been on your own, now you're here, with dozens upon dozens of lynxes. And as High Heir, no less. And with double-training on top of that."

And a friend's life hanging by a claw, she added silently.

"We're still young," he continued. "We need time to hang-out and play and just, well, I don't know." He shrugged.

"I think you're right," she sighed. "But Esafi is pretty intent on having me train."

"Well, she is your mother. Maybe you could ask her for a day off or something." He hesitated.

"What is it?"

"There's also the half-moon. But I don't know if that applies to you."

"The half-moon?"

"It's a day off for novices. Every half-moon, dark moon, and full moon."

Hasefi's mind jumped immediately onto this knowledge. *A day off? I could make a plan to see Kolahn for then.*

You've only got a couple days before that, Sefonis pointed out.

I'll figure something out. I have to. And if this day off isn't for me, I can take up Garfonis's offer and say I want to hangout with friends. She glanced sorrowfully at Nakilon, knowing he had likely mentioned the day in the hopes of sharing the meal she kept promising him. *Maybe I'll have time for that, too.*

If you are to get to the Clan unnoticed, you'll need a gifted, Kilarsa said.

Anyone in mind? she asked. There was no response. *Refarmi, what about your sisters?*

I don't think they'd do anything without the Elder's or Sage's permission, she admitted.

Gifteds are strict in their rules, Kilarsa agreed. *But younger lynxes tend to deviate from them before they understand their nature.*

Are you talking about Salifen? Hasefi asked.

Kilarsa responded with an affirming hum.

But you saw how nervous he was. There's no way he'd help with something like this.

Perhaps you could get to know him better, Kilarsa suggested. *It couldn't hurt.*

Hasefi looked to Nakilon again, wondering if he'd be able to help her. He seemed willing enough, but there was no saying what he'd do if she told him the truth about Kolahn.

I can't risk it, she said to herself. *He's a good cover for now,* she added, wincing. *Okay,* she continued to Kilarsa. *I'll try seeing what Salifen might be capable of.*

"Nakilon?" she asked and the novice looked eagerly to her. "Did you want to share that hare on the half-moon?"

"Yes!" He ducked his head as the mentors aimed their glares at him.

"Nakilon, pay attention and stop distracting the High Heir," one of them scolded.

"Yes, Katrima," Nakilon responded, dipping his head in apology. Then he snuck a glance at Hasefi, his eyes bright.

Hasefi felt her own delight, but it was dampened by the guilt she felt, knowing she would be using him to make sure no one had a reason to be suspicious about her whereabouts, if she needed it.

But I can't let that stop me. This is for Kolahn.

After their lesson, Hasefi said goodbye to Nakilon and left the Cavern on her own. She hadn't seen Arsolin all day and he continued to remain absent when she emerged into the clearing. Knowing novices would be starting their meals, she looked to the fallen tree where a lot of them tended to stay, searching the pelts and various armor pieces.

A flash of white caught her eye and she marched over. Salifen was sitting with two other lynxes, all of them tucking into a deer.

"High Heir!" Salifen greeted the moment she was upon them. He got up to bow, followed by the smallest of them, and then the third lynx who had a hunter's bracer.

"Please, you don't have to bow," she said quickly. The smallest of the three hesitated, while the novice hunter easily returned to a comfortable position. "And call me Hasefi."

"Of course," Salifen responded, passing a look over his silent companions.

"May I join?" Hasefi asked them.

"Do we have a choice?" the novice hunter murmured under her breath, but Hasefi still caught the words. She made no reaction to them, however.

"Of course," Salifen replied again. "This is my sister, Alarni," he introduced the novice hunter. "And this is Ivanus. He's almost old enough for the initiation moon."

"Hello," the kit greeted nervously.

"Hi," Hasefi returned, blinking warmly at him. "I'm Hasefi. Which I already said," she added awkwardly.

"Duh," Alarni growled.

Hasefi passed the novice a questioning look, but the novice was distracted by the mouthful of deer she was tearing off.

There was an awkward silence. Hasefi wasn't sure exactly what it was she was looking for from Salifen but being with other lynxes made it a bit more difficult.

Or maybe not. He might be more comfortable here, she thought as she watched the novice healer who had shown more delight than nervousness.

"How was training?" Hasefi asked as she settled down with the other lynxes.

"It was great!" Salifen replied when the others said nothing. "Well, for me, anyways. I practiced using magic again and learned some neat stuff. How was your day?"

“Tiring,” Hasefi admitted. “But I’ve been teaching some of the other novices some moves I learnt from hunting that could be used in battle.”

“Of course you did,” Alarni sighed.

Hasefi frowned at her.

“Don’t mind Alarni,” Salifen said quickly, giving his sister an uncertain glance. “That sounds really neat,” he added.

“You were teaching the novices?” Ivanus asked.

Hasefi nodded.

“What would you know that they don’t?” Alarni asked.

“I know how to survive on my own, for one thing.”

“Any lynx could fend for themselves,” she argued.

Hasefi fought the urge to flatten her ears. She didn’t feel like her experience was something to boast about, but the novice’s dismissal of her experience angered her. “What about at three moons old? In the high mountains?”

“High mountains?” Salifen asked.

“There.” Hasefi gestured towards the cliff-face and they all turned to look. “The snowy peaks.” Their three gazes returned to her, each with a different expression.

“Snow comes here, too,” Alarni pointed out.

“Have you ever been worried about eagles and hawks? Or mountain lions?” The hunter novice said nothing, but she still held Hasefi’s gaze. “Have you even seen any?”

“Mountain lions are myths,” Alarni scoffed. “And hunter-birds don’t usually come near the clearing.”

“My point exactly,” Hasefi said. “I’ve fought eagles, I’ve taken down prey bigger than myself. I’ve even attacked mountain lions.”

“Wow, look at you. The perfect lynx already.”

Hasefi narrowed her eyes, beginning to realize what Alarni’s attitude was coming from.

“That’s not my point,” Hasefi explained.

“Then what is it?”

“My point is...” Hasefi hesitated, looking at the lynxes before her. Ivanus seemed fascinated by her words while Salifen seemed to be conflicted between excitement and nervousness. Alarni peered at her through narrowed eyes, reminding Hasefi of the Highchief's comment about her constant glaring.

I don't have a lot of time to come up with a plan for Kolahn, she thought. *Let alone recruiting help. Esafi never said I had to be quiet about how I felt.*

Hoping she was right about this narrow-eyed novice, Hasefi decided to show they were on the same side and told the truth. "My point is I don't want to be High Heir," she said quietly. Surprise flickered across Alarni's expression. "I'd rather just be like any other lynx."

Her ears flattened. "Why would you want that? We don't know anything about anything and just do as we're told like good little kits," Alarni hissed, but Hasefi could see the hostility in her expression had lessened.

"Would you rather rebellion?" Salifen asked.

"I'm okay with the way things are," Ivanus added.

"Well, I'm not," Alarni said, then turned to Hasefi. "And I'm sure there's a reason you're here."

"Yeah. I want to make friends."

"I doubt that," the novice scoffed.

"Why?" Hasefi asked, but Alarni just responded with a wordless growl.

"Maybe I shouldn't have invited you to eat with us," Salifen said, giving Hasefi an apologetic look.

Hasefi ignored him, focused on Alarni, knowing that the lynx's distaste for her was probably little different than her own feelings towards how things were done in this tribe.

"You're right," Hasefi told her. "I know things you don't. And, if I had it my way, I would be telling you and every other lynx right now what I know. But I can't, because if I do, I might get you in trouble."

Alarni's expression didn't change, but she was silent.

"But you know what? There are some things I can tell you. So ask me anything and I'll tell you what I can."

The three lynxes were silent, giving her uncertain and doubtful looks. Finally, Alarni spoke.

"Why did you come back?" she asked.

"I didn't mean to. I didn't even know there were other lynxes here—or other lynxes at all, for that matter. But my...friend was taken prisoner by the Clan and I sought to help him. But then I saw my father and...here I am."

"The wolves took a lynx?" Ivanus gasped.

"And you decided he didn't need your help?" Alarni added.

"A single lynx doesn't have much chance against a group of wolves," Hasefi pointed out carefully.

"Point. But...then what? What are you going to do?"

Hasefi hesitated, wondering if she'd made an error opening up so quickly.

"Are you not allowed to answer?" Salifen asked.

"Actually, this is something I won't answer."

"You're going to go after him," Alarni said and Hasefi's ears twitched. "Do you have a plan?"

"I don't know what you're saying," Hasefi tried.

"Don't even try that. You don't want to be Highchief because you don't want to be here at all. But Esafi won't let you leave because she knows you'll go to the Clan, which is the last thing she wants when we're about to march into war with them."

Hasefi stared at the novice hunter, baffled by the accuracy of her words.

"Alarni thinks there's going to be a war," Ivanus explained. "Ever since..." he trailed off and looked apologetically to his paws.

"My brothers were killed," she finished for him.

"Every lynx knows it," Alarni scoffed. "You think Esafi would just let the Clan kill her own kits and get away with it?"

"But there hasn't been war since Resahn's Reign," Salifen pointed out with a fearful twitch of his ears.

Alarni said nothing, turning her scrutinizing stare on Hasefi.

"I've heard the others talk about it," Hasefi admitted carefully. "Like you have, I'm sure. But that's not something I'm allowed to talk about."

"Okay. So, what about your plan?"

"My plan?"

Alarni rolled her eyes. "To save your friend? And who is he, by the way? One of your tribemates?"

"No," Hasefi said slowly.

"Who?"

"I...met him after my tribe died."

"An outsider?" the novice hunter echoed with disbelief. "There are lynxes outside the Tribe?"

"What would the Clan need him for?" Ivanus added.

"Maybe...we shouldn't be asking so many questions," Salifen warned with a nervous chuckle, but the others didn't seem to hear him.

"He was an outcast," Hasefi continued, hoping to offer enough information before she'd have to admit the entire truth.

"What did he do?" Alarni demanded.

"Nothing," Hasefi said immediately before forcing herself to take control of her emotions. "I guess the Clan just didn't agree with him."

"Well, the Clan doesn't agree with any lynx," Alarni murmured. Hasefi pushed down the urge to respond. "So are you still going after him?"

Hasefi didn't reply.

"Are you worried we'll talk?" Alarni asked. "Trust me, any secret the highbloods and champions don't have I'll be happy to keep. And you two won't talk, right?" She turned her gaze on the other two who were giving each other nervous looks. "Don't worry," Alarni continued to Hasefi. "Salifen is too afraid of everything to say anything and Ivanus is loyal to the end."

Hasefi still looked at the lynxes with doubt.

Extra allies would be smart, Sefonis told her. *But there is the danger of building a rebellion.*

I don't want to rebel against Esafi or anything, she assured her uncle. *I just want to save Kolahn and maybe stop her from fighting the wrong enemy.* She frowned thoughtfully. *If I tell them and they tell Esafi, I guess it's nothing she doesn't already know, right? I haven't technically done anything she told me not to do. And surely she knows I wouldn't give up so easily.*

You could risk worse consequences, Gelinaf pointed out.

If she tries to keep me prisoner like Kolahn, we'll show her she's messed with the wrong lynx.

Esafi doesn't keep prisoners, Sefonis told her.

So what, then? She won't cast me out. All she has left is to.... Hasefi stopped, her eyes widening.

"What?" Alarni asked, watching her closely.

"What happens to prisoners?" she asked.

"Um, random, but we don't have prisoners. If a lynx has done something bad, they're punished. Or, if it's too bad, they're killed. But, that hasn't happened in seasons, apparently."

Hasefi resisted the urge to gulp air. *If I talk to them, they might be killed!*

I doubt the Highchief would kill kits, Sefonis told her. *But you would be putting them in danger.*

"Are you alright?" Salifen asked Hasefi.

"I think I need to go. Thanks for the meal." Hasefi hurried away before the others could say anything. She went towards the Highcave, but Arsolin appeared, fully clad in his keeper's armor.

"High Heir," he greeted. "I—"

"I'm not feeling well," Hasefi blurted. "I'm just going to get some sleep. See you tomorrow." She brushed past him and hurried into the Highcave. To her relief, Esafi wasn't there, but she still felt as if the Highchief was watching her. For the first time, she was beginning to feel truly helpless, even with her tribe's strength in consideration.

I should just leave, Hasefi thought. *I'm sure if I went far enough away, they wouldn't bother trying to find me. And there's no one they would blame.*

Your keeper, Arsolin, could be punished, Sefonis pointed out quietly.

Hasefi bit down a whimper. *He wouldn't be killed, would he? What happened to him after Mekonis and Talonis went missing? Why would Esafi even assign him to me? Wouldn't she want to make sure I had a keeper that would keep an eye on me at all times?* She didn't think Arsolin was any less of a keeper for what happened, but she knew the Highchief wouldn't think like that.

It is that very mistake that will make him watch you like a hunter-bird, Gelinaf pointed out, sending a flood of realization through Hasefi.

Then it's going to be even harder to sneak out, she said with a helpless sigh.

Her tribe was silent.

Did Esafi ever kill any lynx when you were here?

Still, her tribe was silent.

Sefonis?

No. But her mother did. And Esafi is much like her.

Hasefi looked fearfully to the entrance of her sleeping cavern. *I won't put anyone in danger,* she said. *I have to do this alone.*

You won't be alone, Sefonis reminded her. *But we can't give you the kind of help you really need.*

A gifted.

More specifically, physical lynxes you can trust and that are willing to help, Kilarsa spoke up, backing Sefonis.

Are you saying I should *risk Salifen and his friends?*

We're saying it's not just up to you whether they should help or not, she pointed out.

Hasefi relaxed a little, knowing the gifted lynx was right.

Okay. But...I want to get to know them a bit better, first. Alarni might be intent to help, but it's Salifen I need.

That is wise, Kilarsa agreed. *But you only have tomorrow before the half moon.*

I know. So I should probably get some rest while I can.

Hasefi put her helmet in its designated spot and tried to fall into sleep and, though she was heavy with exhaustion, her mind wouldn't quiet. Fear of another nightmare didn't help. She shifted around in frustration until her eyes snapped open and she saw light filled paws at the edge of her nest.

"I can't sleep," she sighed, lifting her gaze to meet Sefonis's.

He touched his nose to her head. "Your last few days have been filled with a lot," he murmured. Sefonis pawed off his helmet, making his starlit armor fade. She shifted so he could curl up beside her in the hollow and she began to purr, grateful to feel his warm fur against hers, even if it wasn't quite the same. Feeling like a kit moons ago, she tucked her nose into his flank, closing her eyes.

"I want so badly for you to be here," she mumbled into his fur. "I wish we had found a home and that it was just us and that, somehow, we brought Kolahn into the tribe and we lived happily for seasons and seasons."

Sefonis rumbled with amusement and he gave the top of her head an affectionate lick.

Hasefi lifted her head and met his gaze. "How long do you think it will take for Esafi to choose a time to go after the Clan?" she asked.

"I cannot say," Sefonis admitted, blinking apologetically at her. "But I know it is difficult to wait. Trust me, I do." His eyes glazed over for a moment, before he looked to her again. "Kilarsa is right. It is wise to wait until opportunity arises. If a strike is to be effective, it must be well-timed and well-aimed."

Hasefi sighed. "I'm just worried that every heartbeat that passes is the one that Eilwyn decides Kolahn needs to die. What?" she added when Sefonis's ears twitched.

"Wolves names descend differently than our own, but he shares his with Resahn."

"I asked Kolahn if Resahn was his father, but he said Resahn was before his time."

Sefonis nodded. "I believe he is kin of the Lady," he admitted. "Which may yet enforce her desire to keep him alive."

"But she was the one who ordered black wolves to be killed after being banished," Hasefi pointed out with surprise.

"Eilwyn is firm," Sefonis agreed. "But she loves her Clan."

Hasefi looked at her uncle in surprise. "How do you know that?"

"I was present during Resahn's Reign," he reminded her. "I watched her ascend to the role of Lady. And...as a knight I am to know the creatures around our territory well."

Hasefi nodded, curling up against him again. "What was it like?" she asked. "Resahn's Reign?" Her uncle was silent and she felt a twinge of guilt for asking.

"I would rather not discuss it," he admitted after a while and she made no move to press.

"What about when you were a novice?" she asked. "Why did you choose the knight's Path?"

"I wanted to protect the lynxes I cared about," he told her and she could hear his tone shift. "I felt that, by being the armor of the Tribe, I could help keep them safe. I always wanted to keep them safe."

Hasefi heard the sadness in his voice and she lifted her head. "You can't blame yourself for what happened," she told him firmly. "Besides —you brought them here, to me."

He blinked at her warmly. "You are right, wee lass."

Hasefi lowered her head again and she grew drowsy as Sefonis lapped the fur on her head.

"I remember Garfonis was so sure of his decision," Sefonis continued. "But I was so troubled. I was worried I'd choose the wrong Path. It wasn't impossible to change if it didn't fit, but it would delay training and I couldn't wait to be a full member of the Tribe." Sefonis continued to speak, his words fading as the rumble of his flank soothed Hasefi into a deep, pleasant sleep.

The following day, it was raining. Though she'd gone to sleep early, Hasefi felt she'd hardly slept a wink. She hoped that the weather would mean lynxes would stay in for the day, but her father came to retrieve her, not seeming to notice the rain.

At least I have armor to keep me somewhat dry, she thought as they left the Highcave.

Fortunately, when the knights and their novices were returning to the clearing after the morning, the clouds parted, allowing the sun to shine and warm the damp forest.

Nakilon joined her as usual, though Arsolin hadn't shown up with prey as he usually did. It was another keeper whom she was pretty sure was the same keeper that had accompanied her father from the Clan's ravine.

It was a shame since Arsolin had brought her extra prey, now that Nakilon made a habit of joining her, but this keeper only brought enough for one lynx, though that didn't stop Hasefi from sharing. Especially since her belly twisted with a growing anxiety as to what might have happened to Arsolin.

Surely he wouldn't be in trouble because I brushed him off yesterday? Or is it because he would have overheard everything after my nightmare yesterday?

"Hey!" Nakilon said cheerily when he reached Hasefi, taking her out of her mind.

"Hi," she returned, pleased at the casual greeting. "Sorry I haven't been able to eat with you after training," she added.

"It's alright. I imagine being High Heir keeps you pretty busy."

"You can say that again," Hasefi sighed.

"But at least we have a break now."

"Yeah," she agreed. They chewed their meal in silence for a few moments before Nalikon spoke again.

"Could I ask you something?"

"Of course."

"When you're talking to us in training…." The novice was hesitant, as if not sure which words to choose. "Is there…is there something you're not telling us?"

"I cover a lot of stuff," she deflected with a shrug. "I'm sure there's things I miss."

"I don't mean like that," he said, studying her with an expression she couldn't quite understand.

Hasefi frowned, hoping she wouldn't have to lie to keep Esafi's secrets.

"I just mean," he continued, shuffling his paws. "You just talk about what's necessary for training, right? I…feel like there's got to be more to it than hunting and fighting…." He was studying her closely. "Things that aren't so easy."

Hasefi looked away.

"I'm sorry," Nakilon said, withdrawing. "I don't mean to push. It's just…I see the way your face changes when you talk about it and…keeping it in can't be good."

Hasefi's thoughts immediately went to memories of numbing cold, hunger, and fear. But before she could act upon them, memories of seeing trees for the first time and butterflies and feeling the sun's warmth entered her mind.

"It was…hard," she admitted. "At first. But then I found somewhere that wasn't so bad."

Nakilon's expression was intent, but, though it was clear he wanted to ask more, he didn't.

Hasefi found herself disappointed, which surprised her. Her surprise increased when she spoke impulsively. "You can ask more if you'd like."

"Every time I do, I can see the pain on your face. I feel bad for making you remember unpleasant stuff."

Hasefi shrugged. "It's alright. You're right—it is good to talk about it."

Nalikon just shook his head and was silent.

"Do you know what a mountain lion looks like?" she asked, picking something that scared her, but wouldn't reveal too much.

"They're giant cats with fur the color of blood and eyes like starless skies." He shuddered as he spoke, but a goofy grin came on his face when Hasefi laughed.

"Not quite," she admitted. "They're big, but they're not that much bigger than wolves. Er, I guess they're a bit bigger. Their fur is more brown than red. And there's white, too, around their muzzles, and black. And their ears are kind of round."

Nakilon's eyes were wide with wonder as he listened and Hasefi couldn't help feel a bit surprised.

"Do you believe me?"

"Why wouldn't I?" he asked, caught off-guard by her question.

"A lot of the others look at me like I'm some sunblind kit with too many thoughts in her head."

"I know you're not some sunblind kit," Nakilon told her. "You're blunt, and honest, and—and really brave."

"Thanks," Hasefi said before smoothing her chest fur with her tongue in embarrassment and averting her gaze.

"What about their eyes?" he pressed. "Are their eyes black?"

"Two were," she admitted, remembering the fearsome monster that she had used as her own weapon against the Pack and the mountain lion that had attacked her and Kolahn. "But there was one that had bright green eyes." Her mind brought her back to when her tribe had been killed and a mountain lion had scared off the black wolves that had murdered them. She had been sure it looked at her, even as she fled. But she had seen another mountain lion later with a look so similar she wondered if it wasn't the same one.

"How many have you seen?"

"Three or four," she admitted.

Nakilon shook his head, his eyes wide with wonder and fear. "You are incredible."

"Come on, you two!" Garfonis called, saving Hasefi from having to find a reply. She bounded ahead with her companion until they were following the Emperor back to the clearing.

In the Cavern of History, time moved along at a fairly quick pace with the help of Nakilon's commentary to sustain Hasefi through it. At the end, she hoped Arsolin would be around so she could apologize for brushing him off yesterday, but it was her father who met her outside the Knight's Cave.

"I told you I'm fine," Hasefi sighed when she saw the worried expression on his face. "I've dealt with plenty of nightmares before. This is no different."

"I know," he assured her. "This isn't that. Esafi wanted to talk to you about skipping your training yesterday."

Hasefi winced. When she had decided to retire early, she had hoped it would be overlooked, especially after the night she'd had prior. Now, however, she knew that, while she didn't care what her own consequences were, Arsolin would suffer for her actions.

"It's not Arsolin's fault," she stated firmly. "I didn't give him a choice."

"Then it might be good to talk to the Highchief," he said. "For his sake."

Understanding flowed through Hasefi. She blinked warmly at her father. "Thank you," she told him. "I know you might not feel the same way about him, so I appreciate this."

"You're right," he said with a shrug. "It could have been any lynx on duty with them. Stars, it could have been me." Sadness filled his eyes. "Mekonis was always so clever. He wasn't quite twelve moons, but he could outsmart any lynx if he wanted. And Talonis followed him wherever he went." He sighed.

"I wish I could've known them," Hasefi said, sitting beside her father. "They sound wonderful."

"They are—uh, were. They—they were." He shook his head, his hollow gaze on the ground. "I thought we were done with black wolves. I thought no more innocent lives would be taken."

Hasefi moved so she could sit in front of him, her gaze holding his. "Maybe I'm wrong," she said slowly. "Maybe you can take on the Pack. But what if I'm right? Is it worth taking that risk?"

Garfonis was silent for a few heartbeats before replying. "You want us to ally with the Clan?" he asked. There was a note of disbelief he was trying to smother, but Hasefi caught it.

"I know it seems impossible. But you know what else seemed impossible? Befriending the very thing related to those who took everything

I had away. If I can be friends with Kolahn, certainly the Tribe and the Clan can work things out to destroy the Pack once and for all."

A sudden purr rose in her father's throat, making Hasefi's fur rise self-consciously.

"What?" she asked, ears half-flat.

"You speak like a Highchief," Garfonis murmured, studying her with affection.

Hasefi flinched. "I'm not a Highchief. I just don't want to see anyone else get hurt."

"Nor do I," Garfonis admitted. "But, even if we did fight the Pack, there would be severe casualties, making us vulnerable to the Clan. Not to mention that black wolves continue to be born to them. If another Pack rises, we could very well be stuck in a war lasting generations."

Hasefi hesitated, her father's words striking a pang of fear through her.

"If we fight the Clan," Garfonis continued. "We may be able to stop more black wolves from coming."

"What, by killing them as pups?" Hasefi snapped. "They're not evil because they have different fur. It's something inside them—Kolahn told me about it. It's something he fights every day so he can be a better creature."

"How long can he keep fighting it?" Garfonis pressed.

"Alone, he did well enough for seven moons. But surrounded by friends and family, I believe he could live a happy life." She stepped towards her father. "I promised Kolahn I would never let him turn and he promised the same for me." Hasefi recoiled at her words, but she couldn't take them back.

"For you?" her father asked with a concerned frown. "Why would he promise that for you?"

"It was kill or be killed," she replied quietly. "Sometimes there is no other choice but the worst." She turned away, deciding she was done with this conversation.

"This isn't easy for you," her father said before she could walk away. "It never has been. But, Hasefi, perhaps it will help if you choose one path instead of trying to walk them all."

Hasefi looked back at him.

"You want to save your friend. When we fight the Clan, you will have him. But you also want the Pack stopped. Unfortunately, I don't think you can have both right now. But that doesn't mean there won't be a day where you reunite with him and the Pack has become a memory."

"Do you really believe that?" she asked.

"I do."

Hasefi wasn't sure she was able to agree with him and, despite his words, she suspected there was something else going on in her father's mind that he was holding back. Every moment still felt as if it could be Kolahn's last—if he wasn't already dead. And the Pack could strike tomorrow, or in a season. If they attacked the Clan while Kolahn was there, he'd have no chance. She had to do something. Now.

"Can I ask you something?" Garfonis asked.

Hasefi looked to her father again and he came so he was in front of her. His gaze was serious.

"What is it?" Hasefi pressed.

"This wolf—Kolahn. Do you...do you love him?"

Hasefi blinked, caught off-guard by the question. It took her a moment to come up with an answer. "Not the way you're asking, I don't think. He's like a...a big brother. He's family." She tilted her head. "Can a lynx love a wolf?"

"It has happened before," he admitted. He looked as if he wanted to say more, but he got to his paws. "I've kept you long enough. We should see the Highchief."

Hasefi followed him up onto the Highledge and into the Highcave. In the mainchamber, Esafi was there with Sifara. Arsolin wasn't, but Hasefi didn't know if that was good or bad.

"I was beginning to think I'd have to send a messenger," Esafi said as they padded in. "You took your time," she added to Garfonis.

"My apologies," he said with a bow.

At first, Hasefi was put off by the seemingly cold display between her parents, but she caught a glint in Garfonis's eye that passed to Esafi, making her feel awkward for noticing it.

"Daughter," Esafi began, looking to Hasefi. "I was informed your keeper failed to deliver your training yesterday."

"If that's what you want to call me barging past him so I could get to my hollow early," she replied.

"I assume you are aware by now that Arsolin was the keeper in charge of your brothers."

"I can't imagine how he feels," Hasefi said evenly.

"I am more concerned about your well-being," Esafi told her.

"I'm fine. Or, as fine as I can be while I wait to see if Kolahn is still alive." Hasefi held her mother's narrowed gaze. "If you're trying to imply you want to give me a new keeper, Arsolin is great."

Esafi narrowed her eyes further, but, to Hasefi's surprise, it was the looming Overlord that spoke.

"Highchief, if I may?"

Esafi looked to the tall, black-clad lynx.

"I understand you may question my judgement after my recommendation of Arsolin as keeper of your sons. But I truly think, if the High Heir is confident, that Arsolin can perform this task flawlessly."

Hasefi tried not to wince, knowing she'd need a flawed keeper if she was to indeed find a way to the Clan so she could check on Kolahn.

"Hasefi speaks highly of this keeper," Garfonis added.

"Does she now?" Esafi said with a suspicious look at Hasefi.

"As long as the Pack is alive, I don't think any of us are safe," she replied steadily. "But it's my experience with them that has made me capable. My losses helped me realize what I had to be if I wanted to stay alive. Arsolin understands that. I trust him."

Esafi was silent for a few heartbeats before responding. "That's all very well, but there is still the matter of his knowledge of everything I had asked you to remain quiet about."

"Sorry," Hasefi replied dryly.

"Sifara, can I trust Arsolin to remain silent?"

"Yes, Highchief. I have already briefed him as you have us."

"Very well," Esafi said, getting to her paws. "Arsolin will remain a highkeeper. But he must place each paw carefully if he wants to continue."

Garfonis and Sifara got up on some unspoken signal and turned to leave. Hasefi got up to follow, but the Highchief lifted a paw to stop her.

Stifling a sigh, Hasefi sat down.

"You have had only mere days of training, but I would like to hear what you've learnt," Esafi said.

Hasefi closed her eyes so Esafi wouldn't see her roll them. But the Highchief saw right through her.

"Do you find our history so boring?"

"I just don't see the point in training if you're going to let me leave with Kolahn."

"If you must see some reason, then it is for appearances," Esafi sighed. "But I had hoped you would show some interest in your ancestry and the ways of your kind."

The Highchief's response was expected as Hasefi had known her training was to keep other lynxes' curiosity at bay, but Esafi's latter words sent a sliver of guilt through Hasefi's chest. She did her best to ignore it, remaining silent.

Esafi got up and padded closer. Hasefi lifted her head, bracing herself for a lecture. But the Highchief sat down before her, her expression inquisitive.

"You are a powerful lynx, daughter," she said. "The ancestors chose you to lead a destiny—"

"—across the river. Yeah, I know."

"They knew you would be special," she continued with little reaction to Hasefi's interruption.

Is that why they tried to kill me?

"I can see they were right."

Hasefi looked up at Esafi in surprise.

"If you were Highchief one day," her mother continued, "you would be unstoppable."

Hasefi narrowed her eyes. "Why do I feel like that's not really a compliment?"

"Because it's not. Resahn was unstoppable, too."

Hasefi shivered at the thought of being compared to such a creature, especially when she knew it might not be totally undeserved.

"Our guardians are the closest of us to the Wanderers," Esafi explained. "Sometimes, they will receive signs that can come in many forms. But sometimes, there are lynxes of prophecy that, while they bear no star on their chest, can also share this link with the Wanderers. And sometimes that link is more powerful."

"The Wanderers," Hasefi echoed. "I've heard that title a few times. That's what you call your ancestors, right?"

"*Our* ancestors," Esafi replied. "You speak as if to detach yourself from us. But, raised by a wolf or not, you will always be one of us."

Hasefi flattened her ears but her frustration was directed at herself. While she felt contempt at her mother's words, there was also an unwelcome hope.

I am not *one of them. Kolahn is my home. Not them.*

"What did you dream of, daughter?"

Hasefi blinked, confused by the sudden question. Then realization flooded through her, bringing with it a sense of unease.

"You think my dream might have been a sign?" she asked.

"It is possible," Esafi admitted. "Myafos would be a better judge than I."

The ancestors would never give me a sign, she thought. *But...what about a warning? If they truly wanted me dead, they could send me a warning.*

That nightmare runs along many of the fears you hold in your heart, Hasefi, Kilarsa spoke. *Though I cannot say for sure, it is very probable your nightmare was just that.*

"It was just a nightmare," Hasefi stated, trying not to think that her dream could actually come true.

"Even still, I am your mother," Esafi replied, her tone just short of sounding kind. "Perhaps sharing could help lighten this burden you carry."

Now Hasefi saw through her.

"No," she stated firmly, getting to her paws. "I need to find Arsolin and 'keep up appearances.'"

With that, Hasefi left.

Chapter Ten

Hasefi walked out onto the Highledge, surprised Esafi didn't come after her or call out a protest. She even waited to see if the Highchief would come out at all, but she was left alone outside the Highcave.

A wave of exhaustion rolled over her, making her paws heavy and her shoulders slump. She sat down near the edge of the Highledge to rest and looked down into the clearing.

Most of the novices were by the fallen log sharing their meals. She spotted Nakilon who looked up and lifted a paw in greeting. Hasefi returned the gesture with a small smile, then looked to where she could see Alarni and Ivanus. The novice hunter's gaze was already on her, but it was impossible to read at that distance. There was no sign of Salifen.

Movement nearby caught her eye and she saw Sifara moving towards the Highledge with Arsolin close behind. Hasefi waited, watching as the two ascended the path. Sifara glanced at her before slinking into the Highcave while Arsolin came over.

"I hope she didn't cuff your ears too badly," Hasefi said apologetically.

"Not at all," he assured her. "She told me you argued to have me remain as your keeper."

"Of course," Hasefi said, then glanced away in embarrassment. "Though, I feel like I should be the one suggesting you find a more cooperative charge."

To her utter surprise, Arsolin laughed. She had never heard something like that from him and she held onto it, knowing how rare it probably was, like a precious stone found amongst the common pebbles of a streambed.

"Keepers protect their charges from themselves as much as from other threats," Arsolin said when he recovered, mirth still thick in his voice. "It was very much so with Mekonis and Talonis. The two of them were quite the mischievous pair."

Hasefi chuckled, leaning towards the keeper in the hope he might continue. She wasn't sure if it was alright to ask about her brothers, since she knew how sensitive it was for him.

"You are much like them," he said, his helmet aimed directly at her. "Smart. Brave. Intimidated by nothing and no one. The kind of lynx others would follow without question."

Hasefi's delight faded and she looked away. She knew Arsolin was trying to compliment her, but his words brought a deep ache in her chest.

"I'm sorry," he said. "I didn't mean to upset you."

"It's not you," she assured him. "I just...." She met his gaze. "You heard me the night before. You know everything. I don't want to be here, Arsolin. I don't want to be High Heir. It's not—it's not who I am. I'm just a lynx who...whose friend is prisoner and she's worried sick wondering if she'll be able to save him in time." She looked deep into his helmet, wishing she could see his expression. But she didn't need to. Arsolin lifted his paws and removed his helmet.

"Sifara briefed me on everything yesterday," he admitted, not quite meeting her eye. "It...was a lot to take in."

"You don't have to be my keeper if it makes you uncomfortable," she told him.

He snorted, his whiskers quivering. He stood and padded closer. "If I had been told this before I knew you, perhaps I would have been hesitant. But Hasefi, you are kind and generous and, even though you might not want to be here, you still make time to help those around you." He looked away. "It's a shame you don't want to stay. But my job is to protect you, not tell you what to do."

"Well, it kind of is," Hasefi pointed out.

"Maybe," he chuckled. "But my words are more guidelines. What you do with them is up to you."

Hasefi shrugged. "Do you have training planned today?"

"If you're up to it."

"I am."

By the time they'd finished and left the Cavern of History, night had fallen over the clearing. Arsolin bid her goodnight, leaving her alone. She looked up into the sky, seeing the nearly perfect half-moon peeking over the treetops.

Tomorrow is the free day, she thought. *Though, I still don't know if it applies to me.*

Normally it would, Sefonis offered. *But I cannot say if Esafi has other plans for you.*

Whether she does or not, I need to figure something out. She realized she had already accepted the fact she might be putting other lynxes in danger in order to check up on Kolahn, but she also realized that nothing would stop her from doing so.

One way or another, I'm seeing Kolahn tomorrow.

Though she had entered the clearing ready to fall over with exhaustion, that thought sent a new energy into her.

I need to talk to Salifen.

She padded towards the Healer's Cave, ready to ask one of the healer's outside tending the herb garden if they had seen the novice, but his voice sounded behind her.

"High Heir?"

She turned, relieved she wouldn't have to come up with an excuse as to why she wanted him.

"You're up late," she said as he sank into a bow.

"Aye," he agreed with a tired smile. "Hesilar and I were out training."

Hasefi snorted. "I thought I was the only one training all day." She frowned. "I don't see Hesilar."

"He stayed in the forest," Salifen explained. There was no sign of his usual nervousness, though when Hasefi eyed him, he glanced away.

"Do you remember what we talked about before?" Hasefi asked him, figuring there was no reason to dance around the topic.

"You want to save your friend," he stated, meeting her gaze again.

"Yes. And I think Esafi plans to," Hasefi admitted. "But I don't know how long that's going to take, so I need to check on him and make sure he's okay."

Salifen was silent for a few heartbeats, making Hasefi worried he might ask about the many things she had not explained in full. But he merely nodded.

"You need a gifted," he began. "One you can trust."

"We'd be going behind the Highchief's back," she warned reluctantly. "We could get in big trouble if we're caught."

"Trouble, or the death of your friend," he replied. "If I'm to follow the rules of a healer, I hardly have a choice." Though his words were grave, there was a determined sparkle in his eye.

"Are you sure?" she insisted. "I don't know exactly what kind of consequences would follow."

"I'm sure." He eyed her. "I think it would be good to bring Alarni and Ivanus in, too."

Hasefi was silent, unsure how to voice her doubt.

"Alarni would *not* be happy to find you had talked to me before her," Salifen pointed out. "Not to mention she wasn't included in something the other highbloods and champions didn't know about. Plus, she's clever and knows how to get around guards. And Ivanus would serve as a perfect backup in case anyone is wondering where we are."

"It sounds like you've thought this through," Hasefi observed.

Salifen ducked his head in embarrassment. "Perhaps," he admitted.

"All the better, I suppose. I haven't really given a plan much thought."

"Tomorrow is the half-moon," he said. "We will have time to plan then. With Alarni and Ivanus."

"Okay," she agreed. "And Salifen," she added when he started to turn away. "I really appreciate this. Thank you."

"We don't know why the ancestors choose the lynxes they do for the gift of magic," he began thoughtfully. "But it is believed that each gifted is to serve a particular purpose." His gaze sharpened on her. "Something tells me this is mine."

With a parting nod, he turned and disappeared into the Healer's Cave.

I highly doubt the ancestors want anything to do with my plans, she thought. *But if it's enough to convince him to help, then it's enough for me.*

The next day, she was surprised at first when she found she'd slept for a good deal of time without her mother, father, or anyone else waking her up. Then she remembered the half-moon.

I have the day, she thought with relief.

Hasefi hurried through the bright-lit tunnel into the mainchamber, then out the entry until she was standing on the Highledge. Dismay took over her enthusiasm when she saw the sun had already reached its peak.

There's half a day left, she realized.

They are waiting for you, Sefonis pointed out, guiding Hasefi's gaze to the log at the edge of the clearing. Sure enough, Alarni and Ivanus were there, but there was no sign of Salifen.

Maybe he's still asleep, she thought, knowing he'd been up training as late as she had. *I should go talk to them so they're caught up.*

Hasefi bounded down the Highledge. In the corner of her eye, she saw Arsolin's dark shadow at a distance and knew she'd have to be careful.

"I wasn't expecting to talk to you again," Alarni said when Hasefi was within earshot.

"Do you want in or not?" Hasefi said without delay, her voice low.

Alarni blinked at her in surprise, while Ivanus glanced nervously between them, his gray fur pricking with unease.

"What I talked about before," Hasefi elaborated. "I caught Salifen last night and he said he's in. Now I'm asking you. I can't do this on my own, but if you don't want to take the risk of getting in trouble, I won't make you." She held both of their gazes. "Are you in or not?"

"Do you have a plan?" Alarni asked.

"Not...really," Hasefi admitted.

"Does anyone else know?"

"Just Salifen."

"Then I'm in."

Surprise mixed with warmth made Hasefi's paws tingle eagerly. Then she looked to Ivanus.

"You don't have to do this if you don't want."

"I don't want anyone to get hurt," the kit confessed.

"We won't," Alarni assured him before Hasefi could respond. "This will be just like sneaking through the burrow." Alarni blinked and stared at Hasefi.

"That's how you sneak out of the clearing?" Hasefi asked.

Alarni was silent, her eyes shrewd.

"Good. Then that's one part already figured out."

Relief flashed in the novice hunter's gaze before she looked to Ivanus again. "Are you in? Come on, even my skittish brother is going to help." Despite her words, Alarni's expression was friendly and hopeful.

"I want to help," Ivanus declared, looking to Hasefi. "But, I'm not sure what I can do."

"Well, if some of us are going to be absent, we'll need a cover," Alarni told him. Ivanus perked up.

"Are you sure?" Hasefi asked them. "If you're with me, you're risking trouble."

"I'm counting on it," Alarni said. Her eyes flicked past Hasefi.

Hasefi turned to follow her gaze, worried Arsolin might have crept closer, but it was Salifen approaching.

"Sorry," he puffed, looking as if he'd hardly slept. "I didn't think I'd fall asleep for so long."

"Did you sleep?" Hasefi asked doubtfully.

He shrugged, flicking his ears dismissively, then jerked his head at Alarni and Ivanus. "Have you all talked?"

"We're caught up," Alarni assured him, eyeing her brother with admiration. "I'm impressed, Salifen. Unless you don't realize exactly what you've agreed to. You know, if we get caught, Hesilar could mute you."

"Mute?" Hasefi echoed before Salifen could respond. "What does that mean?"

"Silence a gifted's powers," Alarni explained. "It's what happens to disobedient gifted."

"But it hasn't happened in a long time," Salifen argued, though he was beginning to look a little nervous. "Besides," he continued. "A true mute requires the ancestors' approval and we're doing this to help someone."

"Okay," Hasefi said, deciding it was too late to back out now. "Then let me tell you what's going on." She crouched and so did the others. "I came after my friend which was how Garfonis found me in the first place. The Clan took my friend prisoner and they may kill him." Hasefi paused for a heartbeat. "Esafi is preparing for a battle."

"I knew it!" Alarni hissed.

"Esafi said she'll get my friend then, but I don't know if he'll have enough time before then. I need to make sure he's okay. And I need to do that now."

"Will your friend be coming here?" Ivanus asked. "After Esafi rescues him?"

Hasefi hesitated, wondering if she should give them the full truth or not.

"Of course, silly," Alarni answered before Hasefi could decide. "Where else would he go?"

"So what do you need us to do?" Salifen asked, bringing all their gazes to Hasefi again.

She frowned, deep in thought.

Any suggestions? she asked her tribe.

You've got the burrow, Kilarsa replied. *But it is unlikely you'll be able to utilize it, with Arsolin watching you. But perhaps....* A series of images showed in Hasefi's mind. If it hadn't been her trusted Elder showing them, Hasefi would have thought she was going crazy.

Could Salifen pull something like that off?

One way to find out.

Hasefi looked to the novice healer. "What can you do?"

"What?" he blurted.

"Can you do anything with illusions?" she elaborated.

"I've only been trained in healing magic but..." Salifen glanced warily to the others. "I may have been trying out other things."

Alarni gave her brother a surprised look. "Really? You going outside the rules of a healer? What have you done with my brother?"

"I was just curious. I haven't done anything other than experiment. Besides, Hesilar says we should practice...."

Alarni laughed.

"Okay," Hasefi said. "Is there something you can make to let me pass through this territory and into the Clan's?"

Salifen was silent before nodding, his nervousness slowly replaced by a sharp thoughtfulness.

"I need something that will allow me passage through the territory on both this side and the Clan's side of the River," Hasefi articulated.

"I have an idea," he replied. "It will probably take me the rest of the day, but last night I spent storing my power in case I needed it for something like this." He held her gaze evenly. "I can have something by tonight."

"Great. Now the tricky part."

"Getting across the River isn't tricky?" Ivanus asked.

"My keeper is always watching me," Hasefi explained. "I won't be able to go anywhere unless he's got his eyes somewhere else." Hasefi looked to Alarni. "I need you to pretend to be me."

The novice hunter looked uncertain for the first time. "I think someone might notice."

"I can help with that, too, I think," Salifen said. "But I'll need a part of you," he added to Hasefi.

"Erm, alright. Like what?"

"A claw."

"Right. Um, I'm not sure how we can do that discreetly."

Salifen shook his head and raised a paw. "I can do it painlessly. Here." He wiggled his paw and Hasefi lifted hers. "Extend your claws," he directed.

Hasefi obeyed. The novice's green eyes began to glow, then the light swirled to her paw. She could feel pressure around one of her foreclaws and watched with amazement and discomfort as her claw detached and floated into Salifen's paw.

"I left enough that it'll still grow back," he assured her.

Hasefi unsheathed her claws again, inspecting the missing one, before lowering her paw.

"Go to a guardian and ask them to make you a pouch," he continued before turning to his sister. "You won't be able to, so we'll just have to hide this in your bracer."

Alarni nodded.

"For tonight," Hasefi began. "I'm going to tell my keeper that I'm out with Salifen." She looked to Ivanus. "I don't expect you to stay up—it's probably best you don't, but if anyone does come to you, you're to be our cover."

"What should I say?" the kit asked.

"I'll be looking for herbs with Hasefi's help," Salifen said.

"And it's not unlike me to sneak out past curfew," Alarni said with a wry glance at the others. "Just do what you normally do."

"When Salifen has your illusion," Hasefi said to the novice hunter. "Leave through the burrow. Salifen and I will leave through the main entrance—can you get the illusions done before curfew?"

"Stars defy me if I don't," he assured her.

"We'll need somewhere to meet," Hasefi continued.

Salifen and Alarni passed a glance, then looked to Hasefi.

"We have that covered," Alarni assured her.

"Great," Hasefi replied, grateful she had found what she guessed to be the most resourceful novices in the Tribe. "Alarni, when you meet us, I'll take my illusion and, hopefully, Arsolin won't notice the switch. It'll probably take me half the night to reach the Clan—"

"Half the night?" Alarni interrupted. "I thought the ravine was further."

"I'm used to moving quickly," Hasefi told her, deciding not to finish with 'and back' as she had intended. "When I come back, we'll meet where we did before and switch again. Then we'll return to the clearing as we left it."

"That's solid enough for me," Alarni declared.

"Great. Now, I'm going to spread that cover to one of the novice knights I've been hanging out with, since it's likely someone might go to him about my whereabouts," Hasefi said. She winced, not fond of talking about Nakilon like a tool to be used for her own purposes. But she consoled herself with the fact she actually intended to hang out with him while she could.

"You're sure this is safe?" Ivanus pressed, eyes wide as he watched Hasefi. He leaned closer and lowered his voice. "What if the wolves catch you?"

"I'd like to see them try," she assured the kit with a wink.

"We'll see you tonight, then," Alarni said.

"See you tonight, Hasefi," Salifen added.

Hasefi dipped her head in farewell, then got up to where she'd spotted Nakilon sitting with another novice a few paces away. He'd been eyeing her the whole time she'd been talking to the others and now he got to his paws, eyes bright.

"Hasefi!" he purred. The other novice sank into a bow and Nakilon did the same. "I'm glad to see you have a break, at last."

"Me too," she agreed. "I slept all the way until sunpeak."

"I know. Er—" His ears half-flattened with embarrassment. "I mean, I guessed, since you came out after the sun...." His words ended with a small chuckle.

"I'm going to find my sister," the other novice announced, rolling her eyes at Nakilon. She bowed again to Hasefi before slinking off. Hasefi tried to catch her eye, but the novice seemed determined not to look at her. With her plan in her head, she was too preoccupied to be bothered by it.

Turning to Nakilon, she was surprised to see dismay in his eyes. "Is everything alright?" she asked him.

"Of course," he replied, his expression brightening again. Then he frowned. "I hope I wasn't bothering you," he admitted, though Hasefi suspected it wasn't really what was on his mind. "I know I was kind of staring when you were with your other friends."

"You're fine," Hasefi purred, nudging his shoulder. "I told you I would hang out with you on the half-moon, remember? Now we can finally share that hare."

A purr of his own rumbled in his throat before his expression turned playfully stern. "As long as you promise you've had time to rest and you're not overworking yourself."

Hasefi laughed. "I promise."

They approached the prey-pile and, though a hunting group had just arrived, any hares that may have come were already taken. Nakilon chose a trio of dark-furred squirrels with ear tufts and led her to his spot near the warmrock. He pawed two of the squirrels to her, then settled in front of the third.

"How are you liking it so far?" he asked after they had eaten a few mouthfuls.

"The squirrel?" Hasefi asked with confusion.

"The Tribe," he chuckled. "The knight training, the lynxes, the territory. Are you happy here?"

Hasefi couldn't lie to him, even if she wanted to, for he'd already noticed her hesitation.

"Is it still a lot to take in?"

"It is," she admitted. "I was on my own for a while and, even when I wasn't, there wasn't so much...activity and, well, things to keep track of, I guess. I just feel like I'm always on the go."

Nakilon offered her a sympathetic look. "Even just training as a knight, I feel overwhelmed some days; I can't imagine what it's like to have the weight of the Highchief on your back."

Hasefi shrugged, not knowing what to say. Her back certainly felt heavy, but not for the reasons he was implying.

"I think Esafi wants me ready to be Highchief as soon as possible," she sighed, trying to by humorous, but her words earned her a nervous look from the novice. "Sorry, that was a joke," she amended.

"I'm worried there might be a war," he blurted, then looked down, embarrassed.

Hasefi frowned. *I don't understand why Esafi keeps them in the dark. Every lynx seems to know one is coming—why not just come out with it?*

"You won't be fighting. If there was one, I mean," she pointed out.

"That's what I'm worried about. I won't be there to help my tribe-mates and keep them safe." He looked up at her and his expression eased somewhat. "At least I won't have to worry about you."

"Even if I was fighting, you wouldn't have to worry about me," she chuckled, nudging his shoulder so he couldn't catch her eye and see the truth. To her relief, he laughed, too, returning the gesture.

"Maybe not," he admitted, sobering. "But...I just hope everyone will be okay." He eyed her for a moment before looking away. Hasefi thought she felt something stir inside her, but she wasn't sure if it was her own thoughts or one of her tribemates.

"Don't worry. I'm sure it will work out." Hasefi hoped she sounded sincere, but she could feel her own worry creeping in. *What will happen?* she wondered. *I've fought, but I've never been in a war.* She turned her head towards the River, looking into the sky as the sun descended behind her. *What would happen if we lost and I can't get Kolahn? What would happen here?* She glanced around, replacing the relaxed setting around her with the nightmare that still sat in the back of her mind. Hasefi shook out her fur and hardened her mind.

Whatever happens, I'll get Kolahn back. He's the only one I need to worry about. She looked towards where Alarni and Ivanus were play-fighting. Salifen had disappeared. *And tonight, I'll be able to make sure he's okay.*

Though half the day had already passed, it was agony waiting for the sun to descend to the horizon and drape the forest in a blanket of darkness. When it eventually had, the half-moon was reluctant to rise; this was better, though, as curfew for the novices came in effect once it was visible over the trees. She wasn't worried about coming back late as she'd already informed Arsolin she'd be helping Salifen, who had permission to be out late if he was gathering herbs. Hasefi thought this was a little strange, but decided she would trust the novice. But, if they didn't leave until after curfew, that would cause some problems.

And all she was waiting for now was Salifen.

Ivanus had retired for the night, summoned by his mother once the sun had left. Alarni was curled by the log at the edge of the clearing, her eyes closed as if asleep, but her twitching ears told Hasefi she was alert.

She had said goodnight to Nakilon; securing her cover with him was easy, though it didn't make her feel good. The two of them had taken a walk before dusk and she'd relayed the same story to him as she had with Arsolin, though with some extra details.

Ever since her leg had been broken in the high mountains and she'd discovered Edgewood and its capacity for herbs, she'd gained an interest in them. This wasn't false, but she didn't have the kind of passion for them Salifen did.

"That's great!" Nakilon had told her. "We learn some healing in our basic training, gifted or not. I think it's something every lynx should know. I'm glad you have someone to help you."

He had been his usual genuine and cheery self, which only made Hasefi feel guiltier about using him for her own benefit.

Hopefully I won't have to do this for much longer, she thought.

She'd also used the daylight to see Silvera again, the guardian that had made her armor. She asked the gifted lynx for a pouch and, to her relief, Silvera didn't ask any questions. Now, Hasefi had a black pouch on her right shoulder, ready for whatever Salifen intended to give to her for tonight.

Movement caught her eye. Alarni was getting up, reaching her legs out in a seemingly casual stretch. Following her gaze, Hasefi saw Salifen was padding towards his sister.

Hasefi waited, washing her flank as the two spoke. Then Alarni gave her brother a friendly cuff over the ear and padded towards a part of the clearing that was sheltered from curious eyes. It was where lynxes went to relieve themselves, if they couldn't use the forest.

So that's where it is now, Kilarsa observed. *Clever.*

"Hey, Hasefi," Salifen called. "Are you ready to help me bring some herbs back for Hesilar?"

"Let's do it," she purred.

They walked out into the forest together, Arsolin just a couple paces behind. Hasefi was tense and her heart was beginning to thump in her chest, but the quiet stillness of the trees and the pleasant coolness of the night was comforting and eased her anxiety somewhat.

"I quite like this forest," she admitted to Salifen.

"Are there others?" he asked.

Hasefi nodded. "I've only been in one other, but it wasn't as full as this one is. And it was colder."

"Sometimes I forget you're younger than me," he admitted with a shy glance.

"Not by much," she pointed out with a purr.

"Most of the adult lynxes haven't even been beyond our borders," Salifen told her. "You've seen more of the world than perhaps even the Highchief."

"Is that why no one knows what I mean when I say, 'high mountains'?"

He nodded.

I guess Kolahn came up with that, too, she thought. She knew Edgewood and Darkwood were his inventions, but with the Great River and the Great Forest and even the Broken Peak being part of this tribe's knowledge, she'd assumed they knew the high and green mountains.

He must have come up with 'ocean', too, she thought. *Did lynxes never explore?* she added to her tribe.

There was little reason to, Sefonis replied. *Why leave home when you have everything you need?*

I feel like it would get boring, she admitted. *But maybe not if lynxes are so busy,* she added, thinking of how lynxes were always on the go here.

"Your friend," Salifen said, bringing Hasefi from her mind. "Did he call them 'high mountains'?"

"He did," Hasefi admitted. "He had names for every different place we came upon. He was really creative that way."

"He sounds like a fantastic creature." Salifen went silent, his gaze unexpectedly calm as he watched her.

"You didn't say lynx," Hasefi observed slowly.

"Could I ask his name?"

Hasefi hesitated, intending to say she'd like to keep it to herself, but as she met the novice's eyes, she felt the need to tell him the truth.

"Kolahn."

Salifen merely nodded as if she'd confirmed something for him.

Why did I tell him that? she thought with alarm. *Did he do something to me?*

I don't think Salifen has that kind of power, Kilarsa said. *And gifted are forbidden from using magic on other lynxes without consent. But he does have a particular nature....*

"He's a wolf," Salifen murmured as they padded along a twisting path.

"I sort of thought you'd have a different reaction," she admitted.

"I'm a healer," he told her. "I'm taught to have compassion for every creature—that includes wolves. And...I don't hate the wolves like a lot of the others do." He gave her a nervous look.

"So...you're okay that I'm friends with a wolf?"

"If he did what you said he did, then how can I feel otherwise? He sounds like a good creature and it's obvious you care a lot about him." He glanced into the trees. "I wouldn't tell Alarni, though."

Hasefi nodded. "She's not going to like the idea of us hiding something from her," she pointed out.

"Then we'll just have to make sure she doesn't find out."

Hasefi chuckled softly. "Thanks," she told the novice.

"For what?"

"For your help. You're risking a lot for a wolf—I don't know another lynx that would do that, other than myself, I suppose." She blinked, remembering how easily Kolahn had come to her aid, not caring she was a different creature. "I care a lot about Kolahn and every day I think about being with him again."

Salifen nodded. "I'm glad to help." He smiled. "He's lucky to have you."

Hasefi narrowed her eyes. "He's like a brother to me," she explained. "But, my father mentioned it was possible for a lynx to love a wolf like a mate."

"Aye," Salifen admitted, though he was caught off-guard by her response for some reason and took a couple heartbeats to recover. "Long ago, when the first gray lynxes came to the Tribe." He eyed her. "Could I ask you something else?"

"Of course," she replied, though the intensity of his gaze made her uneasy.

"Do you have a home? Outside the River?"

Hasefi hesitated. "What do you mean?"

Salifen gave her a knowing look. "I can't imagine the Tribe would be too fond of you bringing a wolf into our ranks," he pointed out.

Hasefi kicked a dry leaf along the trail, not sure if she preferred this version or the nervous one of Salifen.

"Did you have a home together before?" he pressed.

Images of the devastated Valley entered Hasefi's mind and she gave the ground a sad look. "He did. Up past the Clan's territory there's a valley. We had just gotten there when a landslide destroyed it." Hasefi found again that she wanted to tell Salifen the entire truth of her experience. The feeling confused her and this time she was able to suppress it.

"So where will you go?"

"I don't know. Wherever he wants to, I guess." Hasefi looked towards the River, her chest aching.

"You'll get him back," Salifen assured her.

She opened her mouth to thank him, but the novice came to a sudden stop.

"Here we are," he announced, nodding ahead.

The trees opened up before them to reveal a glade filled with silver-cast grass reaching up to Hasefi's shoulders. Colorful wildflowers turned white in the light of the moon and stars dotted the grass. It made Hasefi think of the many times she and Kolahn had found spaces similar to this on their journeys and laid on their backs, looking up at the night sky.

"This is where I like to collect juniper," Salifen explained, bringing Hasefi from her memories. "We'll be here for a while."

Hasefi nodded, her heart beginning to pound again. She was silent as Salifen led her into the open space and beneath the moonlight, towards a bush with spiky green leaves and dark berries growing just inside the treeline on the other side of the glade.

They sat down. Salifen showed her how to pick the fruit carefully and she did, though her attention was focused elsewhere.

Okay, she said to her tribe. *Let's see if this works.*

She drew upon their strength but, instead of using it to enhance her own physical strength, she strained her ears, listening through the trees. The rustling around her grew sharper. Salifen's soft, graceful movements were easy to detect and she could tell what he was doing without looking at him. At a distance, she could hear the careful steps of a deer passing through the forest. There was another sound, a soft thumping, and Hasefi was surprised to find it was the deer's heartbeat.

Wow, she thought. *I can hear everything!*

Focus, Gelinaf came to the forefront of her mind. *Listen for Arsolin.*

Hasefi obeyed, angling her ears until she picked up the nearly imperceptible steps of her keeper as he padded a few paces away. He was walking around them, checking the perimeter, Gelinaf told her. She could hear the whisper of his armor and the steady pace of his heart. His breath echoed softly in his helmet, louder as he looked toward her, then soft when he looked away.

Hasefi waited until Arsolin had completed a full circuit, then moved farther away, allowing Salifen and her some space.

"Okay," she murmured, releasing her tribe's strength and turning her attention on Salifen. "We can talk."

There was question in the novice's eyes, but he didn't ask anything when he spoke.

"I have enchanted your claw so Alarni will appear as you do, armor and all, when she has it on her. I placed it on the forest side of the burrow and told her where to find it. She'll be on her way here."

He lowered his head, using his teeth to lift the edge of his collar until a tooth tumbled out and fell onto the ground before them.

"What is that?" Hasefi asked.

"A fox tooth. Hesilar found it while we were touring the border one day and gave it to me. When you keep this in your new pouch, you will appear and smell like a fox. Lynxes nor wolves hunt them for food, but it's still probably a good idea not to be seen, especially since I haven't had a chance to test the illusion."

"Wait," Hasefi interrupted. "How come you didn't look like a fox coming here?"

"I bound this to you," he explained. "Using your claw. I did the same for Alarni, using some fur from her sleeping hollow."

"Really?" Hasefi asked, amused and impressed. "How did you manage that?"

"Apparently I play the blundering novice quite well," he replied, ducking his head in embarrassment, though Hasefi noticed a flash of pride in his eyes.

"I have to admit I may have underestimated you," Hasefi told him.

"Hesilar says I underestimate myself," he admitted. "I'm trying to be braver. I find it's easy to do around you."

"Well, at least that's something I can offer, then," she replied. "And I'm not the only one gaining something out of this."

"You're not," he assured her, but he made no attempt to elaborate.

Before Hasefi could respond, rustling sounded. She tensed, ready to bat the fox tooth out of sight, but the lynx that appeared before them wasn't Arsolin.

She had to blink a few times, feeling as if she were looking at a section of rippling water, before she realized it was a magically-transformed Alarni standing before her.

"Time to go," she said to Hasefi.

Salifen picked up the tooth and, with a nod from Hasefi, put it in her pouch.

"Alright," she said to the novices. "I'll see you soon."

She turned away from them and fled back into the trees.

Chapter Eleven

Hasefi's heart thrummed in her chest with every running step she took. She hoped Salifen's illusion was enough to keep the Tribe's patrols from noticing her scent and that Alarni would be able to play as the High Heir until she returned.

We need to be fast, she told her tribe.

They acknowledged her words by offering their strength. She sped through the forest, running as fast as she had the last time she had sought to rescue her friend, using her tribe's knowledge to pick the fastest routes and keep from tripping over snaking roots and trailing brambles. Her paws got her to the border in what felt like heartbeats. When she paused a few paces away from the waterfall, she could see the moon still hadn't shown itself over the treetops.

There are guards, she said to her tribe. A knight and a keeper sat dutifully near the path leading behind the waterfall. *I would go deaf sitting there,* she thought.

I suspect there is another keeper, Gelinaf warned her. *Usually a patrol is no less than three.*

I can't hear anything, she told him.

Open your mouth, he told her. *Taste the air.*

Hasefi obeyed, breathing in the fresh night air. Scents bathed her tongue, stronger than they ever had before until it was as if she was eating the decaying leaves beneath her paws and drinking the cool water of the River.

There, she thought, trying to pick apart the scents. *A lynx came by this way, not long ago.*

They are far enough away, Gelinaf assured her. *But we must create a distraction for the others before they scent you. Foxes are chased off Tribe territory.*

I can do that.

Hasefi slunk just inside the treeline bordering the little clearing the two guards sat in. A fallen tree had been caught by another, creating a narrow ramp leading into the air in the direction of the waterfall.

Can foxes climb? she asked.

If they really want to. It was Tenarli who replied. *But most creatures could climb that.*

Good.

Hasefi went past the tree-ramp, then stopped again. She was in the eyeline, now, of the two guards, so when she stepped out of cover, the keeper reacted immediately.

Something was said, but the roar of the water behind the guards was too loud for Hasefi to hear what the two lynxes were saying. They both got to their paws, but it was the keeper that approached.

I really hope Salifen's magic is working.

"Get back!" the keeper hissed.

Hasefi ducked backwards, but she didn't retreat until the keeper had sped up and was running at her. She turned and fled, running a wide arc before pelting towards the tree-ramp.

As she scrambled up it, the knight's helmet flicked up and they bounded over, bracing themselves. But Hasefi used her tribe's strength to sail far over their head and land nearly at the entrance to the waterfall.

She didn't miss a beat and ran through, using her claws to keep from slipping on the slick rock. On the other side, there were no signs of wolven guards. She didn't stop until she was in the safety of the trees and, after ensuring the lynxian guards had no intention of following her over, she stepped back out.

How come the wolves aren't keeping guard? she thought. *Wouldn't it be easy for them to keep an eye on the passage if they're determined to keep lynxes out?*

The Clan suffered heavy losses during Resahn's Reign, Sefonis explained. *It's possible they are still trying to recover.*

If that's true, they probably wouldn't have much chance in a war with the Tribe, Hasefi observed. *But if you know that, then Esafi probably does, too. I'm here to help Kolahn, not stop a war,* she added to herself.

She turned, running deeper into wolven territory. As she drew closer to the ravine, she felt as if she was shedding an old pelt for a new, fresh one.

It's hardly been a quarter moon, but I've already forgotten what it feels like to be free like this. She relished the ability to run free through the trees with nothing but her own thoughts and her tribe to accompany her. But, she was still in Clan territory and her friend was still in danger.

I could just get him, she thought. *Then we could leave and put this place behind us.*

Her tribe offered no response, but she was distracted when she recognized the dried up streambed that led to the ravine.

She slowed then, following the slope up, but when the land around her grew steep, she hopped onto the ledge on her right and followed it as the earth gave way to rocky walls, forming the ravine where the Clan lived.

Hopefully Salifen's illusion works for the wolves, too, and any that see me think I'm whatever a fox is.

Hasefi made it unhindered to the same ferns she had hidden in when she had first arrived at the River. She peered down into the ravine, eyes and ears open and enhanced with her tribe's strength, searching for any sign of her beloved friend.

He's here somewhere, she said to herself. *He has to be.*

Do you see that wolf in black armor? Sefonis said, angling her gaze when she couldn't find the wolf in question. *They guard the Clan's prison-den. They wouldn't be there if there was no prisoner.*

But we don't know if it's Kolahn, Hasefi protested.

It is unlikely to be another black wolf, he pointed out. *And, from my information on Lady Eilwyn, she does not hold prisoners.*

What, does she punish and kill, like Esafi?

She is of a kinder sort. It was Dahsefer, her Sage, who answered.

'Kinder sort', Hasefi thought bitterly. *That's what I would describe a creature who throws out wolves because of their fur color.* Guilt tugged at her when her Sage withdrew. *I'm sorry, I don't mean to snap at you.*

We understand, wee lass, Sefonis assured her. *This is not an easy thing. But I am confident when I tell you it is Kolahn within the very stone you stand upon.*

Hasefi drew a breath in, then let it out slowly.

If we are quick, Sefonis continued. *We can make it as the Tribe's guards switch for the next shift. It would be wise to avoid arousing more suspicion, even if they see you as no more than a fox.*

Reluctance made Hasefi's paws heavy, but she knew her uncle was right.

Why should I even go back? she thought half-heartedly. *I could stay and wait for my own opportunity.*

I cannot see a better way than what Esafi has offered, Kilarsa said to her. *Not without hurting a lot of wolves.*

Wolves will get hurt anyways, she pointed out, but she knew it wasn't the same. *Why is Esafi taking so long with this?*

She has a lot of variables to consider, Sefonis reminded her. *Even without the ones you brought along.*

Hasefi didn't reply, straining again as she looked into the ravine. She tried to spot the Lady, but there was no sign of her.

Time grows short, Sefonis warned gently. *If you are going to return, the best time would be now.*

Hasefi dug her claws into the earth, then released her grip. *Don't worry, Kolahn. I'm coming for you. Don't give up.*

She straightened and turned back the way she came, feeling as if she was ripping out her own heart. *Okay,* she told her tribe. *Let's go back. The others will be getting worried.*

On the way back, Hasefi felt numb and hardly noticed the trees going by as she sped through the Clan's part of the forest. Leaving Kolahn with the Clan was like betraying him, but the only way she could get him back immediately would probably break him.

He still won't be happy with the Tribe hurting them, she knew. *But at least it won't be me or the Pack.*

She was distracted by her thoughts, so she didn't notice the rustling of leaves nearby until it was too late. Fortunately, however, her Keeper Overlord acted quickly and took control of her body so he could tuck her under a thickly growing wild rose bush. Prickles scraped her fur and skin, but she was thankful for it when two wolves emerged a heartbeat later.

They were both without armor and were smaller than the full-grown wolves she had seen before. One was hardly bigger than herself. She urged the two to move on, but was dismayed when the smaller one stopped. Hasefi tensed, bracing herself to fight.

"What's wrong with you?" the other wolf asked, returning to his companion.

"How can we be sure?" the first asked, continuing the conversation they must have been having.

"What do you mean?" the second pressed, ears flicking with annoyance.

"How can we be sure that we're safe from…them?" The smaller wolf spoke the last word quietly as if hardly daring to speak at all.

"Please don't tell me you're still afraid of the black wolf," the older wolf groaned.

"I am, okay? I can't help it!"

"You're a tenderpaw now—you can't act like a pup anymore," the bigger wolf insisted, puffing his chest. But his companion was not eased.

"You know the story—even the grown wolves are scared of him!" The younger wolf's eyes were wide with fright. "How aren't you?"

The older wolf was silent.

A mixture of delight and anger made Hasefi's paws prick and her fur bristle.

They must be talking about Kolahn, she thought. *But they have no idea he came to warn them! They're the ones threatening to have him killed!* Despite her anger and desperation, Hasefi was able to keep herself in check and remained silent beneath the wild rose bush.

"What if he's not the only one?" the smaller wolf squeaked.

"Eilwyn said he's not a threat," the older wolf replied quickly, but Hasefi could hear the uncertainty in his voice now.

"But what about the Seer Alpha's prophecy?"

Hasefi's ears flattened. *Another prophecy?*

"'When water recedes, darkness will flow.'" The younger wolf's tone changed as he recited the words, sending a shiver down Hasefi's spine.

That doesn't sound good at all.

The other wolf was silent, his face showing his thoughts weren't all that different from her own.

"It can't be a coincidence that *he* shows up when the stream stopped flowing." The smaller wolf's ears flattened. "What if he caused it?"

"Don't be ridiculous," the bigger wolf barked with forced laughter. "Black wolves can't be gifted. Besides, don't you think something would have happened by now?"

"But it is! Haven't you heard the others? It's like the time right before Resahn. Prey is scarce. The Tribe is getting aggressive. What if it all happens again?"

"You're making up stories in your head," the other wolf snapped, but his voice wavered. "It won't happen again."

"How can you be so sure?"

"Because Eilwyn and the Seer Alpha stopped Resahn. They'll stop anything else from happening, okay? Now, can you stop bothering with this? I want to test my new hunting technique before curfew comes."

The small wolf nodded quickly and straightened. Then he hesitated, his nose twitching. "I smell fox."

"Don't tell me you're afraid of that, too," the other wolf moaned.

"Of course not!" As if to prove his point, the younger wolf hurried ahead and his companion followed, a shadow passing over his face before he resumed the irritated mask he had used to try and appease the younger wolf.

Hasefi didn't extricate herself from the prickly rose bush right away, though not from fear of more sharp scrapes in her pelt. Her thoughts were conflicted with relief, knowing they could only be talking about Kolahn, and frustration at how ignorant the wolves were of Kolahn, but she was aware they weren't much different than she was when she was first on her own.

They never got a chance to know Kolahn.

And they are suffering. Dahsefer observed. *It seems the Pack may be trespassing on both sides of the River.*

That's not surprising, Hasefi thought. *They don't seem like the kind of creatures that would be worried about boundaries.*

It may be wise to leave now, Sefonis reminded her.

Hasefi forced her way out of the rose bush, hardly noticing the sharp pains within her pelt as her mind continued to work. *Surely Esafi knows all this, right?* she asked. *Is that why she's waiting? For the Clan to be at their weakest?*

That may be helpful when it comes to rescuing Kolahn, Sefonis pointed out.

You know that's not what I mean, she said.

As far as I know, Esafi has never led lynxes into battle before, he admitted. *She has no love for the Clan, so why not strike when they can't?*

Which you can't truly blame her for, Dahsefer pointed out. *Her generation suffered the consequences of Resahn's Reign. A lot of lynxes were lost—including her mother. Wanting to avoid casualties is what any good leader would do.*

Good leader? Hasefi echoed. *I thought you all left because you didn't agree with her leadership.*

Just because we didn't agree doesn't mean she's a bad leader, Kilarsa spoke. *You may not think well of her, but you must remember she just lost two of her kits. Such a thing is difficult for any creature. That kind of grief blinds a mother to things that might otherwise deter her.*

But she's their Highchief, Hasefi insisted. *She can't let that get in the way, right?*

A Highchief's champions are there to provide wisdom and suggestion, Kilarsa replied. *But it is still up to the Highchief what happens.*

Hasefi shook her head, once more conflicted. *If this war happens...it won't be right.* She came to a stop, hidden beneath the trees overlooking the little clearing of water-sparkling grass near the waterfall. There were still no signs of wolves. *The Clan is already suffering and lynxes will get hurt for the wrong reason. This isn't right.*

Hasefi's tribe was silent.

Couldn't Esafi try talking to them?

I think that's what Garfonis meant to do, Gelinaf admitted quietly.

Hasefi sighed, deflating. *I'm being pulled in too many directions. What do I do?*

Return to your friends, Kilarsa replied after a few heartbeats of silence. *Then sleep. A refreshed mind will be easier to think with.*

Hasefi let out another long sigh and nodded agreement.

With Sefonis's guidance, she waited until the guard patrol on the Tribe's side of the water changed as the old guards were replaced with new ones. Using the shadows, she was able to sneak through, pressing close to the cliff-side in the grassy clearing until she was under the safety of the trees.

Then she ran, careful not to run into her own keeper. When she found Arsolin, she waited until he was focused on something else, then approached the clearing where Salifen was speaking quietly and Alarni was listening intently.

It didn't take long for them to spot her. Alarni got up, fiddling with her bracer and dropping Hasefi's enchanted claw before slipping back into the trees.

In the same heartbeats, Hasefi pawed the pouch on her shoulder and let the fox tooth fall on the ground.

Salifen was sitting quietly as if nothing had happened.

"Thank the stars you're okay," he murmured when Hasefi joined him.

She pawed the claw and tooth between them, biting back a retort about how the stars had nothing to do with her well-being and was silent.

"Did you find your friend?" Salifen asked, his expression hopeful.

"Not exactly," she admitted. "But I heard wolves talking about him. It sounds like he's still alive." Hasefi noticed a green stone between Salifen's paws. "What's that?"

"It's my energy-stone."

Hasefi's ears twitched with confusion.

"Er, do you know what an energy-stone is?"

"Is it like a soulstone?"

"Sort of. A soulstone's purpose is to hold the essence of a deceased lynx and is made to last as long as possible. But this," Salifen pawed the stone towards her. "Is an energy-stone. Gifted lynxes all have one. We pour parts of our strength in it so that, if we ever need to use more strength than we can offer, we can draw from it. It's what I used to help with those." He nodded at the enchanted pieces between them.

"It must have been pretty strange staring at Alarni while she looked like me," Hasefi observed, but Salifen shook his head.

"I made the magic so it didn't affect me."

Clever novice, Kilarsa murmured.

He might have been better off as a guardian, at this rate, Dahsefer added.

"We should get back to the clearing," Salifen stated, using magic to move the enchanted pieces and tuck them beneath his collar. He gave himself a gentle shake to ensure they were secure, then nodded to two large leaves that had somehow been folded over each other. "Can you help me carry these?"

Hasefi picked up one of the bundles, then walked with Salifen back towards the clearing. They couldn't talk much, with their mouths full, so they returned in silence. One of the healers working through the night took Hasefi's bundle and followed Salifen into the Healer's Cave. The novice offered her a parting nod before disappearing inside.

Hasefi looked around, but there was no sign of Alarni. She risked a glance at Arsolin, just catching his white jaw beneath his helmet as he yawned.

She went over to him, trying to stifle the guilt she felt for going behind his back.

"Thanks for letting me stay out," she said, watching the keeper as closely as she could with his full set of armor.

"You are helping your tribemates," he replied. "You are the one that deserves thanks." His tone was affectionate, without a trace of suspicion.

"Whatever you say," she purred. "Now, I think you're as tired as I am. I'll see you tomorrow."

"Goodnight, Hasefi," he said, a purr in his throat.

She watched him pad towards the Keeper's Cave. Despite his good mood and her relatively successful mission, Hasefi found she only felt worse.

Sleep, she thought, remembering Kilarsa's words. *I'll feel better tomorrow. And maybe I can think about getting Esafi to move on the Clan.* The very thought felt like a betrayal to Kolahn, but she did her best to ignore it, convincing herself the only other alternative was much worse.

She braced herself as well as she could when she entered the Highcave, but it was empty. Relieved she wouldn't have to put on a false face for anyone else, she sank gratefully into her sleeping hollow and into a troubled sleep.

The next morning came much too quickly.

Esafi almost had to lift Hasefi from her hollow before she could stand on her own paws. Her legs protested beneath her weight; she felt more exhausted than she had after returning last night.

I could sleep for a day, she groaned inwardly. *Maybe I shouldn't have relied so much on you,* she added to her tribe.

Esafi might agree to a break, Kilarsa suggested, but Hasefi dismissed the idea with a mental shake of her head.

I just had one. I can't let her be suspicious. Hasefi drew up her head and stifled a yawn, hoping she looked somewhat ready for the day.

"You have lived long without waking to perform daily duties," Esafi observed, scrutinizing Hasefi. "But," she continued, her tone a sliver friendlier. "Staying up late to help your tribemates is one of the many sacrifices a Highchief makes for her Tribe."

Hasefi shrugged beneath the Highchief's imploring gaze. "Kolahn taught me about herbs," she explained. "Salifen offered to teach me a bit if I helped him."

Esafi hummed a response, becoming suddenly thoughtful. However, she moved on, jerking her head towards the tunnel leading out of the sleeping chamber. "Garfonis will be expecting you."

As Hasefi left the Highcave, she made an awkward attempt to smooth some of her sleep-stirred fur before she emerged outside.

At least it's still dark, she thought, licking a stubborn tuft on her chest.

Garfonis came to retrieve her and they headed to the Knight's Pit. They were always up before the novices, so Garfonis would sometimes go over details pertaining to the role of a Highchief and how they tied in with the knights' champion. Normally, he preferred to hangout with her, but today she must have made it clear she was too tired to chat and he dove right into lessons.

When the novices arrived at the Pit, Hasefi was disappointed when Nakilon was nowhere to be found. She learned the novice was taking a sick day after waking up before dawn with a cough.

"Can't the healers just take care of it?" Hasefi asked Garfonis when they had finished their physical training and were on their way to the clearing.

"They help, but it's important to let our bodies fight their own battles, or else they'll never get a chance to be stronger."

Hasefi never really understood the ways of magic, but for once, what her father said made sense, especially since it made her think about the coming war and the lack of battle experience of these lynxes.

That's one way I can see this war, right? As a chance for these lynxes to grow stronger?

The thought wasn't as comforting as she'd hoped.

Arsolin continued her training after Garfonis released her. Hasefi was too tired to eat, so they went straight back into the Cavern of History until, finally the day was over.

Hasefi was tripping over her own paws on the way to the Highcave, but Alarni stopped in front of her.

"By the stars, are they training you this much every single day?" she asked.

"Salifen is usually out late," Hasefi mumbled in response.

"Only if he wants to. Hesilar isn't hard on him." Alarni shook her head, something like sympathy in her eyes. "I couldn't imagine having to work this hard all the time."

"I think it's more to keep me preoccupied so Esafi doesn't have to keep track of me every heartbeat." She straightened a little. "But, obviously, it takes more than that to stop me." She eyed Alarni, finally wondering why the novice hunter had approached her.

"I haven't had a chance to talk to my brother," the novice explained, reading Hasefi's face. "I wanted to know how it went. Did you get to see if your friend was still there?"

"Sort of," Hasefi said, sitting down and trying not to look disappointed that she couldn't retire to her hollow yet. "I heard wolves talking about him."

Alarni sat down, too, clearly intent to talk. "You said Esafi plans to rescue him during the upcoming war?"

Hasefi nodded, sweeping her gaze warily around her.

"Is he your mate?"

"Mate?" Hasefi echoed, wondering why lynxes kept asking her that. "Can't creatures be fond of others without being mates?"

"Of course," Alarni said, looking unexpectedly pleased. "I was just curious. You haven't told us a lot about him."

"I know," Hasefi admitted, prepared for this. She bowed her head, assuring herself that, though her intention was to divert the novice, she still spoke the truth. "It's difficult to talk about him knowing that he...." She shrugged.

"If I were you, I would be doing anything to break out of here and go after him," Alarni said. "You have more control than me."

"I guess it comes from being out there," Hasefi said, jerking her chin vaguely in the direction of the Valley.

"So what's your plan now?" the novice pressed.

"Well, I guess I have to try and find out more about the war Esafi plans on declaring," Hasefi sighed, not really wanting to think about it now. "I just...."

"You just what?"

"I don't know," Hasefi said with a shrug. "I grew up fighting for survival. I just don't see why creatures should choose to fight when they don't have to."

Alarni narrowed her eyes. "The wolves killed your brothers," she pointed out. "I'm sure you know about that by now. Aren't you furious with them?" she added after Hasefi murmured confirmation.

"I want my brothers' killers to pay," she admitted. "I just think it's more complicated than that."

Alarni shrugged, unconvinced. "If a wolf killed Salifen, I wouldn't even give them the chance to be sorry about it." Hate burned in the novice's eyes. It didn't run quite as deeply as Esafi's, but it did make Hasefi think of the Highchief.

"My brothers will be avenged." The words weighed heavily on Hasefi as she thought of facing the Pack once more. "But they're dead. My friend isn't. I need to worry about him, first."

To Hasefi's relief, Alarni nodded agreement and got to her paws.

"You look ready to fall off your paws," she observed. "If you need any more help, don't hesitate to let us know."

"Thanks, Alarni," Hasefi told her, dipping her head gratefully. There was a delighted glow in the novice's eyes before she nodded and turned back towards the Hunter's Cave.

Hasefi let out a long sigh and continued to the path leading onto the Highledge. She ascended, step after trudging step until she reached the top.

A gaze pricking her pelt made her fur twitch until she looked up. Esafi was at the end of the Ledge, but it was the Guardian Elder, Myafos, who was watching Hasefi. His hood shadowed his face, but his eyes pierced the darkness, two golden orbs emitting a soft, ominous light.

Unease shivered down her spine and Hasefi hurried into the Highcave, forgetting her exhaustion for a moment. She immediately thought of the Elder's stare in her dream, disliking how similar it was to what she had just encountered.

Could Esafi be right? she wondered fearfully. *Could my dream be real? Does Myafos know about it?*

Her tribe didn't respond, but they were giving her some distance so she and they could recover from the exertion last night required. However, the silence in her head allowed the images of her nightmare to return, making her wonder if her efforts to get Kolahn would lead to the very thing she was trying to avoid.

I'm too tired for this right now, she decided and slunk into the Highcave and to the sleeping chamber where she sank heavily into her hollow.

Chapter Twelve

"Nice work!" Hasefi puffed as Nakilon stepped off of her and helped her to her paws.

"Sorry, I probably shouldn't have hit you so hard," he apologized.

"I've taken harder blows," she assured him, but she was unable to hide the unsteadiness of her legs. Despite a full night's rest, she still hadn't recovered fully from her mission to visit the Clan.

"Well done!" Nakilon's mentor praised before the novice could say more. The knight gave Nakilon an approving nod. "I think you're the first to master Hasefi's move."

"That's because they're always sparring together," Firalos called from a few paces away.

"Firalos," one of the knights scolded with a growl.

Hasefi stifled a sigh. The older novice had grown increasingly difficult every time Hasefi had a paw to play in their training. Before, he hadn't caused any problems other than boring a hole into her pelt with his gaze, but today he insisted on commenting on every little thing he could.

Maybe he's like Alarni, she thought to herself. *Maybe it's not really me he's upset with.*

"No, he's right," she said aloud, approaching the broad-shouldered novice. "Would you prefer I sparred with you?" she asked him, hoping she looked friendly.

Firalos growled, but lowered his gaze to the ground. In the corner of her eye, Hasefi saw Nakilon's triumphant look, but she wasn't so pleased with Firalos's reaction.

He won't talk freely with Garfonis and all these knights around. How could I get him alone?

Hasefi was hoping for guidance from her tribe, but she was also aware of the many eyes on her and knew she would have to do something soon.

I'm the High Heir, she thought suddenly. *I could pull him aside, couldn't I?*

"I'd like to talk to you," Hasefi declared, causing the novice's head to jerk up in surprise.

"Hasefi, we're in the middle of a training session," Garfonis protested.

"Then train amongst yourselves," Hasefi replied, copying Esafi's authoritative tone, perhaps with a bit of exaggeration. "I'd like to talk to Firalos."

Garfonis hesitated, conflict clear on his face. Mentors and novices looked between him and Hasefi, awaiting his response.

"Please be quick," he said finally.

"Come on," Hasefi told the fuming novice and he trudged after her to the edge of the sand pit.

"So, what?" he growled when they were out of earshot of the others. "You'd rather snarl at me in private?"

"Why would I want to snarl at you?" she asked.

Firalos snorted.

"What have I done to make you upset with me? Surely this isn't from one bad sparring session?"

The novice's face twisted and he recoiled. "Is your head filled with stars?" he snapped. "Or are you just cruel?"

"Cruel?" she echoed with confusion.

"I know you're gifted," he growled. "And I know you used your power on me."

Hasefi stared at him with wide eyes, caught off-guard.

"But no one else does—or maybe they just don't care because you're the Highchief's prophesized daughter with the oh-so-important destiny," he hissed, getting close to her face. "Do you really think using your gift against me proves anything?"

"But I—"

"Save it. I don't care." The novice stalked away from her, rejoining the others. Hasefi frowned after him, disturbed.

It can't be a secret I'm not gifted, she thought. *I came to the Tribe without armor to hide my chest.*

But you are the focal point of a prophecy from the ancestors, Kilarsa reminded her.

A prophecy meant to destroy me.

We know that truth. He nor any others here do.

Hasefi's frown deepened. *Firalos didn't like me from the start.* A sharp pang twisted her chest. *I've never been* disliked *before. At least with the Pack it was simple. Here, it feels like there's something else going on.*

Some lynxes are hard to get through to, Sefonis spoke up. *Not everyone will like you. You've only been here a quarter moon. You are as much a stranger to them as they are to you.*

An outcast, she thought, thinking of Kolahn. *Then maybe it'll make leaving easier.*

Hasefi looked up to where Firalos sat before his mentor. His back was turned to her and she wondered if that was intentional.

I have more important things to worry about than grumpy lynxes, she thought. *I need to talk to Esafi or Garfonis about the war and see if they've made any sort of progress in their planning. Esafi's never around—surely she has something?*

With her tribe silent, Hasefi returned to the others.

"Is everything alright?" Garfonis asked when she stood beside him. "If Firalos is behaving badly—"

"It's fine," Hasefi assured him, not wanting to cause the novice any more harm. "I was just hoping I could see why he was upset with me."

"Did he say?"

Hasefi shook her head.

Her father leaned over, giving her shoulder a comforting nudge with his nose. "Firalos has always been a bit of a hothead," he purred. "He's a formidable fighter and will make a great knight. But he's still young."

Hasefi nodded, eased by his words. Looking to the novices again, she noticed Nakilon's worried gaze on her. She offered a warm smile and he returned it with a goofy one before his mentor lightly cuffed his ear to get his attention back.

"Could Firalos have known my brothers?" she asked when a new thought came to mind.

"Not like you suggest," Garfonis replied. His whiskers twitched with sudden amusement. "Esafi kept a closer eye on them than she does you."

"Really?" she asked in disbelief.

"Your reason for wanting to leave is much more significant, but your brothers were escape artists." His whiskers quivered with suppressed laughter. "They wanted nothing more than to see beyond the walls of the clearing."

"I couldn't imagine being cooped up in the clearing for twelve moons," Hasefi admitted.

"When kits are older, restrictions are lessened as long as they have a supervisor." His mirthful expression darkened.

"You implied they didn't hangout with the other kits," Hasefi redirected.

"No. Even if Esafi wasn't so careful about them, I don't think they would have. Mekonis and Talonis were very independent. It was like they were the only two in the world."

Hasefi found herself looking up into the sky. It was bright blue with wisps of cloud floating across, blown by a gentle morning breeze. She imagined the stars looking down at her and, while the eyes of the ancestors felt like those of a hunter-bird, there were two gazes she pictured that were friendlier.

Garfonis stood with a murmured word and they joined the others in their lessons. Hasefi noticed that Garfonis spent a good deal talking about battle formations before letting the mentors take over and teach their novices new moves.

When sunpeak came and they dispersed, she was so deep in thought she didn't notice Nakilon was with her until she was at the top of the ridge surrounding the Pit.

"Sorry," she told him. Arsolin had come with a pair of hares for them and she absently pawed one towards him.

"It's alright," he replied, watching her intently. Then his expression darkened. "What did Firalos say?"

"Nothing," Hasefi sighed, taking a bite of hare. When she looked up, she saw Nakilon was watching her through narrowed eyes. "What?"

"He's Firalos—he never says nothing. Besides, you looked glum the entire time afterwards." Nakilon's ears angled with sudden embarrassment and he stared at the grass between his paws.

"He thinks I'm gifted," Hasefi admitted. "And he thinks I used it against him."

"Did you tell him you weren't?"

"I wanted to. But he didn't seem to want to listen." Hasefi's thoughts had moved from Firalos to the prospect of war, but she suspected she wasn't hiding her exhaustion as well as she'd thought. She was grateful now that she had tried to talk to the older novice, or else Nakilon might press her about why she was so tired.

"Don't mind him," Nakilon assured her. "I think he's just jealous."

"Jealous?" Hasefi echoed with a sharp, humorless laugh. "Of what?"

Nakilon flinched, his eyes wide.

"I'm sorry," she said immediately, ears flat. "It's just...been a long day."

"Is there anything I can help with?" he asked, concern in his eyes. "I know I'm just a novice...but if there's anything I can do, I'd like to help."

A faint purr rose in Hasefi's throat and she gave his shoulder a grateful nudge with her nose. "I don't think so, but I appreciate that." When she pulled away, she tilted her head, studying him. A sudden desire to tell him everything came over her and she wondered if perhaps he'd be as willing to help her with Kolahn as Salifen, Alarni, and Ivanus were.

Before she could finish the thought, Nakilon slowly shifted, turning his head with a peculiar precision. When he stopped, she realized he was copying her and she quickly straightened herself.

"I like it when you think," he murmured, his eyes fluttering to his paws.

"You...do?" she asked, confused.

"I've never seen anyone tilt their head like that," he continued. "It's funny."

"Funny?"

"I mean, different. It's, uh, it's cute."

"Cute?"

"I'm sorry," Nakilon stammered, getting to his paws. "I'm mumbling nonsense. We should probably get back to the others. I'll meet you there," he added before she could respond. Hasefi was left blinking in utter confusion as the novice disappeared into the trees.

What in all the stars was that about? she wondered. Her tribe didn't offer a direct response, but their amusement washed through her. *What?* she demanded.

"Hasefi?" Garfonis appeared, concern sparking in his eyes when he saw her. But he merely jerked his head towards the clearing. "Ready?"

"Yeah, I'm coming."

When Hasefi was in the Cavern of History, she sat beside Nakilon who seemed to have forgotten entirely about their interaction earlier. As they listened to their mentors, he was his usual self, leaning towards her to murmur a witty comment or joke into her ear and making her struggle to keep a straight face as she pretended to look like she was listening.

Once the lesson was over, Hasefi headed into the clearing, wondering if she'd have a chance to ask her father or perhaps Hesilar or Lisefi about the war. But she didn't have to, as Garfonis joined her in the clearing.

"Did you need something?" she asked.

Garfonis gave her an amused look. "Do I have to need something to be with my daughter?"

"No, of course not," she shook her head. "Sorry, I feel like I'm always on the go."

Understanding flooded her father's gaze and he let out a sigh. "You and me both." He eyed her. "If you need a break, all you need to do is ask."

"As much as I'd love to curl up into a soft, comfy hollow right now, I don't think I can rest until I get Kolahn."

Garfonis nodded as if expecting her response.

Hasefi sat in front of her father, watching him closely. "You were talking about battle tactics in training today."

"Aye," he admitted, not quite meeting her gaze.

"Is Esafi going to announce the war?"

"I don't know," he replied.

Hasefi blinked with surprise. "You don't?"

"She has her paws full," he explained with a shrug. "And war isn't something we've had to prepare for in seasons. But," he added, not quite looking at her. "Preparation is needed." There was a mixture of emotions flitting about his thoughtful expression, making Hasefi wonder what exactly he was thinking.

"You think Esafi should announce it soon?"

"The Tribe is restless," he began carefully. "Kits were killed in our own territory. High Heir or not, such a crime needs to be answered. Even if the real killers aren't known to them." A darkness shadowed his face, twisting his expression with something Hasefi hadn't seen from him before. It sent a shiver through her fur and twisted claws into her heart.

"Is everything okay?" she asked him.

"I don't want you to fight," he said, his dark expression shifting to worry.

"That's not up to you," Hasefi argued, her voice hard.

"You're a kit, Hasefi. Bringing you to a war wouldn't be right. I know you're worried about Kolahn, but I promise I'll make sure nothing happens to him if I can help it." He leaned towards her. "I just don't want you to get hurt."

Hasefi bristled at his words. "I've been hurt," she growled. "Don't you remember what I looked like when I came to you? Have you already forgotten the scars on my pelt?" Hasefi pawed her helmet off, letting her armor disappear. "You know the kind of monsters I've faced —and that's not even all of it!" She intended to continue, but Garfonis's gaze flitted past her and, following it, Hasefi realized she was drawing attention. With a great deal of effort, she swallowed her anger and put her helmet back on, closing her eyes and letting out a long breath.

"Why do you keep them?" Her father's voice was quiet.

"Keep what?" Hasefi asked.

"Your scars?"

She frowned at him. "Because I'm not a soft-furred kit anymore and you need to stop treating me like one."

Hasefi, Sefonis murmured and she quieted, allowing him to speak. *He lost his sons a quarter moon ago. You're all he has and he's trying to do what he can to protect you while he has you here.*

Hasefi deflated. "I'm sorry," she told her father. "I shouldn't be yelling at you. I'm not upset with you."

"I know," he said with a small smile. He was silent for a few heartbeats. "Can I truly not convince you to stay home?"

Hasefi shook her head. "I need to go. But I promise you don't need to worry about me." She held her father's uncertain gaze. "Esafi thinks I'm special because of the prophecy the ancestors gave me," she began carefully. "She's not entirely wrong. There is something special about me. Something that means you don't have to worry about me."

Garfonis's eyes darted back and forth as if he were trying to find the answers on her face. Hasefi's words had made her tribe tense but, instead of asking for further explanation, Garfonis merely dipped his head.

"I know what it's like worrying about someone like you do with Kolahn," he admitted.

"You do?" she asked, tilting her head in query.

"I may have had my pelt fixed, but scars can run deeper than fur and flesh," he murmured.

A pang of sympathy tightened Hasefi's chest, urging her to move close and press her flank against her father's, letting her armor disappear. He did the same and she relished the warmth from his pelt.

"Thank you for understanding," she told him seriously. "All I want is for Kolahn to be safe."

He nodded, lingering at her side for another heartbeat before his armor returned and he got up. "I have some things to tend to before moonrise." His gaze went past her. "I believe the Highchief may have need of you."

Hasefi turned, following his gaze. To her surprise, she saw the Keeper Overlord, Sifara, making her way over. She could also see her own keeper hovering nearby like a wary bee.

"High Heir," the Overlord greeted, sinking into a bow.

Hasefi responded with a curt nod, still not overly fond of her mother's bodyguard.

"May I…speak to you?" Sifara asked, straightening. The black horns on her helmet glinted in the sunlight, curling behind her ears and around so the ends were pointed directly at Hasefi.

"Sure," Hasefi said, confused by the request. "Erm, did Esafi need me?"

"No, I…this is of my own desire."

Hasefi's ears pricked with surprise. The stone-like Overlord's words were hesitant and, though she was much taller than Hasefi, her looming form was suddenly less intimidating. *What could she possibly want to talk to me about?*

"It's about Arsolin," Sifara answered as if she was one of Hasefi's tribemates.

Hasefi had to bite back a growl. "If it's about what happened with my brothers, then don't bother. We've already been over this; I'm not trading Arsolin for another keeper—"

"Yes," the Overlord blurted. "It is about them. But not in the way you're thinking."

Hasefi frowned, tilting her head. "I don't understand."

"I wanted to thank you."

"Thank…?" Hasefi blinked, caught utterly off-guard.

"Arsolin told me of your words to him," she explained. Her head lowered slightly. "I have seen the light in him return since you've come. It has only been a quarter moon and he had been so affected by the loss. But, you've helped him heal."

"I just…did what any lynx would have," she spluttered, baffled by the Overlord's words.

"No." The Overlord's voice changed and Hasefi had no sense of the silent watcher she had seen her as before. "Keepers are trained to control their emotions, but many lynxes believe we learn to forget them. It's easy for them to think that we don't feel. But it's quite the opposite. We do feel. And we rarely get the chance to express that."

"That doesn't seem like a good lifestyle," Hasefi murmured, her mind moving to her own Overlord.

"Being a keeper is a necessary sacrifice for the Tribe," Sifara told her. "Every lynx gives a part of themselves to the Tribe, but keepers give everything."

Hasefi narrowed her eyes, wishing she could see the older lynx's face. "Is he your kin?"

"No," Sifara replied, but she didn't elaborate.

Hasefi narrowed her eyes further, looking between the Overlord and her own keeper a few paces away. "You're mates," she guessed. The Overlord was silent and Hasefi figured it meant she was right. "That's why you care so much."

"Keepers rarely have mates," Sifara said, sounding distracted. "Our duty to the Tribe trumps that of our feelings."

"I don't think that should be true," Hasefi told her. "You should be able to be with Arsolin if you want. Are there rules against it?"

"No, of course not. My apologies, High Heir, but I should return to the Highchief." The Overlord sank into a bow before hurrying off.

Hasefi was left feeling puzzled and didn't realize she had padded over to her keeper until he spoke.

"Hasefi," he greeted with a bow.

When he raised his head, Hasefi touched her nose to the forehead of Arsolin's helmet, making him freeze. "You're a fantastic keeper, you know that, right?" she told him.

"I—" The keeper's voice caught in his throat. Then he relaxed, resting his chin against Hasefi's shoulder as she brushed her cheek along his helmet. "Thank you."

When Hasefi pulled away, she noticed there were a couple gazes on her. She met them and they quickly averted.

It is not often a keeper is openly shown affection, let alone from a highblood, Gelinaf explained quietly.

I think that should change, she said.

"Shall we begin with tonight's training?" she asked her keeper.

"I think we shall," he responded with the rumble of a purr in his throat.

When their day ended and Arsolin bade her goodnight, the sun was still peeking over the trees. Hunger gnawed at Hasefi's belly, but her head was too heavy for her shoulders so she went directly to the Highcave.

Esafi was there, putting away her helmet.

"Daughter," she greeted.

Hasefi didn't reply, hoping to just curl up in the soft feathers and plants that beckoned her from her sleeping hollow.

"Your father spoke to me about the war," Esafi continued.

Hasefi's exhaustion retreated at the words. She straightened, meeting the Highchief's steady gaze. "I'm fighting," she stated. "You can't stop me, even if you've changed your mind."

Esafi shook her head and sat down a few pawsteps away. "Many lynxes passed during Resahn's Reign, especially during the final battle that saw his end. Others have gone peacefully to the ancestors or live their days now as advisors. There are few in our ranks with the experience of combat, let alone against black wolves. The majority of my lynxes are young, the oldest having being kits when the dark times took place."

Hasefi was quiet, wondering if the uncertainty in the Highchief's eyes was something she imagined, so quickly did it appear and disappear.

"Your father believes the lack of threats to my Tribe has made us complacent. And, like you, he believes the Clan is not our priority."

"Well, he's right, in both points," Hasefi replied, a little surprised. "I won't pretend to know more about fighting than the knights or any other lynx in your Tribe, but there's a difference between knowing and experience."

"Aye," Esafi agreed, though her tone was hard. "Which is why you need to let those who have witnessed war plan without hindrance."

Hasefi frowned and was silent, not expecting the Highchief's response.

"Garfonis and I are some of the few left that remember the danger of the black wolves. And we have lived our entire lives with the Clan just across the River." For a heartbeat, her gaze softened. "Garfonis has an empathetic heart; he is the one I trust to ensure my lynxes are happy. But, sometimes, the concerns of others override his better judgement. Especially concerning his kits."

Hasefi recoiled. "You think I'm, what, 'overriding his better judgement' because I'm his daughter? Do you really think so little of him?"

This time Esafi flinched and there was genuine pain in her eyes, but Hasefi was too angry to care.

"Garfonis can think for himself and, honestly, he seems to be one of the few lynxes here that have any sense. I'm done trying to convince you about the Pack—all I want is to get this unnecessary war out of the way since you seem to believe that's the only way to face the Clan so I can get Kolahn and leave!"

Besides her initial reaction, the Highchief showed nothing else on her face to give away what she thought. Then she spoke, her tone even. "After your time here, albeit short time, do you truly still prefer this wolf to your own kind?"

"I, well," Hasefi stammered, feeling trapped by Esafi's word choice. "I wouldn't say that. It doesn't have anything to do with my own kind. Kolahn and I were together for a while. He's my kin through experience. I may have family here, but I don't know anyone. Not really." She shifted her paws, uncomfortable beneath Esafi's narrow stare.

"*Kin*," the Highchief murmured, the word sounding strange with her voice as if she hadn't used it before. "You really have been raised by a wolf."

Hasefi cocked her head in confusion which only seemed to add to the strange expression on Esafi's face.

"You even move like one."

Hasefi straightened her head quickly, thinking of Nakilon's comment earlier that day.

Esafi's expression relaxed and she let out a long sigh. There was something in her expression Hasefi couldn't identify, but when the Highchief turned her yellow gaze on Hasefi, all she could read was a bit of regret.

"I have no intention of trying to keep you here," Esafi admitted. "I may be Highchief, but I am also your mother. Contrary to what you seem to believe, I do care about whether you're happy. And if you don't like it here, then so be it."

"But...what about a High Heir?" Hasefi couldn't stop from asking. "With Mekonis and Talonis...and now me...." She eyed her mother. "Are you...?"

Esafi laughed softly; it was a strange and unexpected sound. "I doubt I'll have another litter of kits. But that will not leave the Tribe without someone to take my place when I pass on."

Hasefi twitched her ears in confusion.

"If the Highchief does not have an Heir," Esafi explained. "The title will move to the next of blood—my siblings or their kits, depending on who remains."

"Do they have kits?" Hasefi asked, unable to suppress her curiosity.

Esafi dipped her head. "Lisefi had a litter moons before I had you." Her gaze darkened. "Only one has survived, though."

"What's their name?"

"Colavir. He's a hunter, like his mother."

Hasefi blinked thoughtfully. *I never really thought about having more family than Sefonis and maybe a mother and father. I didn't even think of brothers, let alone....*

"What would I call him?" Hasefi asked. "I know Lisefi is my aunt and Hesilar is my uncle—what do I call Colavir?"

"He would be your cousin," Esafi told her.

Cousin, she echoed. She focused on Sefonis. *Did you ever have kits?*

No, wee lass, he replied quietly.

"I must return to my duties," Esafi said, bringing Hasefi's attention outwards again.

"Duties?" she echoed, glancing at the cave walls where the magical light was changing from dusk to night. "It's nighttime."

"A Highchief's responsibilities do not disappear with the sun," Esafi said with an amused twitch of her whiskers before padding from the Highcave and leaving Hasefi alone.

For the first time, Hasefi felt sympathy for her mother. *I can barely handle training all day. I can't imagine having to continue duties for even longer.*

A war is no easy thing to prepare for, Sefonis said. *And this will be Esafi's first.*

Hasefi frowned. *What about Resahn?*

Esafi never fought. Her mother kept her safe in case something happened to her. Which...it did.

Hasefi's whiskers twitched with surprise. *Esafi made it sound like she had experience. Should a lynx who hasn't fought before be leading others into a war?*

She has her champions, Kilarsa pointed out. *Myafos has seasons of experience and your father fought during Resahn's Reign. Hesilar healed some of the injured, and Sifara also fought.*

What about Lisefi?

She was held back, too, Sefonis replied.

Did you fight? she asked her uncle.

Aye, I did.

Hasefi could detect that her uncle was reluctant to continue the topic, so she let it go.

There's something about all this that doesn't feel right, she admitted to her tribe.

Aye, her uncle agreed. *Esafi is often secretive about her motives until the last heartbeat. I used to be quite good at reading her, but whatever her endgame is, it's hidden from me.*

Am I in danger?

Esafi cares about you. It was Gelinaf who spoke. *That much is clear. But there is a lot she might be willing to do for the protection of the Tribe.*

That's not very comforting.

Tread carefully, Kilarsa told her. *While I cannot imagine you are in immediate danger, I believe your instinct is correct. Something has yet to be revealed.*

Do you think Esafi might wait to declare war until Kolahn is executed? Hasefi thought suddenly. *Could that be why she's delaying?*

Her tribe's silence alarmed her.

We can't let that happen!

We won't, Sefonis assured her. *Do you recall those pups you saw before you returned to the Tribe? They didn't say anything about an execution.*

Hasefi calmed a little. *You're right. They were scared of Kolahn. Do you think that prophecy they mentioned might be why they're keeping him alive? 'When water recedes, darkness will flow'.*

It is quite possible.

I fear what this 'darkness' might be, Kilarsa added.

Maybe it's just the war. Maybe the Tribe is meant to win. Her words were flimsy, especially since she could hardly believe them herself. *Or perhaps it's not worth thinking about; we all know how my prophecy went.* She straightened, making a decision. *We have four days before the full moon and the novices have another break. If Esafi doesn't announce anything by then, I'm going to check on Kolahn again. But this time, I'm going to get more information.*

Chapter Thirteen

The four days before the full moon passed much more quickly than Hasefi had anticipated. Garfonis had amped up her training alongside the novices and even added some junior knights to refresh their memories on battle tactics. She suspected Garfonis wouldn't normally have the novices so involved, but with her joining the upcoming war, it was the only cover to keep the knights from guessing she would be fighting alongside them. She still didn't like secrecy, but she understood why her father felt the need for this particular reason.

Arsolin kept to her training but, whether obeying orders or acting of his own volition, he, too, changed her lessons to war. Learning of previous battles in the Tribe's history or training in the very basics of combat, she was busy from dawn until dusk.

Before she knew it, it was the night before the full moon.

I haven't even seen Salifen, she thought. *I need the fox tooth if I'm going to the Clan again.*

Though she was ready to collapse and her stomach ached with hunger, Hasefi hurried past the prey-pile and the path leading up to the Highledge and ducked into the Healer's Cave.

"Hasefi!" Hesilar was there, a pair of healers before him. At her arrival, the latter two bowed and hurried off. "To what do I owe the pleasure?" the Sage asked, sinking into his own bow.

"I was looking for Salifen," she explained. "Have you seen him?"

"If I'm correct, he's already retired for the night." He paused. "Did you want me to get him?"

"No, that's alright," Hasefi assured him, hoping she didn't sound too disappointed. "Next time you see him, would you be able to tell him I was looking for him?"

"Of course. Hasefi," he added before she could thank him and leave. "Is everything alright?"

"What?" she blurted, then struggled to recover. "I mean, yeah. Why wouldn't it be?"

Hesilar's eyes were warm as he sat before her. "I'm a healer, lass. I'm trained in ensuring the well-being of my tribemates." His expression was kind and his tone gently inquisitive. "Something is bothering you."

Hasefi was prepared to offer a dismissive answer, but she remembered this lynx was her uncle, just like Sefonis. She sat down, shrugging. "You know my story," she reminded him. "I'm worried about Kolahn."

The Sage smiled sympathetically, showing no sign of the kind of hatred his sisters held for black wolves.

"Aye. It's a heartbreaking situation you're in," he agreed. "But Esafi intends to free him so you may return to your life before. You can trust her word, Hasefi."

His tone was so sincere that Hasefi wanted to believe him. But her suspicion from the last time she had talked to the Highchief was no less prominent in her mind.

"You've been training hard," Hesilar observed. "You should get some rest. The full moon is tomorrow, so you can sleep in."

"Thanks, Hesilar," she said, dipping her head respectfully before she turned and left. Figuring there was not much else she could do, she intended to heed his words. But, as she returned to the clearing and started in the direction of the Highledge, a raised voice caught her attention.

On the adjacent side of the clearing where the log stretched across the ground, a group of novices were standing together, their fur bristling. She recognized Nakilon and Firalos and a couple other novice knights. A frown twisted her lips when she noticed her friend's stance indicated he was facing a threat.

Altering her path, she made her way over to the group, angling her ears so she could catch their snarled words.

"If our mentors were here, they'd cuff you over the ears for saying that!" Nakilon was hissing.

"Is that what you're going to do?" Firalos sneered. "Tell on us?"

"I'm not some tattling kit," Nakilon spat.

"So what are you going to do, then?" one of the novices with Firalos scoffed.

"I'm not going to let you get away with this," Nakilon growled.

"Alright then, do something," Firalos taunted.

Nakilon hesitated, his tail twitching angrily. Hasefi picked up her pace before someone got hurt.

"What's going on here?" she demanded, moving to Nakilon's side. The novice gave her an apologetic look.

"None of your business," Firalos snarled.

"She's the High Heir," Nakilon snapped. "Of course it's her business. Besides—it's about her!"

"So you are telling on us!" Firalos sneered.

"It's late, shouldn't you be going to your sleeping hollows?" Hasefi interjected, stepping between him and Nakilon.

"It's not even curfew," one of the other novice knights scoffed.

"Let me try that again," Hasefi said, leaning towards the three. "Leave. *Now.*"

The novices gave her scornful looks but, when Firalos turned away with a muttered growl, they followed, slinking after him towards the Knight's Cave.

Satisfied they wouldn't be coming back, Hasefi turned to her friend who was staring miserably at the ground. "Are you alright?" she asked him.

"*I'm* fine," he growled.

Hasefi frowned and sat down, blinking questioningly at him when he met her gaze. Nakilon seemed hesitant to speak, but, after a few heartbeats, he let out a sigh.

"Those *cowards* were talking behind your back."

"Does that surprise you?" she asked.

"Well no...but they shouldn't be doing that. If anyone talked about the Highchief that way, they'd be punished."

Hasefi shrugged. "Lynxes can have opinions. They don't have to like me—as long as they don't hurt anyone, it shouldn't matter."

"But what if they tried to do something?" Nakilon asked, looking worried.

"Do you think they would?"

The novice gave a small shrug.

Hasefi smiled sympathetically at him, nudging his shoulder. "Don't worry about them—they're not worth your time." She drew back, blinking warmly. "Thanks for standing up for me."

Nakilon glanced away, giving his chest a lick. "It was nothing," he murmured.

Hasefi let out an amused purr which strengthened when the novice knight traded his frustrated expression for a happy one. Then his ears went flat and he glanced diffidently at his paws.

"Hey, can I—"

"Hasefi!"

Nakilon was interrupted by Alarni who was trotting over.

Hasefi got up to meet Alarni, flashing the novice knight an apologetic glance. There was disappointment in his expression, but he stifled it as he got up to join her.

Alarni eyed Nakilon when the three were together. Hasefi swallowed her guilt as she turned to the novice knight.

"Hey, I'm going to chat with Alarni for a bit, if that's alright."

"Of course," Nakilon replied, though disappointment returned to his face. "I'll see you tomorrow?"

"Yes," she replied.

Nakilon grinned. He started to turn, then hesitated as if he meant to say something, but merely jerked his head in a nod and padded off towards the Knight's Cave.

Looking back to Alarni, Hasefi noticed the novice hunter was still eyeing Nakilon.

"Everything alright?" Hasefi asked her.

"Does he know?" Alarni demanded, turning her narrow stare on Hasefi.

"No," Hasefi replied. "Why do you think I sent him away?"

Alarni seemed satisfied by her words and relaxed. She looked at Hasefi expectantly.

"Erm, was there something you wanted?" she asked the novice hunter.

Alarni rolled her eyes. "I saw you come out of the Healer's Cave. You hardly talk to us, so I figured you were planning something else."

"It's not that I don't want to talk," Hasefi said defensively, unexpectedly offended by the remark.

"I know," Alarni admitted, her expression relaxing. "You look ready to fall over."

Hasefi shrugged, then responded to the novice's previous statement. "You're right. I was hoping Esafi would announce something about the war, but she hasn't and I…I want to check on my friend again.

Alarni's narrow stare returned. "There's something else."

Hasefi opened her mouth to argue, but she knew by the novice's scrutinizing stare she wouldn't be able to get past Alarni without giving her something.

"I'm worried there's more to this war than just what happened to my brothers," she admitted, which was entirely true, if not the intended truth.

Surprise glittered in Alarni's eyes. "Really? Like what?"

"Can I trust you?" Hasefi asked.

"I think I've proved that already."

Hasefi nodded, knowing it was true. "I'm going to fight when it happens."

Alarni eyed her doubtfully. "I can't say I believe Esafi would let you."

"That's just it—she is," Hasefi said. "And I didn't have to fight very hard for that. Plus, she's always gone and it's been, what, a whole half moon since my brothers were killed? If I was in charge, I would have done something by now."

Alarni nodded, agreeing. "Any ideas what she might be planning?"

"No, unfortunately," Hasefi admitted. "Esafi has been surprisingly open with me, which worries me as to what it is she might be keeping from me."

"Welcome to the Tribe, Hasefi," Alarni sighed, then glanced towards the Healer's Cave. "What did Salifen say?"

"I didn't talk to him," Hasefi told her. "He's asleep—I don't want to disturb him," she added when Alarni started getting to her paws. "Hesilar said he'll let him know I was looking for him."

"Good," the novice said. "He'll come to us, then. I'll be with Ivanus tomorrow." A spark lit her eyes. "He's going to be a novice any day now."

Hasefi's ears perked up. "Does he know which Path he's going to follow?"

"Not yet," Alarni said. "But he still has another moon to choose. The first moon is just basic training and history."

"Right."

They fell into silence.

"What if you could help him?" Alarni asked.

"Ivanus?" Hasefi replied with confusion.

"Your friend," she corrected. "If you could get to him rather than just checking on him, would you?"

Hasefi frowned. "I feel like that goes without saying. But I can't risk getting caught by the Clan."

Alarni nodded, uncharacteristically quiet.

"What is it you're not telling me?" Hasefi asked.

The novice hunter's ears went half flat with dismay. "I'm not trying to hide anything," she assured Hasefi. "It's just…." She stared at the ground, her eyes darting back and forth as if searching the earth for the words she needed. "When I was a kit, I was really jealous of Salifen because the ancestors chose him to be gifted. It's not a problem anymore," she added quickly when Hasefi frowned. "Gifted or not, every lynx has their purpose." A sharp intrigue entered her gaze with an intensity that made Hasefi think whatever Alarni was trying to say had been on her mind for a while. "But you were given your own prophecy."

Hasefi's ears went flat as she bit back a retort.

"There's more to your story," Alarni continued. "You haven't told us everything—in fact, you've told us very little."

"You're right," Hasefi admitted. "But there are some things I just can't talk about." To her surprise, Alarni nodded agreement. "I sort of thought you wouldn't be happy with that."

"I don't believe in everything being common knowledge; every creature needs their secrets. I just don't believe in keeping others in the dark. What good does hanging the anticipation of war over the Tribe do? We know it's going to happen. And your friend—no one else knows there's a lynx prisoner in the Clan. Why hide that? But you and your life outside the Tribe, the ancestors led you on that quest. Plus, clearly you don't feel the need to hide things that are important."

"I'm not sure I understand what you're trying to get at," Hasefi replied carefully.

"You're not gifted." Alarni's words were half question and Hasefi confirmed them with a shake of her head. "But you can do stuff normal lynxes can't. Not easily anyways."

"Like what?" Hasefi hoped her dismissive snort was convincing.

"You barreled past a keeper like he was a pile of leaves and the novice knights still haven't stopped talking about how you flew into the Pit."

Hasefi shrugged, unable to meet the novice's inquiring gaze. "I lived out in the wild for most of my life. I guess I have a certain...toughness."

"Mhmm," Alarni replied, clearly unconvinced. "Whatever it is, I think you should take advantage of it."

Hasefi didn't reply, unsure how and unable to even begin trying to explain her situation to Alarni.

Clearly she thinks as highly about the ancestors as every other lynx here. And if word of my tribe gets out there, it could cause more trouble than what's already going on in this tribe.

"Ivanus and I will be by the log tomorrow," Alarni announced, bringing Hasefi out of her mind. "I'll let Salifen know, too."

Hasefi nodded, relieved to move on to a different topic. "I hope we can do this earlier this time," she said. "So we don't have to worry about curfew."

A tiny smirk made Alarni's whiskers twitch, but she merely nodded. "See you tomorrow, Hasefi."

Hasefi returned the nod, watching the novice hunter retire to her respective cave. She sat alone in the clearing for a time, deep in thought.

I can feel your unease, wee lass.

I don't like hiding things, she told her uncle. *I understand not telling anyone about you, but Kolahn...Alarni can't know who he is and that...that I'm going to be leaving. If she knew, she'd probably ruin everything.*

Is that all that's bothering you?

Hasefi hesitated. Then she hardened her mind. *Yes.*

Without another thought, she marched to the Highcave and went to her hollow.

With great difficulty, Hasefi managed to get up much earlier on the day of the full moon than the last time the novices had a break. The Highcave's sleeping chamber was empty, save herself, so she grabbed her helmet and hurried through the tunnels until she was on the Highledge.

The sun had risen above the treeline, casting golden rays through their leaves and creating a pattern of light and shadow across the clearing. Lynxes flitted about; entering and leaving caves, taking prey, standing guard.

She caught sight of her keeper sharing a hare with Sifara. Though they could eat with their helmets on, they had taken them off, allowing Hasefi to see the Overlord's face for the first time.

She was a dark lynx, with pale brown fur and a pretty pattern of dark stripes and spots upon her head. Her eyes were golden and, as she lowered her head to take a bite, they blinked affectionately at Arsolin.

Gelinaf's surprise was stronger than her own.

Your words to the Overlord have had a great effect, her own Overlord observed. *Though I am many moons younger, this is the first time I have seen Sifara thus.*

Look at Arsolin, too, Hasefi added, her heart swelling as she watched her keeper grin with delight at his companion. *He looks so happy. I don't think I've ever seen him like that before.*

As if feeling her gaze, Arsolin's head turned until he saw her. He murmured something to Sifara, then picked up an untouched hare at his side before trotting over to the base of the path leading to the Highledge.

Hasefi hurried down to meet him.

"Sorry," she said when she was on the ground. "I didn't mean to spy."

"No worries, Hasefi," he assured her, lacking his normally calculated keeper's tone. He paused and took a breath, composing himself. "I saved this hare for you."

"You are my hero," she purred. "I'm going to hang out with some friends for the morning, so you can go back to Sifara if you want."

Arsolin dipped his head, blinking gratefully at her before trotting back to where the Overlord was stretching in the sunlight. A smile made Hasefi's whiskers twitch before she picked up her hare and turned away.

At the end of the clearing where the log was, Hasefi could see a pawful of novices. Two novice knights were practicing their moves, while a novice hunter crept forward, hunting a butterfly that was sunning its wings.

Towards the Healer's Cave, the stump that had likely once held the log was crawling with kits of all ages. It seemed they were trying to climb to the top and hold it for their own, but too many adversaries made it nigh impossible.

One kit in particular who was hardly younger than herself sat contentedly a pace away. Ivanus had his ears pricked as he listened to Alarni who was explaining something with enthusiasm. The kit's gaze flicked over to Hasefi as she padded over.

"Good morning," Alarni greeted, turning to face her. "I wasn't sure when to expect you."

"I'm surprised I managed to get up before sunpeak," Hasefi admitted, dropping her hare on the ground. "But I feel rested enough." She nodded to the hare, offering it to both of them. Alarni shook her head, but Ivanus settled across from Hasefi and took an eager bite.

"Alarni said you had another plan," he told her, looking both excited and nervous at the same time.

Hasefi nodded, glancing in the direction of the Healer's Cave. "Have you two seen Salifen?"

"No," Alarni replied, following her gaze. "He retired before we did last night. If you managed to get up, he should probably be up by now, too. Right?" She passed Hasefi an uncertain glance.

"Maybe he's trying to get all the sleep he can," Ivanus suggested. "He does use his gift a lot." Concern rounded his eyes. "You don't think he got into any trouble, do you?"

"If he was, we'd all be in trouble," Alarni said, but her tone wasn't confident.

"Salifen wouldn't mention us," Hasefi guessed. "He'd try to protect us, if he could."

Alarni nodded agreement.

"I can go look for him," Hasefi offered. "Hesilar already knows I'm looking for him."

"No," the novice hunter said. "If he's not in trouble, we don't want to raise suspicion. Let me check on him. They won't wonder why his sister is curious about his whereabouts." Without waiting for a reply, Alarni hurried off to the Healer's Cave, leaving Hasefi and Ivanus alone.

The kit's fur pricked nervously as he watched the novice disappear into the cliff-face. Hasefi spoke, hoping to distract him from his worry.

"Do you want to help me bring these bones to the Guardian's cave?" she asked, gesturing to the cleaned hare bones between them.

"Sure," he replied.

They picked up the remains and moved in silence, unable to speak much with their mouths full. Once they had dropped off the bones, they made their way back and Hasefi tried to make conversation.

"Alarni mentioned you'll be made a novice soon," Hasefi said.

He turned to her, excitement replacing the concern on his face. "Aye. I'm looking forward to it."

"Do you have an idea of which Path you might follow?"

Ivanus looked up, his eyes narrowed thoughtfully. When he returned his gaze to Hasefi, he shrugged. "I think I'll have to see what each Path is like before I know," he admitted. "What would you be, if you weren't High Heir?"

"Me?" Hasefi asked. She tilted her head. "I'd probably be a knight."

Ivanus nodded.

"You don't seem surprised."

"Knights are brave. You're one of the bravest lynxes I know."

Hasefi blinked in surprise, caught off guard by the compliment.

"You also seem really good at fighting, from what the other novices say." His gaze darkened.

"That's not all they say, is it?" Hasefi asked, remembering Nakilon's encounter.

Ivanus gave her an apologetic look.

"Don't worry about them," she assured him. "A few mean words don't mean anything to me."

He smiled, looking relieved.

Movement caught Hasefi's eye and she was glad to see that Alarni was returning with her brother close behind.

"Everything's alright?" Hasefi asked the two when they reached her and Ivanus.

"Yeah," Alarni replied, her tail twitching irritably. "Hesilar doesn't seem to think Salifen needs a break like the rest of us, for some reason."

Hasefi turned her questioning gaze on the gifted novice.

"He had me experimenting with some herbs," he explained, sounding breathless. "I think he's trying to test me."

"What for? Your Healer evaluation isn't for moons," Alarni pointed out.

It is likely Hesilar has detected the power in this young lynx, Dahsefer murmured.

"It could be he knows how powerful you are," Hasefi said before she could stop herself. The three of them looked at her with confusion and she reached desperately to find more words. "I mean, well, you seem like a pretty powerful gifted. Healers don't normally make illusions and stuff, do they?" To Hasefi's relief, Alarni nodded agreement and looked back to her brother.

"It could make sense," she told him.

"You think so?" he asked, looking at Alarni with surprise.

"Why not?"

A sheepish look came onto Salifen's face and he ducked his head. "Well, perhaps it's possible. I mean, Hesilar always wants to be the one to train me. I thought perhaps he suspected what I was doing, but he was like that before I met you." He nodded to Hasefi.

"Either way, we'll need to be careful," Hasefi pointed out. "Clearly he's got an eye on you."

Salifen nodded agreement, then his expression twisted with apology. "Sorry I missed you last night. I asked Hesilar to retire early."

"Don't be sorry," Hasefi told him. "You're probably more exhausted than I am if Hesilar keeps testing your gift."

His sheepish look returned. "It is tiring," he agreed. "But I wasn't sleeping." He eyed her. "I thought you might be needing more help soon, so I added to the fox tooth."

Alarni purred loudly with amusement, nudging her brother's shoulder. "Look at you go! At this rate, you'll be your own champion!"

Salifen's ears flattened with embarrassment, but his eyes glowed.

"That's perfect," Hasefi told the novice, her own purr in her throat. "It's been another quarter moon and I was hoping I could get some information on what the Clan means to do with my friend.

"Won't it be more dangerous in the day?" Ivanus pointed out, nervous again. "If the lynxian patrols don't spot you, won't the wolves?"

"Earlier will be better," Hasefi replied. "But I think I can make it to and from the Clan before curfew if we leave the clearing just before the sun lands."

The kit was doubtful, but he didn't press further.

"Is it the same plan as before?" Alarni asked.

"Essentially. We'll be a bit more prepared this time, though. I want to get to the River when the patrols are changing."

"The fox tooth will be more effective," Salifen announced. "But you'll still want to be careful." He turned to Alarni. "And Hasefi's claw should change your voice, I think." He narrowed his eyes. "But it might be good to test, if we can."

"I doubt I'll be able to go anywhere without Arsolin following," Hasefi admitted, thinking of her brothers. "But I trust you. They worked before—they'll work again."

Salifen nodded, his expression confident.

Looking past the novice healer, Hasefi noticed Nakilon had entered the clearing and was glancing in her direction. He turned away as soon as she noticed, bringing a purr to her throat.

"That novice knight is determined to spend every waking moment with you," Alarni observed, following Hasefi's gaze. There was disapproval in her tone.

"I can have other friends," Hasefi pointed out, wondering why Alarni was intent on disliking Nakilon.

"What if he gets in the way?" the novice hunter replied.

"He won't," Hasefi assured her. "But," she continued, looking to Nakilon again. He was studying something on the ground with great interest. "I should hang out with him, or else he might come looking for me later."

Alarni rolled her eyes with a snort, not replying.

"When the sun touches the treetops, we'll come back here," Hasefi announced, choosing to ignore the hunter novice.

"We'll be here," Ivanus assured her cheerily.

Hasefi looked to Salifen. His head was bowed, but he lifted it to meet her gaze and gave her a jerky nod.

"See you later, Hasefi."

Hasefi murmured farewell and walked over to where Nakilon was pawing at the ground. The novice lifted his head when she approached, allowing the beetle beneath his paw to escape.

"You are not subtle," she purred, giving his shoulder a teasing nudge.

"I'm sorry," he replied, ears half flat, though his expression only showed delight.

"Have you eaten?" she asked him.

"Aye. I was up early; I just got back from being outside." He jerked his head towards the fern entrance, his gaze everywhere but on her.

What is with everyone's weird mood today? she wondered.

"Well, in that case, did you want to do something?" she said aloud. "I wouldn't mind exploring the forest a bit."

"That would be great! I could show you my favorite spot. If you wanted," he added diffidently.

"Yes," she purred. "Come on; I'm just going to let my keeper know."

To her relief, Arsolin was on his own now, sitting dutifully at the edge of the clearing. He joined Nakilon and her as they entered the forest, trailing a few paces back.

They walked in silence for a while, passing slowly beneath the cool shade of the trees while a gentle breeze rustled their leaves. Hasefi let Nakilon lead the way, content to follow. A grateful breath left her mouth when the heaviness weighing on her back lightened, even if only a little.

It's almost like being back beyond the territory with Kolahn, she thought to herself. Closing her eyes, she could almost convince herself that the padding steps beside her were her beloved companion's and the forest they walked through was the one in which his Valley was located.

A soft touch on her shoulder made her eyes snap open. Her nose was hardly a whisker-length away from a tree. Nakilon was beside her, a paw out.

"Sorry," Hasefi mumbled, her ears flicking self-consciously.

"I've heard of sleep-walking, but I don't think that's what that was," Nakilon replied, amusement and concern flickering in his golden eyes.

"No. I just...." Hasefi shrugged, her gaze flicking past him towards the River.

Nakilon sat down, his eyes intent upon her. "That's where you came from, right? From the land above the Clan's territory?"

"Yes," Hasefi replied, sitting with him.

"You miss it."

Not knowing how to reply, Hasefi was silent, unable to meet Nakilon's searching gaze.

Movement flickered in the corner of Hasefi's eye and, to her surprise, she felt Nakilon's gentle paw beneath her chin, urging her gaze back up.

"Can I ask you something?" he said softly, leaning towards her.

Hasefi waited, having no idea what it was he might say.

Nakilon was quiet for a several heartbeats. Then he withdrew his paw and straightened. "Did you have someone? Out there?" He jerked his head towards the River.

"What do you mean?" Hasefi asked, unsure exactly what he was asking.

"Well, I just, I feel like you would be different if you'd been on your own," he explained. His eyes narrowed as his gaze went inward, like he was trying to glimpse his own thoughts as he spoke them. "I know you had your tribe, but, from what it sounds like, you were without them for quite some time. But, I can't help but feel as if you weren't alone."

Hasefi blinked, surprised at how well this novice was able to read her. *Or maybe I'm not as good at keeping secrets as Esafi wants me to be.*

"I don't mean to pry," Nakilon continued. "I just, whenever I'm with you...." He trailed off, his ears going flat.

"What?" Hasefi asked.

"You always look so worried. And...and angry. Not outwardly," he added hastily when she flinched. "Like something inside trying to get out, if that makes sense."

It's like he's in my head with the rest of you, Hasefi thought.

You have a knack for finding clever friends, Sefonis purred. *A burden it may seem at times, but you will not find better.*

Kolahn was clever, too, she thought with an inward sigh.

"There," Nakilon blurted. "That look, right there. Something went through your head, didn't it?" He recoiled before she could respond. "I'm sorry, it's not my business. I'm just—"

"Worried?" Hasefi guessed with a hollow chuckle.

Nakilon nodded, his eyes alight with apology.

"You don't have to be," she assured him with a touch to his shoulder. "I've barely been here a half moon. I'm just...adjusting. It'll take time."

The novice nodded again, though there seemed to be unspoken words in his gaze as he watched her. But he blinked and they left, making way for his usual bright-eyed cheeriness.

"I'll do everything I can to help," he said determinedly. "Before you know it, it'll be like you were always here!" He got to his paws and head-butted her shoulder.

"Thank you," Hasefi purred, batting him with a playful paw.

The novice knight ducked, then bounced away, deeper into the forest. The moment he was gone, the purr in her throat came to a stuttering stop and she felt as if she were being torn in two directions.

I'm checking on Kolahn tonight, she assured herself. *But I need to pass the sunlight.* She looked ahead to where the bushes still shifted with Nakilon's passing. *I can hangout with Nakilon. I can do both.*

Refusing to acknowledge the uncertainty growing in her mind, Hasefi ran after her friend.

The day went by quickly with Nakilon. He showed her a narrow stream that ran from the River into the Tribe's territory and the unknown woods beyond. A bed of pebbles carried the water along, their silvery smooth surfaces glistening in the sunlight that shone down between the treetops.

The land on either side of the stream was relatively flat until, in the direction of the falling sun, one of the banks rose up into a small rock wall with stubborn brambles and bushes clinging to its sides. Facing the River was a little opening where a small lynx could wriggle in. Despite the small entrance, there was room enough inside for at least three full-grown lynxes.

"It's a nice place to sit and think away from everyone else," Nakilon told her when they sat within the shadowy space. "I come here every morning on our break-days, though," he added with a wry glance at the entrance where light was spilling in. "I don't think I'll be doing that much longer."

"You could always ask a gifted to open it wider, couldn't you?" Hasefi pointed out.

Nakilon shrugged. "Gifteds don't usually use their powers for trivial things. Besides, I like this because it's...."

"Natural?" Hasefi suggested.

The novice knight nodded.

When the sun was falling from its highest point in the sky, Hasefi announced it was time for her to return to the clearing. On the trek back, she thought about Nakilon's space and how much it reminded her of the caves she used to dwell in during her time in the high mountains, if not as cold.

I almost wish I was back there, she thought. *Things were tough. But they weren't so complicated.* She glanced towards the River. *It was much better with Kolahn.*

When they reached the clearing, Nakilon bid her farewell. The novice had become suddenly distracted, but he didn't give Hasefi a chance to see if everything was alright. Herself distracted, she put aside her concern for her friend and approached the two lynxes chatting by the log on the far right side of the clearing.

"Where's Ivanus?" Hasefi asked when Salifen and Alarni greeted her.

"He's hanging out with some of the other kits," Alarni replied, glancing in the direction of the tree-stump to her right.

"He is prepared, as are we," Salifen assured Hasefi.

As if his words were a signal, Alarni got up and went to where Ivanus was chatting with a pair of kits not much smaller than he was.

"No idle chat, huh?" Hasefi asked, more put off than grateful by their willingness to go through with their plans.

"I think Alarni is almost as eager as you to save your friend," Salifen admitted, nodding towards the entrance of the clearing.

Hasefi got up and padded with him towards the ferns, a frown on her face. "I appreciate it," she said honestly. "But I'm not sure I understand."

"Alarni likes to be important," the novice healer explained. "You both don't like how little the Highchief and her champions say about the important matters going on around the River, but I think it is for different reasons."

"Wait," Hasefi breathed at a word from her Keeper Overlord. Looking past Salifen, she saw Arsolin coming directly towards them.

Taking on an impressively innocent look, Salifen followed her gaze, watching her keeper curiously.

"High Heir," Arsolin greeted Hasefi with a bow.

"Everything okay?" she asked, hoping she appeared as nonchalant as her companion.

"Aye." He paused and, while Salifen flicked one of his ears uneasily, Hasefi knew her keeper was feeling a bit awkward. "I don't intend to pry, but you haven't eaten since this morning."

Hasefi looked to the sky where the sun had descended to the treetops, casting golden rays and the long shadows of trees into the clearing. She pretended to look surprised, hoping to mask her relief.

"I suppose I haven't." The thought made her belly tighten hungrily.

"We could take something to the Old Oak," Salifen suggested. "I can collect leaves while you eat, I don't mind."

"Are you sure?" Hasefi asked.

"We aren't in a rush." Salifen spoke just a little loudly and, with a discreet glance, Hasefi could see that Alarni's ears were angled towards them.

"There are no hares," Arsolin admitted. "But I will find something to be carried to the Old Oak."

"Thank you," Hasefi purred.

Arsolin bowed and went towards the prey-pile. Hasefi and Salifen waited until he'd chosen a plump ptarmigan, then went out into the trees.

Saying little, Salifen led her in the general direction of the River. It didn't take long before she could hear it through the trees, but the novice healer didn't stop until she could catch glimpses of the running water glinting in the fading light.

Salifen angled their path to walk in the same direction as the water. They were closer to the waterfall than they had been a quarter moon ago, but now they were moving away from it and each step made Hasefi more and more anxious. But it wasn't long before the trees gave way to a clearing that stretched all the way to the waterside.

In the middle of the clearing, a magnificent tree stood, its bole thicker than five lynxes standing together and its branches reaching high and far. She had seen this tree, the Old Oak, before, in her learning of the borders with Arsolin, but it was no less amazing to see again.

"I thought once that the scraggly old pines at the borders of Edgewood were amazing," she murmured, staring at the giant tree.

"It is impressive," Salifen agreed, leading her towards it. "Not to mention its healing properties."

Before he could continue, Arsolin emerged behind them, the ptarmigan hanging from his jaws. He laid it before Hasefi.

"I'll be in the trees," he stated before bowing and slinking back into the lengthening shadows.

Hasefi carried the brown-feathered bird closer to the broad trunk of the Oak and settled before it while Salifen began pawing a loose pile of leaves and bark together nearby.

A silence fell between them as Hasefi ate. Though she was hungry, it was difficult to swallow each mouthful. Every heartbeat brought her closer to returning to the Clan and, with her determination to find any useful information, she was afraid of what exactly she might find.

Salifen was preoccupied with his own thoughts, too, though whether it concerned Hasefi's situation or not, she couldn't say. Neither of them said much when rustling came from the direction she and Salifen had emerged from the trees.

In one smooth motion, Salifen came over to Hasefi, waving a paw and letting a flash of white that wasn't there before fall from it. Hasefi picked up the tooth, put it in her pouch, and hurried off without a word.

Chapter Fourteen

Silence enveloped Hasefi as her mind narrowed with concentration. Her tribe's strength heightened her senses, allowing her to dodge stealthily around her keeper and run swiftly through the trees like a shadow beneath the growing darkness of the forest.

The waterfall was guarded, but the patrol changed almost as soon as Hasefi arrived. While words were exchanged, she crept along the cliff-face where the rock cast sharp shadows in the dusk-light and slunk under the cover of the falling water.

Hasefi came to a sudden halt when something flashed just outside the waterfall on the Clan's side of the River. A wolf in silver armor shifted, their head twitching as if they'd heard something above the crashing of the water.

Hasefi tensed, prepared to run past and rely entirely on Salifen's magic, but the wolf's mouth moved and she realized their attention was on something else.

Can I get a little help? she asked her tribe, angling her ears towards the wolf. Sound rushed to her, but the waterfall silenced all else until she thought she would go deaf with the noise of it.

You're going to have to get closer, Gelinaf told her.

It may not be worth the risk, Sefonis interjected. *Even if you can get past them, coming back will prove more difficult.*

Hasefi made no reply, creeping closer to the exit of the waterfall-path. She was hardly a pace away from the warrior when she stopped, allowing her to see another warrior pacing back and forth anxiously with a third wolf, this one clad in black, watching intently.

Angling her ears again, she was able to pick some words up, this time without the help of her tribe.

"...not much longer, now," the wolf closest to Hasefi called above the sound of the water. "The moon is almost up."

"I hate this," the pacing wolf responded. "I feel like we'll be attacked at any moment." He shook his head as if trying to get rid of a stubborn fly. "We're vulnerable."

"Maybe," the first wolf agreed. "But if the Tribe does come through, Jaylen will warn the Clan."

"That's right," the black-clad wolf answered, puffing his chest out proudly.

"Still, what about us?" the second wolf asked.

"We need to protect the Clan," the first wolf explained. "It's what we're sworn to do. Surely you haven't forgotten?" Her tone wasn't unkind.

"Of course not. I'm just..." The wolf trailed off into something Hasefi couldn't hear.

They're on edge, Hasefi thought. *They know the Tribe wants to retaliate. So why does Esafi wait? That just gives the Clan more time to prepare.*

The wolf before Hasefi shifted, making her go rigid. But the warrior got to her paws and approached her anxious companion.

"I'm scared, too," she admitted, stepping before the pacing wolf and forcing him to come to a stop. "But Lady Eilwyn chose us because she knew we could do this. Besides, the Tribe may never even show up! All they've done is accuse us of stealing prey which isn't even true. I think they're just looking for trouble."

"But you heard the Emperor," the other warrior protested. "He said he'd bring a whole army!"

"Of course he did," the wolf called Jaylen replied, joining the warriors. "He was surrounded. He was just trying to scare us."

"Well...it worked." The second wolf bowed his head and glared at the ground.

A look passed between the first warrior and Jaylen before the latter spoke again. "Would it make you feel better if I scouted the River?"

"No!" the anxious warrior barked. "You can't go alone! What if you go missing, too?"

Missing? Hasefi echoed silently. *The Clan is losing wolves?*

"You think a lynx could catch me?" Jaylen scoffed. "I'm one of the fastest wolves in the Clan!"

"It's too dangerous," the warrior insisted.

"We shouldn't have to be afraid in our own territory," Jaylen growled, his tone becoming defiant. "I won't be more than a few heartbeats." The black-clad rogue turned and disappeared into the shadows of the forest.

The nervous warrior muttered something Hasefi couldn't hear.

"Jaylen's right," his companion said, her tone firm but kind. "We shouldn't have to be terrified in our own home."

No more words came from the wolves. Hasefi strained her ears, wondering if they were speaking more quietly now, but still, she heard nothing. The anxious warrior remained where he was, but he kept looking into the trees, his tail twitching with agitation. His companion was calmer, but she, too, was beginning to glance in the direction Jaylen had gone.

Fallen stars, Hasefi thought. *How long will they be here? Didn't one of them say something about the moon coming up? Maybe they'll be switching out soon.*

Lingering is dangerous, Gelinaf warned. *If one of the Tribe notices fresh fox-scent, they might look in and see you.*

I have to get to the ravine, Hasefi told him. *I hate lying to everyone. I have to do this now.*

There may be little choice, Sefonis responded gravely.

Anger ripped suddenly through Hasefi making her claws curl and scrape against the stone. *There's always a choice! And I've chosen your way, but this stupid war is hanging in the air like a triumphant bird! This is all*

I have to make sure Kolahn is still alive, but every day that passes could be the one where that white wolf decides to execute him! I have to do this! Hasefi drew in a stabilizing breath. *These wolves are worried about the Tribe. Salifen said the illusion was stronger; maybe they won't pay attention to a fox coming through.*

Hasefi, I don't think—

Hasefi wasn't listening to her uncle, but still she hesitated. The anxious wolf had begun pacing again, but now he stopped, peering past his companion into the trees.

Did he see something?

"It's been too long," the nervous warrior said.

"Hush. You're just worrying," his companion responded.

A few more heartbeats passed.

"He should be back by now," the other warrior fretted.

The first warrior didn't respond. Hasefi could see her shifting uncomfortably.

"Should we go after him?" the anxious wolf pressed.

"We can't leave our post unguarded," she pointed out.

"But what if something happened? What if the Tribe is already here and they took him?"

They think the Tribe is taking wolves? Hasefi thought.

"Do you really think it's them?" the first warrior asked, almost too quiet to hear over the waterfall.

"I don't want to think of the alternative," he admitted.

Hasefi's mind darkened. *The Pack is taking wolves. Killing them, no doubt. Does that mean they're already trying to work their plan to take back the River?*

It may be wise to turn back, Sefonis suggested quietly.

No. A low growl rose in Hasefi's throat. *I won't let the Pack keep me from Kolahn.*

"We can't ignore it," the first warrior told her companion, looking both frightened and determined. "We're warriors. If it is the Pack, we need to help fight them off."

"You believe him, then?" the nervous wolf asked. "You think the black wolf might be telling the truth?"

"Why would he try and out his kind?"

"But there's only been lynx scent," he pointed out. "No strange wolf-scents have been found."

Really? Hasefi thought with surprise. *Why would there be lynx scent? Could it be mine?*

Esafi might have spies, Gelinaf explained. *Though normally a gifted can mask their scent—just as yours is—but the Clan also have their own gifted who can detect that.*

Hasefi's fur prickled. *Could they see through my cover?*

Likely.

Then I need to move quickly.

"We need to go," the anxious warrior spoke with the same urgency Hasefi felt. "We can explain what happened to the Lady—she'll understand."

The first wolf hesitated for a few heartbeats before nodding her head. "Okay. But we need to follow Jaylen's trail. He could be on his way back even now." She got up and went to where their rogue companion had left the clearing.

"Or he found something that had to be reported," the other warrior muttered before following.

Hasefi waited until the brush had stopped rustling from their departure even though her paws itched to take her flying out from beneath the waterfall and deep into the forest.

When it looked clear, she stepped out carefully. After a moment to take in her surroundings, she heeded her paws and darted into the trees.

Her tribe's strength and skill took her swiftly and quietly through the brush, no more than a shadow flitting through the forest. She was about halfway to the ravine when a short cry reached her ears. It was cut off almost immediately and she knew she wouldn't have heard it if she hadn't been using her tribe to keep alert for danger.

What was that? she thought, slowing her pace.

Hasefi, it's too dangerous, Sefonis warned.

When did that ever stop me?

What good will it do Kolahn if you aren't alive to help him? her uncle insisted.

I'm not going to die, she growled, frustrated by her tribe's unrelenting hesitancy. *Not while you're in my head.*

Her uncle didn't respond, but she could feel that he was afraid. She was prepared to push forward into a sprint again, but another sound brought her to a full stop. Something heavy fell to the ground, though it was some distance away, back towards the waterfall. She stared in that direction, feeling as if claws were tugging her fur in opposite directions.

We cannot linger, Gelinaf warned again.

An anger directed inwards made Hasefi curl her claws into the earth. "Broken stars," she muttered.

Hasefi....

Something happened to those wolves, she told her uncle. *If I'm right and the Pack is taking wolves like they took my brothers, then I have to do something.*

Her mind made, she ignored the protests from her tribe and snuck back the way she had come. Despite their hesitation, her tribe lent her their strength so her senses expanded further, letting her pick up the faintest of noises, smells, and movement as she prowled through the undergrowth.

There, she thought as a shadow flickered ahead. It was barely noticeable, even with her enhanced state, but she was able to hear soft steps and she followed them. After a few heartbeats, she found a narrow path ahead. She did not use it, but stalked beside it, her eyes searching. Then she caught a glint of light that made her stop.

Armor.

She slunk forward until she could see where the path widened. The two warriors were there, one farther down the path while the other lay between two shadowy figures.

Hasefi's fur rose with anger and fear as she stared at the large black wolves. Seeing them was like walking back into a waking nightmare that had only gotten worse. These wolves seemed bigger than ever and their glaring yellow eyes pierced the shadowy darkness with a malice that crept up her spine.

They're here.

No scent was present as if they were mere ghosts. Upon inspecting them further, Hasefi realized their fur was caked with mud, spiking it and making them look larger.

This isn't some raid, she thought. *This is planned.* Crouching low, Hasefi focused all her attention on the pair.

"Nice work," one of them grunted, nodding at the motionless warrior at their paws.

"You're sure no one heard her?" the other growled.

"She barely opened her jaws. But we should get them out of here, just in case."

The other responded with a grunt, then lowered their head and helped maneuver the lifeless body onto the first wolf's back.

They moved a few paces ahead, where the other warrior lay, and put him on the other Pack-wolf's back. Then they padded quietly through the forest in Hasefi's direction.

She was hidden and they passed without any sign of noticing her. Still, she remained where she was until they were out of sight. Using her other senses, she followed the wolves while also battling the conflicting fear and anger within her.

The Pack is here, killing wolves, she thought. *But something's different. They move like shadows and kill like hunters. I'm not sure if I prefer this or the raging monsters that attacked us in the first place.*

Despite the weight they carried, the Pack-wolves moved effortlessly through the forest, lengthening the distance between them and her. If it weren't for her tribe's strength, she wouldn't be able to hear their receding steps.

I should warn the Clan, Hasefi thought. *Kolahn has warned them, but they clearly don't seem to trust him enough to act. Maybe I can help them realize the real danger they're in.*

The Clan isn't likely to heed the words of a lynx any more than a black wolf, Sefonis pointed out. *Remember Eilwyn's warning when you first arrived.*

Hasefi's ears went flat and she stopped. The black wolves had passed across the dry streambed leading towards the Clan's ravine. *What do I do, then?* She stared in the direction of the Pack-wolves, then turned her gaze towards the ravine. This time the claws pulling her fur in different directions yanked almost painfully until all she wanted to do was curl up and wrap her paws around her head.

I can't ignore the Pack, she thought, thinking of some of the warrior's final words to her anxious companion. *But I can't forget Kolahn, either, even though I know that's exactly what he'd want me to do. If I could just know he was safe, then maybe I can do something about the Pack.*

A sudden light made her look up. The full, bright moon cast the forest with a silver light, making the empty streambed glitter before her. It looked as if stars had fallen onto the path leading to the ravine.

Taking it as a sign, though she knew not which ancestors would offer her such, she drew in a steadying breath and, with a great effort, turned her paws towards the ravine. Each step felt like a betrayal, but to whom, she did not know.

Despite being distracted, Hasefi didn't run into a single wolf, Clan or Pack, as she rounded the front of the ravine and slunk along the edge.

It's almost like the forest is empty here, she thought. *And yet I feel like every shadow has eyes.*

Arriving at the same spot where ferns grew just outside the ravine, Hasefi hunkered down and peered into the open space below.

A guard outside the Clan's prison-den was present, which eased Hasefi a little. She looked about, hoping to find the white wolf, Eilwyn, to overhear anything useful the Lady might say.

A disturbance at the entrance of the ravine sent a burst of adrenaline through Hasefi. She shot up, prepared to see a host of dark wolves pouring into the Clan's home, but it was a single wolf, gray, clad with silver armor bearing a black wolf's print on the chest.

Kowvis, she thought, recognizing the Warrior Alpha from her first visit of the ravine. *I never thought I'd be relieved to see him.*

That thought dissipated quickly, however, as the Alpha marched over to the prison-den, shoving his face into the guard's.

"Bring him out," Kowvis snarled.

The guard hurried away towards a path across the ravine leading up the rocky wall and into a cave.

Wolves were beginning to gather, drawn by the commotion the Alpha was causing.

He wants Kolahn, she thought. *Why? What is he going to do?* Adrenaline still coursed through her, keeping her upright, half out of the ferns. Her muscles were tense, poised to act should there be any sign her friend was in immediate danger.

The guard appeared at the mouth of the cave they'd gone in with a golden-clad wolf following behind. They descended and hurried back to Kowvis. The seer moved close to the wall, a magical pale green glow emanating from them. Then, to Hasefi's surprise, the seer moved into the wall with the guard close behind.

No amount of brute force is going to help me break into that prison, she thought, deflating a little.

When the seer and the guard came back out, Kolahn was between them. Never before had Hasefi's paws yearned to move so eagerly, but she forced herself to stay put with the single thought that, if she acted, she might lose her only chance at getting him back.

She had hardly caught sight of her friend when Kowvis lurched forwards and sank his teeth into Kolahn's scruff, dragging him to the ground.

You mangy dog! Hasefi's mind roared. Before she could act, however, a voice rang through the ravine, sharp even without her enhanced senses.

"Kowvis!" Eilwyn's clear voice cut the air and every head turned to her. She was at the opposite end of the entrance, emerging from a hole behind a tall rock where once had been a waterfall. Her fur blended with the snow-white robes she wore, both a brilliant silver with the moon peeking over the cliff rising high above the ravine. A large gray wolf was at her side, his armor white like hers, but plated. He trotted ahead and shoved the Alpha away, his teeth bared. Eilwyn joined the other wolf, glaring at the Alpha with her uncanny blue eyes. "What is the meaning of this?"

"Two of my warriors were supposed to return with a rogue at moonrise. I went to check on them but the waterfall is unguarded!" Kowvis threw an accusing stare at Kolahn. "Your Pack is doing this, aren't they?"

"So that gives you the right to torture a prisoner?" Eilwyn snapped.

"Wolves are *missing*," Kowvis snarled back, surprising Hasefi.

If any lynx talked to Esafi like that....

"I'm aware!" Eilwyn growled vehemently, making the fuming Alpha flinch. The gathered wolves were silent, looking between each other and the Lady. With her enhanced senses, Hasefi could see the fear in each of their gazes and the hopelessness that sagged their shoulders.

Eilwyn drew in a long breath and sat, composing herself. The white wolf's gaze looked down to the pile of dark fur lying at her feet. Kolahn didn't move and, if it weren't for her tribe's strength, she wouldn't have seen the faint rise and fall of his flank and assumed he was already dead.

He looked okay otherwise, she thought hopefully. *Why doesn't he get up?*

"I know you want answers," Eilwyn murmured, turning every gaze on her. "The Tribe is hostile and the threat of this Pack dangles above our heads. Prey dwindles even as the light of the warm season spreads, and our friends and family are vanishing. Once more, the Clan of the Gray Wolf is flanked with hardship."

The wolves bowed their heads with defeat. Some gazes were dark with memory while others were alight with a terror of the unknown.

This isn't a Clan that can fight back, she thought suddenly, sweeping her gaze through the ravine. It was likely more wolves were hidden in the caves, but she was sure that many of the Clan were about now, listening to the Lady.

There were hardly thirty.

A war would ruin them, she thought. *No wonder those wolves were so terrified. Not even their own home is safe anymore and they hardly know why.*

"Things may be just as bad as they were before my brother's reign, perhaps worse," Eilwyn continued, taking Hasefi's attention again. "And it's easy to think that the darkness of his rule may return. But Resahn was defeated. The Clan pulled through once before. I know that we can do so again."

Some of the wolves nodded and murmured agreement, but many remained dejected.

"We are strong," Eilwyn continued. "Our history is laden with hardship, but we are still here. And we are not alone. Even now, the light of the full moon shines upon us. The Watchers are with us."

"Will you sing, my Lady?" a wolf whispered.

"Yes, Ahlkir," the white wolf said. "I will sing."

The guard and the seer hovering over Kolahn moved to grab the black wolf, but Eilwyn stopped them.

"Fetch him prey and let him listen," she told them.

The guard did as she bade while the seer remained at Kolahn's side. Hasefi's friend still hadn't moved, but when the guard returned with a young mountain sheep, he lifted his head.

The small movement sent a relieved thrill through Hasefi. For once, she was grateful towards Eilwyn.

He's being fed, at least, she thought. *I can't imagine she'd waste prey on someone she intended to execute anytime soon.*

As Kolahn picked slowly at his food, the guard and seer sitting dutifully on either side, Eilwyn moved to the tall rock at the end of the ravine. There was a spiral path going up the sides until it reached the top where it was flat and big enough for a pair of wolves the sit with space to move. There, Eilwyn and the other white-clad wolf sat, their gazes turned on the full moon above.

"Watchers, give me strength," Eilwyn breathed, only loud enough for her companion and Hasefi's enhanced ears to hear. Then she tilted her head back and opened her jaws in a lone, forlorn howl.

I howl, I howl, to the full moon this night,
To the bright white light of the ancestors.
Full moon, full moon, hear my words this night.

A claw of grief tore Hasefi's heart. The words were almost exactly as Kolahn had sung them all those moons ago. She saw herself back in that pit, dragging herself half dead to the edge just to hear the eerie voice. He had been singing for her, praying his ancestors would give her strength. And perhaps they had, else she may not be there at all.

Eilwyn's next words, however, were different and, though Hasefi was wrought with the lingering thoughts of the Pack and her desperation to save her friend, a calm peace settled over her, allowing her to relax until she was settled comfortably at the edge of the ravine.

Once more through darkness we strive,
Wondering when we might thrive,
Like the ages of old,
Where once we stood bold.
So I ask this night for your light;
Shine upon us so that we may see,
Our future bright for which we fight,
And wolves once more stand free.

Suddenly all the surrounding wolves, save Kolahn, lifted their heads to the moon and added to their voices to the Lady's.

We howl, we howl, to the full moon this night,
To the bright white light of the ancestors.
Full moon, full moon, hear our words this night.

Once more Eilwyn sung, repeating the next set of words, and so the howling continued. Hasefi was moved, drawn by the beauty of their high voices, and stricken with grief by the desperation in each note. Yet, still, a strange calmness continued to roll over her and it seemed the same fell over the ravine below, for the howling voices gradually lost their pleading notes, strengthening with a resolve building now, too, in Hasefi.

Could it be the Watchers? she asked no one in particular as she looked up to the moon. It was barely over the cliff-face towering high above the ravine, but it was nearly at its highest point in the sky.

I've been away a long time, she thought, though she remained tranquil, unable to be disturbed by worry or fear, even concerning the Pack.

Looking to Kolahn, she saw that her friend had forgotten his meal and was watching, enraptured by the voices of the Clan. Without seeing his face, she knew every part of him wanted to join, but he was silent.

As if on some unspoken cue, all the wolves grew silent, their voices echoing upon the rocky walls. Then the white-clad wolf sitting with Eilwyn raised his head once more and his lone howl rose high into the night air.

The night grows old, we cease our howling,
Thank you, full moon, for listening.

Silence descended upon the ravine once more, though the air felt charged with a reassuring strength. Hasefi almost felt as if she could walk down into the Clan's home and pick up Kolahn without hindrance. By the sparkling gazes below, she knew the same confidence burned within each of the wolves below as if all that had heard the howled words were blessed by the Watchers above.

Then the wolves got up and, without further words, departed, some disappearing into caves, other returning to duties. Kolahn's guards urged him back into the prison-den, their movements gentle. For a heartbeat, Hasefi saw his face and, like the others in the ravine, saw the heartened look in his eyes. Yet, just like in her own heart, a shadow hung there. No amount of mystical confidence could erase the darkness looming so frightfully near. But, for once, Hasefi didn't feel so afraid of Kolahn's fate.

Maybe there doesn't have to be a war, either, she thought hopefully. *Maybe there's a way this could all end peacefully.*

She thought again of her request to Esafi to somehow join forces with the Clan to face the Pack. Saying it then, even she had felt the flimsiness of the idea. But sitting there now, the thought didn't seem so impossible. *If Esafi would just talk to Eilwyn, maybe things could work out. We can defeat the Pack once and for all and I can get Kolahn.*

She stifled a long sigh. The strange comfort brought by the wolves' singing remained, but the reality of what lay directly before her was not forgotten. Returning her attention to Eilwyn and her companion, she watched the two descend the tall rock only to sit at its base, heads close together.

That is Lord Morvak, Sefonis explained when Hasefi wondered of his significance. *Eilwyn's equal and mate.*

Hasefi angled her ears towards the pair, straining to hear their hushed words.

"I'm lost, Morvak," the white wolf was sighing. "I don't know what else I can do."

"We are strong, as you said," the Lord told her. "But we may need a different strength if we are to pull our Clan out of these dark times." His words were slow as if emphasizing some sort of meaning, but the Lady's gaze only darkened. "Perhaps you should talk with the Seer Alpha."

"I have," she breathed. "So many times. But all he has are prophecies of misfortune." Eilwyn hung her head in utter defeat. Somehow, it seemed she had been untouched by the mystical calm bestowed upon the ravine. "I never asked for this."

"I know," Morvak said gently, giving her shoulder a soft touch with his nose. "But I am here, to bear whatever burden I may."

Eilwyn looked up and, though her gaze was filled with affection, it was the same kind Hasefi might give to Kolahn, an expression of love given to a loyal friend.

"Ever strong, even in such dark times," she murmured. "You are my strength."

"And you, mine, Eilwyn. We will get through this." Morvak lowered his head a little, his tail twitching once. "Have you decided what to do with Kolahn?"

"No," Eilwyn admitted, her shoulders sagging again. "How can I?" She looked towards the prison-den, looking unexpectedly torn. "I had hoped to end the blood and death of my brother's rule by banishing his kind. And yet they kept coming, and now their darkness has returned."

"If Kolahn speaks truth," Morvak pointed out gently.

"I believe him and so do you," Eilwyn growled softly. "But I cannot let him go, nor can I have him...." She shook her head.

"Action must be taken soon," Morvak urged. "Wolves are missing and lynx scent is all over our territory beyond the Rockmead. We cannot take both."

"Can we take even one?" Eilwyn whispered.

Morvak lowered his head a little, hesitating before he replied. "We will have to try."

Eilwyn closed her eyes. At length, she opened them, seeming to have come to some sort of decision. "Okay," she sighed. "I'll talk to Lirvas. Maybe he will have cheerier words this night."

The two parted. Eilwyn disappeared into the cave the seer had come from before while Morvak retreated into the one behind the tall rock. Still under the spell of the Clan's song, it was some time before Hasefi felt the need to leave. Her tribe, too, had eased, forgetting their urgency.

Kolahn is okay, she thought. *And I don't feel like Eilwyn has any intention of harming him. But I can't be certain.* Though she felt calm, the reality of her situation was as present as ever. *The Clan can't handle a war. I'd get Kolahn back, but I can't leave them for the Pack.* She bowed her head, seeing her friend's expectant gaze in her mind. *He'd want me to stop them. I have to do this. For him.*

She lifted her head and looked into the ravine again. The activity had quieted. The wolves still about were relaxed, but alert. Hasefi realized she was lying casually within the ferns of her hiding place, not well concealed at all.

Getting to her paws, she crouched, preparing to leave the ravine's edge and make her way back towards the Tribe's side of the River.

Eilwyn seems reasonable enough, she continued to herself. *I wasn't expecting that. But if I could just convince Esafi to talk to her, maybe we can avoid this. Or perhaps Garfonis could help....* Hasefi slunk out of the ferns, hurrying along the narrow strip of grass and back into the trees. No signs of wolves of any kind were present and she continued quietly towards the River.

The Pack's presence is strong here, Kilarsa observed.

They hide their scent, Gelinaf added. *They move in darkness. A plan is in motion.*

The *plan,* Hasefi said to them. *The same plan Kolahn sought to warn the Clan of. But even if they were willing to act on his word, there's not much they can do. We have to help them, somehow.*

Esafi is not fond of the Clan, Sefonis pointed out.

I know. But maybe she hates black wolves just a little more. She's scared of them, that much is clear. Maybe I can play on that. I...can't exactly tell her they're here now. That would risk Salifen and the others.

Such a risk may not seem like much in the face of this particular evil, Kilarsa pointed out.

Maybe. But I still have some options to try. I think, she continued slowly, intrigued by the direction of her next thought. *I'll talk to Salifen first to see what he thinks. I trust him.*

First, you must return to the Tribe, Sefonis said. *The Clan may not have guards, but the Tribe certainly will.*

There really isn't any other way across the River?

Not that we are aware of, he replied.

I have an idea, Dahsefer, Hasefi's Healer Sage, spoke up suddenly. *Though I'm not intent on being the one to see it through.*

Out with it, then, Kilarsa purred.

While we are bound to Hasefi, the Sage began, *we can still walk the physical world in our ethereal forms. Ghosts are not unheard of...perhaps we could create a distraction.*

Aye, because a starlight lynx dashing out of the waterfall is less surprising than a fox charging into it, Kilarsa snorted softly.

No, Gelinaf agreed, his voice soft. *But it could redirect attention and, additionally, take minds off the Clan for a time.* Hasefi's tribe directed their attention to the Overlord as Hasefi continued towards the waterfall. *Not every lynx believes in ghosts,* Gelinaf continued. *But they do believe in the ancestors. This won't be something a gifted can conjure. A strange fox raises suspicion against lynx and wolf. A sighting of a ghost or ancestor is something else entirely.*

I don't think I'll be returning to the Clan like this again, she said to her Tribe. *This may be the last time we have to get past the guards.*

It is dangerous, Sefonis warned. *Not just because of the potential discovery of us by the Tribe, but of how the ancestors may retaliate.* His unease was almost enough to overcome to peaceful state still lingering in Hasefi's mind. *They have been quiet, but I fear that may prove for the worst.*

Well, I don't know how to stop the ancestors, Hasefi pointed out. *So there's no point in worrying about them. What I can do is try to stop this war and turn these lynxes and wolves to the real enemy.*

You are our Highchief, Sefonis conceded. *We will follow.*

Who is the fastest? Hasefi asked her tribe.

I will run. Tenarli, her Huntmaster, spoke. *Once you are free of the guards, I will find you.*

Are you sure? Hasefi asked. *I might have to take a detour in order to avoid them. I could go anywhere.*

Our bond to you pulls us. It was Sefonis who spoke now. *We will always be able to find you.*

Alright, then. Hasefi came to a halt. The wolven side of the waterfall-path was empty. *After you.*

A flash of bright white light passed before her, forcing her eyes into a narrow squint. Tenarli stood before her, green and brown armor decorated with starlight. Her golden eyes blazed with silver.

"These lynxes are about to get quite the fright," Tenarli chuckled over the roaring of the waterfall. Then, without another word, she sprang into the path behind.

Hasefi followed, keeping to the darkest shadows as they danced like black flames around Tenarli's glowing figure.

The Huntmaster flew out from behind the waterfall and burst into the clearing where two keepers and a knight were keeping watch.

The knight let out a cry and crouched like cornered prey. One of the keepers went rigid while the other leapt into action and pursued Tenarli. They disappeared into the forest, silver light glittering strangely beneath the treetops.

The frozen keeper snapped out of their shock and pelted after them. The knight remained where they were, claws deep in the earth and eyes wide.

Hasefi was able to sneak past undetected, following the cliff-wall and slipping past the terrified knight. When she was in the trees, she ran towards the Old Oak.

Tenarli's light flashed through the trees, but it only grew fainter. Hasefi slowed as she neared the spot where she had left Salifen and Alarni, knowing she couldn't risk them or Arsolin seeing her star-fused tribemate.

Just as she began to think she might have to go after the Huntmaster, the silver light strengthened and the sound of rapid steps approached. Tenarli sprang out of the brush nearby and washed over Hasefi with a flash of blinding light. Hasefi flinched, blinking, trying to adjust to the sudden change in light and darkness.

That keeper will be running circles until the sun rises, the Huntmaster gasped.

What about the other one? Hasefi asked, hastening to the Old Oak once more.

You do not catch prey by hesitating, Tenarli purred.

Hasefi responded with her own purr, but it died in her throat as she emerged into the clearing where the massive oak stood beside the River.

They're not here, she almost said aloud.

Her tribe's strength poured into her as she scoured the clearing. She had hardly taken a few steps, however, when Salifen stumbled before her.

"Salifen," she gasped. "What's going on?"

"The Highchief," he replied, his voice steady despite the alarm on his face. "She sent a keeper out for you. We tried to stall for as long as we could—"

"How long ago was this?"

"Alarni is with the Highchief." Terror turned Salifen's words into a hiss.

"Broken stars!" Hasefi gasped.

"Your keeper didn't seem to see through the illusion," Salifen continued, making an effort to control his wavering voice.

"Then I can't go back, not while there's a chance Alarni can get out."

"We have a plan," Salifen agreed. "It's not much, but it's the best we can do. If Alarni's cover isn't broken, she's going to feign being sick and slip through the burrow. We need to wait here."

"What about you?" Hasefi insisted. "It's past moonpeak. Shouldn't you be back?"

Salifen shook his head. "I'm just an herb-gatherer," he said. "I get overlooked."

"You should go back," Hasefi pressed. "That way, if something goes wrong, you have a better chance of getting out of it."

The novice shook his head again. "If Alarni is caught any gifted can read that the illusion uses my magic. Besides, I can't just leave you here."

Hasefi let out a small breath, but the tension inside her was only growing.

Is there anything we can do?

No, Kilarsa replied. *All we can do is wait to see if she is discovered. But Hasefi, if any gifted come upon her....*

Right. Okay. Well, whatever happens, we can deal with it. But this doesn't change the fact that the Pack is roaming just across the River. Maybe I can try and work this out while we wait, instead of just sitting here wide-eyed and waiting.

"The Pack," Hasefi blurted.

Salifen's frightened expression was mingled with confusion.

Taking a moment to try and calm herself, Hasefi drew in a breath and sat. "If we have to wait, then we may as well do something with our time," she explained.

The novice gave a tiny nod, fear still bright in his wide gaze.

"I haven't told you everything," Hasefi continued. "My tribe, they were killed by black wolves."

Salifen's eyes went even wider. "Like...the ones that nearly drove the Tribe from the River?"

Hasefi nodded. "They're back. They were hunting me until maybe a moon ago. Or maybe they're still looking for me. But they're here now and they want revenge on the Clan."

The novice healer's ears went flat. His eyes darted back and forth, studying something only he could see. Whatever it was, it gave him a confidence that straightened his hunched shoulders.

"The Clan can't take a war," Hasefi continued, holding his gaze. "Nor do they deserve one. Everything the Tribe thinks the Clan is doing, is just the Pack."

"What do we do?" Salifen asked.

"I'm not sure," Hasefi admitted. "But I need to find a way to convince Esafi to call off the war and tell the Tribe about the Pack. She thinks it's too much for them to handle but...even if it is, what is keeping them in the dark going to do?"

"What about the champions?" Salifen offered. "If you can't convince Esafi, maybe they can."

Hasefi shrugged. "Why would they listen to me?"

"Because I think they agree with you."

Hasefi blinked, surprised.

"At least Hesilar does," he continued. "I hear him mumbling sometimes. I didn't know about the black wolves being back, but he did mention 'the Pack' and he seems to think going against the Clan is unwise."

"I think Garfonis is the same," Hasefi stated, heartened by this discovery. "But they seem too afraid of Esafi to do anything."

"Could you talk to the other champions?"

Hasefi twitched her ears doubtfully. "Lisefi seems a lot like Esafi and Sifara is hardly ever apart from her. That just leaves...." Hasefi shuddered, thinking of the Guardian Elder and his eerie, lingering stare.

"Esafi is often with Myafos," Salifen said. "She listens to him. But I have no idea where he stands. In fact, I don't know much at all about the Elder." Salifen looked just as uncomfortable as Hasefi felt.

What about you? Hasefi asked her tribe, unbothered by the novice healer's gaze intent upon her. *What can you tell me about Myafos?*

Not much, Kilarsa admitted. *He has changed little even since I was a kit. He's always been a mysterious figure in the Tribe. He has seasons of experience and powerful magic, spending most of his time advising the Highchiefs or studying.*

Aye, Sefonis, who was the oldest of Hasefi's tribe, added. *Myafos has always been present. But he keeps to himself, when he is not advising.*

He might be my last chance, then. I'll have to try.

Rustling sounded. Salifen jumped from the ground and scrambled over to Hasefi, his flank pressed against hers as he cowered. Hasefi lifted her head, determined to face whatever consequences awaited.

The lynx that emerged into the clearing was foreign to Hasefi at first. They wore silver and black armor with a pouch on one shoulder. The face was gray, with three lines stretching from brow to cheek across the nose.

"Alarni!" Salifen gasped, collapsing. "Thank the stars!"

"It worked?" Hasefi asked, finally comprehending that she was looking at herself.

"Aye, so it seems." The voice that came from Alarni was also strange to Hasefi's ears, yet with an uncanny familiarity.

Is that my voice?

Quite close to it, Kilarsa replied, her tone thick with fascination. *Your novice friend has quite the talent.*

For a guardian, Dahsefer interjected. *Still, I wonder why he chose the Path of the Healer.*

Alarni lifted her leg and grabbed something with her teeth. As she tossed Hasefi's enchanted claw, the illusion vanished, returning Alarni to her normal self.

Realizing she still had the fox tooth, Hasefi took it from her pouch and pawed it over to Salifen.

"There's a lot that needs to be said," Hasefi said to Alarni. "But I don't think we can risk that right now."

The novice hunter nodded. "You'll want to go through the burrow. It's beneath the roots of the maple tree growing on the side of the clearing towards the River. It's easy to miss, but its under the maple."

With a quick nod, Hasefi bounded away, summoning once more the strength of her tribe.

She reached the clearing's borders quickly, using her tribe's knowledge to find the tree Alarni indicated. It stood on a tall, narrow trunk and spread its branches above wide, its green leaves turned silver in the bright moonlight.

Beneath its bole, twisted roots had been uncovered by the earth falling away down the gentle slope leading to the Tribe's home's borders. If Hasefi hadn't been looking for it, she wouldn't have noticed that the space between two of the spindly roots was actually a compact tunnel curving into the ground. She dove into it, her armor sending small tumbles of dirt falling around her.

After clawing her way through, she emerged into the private spot of the clearing where lynxes relieved themselves. The tunnel was just as difficult to see here in the dim lighting. Shaking her pelt, Hasefi left the space and entered the clearing, hoping she didn't look as tense as she felt.

"High Heir?"

Hasefi nearly jumped out of her pelt as a keeper approached.

"Is everything alright?" they pressed.

"Yeah, sorry," Hasefi gasped, making an effort to smooth her fur. "You startled me is all."

The keeper leaned towards her. "You were in quite the hurry," she explained. "Are you feeling well?"

Hasefi took a small breath in and let it out. "I am now, yes," she assured the keeper. "I must have eaten something."

"Would you like me to fetch a healer?"

"No," Hasefi said, wincing when it felt a little too quick. "I'm fine now."

The keeper was silent, the eyes of her helmet directly on Hasefi.

"I should return to my sleeping chamber," Hasefi continued with a yawn. "Early training tomorrow."

To her relief, the keeper sank into a parting bow, murmuring goodnight. Trying not to hurry, Hasefi went to the path leading up to the Highledge. When she passed through the Highcave and used her Tribe's strength to determine the cave system was empty of Esafi or any other lynx, Hasefi ran through the tunnels until she was in the empty sleeping chamber.

Too close, she thought, collapsing into her bedding. *That was too close.*

I do not think we are out of danger yet, Sefonis warned. *The consequences of tonight may yet be revealed.*

Let's hope it worked out, despite everything. I'll get the chance to talk to Alarni tomorrow. Hopefully whatever Esafi said to her doesn't come up again until after then.

Chapter Fifteen

The next morning came too quickly. If it weren't for Garfonis waking her, Hasefi was sure she would have laid like the dead until someone else found her. Her tribe offered to give her the strength needed to get up and make it through the day, but she refused, knowing she'd have to recover on her own, especially if she wanted to preserve the precious strength of her tribemates.

However, when she made it to her paws, she could go no further.

Her father was immediately worried, seeing through any mask she tried to put on to ease him. Even after admitting she was out late with Salifen, he was unconvinced, so she tried another direction as she tried to step out of her hollow.

"I wasn't feeling well last night," she told him, trying not to wince as she lied. "I felt better after a trip to the private-bush, but…." She shrugged.

"Have you seen a healer?" he pressed.

"No."

"Then I will send your keeper to fetch one."

"I'm fine," Hasefi insisted, wondering if a gifted could somehow discover the true nature of her exhaustion. "I just need some rest."

"It's better to be safe than sorry," Garfonis argued. "Even if it is nothing, at least we will know." Before she could respond, he hurried off into the tunnels leading out.

Hasefi wanted to collapse, but she knew she wouldn't be able to get up again if she did. Her mind spun and she felt as if she were lifting the weight of a boulder. Her formerly broken leg was as strong as the others now, but they all shook, protesting greatly against her own weight. Despite it all, she tried to come up with a plan to get through the day without rousing suspicion.

Maybe if I can get away and just rest for the day, I can avoid any interactions until I can talk to Alarni and Salifen.

Eyes will be on you, Sefonis warned. *It may be better to stay away from them for a time.*

Perhaps not, argued Gelinaf. *Hasefi has spent much time with them, especially the novice healer. To suddenly avoid them may be seen as strange, too, at least from a keeper's point of view. Not to mention whatever information Alarni has is too important to delay.*

Aye, Sefonis conceded. *But be wary, wee lass,* he added to Hasefi. *My instincts tell me the rising tensions are nearing their peak.*

Hasefi nodded, looking to the tunnel her father had disappeared down. It felt like an eternity since he had left. She was wondering how long she could stand before her legs gave out when he appeared again.

Setting his helmet aside and letting his armor disappear, he returned to her, concern twisting his expression.

The strength of Hasefi's legs failed just as he reached her. With impressive speed, Garfonis used his shoulder to hold her weight, keeping her upright.

"Don't sleep," he told her, trying to nose her onto her paws. "Not yet."

"Sorry," she said through a massive yawn. "But I promise I'm fine." She bent her legs beneath her, settling on the ground. She was aware of her father's voice beside her and warm fur brushing her own, but in her head it was Sefonis curling up beside her. With a purr, she lowered her head, her nose filled with the comforting scent of family, and drifted off into a deep, dreamless sleep.

Hasefi. Hasefi, wake.

Hasefi's eyes slowly opened to slits. Golden brown fur filled her vision. Her father's scent was strong in her nose. But it wasn't his voice she'd heard, if similar. Opening her eyes further, she could see

Garfonis was settled with his head up and his eyes closed, his breaths coming softly.

What happened? Hasefi asked her uncle.

The day has passed, he explained. *The sun nears the treetops.*

Hasefi lifted her head in surprise, alerting her father. His eyes opened and he turned to her, relief and worry mingling in his gaze.

"Hasefi, you're awake." His eyes darted back and forth as he studied her. "How do you feel?"

"I'm okay." She blinked, confused by his concern and why she had slept so long. It was a few heartbeats before her mind caught up. When it did, she had to make an effort to stifle the urgency and apprehension that suddenly flowed over her. "I'm feeling better."

"Good."

Hasefi jumped at the sound of Esafi's voice. She whipped her head around to look at the Highchief. It was impossible to read her expression, though Hasefi thought that might be a good sign.

"Sage Hesilar said you've been overworked," Garfonis explained, giving her ruffled fur a fatherly lick. "I'm sorry. I should have paid closer attention."

"Nay, you were following orders." Esafi's expressionless visage softened. She padded over and sat beside the hollow where Hasefi and Garfonis were curled up. "I have given you a schedule only the most committed lynxes could follow," she said to Hasefi.

They didn't find out about you, Hasefi thought with relief.

We are still in dangerous territory, Gelinaf reminded her. *There is still daylight left. Your friends will be looking for you.*

Hasefi gave a mental nod, then returned her attention to her parents.

"Though," Esafi continued, studying Hasefi closely. "Late nights don't help."

Hasefi said nothing, turning her gaze straight ahead. Exhaustion still tugged at her and she would have been happy to sleep until the next morning if it weren't for her need to get to her friends. She did not have the energy to play the Highchief's games.

"A strangeness has fallen over you," Esafi observed, bringing Hasefi's attention back to her. "Last night you were not yourself and today you are silent."

"What do you want me to say?" Hasefi asked. "You know what I want." Silent, deadly shadows entered her mind, reminding her of what she had witnessed just last night.

"I do," Esafi replied. "And you do not have to wait much longer for it."

Alarm drove Hasefi to speak. "Wait. I don't think—"

"Let me finish," the Highchief said, lifting a silencing paw.

Hasefi swallowed an irritated hiss.

"My champions and I are nearly ready to take the first steps into war with the Clan. I will be announcing it before the shrinking halfmoon; I intend to bring battle to the gray wolves on the night of the dark moon."

Shock rendered Hasefi speechless. Naught but a halfmoon was all that lay before the war she had been anticipating, yet now it was fear and not relief that struck her.

They can't go to war.

"What was it you wanted to say?" Esafi asked.

I have to convince her to stop this, Hasefi thought. *But I don't want to say too much in case whatever happened last night comes up and I put Alarni and the others at risk.*

Talk to them now, Sefonis told her. *There is time yet to talk to Esafi.*

"Daughter?"

"Forget it," Hasefi said to the Highchief. "Can I go?"

"The day is nearly over," Esafi replied with narrowed eyes.

"I know. But I promised my friends I'd see them today and they're probably worried about me." Hasefi rose slowly from her bedding, trying not to wince at the stiffness in her legs.

"Their concern can wait," Esafi said. "It's clear your still need rest."

"I slept for an entire day," Hasefi argued. "Sitting here miserable isn't going to make me feel better." She flattened her ears, aware of her father's nearby presence. "Not that I don't like being with you," she added to him.

But his gaze was focused on Esafi with an expression that Hasefi couldn't understand. It wasn't a hostile look, but something burned in his eyes as he looked at the Highchief. He stood, too, and spoke before Esafi could respond to Hasefi's words.

"Let her go see her friends."

"Are you giving me orders, Emperor?"

"No," he replied, though his tone was still firm. "But neither do I speak as one right now. You are my Highchief, Esafi, but you are also my mate and in that we are equal." Garfonis looked to Hasefi. "Our daughter is capable of making her own decisions." He looked to Esafi again. "But if you insist on overriding them, then I will make my own." Sorrow and grief entered his gaze and his words came more softly. "I know why you want to keep her close. Only half a moon ago we lost our sons. Hasefi is not going to be here for long—we should be grateful for the time we have with her instead of trying to control it."

Hasefi was expecting anger from the Highchief, but Esafi's gaze darkened as if some shadow had passed through her mind. There was uncertainty in her eyes, but it changed suddenly, masked once more by impassiveness.

"I expect you before curfew," Esafi said finally to Hasefi.

Surprised and unsure if she should be pleased or worried by her father's willingness to stand up for her, Hasefi hesitated before dipping her head awkwardly and stumbling towards the tunnel.

"I'll be back," she mumbled before hurrying out.

The tunnel was empty, so Hasefi burst into a run, ignoring the protest of her stiff and sore limbs.

Just before the entrance, she slowed, and padded casually out onto the Highledge. Immediately, her gaze caught the golden gaze of Alarni where she was with her brother near the prey pile.

Resisting the urge to run down, Hasefi lowered herself into a stretch before trotting down the path to the ground.

Buzzing with apprehension, she finally reached the siblings.

"Hasefi." Salifen's tone was carefully calm as he greeted her with a welcoming twitch of his ears. "It's good to see you."

"Is Ivanus around?" Hasefi asked after offering Alarni a nod.

"I told him to hang out with the other kits," the novice hunter said, jerking her head to where the younger lynxes were playing at the edge of the clearing by the stump. "I was hoping we could go for a walk before the sun lands." Her words were even, but her gaze was intense.

"Sure," Hasefi told her, wondering if it would upset the Highchief if she left the clearing. "I should probably let my keeper know, though." As she spoke, she looked around the clearing, catching sight of a familiar gray face. Arsolin was sitting beside a clean pile of prey bones, his helmet beside him and his armor gone as he washed his flank. One eye was open and on her.

"I'll meet you at the entrance," she said to the two before approaching her keeper.

"Hasefi." Arsolin straightened and scanned her closely. "I was told you were ill."

"Just overworked," she assured him.

Something passed through his eyes, but it was gone as quickly as it came and there was nothing to read but sympathy.

"I think today I'm going to go for a short walk with my friends before resting again for the night."

"A walk will be good," the keeper agreed. "I could do with one myself."

Hasefi was pleased by his words and let out a short purr. Arsolin returned it, then put on his helmet before she led him towards the ferns at the front of the clearing.

Salifen and Alarni were there, silent. They got to their paws as Hasefi joined them, but their gazes suddenly went past her.

"Hasefi!" Nakilon's voice sounded, followed by rapid steps. Hasefi's heart sank, making her feel guilty that the sound of her friend's voice would cause such a reaction.

"Nakilon," Hasefi greeted him. Despite her initial reaction, she was quite pleased to see him, even if his expression was fraught with worry.

"You weren't in training today," he said with an absent glance at the other novices. "Some were saying you were sick."

"I'm alright. Just been working hard, is all."

He studied her closely before relaxing a little. "Where are you off to?"

"I was just going to take a short walk for a bit," Hasefi explained haltingly, reluctant to lie to him.

"Salifen and I wanted to show Hasefi the pool near the far border," Alarni added smoothly.

"Cool! Can I come?"

Hasefi's chest tightened. "I promised I would go with them…."

Disappointment dulled Nakilon's gaze, though he made an attempt to hide it with a grin. "That's alright. Will I see you tomorrow?"

"Yes," Hasefi assured him.

"Great!" He leaned forward and touched her ear with his nose. The unexpected gesture brought a warmth that eased Hasefi's guilt. Nakilon recoiled, embarrassment alight in his eyes. "Uh, goodbye." He turned and hurried away.

"Are we going?" Alarni's tone was hard.

Hasefi turned. The novice hunter was glaring after Nakilon while her brother had his back to them and was staring off through the entrance as if impatient. Urgency returned to Hasefi and she led the way through the entrance.

In the forest, Salifen took the lead while Alarni and Hasefi followed side-by-side. They were quiet, aware of Arsolin's presence close by. Hasefi listened to him, using only as much of her tribe's strength as was necessary to determine when he was out of earshot.

"Okay," Hasefi said, turning her gaze on Alarni. "It's safe to talk. Tell me everything."

"A keeper came to yours saying Esafi wanted you," the novice hunter began immediately. "I asked if it could wait, but the keeper was insistent. I did my best to delay and help Salifen bring some leaves to the clearing, but I couldn't do more than that. If a gifted saw me…." Fear passed through her eyes.

"Did one see you?" Hasefi asked, unnerved by Alarni's tension.

"I went to the Highcave with Arsolin. He didn't say much, though he knew something was off, I think. He asked me if I was okay a couple times. If I hadn't been so terrified I might have been annoyed."

"He means well," Hasefi said, trying to be patient.

"I met with the Highchief. She—she wanted to talk about your prophecy."

Hasefi blinked in surprise. *My prophecy? What does that have to do with anything? I thought it was over.*

"'The first Heir to the Highchief will lead a destiny beyond the River.' That's it, right?"

Hasefi nodded.

"She said that they had read it as being the Wanderers' sign for the next Divide. That you were going to lead this new tribe to their home. But when you came back, they realized they were wrong. Instead, they think your return was to warn us about the Pack." Alarni's gaze sharpened. "Hasefi, what is the Pack?"

Hasefi looked ahead to where Salifen was picking his way through the brush. His ears were angled back as he listened and she could tell by the anxious twitching of his tail that he was thinking about what she'd said last night.

He didn't tell her anything.

"I'll explain when I talk about what happened to me," she assured Alarni. "Is there anything else?"

"She thought that would make you feel better about what happened to your tribe." Alarni hesitated.

"What else?" Hasefi asked, worried and hating that she was worried at what else Esafi may have revealed to the novice.

"The Guardian Elder," Alarni said. "He—was there."

Hasefi's alarm combined with her tribe's.

The Elder would know the illusion the moment he saw it, Kilarsa said. *There is no possibility of him missing the deception.*

Then Esafi must know, Sefonis said. *Yet she said nothing. That is not Esafi's way.*

"He didn't do anything?" Hasefi asked her friend.

"Not while I was there. I could feel his eyes on me, but he didn't say a word. I don't even think he moved. I was sure the Overlord would be coming for us today."

"Esafi didn't say anything," Hasefi said. "Myafos must have known. But for some reason, he said nothing, or Esafi has other things to worry about." She shook her head, unable to wrap her head around what could have allowed Alarni to get away.

Esafi would have confronted me if she knew. But what about Myafos? I hardly know anything about him.

"What about you?" Alarni pressed. "What happened to you? And what is the Pack?"

It was difficult for Hasefi to change her thoughts from Esafi and the Guardian Elder, but she knew she needed to tell Alarni about the Pack. "The Pack was hunting me in the high mountains. They killed my tribe. They're the black wolves the Clan cast out."

Alarni stopped in her tracks. Her jaws opened as if to cry an exclamation, but she shut them and lurched forward again.

"They still exist?" she hissed quietly. "I thought they were gone."

"Unfortunately, no," Hasefi sighed. "And they're a threat to every creature around the River. They're in the Clan's territory now, taking and killing wolves in silence."

Now Salifen came to a stop, turning to look at them both.

"We cannot fight the Clan," he said to Alarni. "It will be the perfect opportunity for the Pack to strike."

"Maybe that's exactly why we should fight," Alarni said. "To show the Pack we're strong. Besides," she added with a hiss. "If the Clan is weak, maybe the Pack will go after them and give us time to prepare."

"No!" Hasefi hissed. "If the Clan falls, then so do we. We need their help."

"Help?" Alarni echoed in disbelief. "From wolves? They're the reason this problem exists!"

"Don't pretend you know better," Hasefi hissed. "*I* hardly know what's going on. But what I do know is that the Pack is strong and they will tear through everything until the world is drowned in blood. Wolf, lynx, it doesn't matter. Which is why the Tribe and the Clan need to put aside their differences."

Alarni was quiet. She and Hasefi had stopped before Salifen, who was looking between them.

"You reminded me of something else," Hasefi continued, slowly and quietly. "The wolves had a prophecy, too. 'When water recedes, darkness will flow.' The stream in their ravine dried up shortly before I arrived. I don't think much of prophecies, but clearly it speaks truth. And it may be enough for me to convince Esafi."

Silence hung between the three of them. Salifen and Hasefi waited for Alarni's response. Whatever it might be, Hasefi knew what she had to do, but it would help if she could have the novice hunter's aid.

"The war was the only thing that would get your friend back," Alarni pointed out. "But you'd leave him for the sake of the Clan?"

"Not the Clan. Life. This is bigger than them and us."

Alarni frowned at the ground, boring a hole into it with her eyes. Then she lifted her gaze and met Hasefi's. "If you're willing to risk your friend for this, then it has to be important. What do you need from us?"

Hasefi bit back a relieved gasp. "Nothing at the moment. I want to tell Esafi about the prophecy—I can do it without revealing our cover," she added at Alarni's doubtful look. "If that doesn't work...I was also thinking I could speak to the Elder."

The novice's ears flattened. "That seems like the last thing you should do."

"There's little choice. Besides, if he knows, what harm is there in facing him?"

"So our rescue mission turns into a save-the-world mission," Alarni chuckled dryly. "We are in way over our heads, but I guess this is what I volunteered for."

"Me too," Salifen added.

"You don't know how grateful I am," Hasefi told them.

"Just think of us when you're choosing your champions." Alarni winked, but the words sounded forced. "Now, come on," she continued, moving ahead again. "Let's check out that pool in case your stubborn knight friend asks you about it."

Every heartbeat after added to the rising urgency welling up within Hasefi. But she knew she couldn't give Arsolin reason for alarm. However, when they finally returned to the clearing and she'd said goodnight to her friends, Hasefi ran towards the Highledge, up the path, and into the Highcave.

Esafi was in the mainchamber with Garfonis. They were sitting close, their heads together and faces intense as they spoke.

Hasefi came to a skidding stop before them, causing them to start in surprise.

"While I appreciate your haste, daughter," Esafi began. "It would do you well to show a wee bit more grace."

"We can't fight the Clan," Hasefi declared.

Esafi gave her a bemused expression. "Why is that?"

Hasefi hesitated again, trying to collect her thoughts and think of the best way to convince Esafi of her words.

"When I went to the Clan, I heard something there and I didn't think about it until you mentioned my prophecy last night." She straightened, speaking her next words slowly. "'When water recedes, darkness will flow.'"

Esafi narrowed her eyes while worry twisted Garfonis's expression.

"It's a prophecy from the Watchers."

"Why should we heed any words from them?" Esafi asked with a snort.

"Because we both know that the darkness is the Pack. If you're right, then your ancestors—"

"They are your ancestors, too, daughter."

"—*and* their ancestors are warning you about them. If they can agree on something, surely the Tribe and Clan can put aside their dislike?"

"You still insist on allying with the Clan?" Esafi asked. She got up.

"What if the Pack is already here?" Hasefi blurted before the Highchief could turn away.

Esafi's eyes narrowed to slits. "What would make you say that?"

"A feeling?" Hasefi tried. "I've been running from these wolves since I was three moons old. Something isn't right. Please, you have to believe me."

Garfonis turned his head to the Highchief, words unspoken in his gaze.

"Half a moon and my champions are already lined with you," Esafi growled to Hasefi.

"This isn't about me," Hasefi snapped. "This is about the Pack. If they agree with me, it's because they see the real threat which you choose to ignore."

"I have no intention of ignoring the Pack!" Esafi returned. "But if we fight them and leave the Clan, we will only find ourselves facing yet another Pack. Eilwyn is too soft to eliminate them. As long as the Clan remains, so will the Pack."

"What does that mean?

"War with the Clan is necessary," Esafi stated, her tone accepting no argument. But Hasefi refused to back down.

"The Clan is weak," she insisted. "I saw it before Garfonis came," she added when Esafi frowned. "I doubt they could even take a war. Besides, don't you think Eilwyn would learn that casting the pack-wolves out wasn't the way?"

Esafi was silent, her expression guarded. But Hasefi could see through it this time.

"You know the Clan is weak," she realized. "And the dark moon; you want to fight them at their weakest."

"Strategy is a part of war."

"Is that what you call this?" Hasefi scoffed.

"It is strange you would argue against this war," Esafi said. "Have you forsaken your wolf friend?"

"Of course not! If I had it my way I would—" The words stuck themselves in Hasefi's throat. She'd intended to say 'I would get him myself and let you deal with the Pack', but she knew, even if she could get Kolahn right then and there, she would remain at the River until the Pack was dealt with once and for all.

"The Pack has taken too much," Hasefi said instead. "And not just from me. Kolahn is a better creature than I am; he didn't hesitate to warn the wolves that cast him out. Even as I warn you, I don't do it for you. I do it for him. And I won't rest until the Pack is stopped once and for all."

"The Pack killed our sons," Garfonis spoke quietly. "Every lynx that is aware of the Pack knows this. The Clan has always been our enemy, but they are not kit-killers. They are bound by a code not so different from our own."

"Sympathy for the enemy," Esafi growled, a sudden feverish light in her eyes. "The wolves, gray or black, are not our friends."

"They don't have to be," Hasefi pointed out. "But if the Pack is to be defeated, you need to put aside this war and form an alliance. Talk to Eilwyn. Maybe she's more reasonable than you think."

"You know nothing of the Clan," Esafi said, shaking her head. "We fight the Clan. Then we fight the Pack. I have humored you long enough. You may have dealt with these wolves before, but there are more lives at stake than your own, now." Esafi turned and headed out of the mainchamber, leaving Hasefi and Garfonis to watch after her.

"She's making a mistake," Hasefi growled, raking her claws across the stone.

"Maybe not," Garfonis said, coming to sit beside her. "There may be more that she knows."

"Then why keep it secret?" Hasefi snarled, whirling on him. "The whole Tribe is apprehensive. They know war is coming. Telling them or not isn't keeping them happy. And when the Pack strikes—which they will—it'll be too late. They'll be caught revelling in their victory against an 'enemy' that could hardly fight back."

"We are not blind, Hasefi," Garfonis said sternly.

"Then open your star-broken eyes and *do* something!" Hasefi turned away and stalked out of the mainchamber and into the tunnel leading out. Before she reached the Highledge, she already regretted her words, but she was becoming too desperate now to care.

Myafos, she thought. *He's my last chance.*

Esafi spends much of her time with him, Kilarsa spoke. *He may have the most sway.*

Then let's hope he has some sense.

Hasefi hurried down the ledge and went over to the Guardian's Cave. She leapt up the zigzagging path and passed into the softly glowing mouth. The cavelight was dimming, taking on a silver hue as the shrinking moon outside shone behind the mountains.

There was not a single lynx within the mainchamber. Hasefi looked to the tunnels lining the back, wondering if she should wander about until she either found the Elder or a guardian that could get him. But just as she chose a random tunnel to go down, Silvera, the guardian that had made her armor and pouch, came in behind her.

"High Heir," she greeted with a quick bow. "I saw you enter." She scanned Hasefi's armorless pelt. "Is everything alright with your armor?"

"It's fine. I actually wanted to talk to Myafos. Do you know where he is?"

"Aye," Silvera admitted. "But he is a very busy lynx." She studied Hasefi another heartbeat. "I can mention you'd like to talk. Wait here." She turned and ducked down the leftmost tunnel.

Alone, doubt crept into Hasefi's mind as she thought of what she could possibly say to the mysterious Elder.

If you're right about him being able to sway Esafi, wouldn't he have already done so if he were inclined?

We do not know where he stands, Kilarsa admitted. *It is possible he is why Esafi is so adamant. But you are right, Hasefi. This war cannot happen. We must convince him.*

How?

Her tribe was silent, but she wouldn't have paid attention to their response anyways. Myafos stood before her, though Hasefi didn't see him emerge from any tunnel. Nor did she see Silvera again.

"Myafos," she gasped, jumping to her paws.

"High Heir," he replied, slowly lowering himself into a bow. When he rose, Hasefi caught a glimpse of glowing eyes beneath his hood, piercing deep within her.

Is he thinking about Alarni's illusion? she wondered. Another fear struck her. *Or can he see you?*

I do not think any but you are aware of us, Kilarsa said, though her words seemed to be for herself as much as they were for Hasefi.

"You have need of me?" Myafos prompted, making Hasefi jump again.

"Er, yes," she stammered.

Myafos rose and moved into the rightmost tunnel without a word. Hasefi hesitated before following him.

He led her into a cavern with a single hollow. It was surprisingly bare compared to the other gifted caverns she had visited. There wasn't even a spot to put armor.

"Any distraction can keep a mind away from sleep," the Elder murmured.

Hasefi gave him an uneasy look. Even though his back was to her, she quickly looked away, wondering if he knew she had been looking at him. When he turned, his head tilted until the darkness beneath his hood was aimed at her.

"What is it you'd like to share?"

"Um...." Hasefi swallowed, her mouth dry. "I wanted to talk about the war."

Myafos was silent.

"I don't think Esafi should go through with it." The Elder still said nothing, so Hasefi continued. "It's the Pack that poses a real threat—not the Clan. If we fight the Clan, we may be dooming them. The Pack wants their territory—it'll give them a chance to strike." Hasefi's unease grew when the Elder continued to say nothing. "I don't expect you to have sympathy for the Clan. But if the Pack turns to the Tribe, we won't have anyone to look to for aid. I already talked to Esafi, but she won't listen to me. I...was hoping you might convince her—"

"Convince who?"

Dread rippled down Hasefi's spine when the Highchief's voice sounded behind her. She turned to meet Esafi's narrowed gaze before it jerked to Myafos.

"Why are you speaking to him?" she demanded, looking back to Hasefi. Uncertainty itched beneath Hasefi's pelt, but she pushed the feeling aside and hardened her gaze.

"If you won't see reason, then I thought maybe your champions would!" Hasefi snapped.

Esafi's lips twisted back in the beginnings of a snarl. "My decision is final," she hissed. "And did you really think my champions would go behind my back?"

"They didn't—"

"I am disappointed in you, daughter."

"Perhaps you shouldn't be."

Both Hasefi and Esafi looked to Myafos as he spoke, silenced by surprise.

"The High Heir has taken initiative to enforce what she believes in, despite the risks," the Elder said. His words were slow as if each was calculated to serve its own purpose. "Is that not what you were training her predecessor?"

"You twist my words!" Esafi growled. "And Hasefi goes behind the back of her Highchief!" Though Esafi's anger wasn't surprising, Hasefi knew by the rising fur along the Highchief's spine that Myafos's words bothered her.

"You are *not* my Highchief," Hasefi growled, her anger changing suddenly from a raging boil to a cold stillness.

Esafi looked at her with surprise, the fur on her spine still spiking.

"And this is not my tribe," Hasefi continued. "I'm only here because you've kept me here. I've played along for long enough."

"If you're so tired of being here, then why are you fighting so hard against your one way out?" Esafi snarled.

"You know why!" Hasefi's muzzle was inches from her mother's.

Something flashed in the Highchief's gaze and Hasefi thought she might attack, but she took a step back, composing herself and glaring down at Hasefi.

"We will fight the Clan," she said simply. "Join, if you must, or stay. After the dark moon, you will be released." Esafi glanced once more at the Elder before exiting the chamber.

Hasefi stared, blinking after Esafi. Something about the reaction abated her fury somewhat, replacing it with a sense of unease. Her tribe shared it and she wondered if her father's words were right.

Does Esafi know something we don't? Is there something else going on?

Myafos's presence, though the Elder was silent, was as loud as a crash of thunder.

"Er, I...."

The Elder showed no reaction. It was impossible to figure out what the silent, shrouded lynx might be thinking. For a heartbeat, Hasefi thought about asking him why he said nothing about Alarni's illusion, but she quickly decided she had bigger problems to deal with.

"I'm...sorry," she mumbled, stumbling to the exit with an awkward dip of her head, for it felt necessary, then slipping out of the chamber.

Passing through the guardians' mainchamber and back out into the clearing, Hasefi walked slowly down the zigzagging path, her mind lost in thought.

That went terribly.

At least you tried, Sefonis offered. *Esafi has always been stubborn. I have been in your place many times.*

Hasefi shook her head. *No, I can't give up yet. There's one more thing I can try.* She let the words hang, allowing her tribe to see fully into her mind.

They were silent, at first. Then their combined uncertainty rose until Hasefi's own fur pricked uneasily despite her growing resolve.

That is a dangerous path, her uncle warned.

It could make things much worse, Dahsefer agreed.

Esafi has given me no choice, Hasefi stated. *I have to try.*

Chapter Sixteen

Hasefi slept little. Though she still had yet to recover from her exertion across the River, her mind was awhirl. The words spoken since she'd woken that evening played over and over in her head.

Esafi is going forward with the war, even with the black wolves across the River. If I told her I'd seen them, she'd be more worried about how I got there. It's not enough to put Alarni and Salifen in danger, not yet.

Perhaps a war would throw the Pack off, Tenarli pointed out. *Their plan was to eliminate the Clan. Alarni may have a point. If the Pack sees the Tribe take on the Clan, they may hesitate. If they had the strength to take on the Clan, they would have done it by now. Perhaps their strength has not recovered, since they last saw you, which is why they keep to the shadows.*

That would be the best case, Hasefi thought. *And I really hope it's the truth, but we can't possibly be sure.*

You have not spoken to all the champions, Gelinaf said. *Your father is on your side. There is still the Sage, Huntmaster, and Overlord.*

Two of which are tied by kin, Hasefi sighed. *And the other, duty. I only have one option left.*

It may not be worth it, Sefonis said. *It is a huge risk.*

If it fails. But if it works, it could save the River. The risk, I think, is worth it.

Her tribe withdrew, their unease leaving Hasefi agitated. She did her best to try and settle in her hollow but, when she sensed the sun was not far from rising, she gave up. Esafi hadn't shown up at any point in the night, so the chamber was left empty after she grabbed her helmet and made her way out to the Highledge.

Dawn had yet to come. Deep shadows obscured the clearing below. A figure here and there moved about; keepers on duty, a restless hunter, a guardian still at work.

For a moment, Hasefi saw the clearing as it had been in her nightmare. She thought about Esafi's words, dreading the idea that it could be some sort of vision.

If it is, then I have to do everything I can to stop it.

The sun was slow to rise, yet to Hasefi it felt the day couldn't start faster. A plan was forming in her mind. Unlike her other endeavors, she was determined to think this one through.

I can't fail.

At length, when the sun's rays turned the back of the mountains to her left orange, reminding her of the fire she and Kolahn had seen, Garfonis emerged from the Knight's Cave. Hasefi padded down the path to meet him, causing him to blink at her with surprise.

"I'm sorry about what I said to you last night," she told him. "I was angry and took it out on you, which isn't fair."

He blinked warmly at her and nosed her shoulder. "No worries, wee lass. It takes a bit more than angry words to get through my pelt." His words rumbled with a purr before it broke off and he studied her closely. "Is everything alright? Did you sleep well?"

Hasefi shrugged, then nodded to the entrance. "Shall we?"

Whether from her father's concern or pure chance, they did little sparring that morning and more learning new moves. She stayed with Nakilon most of the time, which she was grateful for. Firalos gave his usual narrowed glares, joined by some of the other novices when mentors weren't looking, but they did nothing else, leaving her alone.

On the way back to the clearing, her exhaustion caught up with her and it took everything she had to keep her paws moving back to the Tribe's home and down into the Cavern of History. But sitting still proved even harder to endure. It was difficult to keep her eyes open.

Her head was lolling when Nalikon inched to her side and gave her shoulder a gentle nudge.

"You okay?" he whispered when she jerked up straight.

"Yeah," she said quickly but Nalikon's concerned look didn't change. "Just a bit tired, is all." Her stomach growled and his face twisted further with worry. She'd shared a hare with him earlier, but her hunger was often great after using her tribe's strength.

"Maybe you could try asking for a break," he told her. "I know you were off yesterday, but I don't see why you wouldn't be allowed if you're still not well."

Hasefi gave a soft snort. "I do."

Nalikon gave her a confused look but she didn't elaborate.

Later, when their lessons were over, Nakilon found a plump turkey for her to eat. It satisfied her hunger, but exhaustion continued to weigh heavily down on her. Arsolin came shortly after she finished, bringing her back into the Cavern of History.

It was even more difficult to stay awake and this time she didn't have Nalikon to help her.

"High Heir?"

Hasefi jerked up straight, realizing she had started to doze off while she leaned against the wall. "Sorry. We were talking about the first dark lynx Highchief, right?"

The keeper was silent.

"I'm sorry," Hasefi said again. "What did I miss?"

"I think we are done for today," he told her.

"What?" she asked.

"You should retire for the night."

"Wait, Arsolin—" To her surprise, the keeper slunk past her, leaving her alone. She blinked with bewilderment at the entrance where he had disappeared.

Is he offended that I fell asleep? she wondered.

I think he's concerned, Sefonis said.

About what? Do you think he suspects something?

He's concerned about you, wee lass, her uncle explained with a soft chuckle.

Hasefi looked to the entrance again, knowing he was probably right. But he'd never abandoned his duty like that with her.

He's right, Sefonis continued. *You should get some rest.*

I can't. The Pack is here now. We don't have time to spare.

Rest, Hasefi, Dahsefer spoke up, his tone firm and leaving no room for argument. *Your bravery is commendable, but if you march into danger hardly able to keep yourself upright, you will meet death and that will help no creature.*

Fine, she conceded. *But I go tomorrow. And...* she continued. *I can't get the others involved this time.*

Her tribe responded with silence. She padded through the Cavern until she reached the tunnel leading into the Highcave. From there, she went to the sleeping chamber and, this time, she fell easily into sleep.

"Wow," Hasefi murmured, looking to the lynxes gathering below the Highledge. "There must be at least a hundred lynxes down there."

"One-hundred-and-twenty-two," Garfonis said, coming to stand beside her. "Well, there will be less since that's counting kits, and patrols are out, hunters are out, and some lynxes might be busy with other duties or sleeping."

"Wow," Hasefi breathed again.

"We used to be bigger," Garfonis continued. "During your grandmother's reign, we were almost two-hundred."

"Two hundred!" Hasefi cried, trying to imagine twice the amount of lynxes below. "How did they even fit in here?"

"With difficulty," Hesilar said, joining them. "Hence the First Divide."

"The First Divide?" Hasefi echoed.

"The first time our tribe split apart," Garfonis explained. He glanced back into the Highcave. "Come, the Highchief will be with us soon. We should take our places."

Hasefi followed her father and her uncle to the back of the Highledge. The other three champions were already there, lined up against the cliff wall around the Highcave. The Highchief emerged just as Hesilar and Garfonis took their spots. Hasefi moved in front of the Highcave and watched Esafi pad slowly out to the end of the Ledge. The noise below quickly faded.

"Good morning, my tribe," Esafi greeted, her voice loud and clear. "It is always a pleasant day to stand before you to represent the next lynxes that will help our tribe thrive." Esafi's ears flicked.

Below, near the path leading onto the ledge, a gray-furred lynx with gleaming yellow eyes sat below, joined by a darker-furred lynx with little black spots spattered across their pelt. Between them, Ivanus had gotten to his paws and was padding quickly and carefully up onto the Highledge.

When he reached it, he glanced at Hasefi, who gave him a reassuring nod. Ivanus flicked his ears, then went to stand with the Highchief.

"The lynx I present to you is the only of his litter," Esafi announced to the lynxes below. "Ivanus, from this day you will hold the title of Novice. For this following moon, you will learn of the three Paths available to you so that you may choose which to follow."

Ivanus sank into a bow until his nose touched the stone at Esafi's paws.

"Tribe, help me welcome Ivanus to his new title."

Hasefi listened as the clearing filled with cheering and calling. It was so loud she had to flatten her ears, wondering if the Clan could hear from across the River. The sounds were heartening, however, and she was able to forget for a moment the nervous twisting in her gut.

After some time, Esafi murmured into Ivanus's ear and he scampered back towards the path down. Hasefi smiled at him and he returned it before skipping happily back to his parents below.

The Highchief raised a paw, quieting the crowd below.

"I have another announcement," she began, her voice suddenly somber. "We are fortunate in the plentiful amount of novices we've had during the start of the warm season," she said. "We have lived long without conflict. But that time is coming to an end."

Some of the lynxes visible to Hasefi passed looks between each other. Anticipation hung in the air and she suspected they were all waiting for the same thing she herself was.

"It has been over half a moon since High Heir Mekonis and Talonis were lost to us." Esafi's voice was steady, though a hint of anguish rang clear. "The only obvious answer is the actions of the Clan, whom we have tolerated spies and thieves for moons. But now they have labeled themselves as murderers."

Hasefi flattened her ears, baring her teeth at the Highchief's back. Garfonis shifted closer, his armor clinking against her own.

Why lie? she growled silently. *If she plans to face the Pack at all, then she'll have to come out with the truth anyways.*

There is little motivation needed for hostility against the Pack, Sefonis pointed out to her. *But the Clan may require a little more if they are to go to war. Without the deaths of your brothers, many more of these lynxes may feel as you do.*

I find that hard to believe. They hate wolves.

Yet they know little more than what decorated walls and magical images can show them.

"It is time to show the wolves their mistakes," Esafi called, retaking Hasefi's attention.

The clearing exploded with noise, but this time there were battle cries and shrieks of anger towards the wolves. A growl rumbled in Hasefi's throat.

There is nothing you can do about it right now, Sefonis told her before she could step towards the Highchief.

"Ever since the Lost History, where the wolves came to the River, there have been problems. Thievery, spies, violence. Not to mention the worst danger we have ever faced." Her last words brought a silence over the Tribe. Hope surged through Hasefi at the thought that Esafi might actually tell the truth.

"My mother swore to protect her lynxes and she did, to her dying breath," Esafi said. "Since then, I have vowed to keep every one of you from harm. And so I have, until this moon." The Highchief stepped forth until she was at the very edge of the Ledge, her claws curled over the lip of stone. "There is only one course of action to be taken for the murder of not only sons of the Tribe, but highbloods. The Clan is no longer welcome here."

The air was thick with anticipation now. Hasefi couldn't tell what the lynxes below might be thinking, but horror filled her own heart.

She wants to drive them out of their home? Hasefi was too stunned to react, rooted by her tribe's shock.

"For the next half moon," Esafi continued, filling the silence. "We will prepare for war. When the night is darkest and the Clan's ancestors are farthest, we will strike their home. Once more the Tribe shall rule the River."

Cheers erupted again, more fervent than before.

That must be why she offered to save Kolahn! Hasefi thought. *She wants to take everything they have!*

"The wolves will meet us with their full might," Esafi continued, her voice rising. "And we will do the same!"

Another cheer filled the air, turning Hasefi's blood to ice.

We can't let this happen! I have to stop her!

Wait until she is alone, Sefonis spoke urgently. *Speaking out in front of the Tribe will do little good.*

Hasefi gritted her teeth, watching the Highchief revel in the eager cries and shouts below.

"My champions will guide you," Esafi said after some time. "Report to them for your new orders." With that, she turned away and padded towards the Highcave. Hasefi had to duck her head lest she let loose the words clawing to free themselves from her jaws.

All of the champions left the Ledge, so Hasefi was alone with the Highchief when she followed her into the cliff-wall.

"I assume you are unhappy with my words, daughter?" Esafi spoke, turning. "That tends to be the case when I feel your glare burning the fur on my neck."

"You lied to them!" Hasefi screeched. "And now you want to drive the wolves out? Just like Resahn tried to do to the Tribe? When they're not even to blame?"

"Do not speak to me of Resahn!" Esafi snarled, her golden eyes flashing. "I do this *because* of him." She drew back, composing herself. "It is your words that have brought me here. If the Pack intends to take revenge on the Clan, removing the gray wolves from the River will redirect their attention. And should the black wolves return, we will be as strong as we were in the old legends."

Hasefi shook her head, unable to believe the words coming from the Highchief's mouth. "Can you even hear yourself? You want to eliminate the only ally we have against the Pack! Even if you're right and the Tribe gets stronger, so will they! And they'll do it faster. They train their pups. Each wolf matches the strength of three lynxes, at least. They have no rules to hinder them."

"Did you not tell me the Clan was weak?" Esafi pointed out. "What aid could they offer?"

"Experience. They've *lived* with wolves from the Pack. Not to mention it was their gifted champion that eliminated Resahn. Besides, if you drive them out, how is that better than what the Pack wants to do?"

"We do not fight to kill," Esafi said, straightening her shoulders and lifting her head proudly like a novice trying to impress their mentor. "The Clan will have a chance at life outside the River."

"No they won't! You just said the Pack may go after them!"

"You seem to have a lot of care for the Clan," the Highchief returned, aiming a scrutinizing glare at her. "Do you share more than their coat, I wonder?"

"This isn't about the Clan!" Hasefi hissed. "This isn't even about Kolahn anymore! Even if it were, I still wouldn't agree to driving the Clan from what has been their home for more moons than you or I could count!"

"And yet the Tribe existed here longer than that."

"We can't drive them from the River," Hasefi insisted, taking on a pleading tone. "Please, at the very least, *try* and talk to Eilwyn!"

"My words are final," Esafi replied shortly. "You do not have to agree with this war, daughter. There will be nothing you can do when you watch us leave."

"Oh, don't think for a heartbeat I won't be there," Hasefi snarled. "Otherwise what else would stop you from killing Kolahn?"

Esafi didn't respond, but Hasefi was finished with the conversation. She turned and stormed out of the Highcave.

She won't listen, she said to her tribe. *And I'm done trying to convince her.*

Outside, the clearing had returned to relative normalcy, though there was an eagerness in the air now, one Hasefi could not share. Still fuming, she descended the path and reached the ground where a knight approached her. It took Hasefi a moment to recall her name was Katrima; she was one of the mentors she'd worked with.

"High Heir," she greeted, sinking into a bow.

Hasefi responded with an inquisitive flick of her ears, trying to check her anger.

"The Emperor wanted me to inform you that he is pausing your knight training for the time as he preps his lynxes for war."

Surprise abated her frustration. "Really? I thought training would be more important than ever now."

"Most novices will find their training subdued for the time," she admitted. "But that hardly means they'll be bored. War brings many tasks."

Hasefi was silent, realizing no lynx other than the Highchief and her champions knew that Hasefi would be joining the fight. She wondered if Esafi meant to inform them, or if she was content with letting them find out the night they set forth.

Unless she's just been humoring me. But it doesn't matter.

"Thank you," Hasefi said to the knight who offered another bow and retreated.

As she watched the knight move off, Hasefi's pelt began to itch with another lynx's gaze. Looking about, she saw Arsolin in the shadow of the Highledge, his head bowed and turned towards her.

His posture was strange to her, making her anxious. With an effort of will, she padded over to him. He straightened, resuming his usual, stone-like bearing.

"Are you okay?" she asked when she'd reached him.

"Of course," her keeper responded. It was very subtle, but Hasefi detected the difference in his tone.

"That's not true," she told him. "What's wrong?"

Arsolin lowered his head. Then, to Hasefi's surprise, he took his helmet off and met her gaze, his frustration unmasked.

"You've done nothing but train in this last half moon. Even keepers don't work this hard."

"It's alright," she assured him. "I—"

"No, it's not." His tone bordered on a growl. "You're still young—you should be able to spend time with lynxes your age and not have to rush through meals to start the next lesson."

"It's okay," she tried again. "I've been through worse, really. Honestly, this is quite a bit better than the life I had outside the Tribe." *Before meeting Kolahn, of course.*

Arsolin narrowed his eyes. "You're not being truthful."

Hasefi twitched her ears uneasily, but his expression relaxed and he gave her a sorrowful look.

"If you were, you'd have little reason to leave." He sighed. "You've been through too much for a lynx your age."

Hasefi's wariness vanished and she blinked warmly at the keeper. "I'm absolutely fine," she assured him. She stepped forward and gave his cheek a gentle touch with her nose. "I appreciate you caring, though." When she drew back, she was pleased to see the warmth shining in his eyes. "And don't worry about training," she continued. "My father is busy now, so as far as I know, you're the only one training me."

"Aye," he agreed. "Though I've been given little instruction."

"Well, you know I'm joining the battle, right?"

He nodded.

"Then help me with that. I've fought, but I've never been in an all-out war like this."

"I have not fought in my own battle, but I will offer what knowledge I can." He put his helmet back on and stood. "If you are ready, there is a glade not far from the Pit we can use."

"Sure." Hasefi rose to her paws and began to follow him towards the entrance. She noticed there were some gazes on them, but neither she nor Arsolin paid them much attention as they left the clearing.

Her keeper brought her in the direction of the Knight's Pit. Indeed, it was close, for he didn't turn off the path until long after Hasefi could hear the grunts and calls of sparring knights and the clanging of armor against armor echoing through the trees.

When he did lead her away, they went left, putting the Pit behind them. After a short time, the trees gave way to a small glade turned bright by the sun above.

The ground sloped up away from them where a trio of birch trees stood at the treeline ahead. Grass had worn away to earth, showing it was a common spot for creatures to come and, from the claw and skid marks in the dirt, Hasefi suspected it was where lynxes came to train in silence.

"I will begin with combat," Arsolin announced after leading her to the top of the slope and sitting before her. "I will merge some of the basic training with that of a keeper's training."

"I thought we'd talk more about how war works," Hasefi admitted. "I don't think fighting is my weakness."

"All due respect, but, while you fight well as a knight, combat as a keeper is much different."

"How?"

Arsolin took off his helmet, revealing his intense gaze. "It is subtle and quick. We aim to incapacitate our opponents without delay. We strike without being seen. Getting caught in a fight is a time for retreat, to allow the knights to take over."

Hasefi tilted her head. "So it's the knights and keepers that fight, then?"

"Every Path plays a part in battle."

"Garfonis has said that knights are the frontlines and it sounds like keepers act as their shadows...what about the others?"

"Guardians subdue enemy gifted or, if able, will use their abilities to aid those who use claw and tooth to fight. Healers fix injuries and offer protective magic where they can. And hunters serve as protectors to our gifted."

Hasefi blinked, imagining what it would look like for the entirety of the Tribe to be assembled for battle. "What about the clearing?" she asked. "There will be kits left behind, and advisors."

"Aye," Arsolin replied, a pleased gleam in his eye. "There will be guards. A champion will probably remain to ensure our home is secure."

Hasefi thought of Nakilon and his worry for those going to fight. He still didn't know she would be part of the battle, but hope for her final plan kept her from saying anything, lest things work out and the war with the Clan is avoided.

Her paws tingled. It was near sunpeak now. Night drew ever closer.

"Hasefi?"

"I'm listening, sorry." Hasefi shook out her fur. "Alright, teach me what you know."

They spent most of the day in the glade. Hasefi was nearly recovered after last night's rest, but the first sign of fatigue she showed, Arsolin ended their combat training and brought her back to the clearing to eat. After that, he took her into the Cavern of History and told her of old wars in the Tribe, most of which were against the Clan. Hasefi was surprised, however, to find the Tribe had fought other creatures, too, though none organized like the two groups living by the River. At one point in their history, an invasion of coyotes had put their home in danger and another time battle was brought to a pair of particularly aggressive brown bears.

Arsolin went over strategy and the weaknesses of both lynx and wolf. Though Hasefi often got quite bored in the Cavern, she found herself absorbed by her keeper's lessons and was unaware of the time until Arsolin declared it was nearing dusk and that the day was over.

"There is time for you to visit your friends," he told her. "I am to report to Sifara before the light fades." He dipped his head, blinking warmly at her as he replaced his helmet. "I'll see you tomorrow."

Hasefi murmured goodnight then, after a few heartbeats, followed his steps out of the Cavern.

Her first thoughts were of Nakilon. Anxiety pricked her pelt, now, as the day made way for night and she knew her best comfort would come from the novice knight. But another part of her told her she should talk to Salifen.

Looking across the clearing, she found the novice healer settled on the ground with Alarni and Ivanus before him. The newly made novice was chattering excitedly and Hasefi knew he was talking about his first day of training. Her paws tugged her towards them, but she resisted.

Salifen would understand, but Alarni won't, she told herself. *And I don't want to lie anymore.*

She tore her gaze away and looked to where Nakilon was practicing a move with another novice knight. Making up her mind, Hasefi trotted over to the pair.

Before she reached them, movement in the corner of her eye made her look and she noticed Firalos skulking by, throwing a sneer at her. She ignored him, only to hear him hiss.

"Wolfcat."

Shock froze Hasefi's paws to the ground and she looked to the older novice again. "What did you call me?"

He seemed surprised, then his face twisted into a snarl. "You heard me," he sneered.

"Yeah, I did." Hasefi turned and went over to him. "How do you know that word?"

This time he gave her a baffled look.

"Hey!" Nakilon bounded over, his sparring partner nowhere to be seen. The novice's gaze flicked between Hasefi and Firalos before settling on the latter with a glare. "Leave her alone."

"I can fend for myself," she told her friend and he ducked his head in embarrassment.

"Yeah, back off, kit," Firalos sneered.

Nakilon threw him a glare, but Hasefi stepped in front of him before he could retaliate.

"Why did you call me that?" Hasefi demanded, taking another step towards Firalos. Uncertainty took over the novice's expression and he looked away.

"What did he call you?" Nakilon asked.

"Wolfcat." To her dismay, her friend flinched as if she had struck him.

"That's not a word that should be uttered," he whispered. Then he threw a smug glance at Firalos. "You're going to be in so much trouble."

Firalos's uncertainty became nervousness.

"Wait," Hasefi asked. "Why?"

Nakilon gave her a confused look. "Don't you know?"

Hasefi shook her head.

"It's...." Nakilon glanced towards Firalos, then to his paws.

Wolfcat was an insult used towards lynxes with our fur color, Gelinaf explained. Hasefi's eyes widened.

Really? Why? Kolahn called me that, she thought with confusion.

It's unlikely he knew the weight of the term to our kind, Gelinaf assured her. *Its origin can be found in the story of the first gray lynx to join the Tribe.*

Hasefi returned her attention to Nakilon. "Come on," she told him, jerking her head towards the entrance of the clearing.

"What about him?" the novice knight asked, flicking his ears at Firalos.

Hasefi turned her gaze on Firalos. He was quiet and his normally narrowed eyes were wide with unease. "My best friend called me

Wolfcat once, but as a compliment. Whatever it means to you is irrelevant to me." With that, Hasefi moved past him.

Nakilon threw a final glance at Firalos before following her. When they left the clearing and reached a quiet spot, Hasefi turned to her friend. "Is wolfcat really that bad?" she asked.

Nakilon lowered his head. "Maybe it would be better if you asked one of your mentors," he suggested without looking at her.

"I'm asking you."

Hasefi, I can—

Give him a chance, she told her uncle.

"Well, you know the different lynxes, right?" Nakilon asked hesitantly.

"Golden, dark, and gray," she answered.

"Well, gray lynxes came last. And...they weren't exactly welcomed into the Tribe."

"Why not?" Hasefi asked.

"Because...well, partly because they looked like wolves."

Anger boiled in Hasefi's belly. "Really?" she growled. "So we're no better than the Clan, then?"

Nakilon flinched. "I feel like I'm not the right lynx you should talk to about this," he stammered.

"Why not?"

The novice hesitated. "Well...my fur is...."

"I don't care what color your fur is," she sighed. "Why can't we all just stop caring about that?" She narrowed her eyes at Nakilon. "Is that what you notice about me?" she asked.

"Of course not," he said quickly. "And it's been countless seasons since gray lynxes have been accepted. I...don't think that's why Firalos called you that."

Hasefi's ears perked. "Then why?"

"Well...according to some of the older lynxes...you sort of sound like one."

Hasefi let out a sigh, remembering again Esafi's words to her.

"I'm sorry," Nakilon said.

"Don't be," she told him. She thought of when she and Kolahn had just escaped the wrath of a mountain lion and he'd tucked her into a small space to keep her safe. It was the first time he'd called her a wolfcat after wondering if his ancestors, the Watchers, could accept a lynx.

Let's hope so, because they might be all I have left at this point.

"You're upset," Nakilon fretted, reminding Hasefi where she was.

"I'm fine," she assured him, though she knew her tone betrayed her. "I just..." she let out another sigh and shook her head. "I don't belong here, Nakilon." When she looked back up at him, she saw pain in his eyes.

"What do you mean?"

"I..." Hasefi wanted to tell him about Kolahn and her plan, but she found the pain in his expression was too unbearable. "I'm just used to being on my own, you know?" The pain in his eyes changed to sorrow and he gave her shoulder a comforting nudge with his nose.

"It hasn't even been a moon yet," he assured her. "I'll help you feel at home." He blinked warmly at her and she could do nothing but nod. He pressed his flank against her armor and she leaned against him, feeling an ache in her heart.

I wish I had never come here, she thought. *I wish Kolahn and I were still in the Valley, warming our fur in the sunlight. Then I wouldn't have to feel like this....*

Her tribe offered wordless comfort, easing her anguish a bit.

Soon, she thought. Her eyes opened again and she looked towards the River. *But there's one thing I have to do, first.*

Chapter Seventeen

I have to.

Hasefi, this is not wise, Sefonis said. *Please, rethink this.*

All of this is wrong, Hasefi told him. *I have no love for the Clan and...little more for this tribe. But I won't let one destroy the other and make things easier for the Pack.*

You risk creating a worse disaster, Sefonis insisted.

And what do I risk by not doing anything?

Her uncle was silent.

Esafi may not have ordered fight to kill, Hasefi admitted. *But driving the Clan from what has been their home for seasons upon seasons just so the Pack can pick them off makes the Tribe no better than the Pack themselves.*

Esafi is acting on emotion, Kilarsa pointed out. *Perhaps there's a way yet unseen to make her understand.*

I've tried to make her see sense! You know I have! But she won't listen. Hasefi looked up from the ground. She had returned to the clearing with Nakilon, who had retired to his sleeping chamber. Night had fallen over the clearing, the waning moon still hidden behind the cliffs beyond the River marking the Clan's border. *This is my only option,* she told her tribe firmly. *Besides, if all works out, I might finally be able to get Kolahn to safety.*

Are you sure you aren't acting on emotion? Sefonis asked quietly.

Of course I am! Hasefi growled silently. *Ever since I met the moon-eyed wolf I've acted on emotion. But I'm not a Highchief.*

You are to us, Gelinaf reminded her.

That's not what I meant. I'm not leading lynxes into a stupid war when a deadlier threat looms over them. But if Esafi insists on being blind, then I have to try to do something. *After this, though, I'm done. Whether I fail or not, I'll be getting Kolahn. And then whatever happens here after doesn't matter to me.*

Do you really believe that? Kilarsa asked.

Of course! Her nightmare flashed through her mind again and she knew her tribe could see it, too. *The Pack needs to be stopped,* she said, trying to control her anger. *But no one here will listen. After this, I'll have done everything I can. If Eilwyn is like Esafi, then what else can I do?*

Her tribe offered no answer.

Kolahn sacrificed everything to warn the Clan. I can't say I've done the same, but I don't know what else to do but to do what I came here to do. And that's save his furry tail. He's all I have.

Is that still true? Gelinaf asked.

Anger surged through Hasefi again. *I'm done discussing this! I'm going to talk to Eilwyn—that's it. Are you with me, or not?*

We are always with you, Sefonis assured her, allowing her to relax a little.

Arsolin is busy with Sifara, she thought. *This is the best time to go.*

Hasefi stood, but a voice stopped her, making her heart drop.

"Hasefi." Alarni bounded over, Salifen and Ivanus in tow. The novice hunter stopped before Hasefi, a glint in her eyes as she scrutinized her. "We've hardly seen you since...." She jerked her head towards the Highcave. "Everything alright?"

"Of course," Hasefi replied with a feigned smile.

"Really?" Alarni asked disbelievingly. "You haven't come around to congratulate Ivanus yet."

"It's okay," the new novice said quickly. "It's really not necessary."

"No, she's right," Hasefi sighed. "I'm sorry, I've just been a bit preoccupied."

"So has everyone else," Alarni pointed out. "The Tribe has less than half a moon to prepare for war." Her hard gaze narrowed on Hasefi. "What's going on?"

Hasefi hesitated.

"Alarni, maybe we shouldn't—"

"There's something you're not telling us, isn't there?" Alarni asked, ignoring her brother.

"I was in the high mountains for moons," Hasefi pointed out. "There's a lot I haven't told you."

Alarni leaned towards Hasefi, her stare intense. There was something in her gaze that made Hasefi uneasy. Even Salifen and Ivanus were glancing nervously at the novice hunter.

"You're planning to leave us," she whispered.

"What?" Hasefi blurted.

"That's what the Highchief said," Alarni continued. "With your prophecy fulfilled, you served no more purpose to the Tribe and were free to go when your friend was rescued."

Hasefi recoiled. Salifen did the same, while Ivanus's eyes widened.

"Were we just tools, then?" Alarni demanded.

"No, of course not," Hasefi told her. "But—" she glanced towards the Keeper's Cave, half expecting to see Arsolin walking out. "I can't talk about this now."

"No," Alarni hissed, barring her way towards the entrance. "We deserve better than that. You trusted us before—why not now?"

Because even my own tribe questions me.

Having other opinions may be useful, Kilarsa pointed out.

You just want her to talk me out of it.

Hasefi let out a sigh, looking once more to the Keeper's Cave before replying to the novice hunter.

"I tried talking to Esafi and even to Myafos. But the war is still coming, obviously." Hasefi looked to Ivanus.

"Alarni told me about the Pack," he said quietly before she could ask anything. "Did you really see black wolves?"

"I fought them."

"How?" he gasped. "They're much stronger and bigger than normal wolves."

"They were normal wolves for me," Hasefi pointed out.

"Explains why you swatted tail in your knight training," Alarni said, but her voice was hard. "You've fought *monsters.*"

"So...was it the Pack that killed the High Heir?" Ivanus asked. "Mekonis, I mean? And Talonis?"

"I don't have proof," Hasefi admitted. "But it makes the most sense. They killed my tribe for practice and they clearly have no love for lynxes. I'm sure any reason would suffice for them."

The wolf, the one called Vek, he doesn't seem like a careless creature, Sefonis pointed out. *Remember how he reacted to what Sal did to us?*

Sure, but he was the only wolf that had some sense beyond violence and rage and we don't even know if he's alive. Even if he is, how would killing my brothers help him?

I haven't a clue, he admitted.

"You haven't given us anything," Alarni broke Hasefi's thought. "Why do you want to leave? Why not bring your friend here?"

"Alarni," Salifen said, stepping between her and Hasefi. "You're being aggressive."

"So you're in on it, too, huh?" Alarni looked to Hasefi again. "I have a theory."

Hasefi was silent. A part of her was terrified of everything falling apart before her, but urgency made her impatient for the novice hunter to be out with whatever was making her so angry.

"You won't bring your friend back here because he's a wolf."

Ivanus let out a gasp. Salifen looked to Hasefi, hiding his alarmed expression. But Hasefi kept her head up, meeting Alarni's glare.

"You're right," she admitted. "He's a wolf."

"But not just any wolf," Alarni hissed. "What wolf would the Clan cast from their home but one with black fur? Your friend is a black wolf!"

Now Hasefi recoiled. Though Alarni's words were hushed, she couldn't help but glance around to see if anyone was paying attention to them.

"The older lynxes are right," Alarni continued. "You're a *wolfcat*!"

"Alarni!" Salifen growled.

"What does it change?" Hasefi snapped at the novice hunter. "Kolahn saved my life. He's the only reason I'm here. What does it matter that his fur is a certain color? You didn't have a problem with mine until now."

"This has nothing to do with fur," Alarni snarled. "You choose a wolf over us!" Her eyes narrowed to slits. "You were going to leave just now. Why? To go to the Clan again, without your illusion?" Her eyes widened suddenly. "Are you their spy? Were you going to *warn* them?"

Hasefi's mouth worked, but no words came out.

"Hasefi is not a traitor," Salifen said to his sister. "You don't understand what's going on here." Despite his words, it was clear he was caught off-guard about Kolahn's nature.

"Oh, and you do understand?" Alarni scoffed. "Did you know Hasefi was going to warn the Clan?"

Salifen didn't respond.

"I don't care about the Clan," Hasefi told the enraged novice. "But Esafi is making a mistake. The Pack is here *now*. If she's not going to see reason, then maybe Eilwyn will. I'm doing this for you—all of you."

Alarni snorted. "Whatever happened to you beyond the River has filled your head with stars. Go, then. Get yourself killed by wolves, black or gray, I don't care." She turned and stalked away.

She might warn the Highchief, Sefonis alerted Hasefi.

She doesn't care for Esafi.

At the expense of the tribe?

Hasefi flicked her ears nervously, watching the novice slip away into the Hunter's Cave.

"Hasefi."

She realized Salifen and Ivanus still stood before her. She looked to the novice healer, who had spoken.

"I don't think this is a good idea," he admitted.

"Do you think I do?"

"Will the wolves try to kill you?" Ivanus asked.

"Not the Clan, I don't think," Hasefi assured him. "And I've been dodging pack-wolves for a very long time."

"But...you'll be going to their home," the new novice pointed out. "What if they take you prisoner or—" He drew in a sharp breath. "They *hurt* you for information?"

"They won't," Hasefi assured him, trying to sound light-hearted. "Even if they tried, I've got some tricks hidden in my fur."

"You can't do this alone," Salifen murmured. There was fear in his eyes, and doubt, but there was determination, too. Hasefi wondered how the novice could still possibly have faith in her.

"I have to," she told him. "There's nothing either of you can do except watch your own tails. If this goes well, there may be no need for war."

"Hasefi...what if it doesn't go well?" Ivanus asked. "What if—"

"You'll see me in the morning—I promise." She winced inwardly at her final words, knowing that, if all went well, none of them would see her again.

"Wait," Salifen said suddenly. He dashed away, leaving Hasefi and Ivanus alone. She was too distracted by the keepers coming in and out of the Keeper's Cave to pay attention to Ivanus, but he, too, seemed preoccupied in his own mind. Before long, Salifen returned. Hasefi thought he might have gone to get the fox tooth, but what he dropped on the ground was a small, sparkling stone. It looked like a star pulled from the sky.

"I was going to get a guardian to attach it to this," he said, raising a paw to his collar. "But I want you to have it."

"What?" Hasefi blurted. "But it's yours."

"It only took a few days to make," he said with a shrug, not quite meeting her eye. "I can make another."

Hasefi looked at it for a moment, bewildered. It matched perfectly the silver lining of her black armor. "Are you sure?" she asked the novice healer.

"Absolutely." He stepped towards her with a questioning look and, when she nodded, he scooped up the stone and put it into the pouch on her shoulder.

"Will it protect her?" Ivanus asked hopefully.

"It's not enchanted," Salifen admitted. "But maybe it'll give you some luck." He caught Hasefi's eye and she knew he was aware that this might be the last time they saw each other.

"Thank you," Hasefi told him, trying not to wince at the guilt building up in her stomach.

"Be careful," he told her.

Hasefi nodded, her throat tightening until it was difficult to speak. Ivanus was staring at her with scared eyes. She wanted to comfort him, but the only words she could find were flimsy. She turned away from him so she didn't have to lie to his face anymore. "I'll see you tomorrow."

Without looking back, Hasefi padded out of the clearing.

What is your plan? Sefonis asked.

Hasefi stared at her reflection in a pool of rainwater that had collected some time ago. The face that looked back bore the same three-lined scar across its face as she had, but she wasn't sure she recognized herself.

You know my plan, she said to her uncle.

I do. But going over it keeps it fresh in your mind.

Hasefi was silent for a time. She was still on Tribe territory, but the urgency she'd felt had not followed her out of the clearing. At length, she responded.

I'm going to offer the Clan information about the Pack and the Tribe's plan of attack if they give me Kolahn.

They may attempt to take you prisoner, as the young novice suggested, Dahsefer warned.

Or hurt you, Sefonis added. *They may be more inclined to bite first and ask questions later.*

If at all, Gelinaf spoke. *With the threat of the Pack and of the Tribe on each side, the Clan may be more prone to kill out of fear.*

They could try *to kill me,* Hasefi said. *If I get to talk to them, though, is there a chance they'd go against their word?*

That's assuming they take the deal, Sefonis pointed out.

I think they will. Kolahn's alive, which means they want to know more about the Pack. And I'm sure they'd like to avoid a war seeking to drive them out of their home.

Would it not be enough to give just info on the Pack? Gelinaf asked.

Hasefi shook her head. *Kolahn went to warn them of the danger to their home. I owe it to him to do the same. Besides, if Eilwyn does listen, maybe she'll be able to convince Esafi to talk.*

Doubt was clear in the Overlord's mind, but it was Sefonis who spoke.

The Clan respects honor as much as we do. If Eilwyn and Morvak agree to your terms, they will uphold their end.

Great. That's good enough for me.

Hasefi lingered at the little pool for a couple more heartbeats before she straightened and looked ahead towards the River.

Rustling sounded, joined by loud, frantic pawsteps. Hasefi crouched, unsure what she meant to do. Thoughts of incapacitating whoever was rapidly approaching came to mind, but she didn't think she could bring herself to do it. Especially since there was a chance she'd be returning and explaining herself would be nigh impossible.

Her tribe lent their strength and she directed her senses towards the noise. At the same time, she thought of what she might say, guessing it was Arsolin and he'd realized she was no longer in the clearing.

But just before he broke through the brush, Hasefi's senses picked up a different lynx's scent.

"Salifen?"

The novice healer emerged and came to a stumbling halt in front of her. He was panting and his eyes were alight with fierce determination.

"I couldn't let you go alone," he gasped. "I know that you're going to try and get Kolahn and, if you do, you'll leave," he added before she could argue. "But something in me is telling me to help you. I want to, Hasefi, but I also have to, I think." He looked up into the sky. Leaves and branches blotted most of it out, but there was a small clear spot where a pair of stars could be seen glittering. "Maybe it sounds vain, but I think it is the will of the ancestors."

Salifen's words made Hasefi uneasy, but when he lowered his gaze back to her, something in it encouraged her and she was relieved at the thought of having him with her.

"It's dangerous," she reminded him. "I know what I said to Ivanus, but the Clan may try to hurt us. And that's assuming we don't run into the Pack."

"All the more reason to have a gifted, no?"

Hasefi snorted softly, admiring the formerly timid novice's courage. She wasn't sure what exactly encouraged him to follow her, but she was glad for it.

"Alright. The lynxian patrol will be changing soon. We'll want to hurry if we want to slip by."

"I'm ready."

Hasefi leapt into a run, leading Salifen towards the River. She kept her senses sharp with her tribe's strength so they didn't accidentally run into any lynx.

They reached the Great Fall just as the new patrol arrived. Two of the lynxes already there went to meet them. One, however, a keeper, remained close to the path leading to the Clan's territory.

"Fallen stars," Hasefi breathed, slinking along the edge of the clearing.

Salifen came beside her, brushing her armor lightly to signal for her to stop. She did, crouching low as the novice healer looked ahead.

His eyes began to glow, but he shut them, hiding the light. Hasefi waited, but when he opened his eyes again and they were normal, nothing seemed to have happened.

"If we pass beneath the shadow of the cliff, they will not see us," he whispered close to her ear so she could hear over the pouring water. "I have put shadows in our fur."

Hasefi glanced at him, but she saw nothing different. Nonetheless, she trusted him, and went the short distance to the cliff-wall.

The new patrol and the pair that had joined them spoke softly, reporting the events of their shift. Hasefi caught some words about the Fall being haunted or that the ancestors had sent an ill omen regarding the upcoming war by sending the image of a starlit lynx fleeing home. Hasefi was a little relieved that Tenarli's plan not only continued to distract the lynxes, but seemed to dissuade them against war. She wondered if any lynx had told the champions or Esafi herself.

It's too late to try and convince Esafi, she reminded herself, focusing ahead as she and Salifen stalked by a few paces away from the guards, unseen and unheard.

Hasefi and Salifen reached the path where the keeper still sat. Their posture was straight and still. As the two of them neared, the keeper twitched, but their helmet turned away from them, allowing her and Salifen to slip by unnoticed.

Not wanting to call over the roaring water passing by them, Hasefi blinked gratefully at Salifen, knowing she would have had a difficult time getting past on her own, especially without the fox illusion.

Hasefi continued beneath the Fall, stopping just before the exit. She glimpsed black nearby and a flash of silver a little farther off. To Salifen, she twitched her ears, indicating there were wolves ahead.

He nodded understanding.

Hasefi straightened and padded out from the tunnel with Salifen close behind.

"Hey!" The nearest rogue whirled on her, surprise and a hint of fear widening their eyes. The call brought out two more rogues and a warrior, surrounding Hasefi and Salifen.

Hasefi stood calmly, silently pleading the wolves not to attack. Fortunately, the four looked more shocked than angry to see the two of them there.

"What are kits doing by the Fall?" one of the rogues asked.

The warrior stepped forth, his gaze hard. "The Lady has ordered all lynxes to be chased from our territory," he growled.

"Whether you're High Heir or not," another rogue added, baring her teeth. Salifen shrunk against Hasefi, but she held firm.

"Who else is with you?" the fourth wolf demanded.

"We come alone," Hasefi assured them.

"Yeah, right, you star-gazing cat," the warrior snorted. "Who else is with you?"

"It's just us," Hasefi said again, trying not to lash out in anger. "I want to speak to Lady Eilwyn."

"Why?" the second rogue snarled. "Just so you can throw more accusations? Get lost."

"I have valuable information on the Pack," Hasefi said.

The wolves were silent now, fright bright in all their gazes. The one who seemed to be in charge, the warrior, spoke again, his tone subdued.

"We will bring you to the ravine and let the Lord and Lady determine what to do with you."

"Thank you," Hasefi sighed.

"Don't you try anything," one of the rogues growled at Salifen.

The novice made no reply, his eyes wide with fear as he padded with his fur pressed against Hasefi. She caught his gaze and gave him a reassuring blink. His jaws parted to release a breath and he lifted his head a little higher.

The wolves flanked them closely, leading them alongside the River. It took much longer to reach the ravine at this pace, but Hasefi ignored the apprehension tightening her gut at the thought of Arsolin realizing she was missing and the series of events that would follow, knowing there was nothing she could do until she returned.

If *I return,* she thought. *But even if I don't, Salifen will and I'd be subjecting him to whatever trouble I've caused.* She glanced at her friend, who was staring wide-eyed at the rogue closest to him. *I'll figure that out later,* she told herself. *First, I have to talk to Eilwyn.*

The moon, a pale oval in the sky, climbed above the cliff to their left and shone brightly down into the trees. Despite its light, a darkness hung about them, reminding Hasefi of the Pack.

The Clan increased their guards, she thought. *Even the Pack would struggle to take and kill four wolves without detection.* Inspecting their escort, Hasefi saw that the wolves kept their eyes and ears moving, watching their forest as if they walked in unfamiliar territory.

Eventually, they reached the dried-up stream leading from the ravine. The wolves turned to follow it, bringing Hasefi and Salifen up the gradual slope.

When the ground before them gave way and the rising earth around it became rocky, creating the entrance to the wolves' home, Salifen hesitated, fear blazing in his eyes. Two warriors stood ahead and more wolves could be glimpsed beyond.

"As long as you're with me, you'll be safe," she whispered to him. "They won't hurt you."

Salifen didn't look at her, but he lurched forward before the wolf at their rear could push him on.

The pair of warriors approached, stopping the escort. They cast loathing glares over Hasefi and Salifen which was unexpectedly chilling to Hasefi. She was used to the hatred of the Pack, but theirs was wild and driven by rage. The hate and anger of these wolves was cold and something different altogether. It was much older.

"The Lady ordered all lynxes to be removed from our grounds," one of the guards said, her stare boring into Hasefi.

"She claims to have information on the Pack," the leader of the escort said. The guard narrowed her eyes at Hasefi before stepping out of the way.

The warrior leading Hasefi and Salifen muttered something to the rogue beside him. The black-clad wolf raced ahead, disappearing into the ravine. Then the warrior followed, bringing Hasefi farther into the wolves' home than she'd ever been.

They passed between the narrow entrance and emerged into the wide, rocky clearing that stretched to the back of the cliff where the rock had been smoothed by the water that had once fallen there.

At the bottom, the ground had been carved, allowing a pool to form. The dry streambed led away from it, its path leading down the gentle slope of the ravine until it left, making its way to the River.

Around them, paths not unlike those in the Tribe's clearing led to caves dotting the walls, though they were lined with ledges, allowing wolves to peer down from all around to glare at her and Salifen.

Hasefi aimed her gaze ahead, trying to ignore the prickling of her fur with so many unfriendly eyes on it. Salifen was pressed close, his ears flat and his head ducked. She hoped that by appearing confident, it helped him overcome the fear he had of being in the heart of Clan territory. And that it hid her own.

The tall rock where Eilwyn had howled last time Hasefi had come stood before her as the escort came to a stop. The rock was much bigger now than she had thought when she'd been looking down at it from above.

The white wolf appeared, coming around the rock. Her fur and robes glowed like the moon itself beneath its light. Morvak, the Lord, was with her, though his dark gray fur held a more ominous light.

"I'm assuming you have good reason for bringing these lynxes into our home," Eilwyn growled softly to the warrior, though her gaze and anger were directed at Hasefi and Salifen.

"My apologies, my Lady," the escort leader said, bowing. Hasefi noticed that the other wolves showed no sign of bowing before their leaders, nor did the wolves around seem afraid to approach to see what was happening. "She insisted on seeing you and claims to have information on the Pack."

"Is this true?" Eilwyn asked Hasefi.

"Yes. Lady," Hasefi added, offering a bow. The gesture surprised the wolves, but the hard light in Eilwyn's stare did not dim.

"Why would Esafi send two adolescents to bring this information?"

"She didn't," Hasefi admitted, holding the white wolf's gaze. "We are here of our own volition. Esafi doesn't know."

Both of the leaders' eyes widened in shock. The wolves around them muttered to each other, their hostile glares shifting with uncertainty and suspicion.

"Speak, then," Eilwyn demanded.

Hasefi looked at her with surprise. "Wouldn't you want to go somewhere more private?" she asked.

"Whatever you have to say, you can say before the Clan. What do you know of the Pack?"

"As much as the wolf held prisoner here does," Hasefi said. Muffled gasps sounded around them.

"What do you know of *him?*" Morvak asked.

"I spent five moons of my life with Kolahn," she said. "He saved my life."

"What was an outcast doing helping the Tribe?" the Lord asked.

"Not the Tribe," Hasefi said. "I didn't even know this tribe was here until half a moon ago."

"You are Hasefi," Eilwyn said. "You are the one he spoke of." Her eyes narrowed. "You were the kit that came with the Emperor." She frowned. "And you are suddenly the High Heir? I thought Esafi had sons."

"I came after Kolahn," Hasefi corrected. "I knew he was putting himself in danger." She eyed the two leaders before continuing. "I'm Esafi's eldest kit, but my brothers are dead."

Eilwyn's eyes widened in dismay.

"Perhaps it would be wise to speak elsewhere," Morvak murmured to her.

"Yes," she agreed. "Come," she added to Hasefi and Salifen.

Eilwyn turned to lead them away while Morvak came up behind. Hasefi was surprised at the lack of disappointment and protest the other wolves gave.

They're not afraid, Hasefi thought. *They just trust her.*

They rounded the tall rock and came to the cavemouth where the waterfall had once been. Inside, Salifen relaxed a little and straightened as they moved along a curve that opened up into a cavern that made Hasefi think of the mainchamber in the Highcave. Magical light made the walls glow here, too.

"You have truly come against Esafi's knowledge?" Eilwyn asked when she was sitting before them. Morvak settled beside her.

"Yes," Hasefi admitted.

"That's a serious offense, especially in the eyes of your leader," the white wolf observed, studying her and Salifen.

"She is not my leader," Hasefi said, not entirely meaning to.

Question entered Eilwyn's gaze.

"I had a tribe," Hasefi explained. "They may not be here anymore, but they will always be my tribe. I don't belong with this one." Guilt pricked her heart when Salifen flinched.

"Another lynx tribe," Eilwyn murmured. "We heard once that your kind split off when your numbers grew too high. Is that...?"

"Not quite," Hasefi replied. "My tribe was the Second Divide."

"How does this relate to the Pack?" Morvak demanded.

"My tribe was killed by them," Hasefi explained. "If anyone knows them, it's me." She hesitated.

"And?" Eilwyn pressed.

"Kolahn has already warned you," Hasefi said slowly.

"He has."

"Which is why you keep him alive?"

The wolven leaders were silent, their stares intense, but Hasefi was unbothered.

"If my words match his...would you let him go?"

Their ears flattened.

"Kolahn returned knowing the consequences," the Lady said, but Hasefi could hear the flatness in her tone.

"To warn you of a great danger," Hasefi pointed out.

"We are aware of his involvement with this Pack," the Lord pointed out. "We cannot trust his words."

"Fine. Then trust mine."

Hasefi settled herself as she began her story from the very beginning when Sal had first made himself known to her. She described briefly the attack and how he continued to hunt her for the following moons. She explained how this had led to Kolahn finding her and saving her life and how, after she was crippled, he continued to provide for her and taught her of the different places in the world and how to survive in them.

Salifen listened as intently as the wolves, his eyes widening when she described her encounter with the mountain lion that had attacked Kolahn and his ears flattening when she recounted Kolahn's near death experiences with the Pack and after the landslide.

There were some details Hasefi left out, like the rising sun and the prophecy that had started her tribe in the first place. But nearly everything concerning Kolahn she offered, hoping to emphasize how he had saved her countless times and how insistent he was on not being like the Pack.

"He lied to you," the Lord was first to speak after she had finished. "About who he is. It's clear you care for him, but his desire lies elsewhere."

"Kolahn's desire was to find a creature that didn't immediately hate him because they thought he was evil," Hasefi replied evenly. Eilwyn flinched, but Morvak was undeterred.

"There is a darkness in these wolves—"

"One that he fights every day!" Hasefi blurted. "And now he has to do that alone in some dark prison-cave because he was too selfless to worry of what would become of him."

"The Pack," Eilwynn said before Morvak could respond, "is exactly as Kolahn described." She paused. "But what benefit would telling us provide you?"

"I told you," Hasefi said. "Kolahn is my friend. I want him back. Then we'll go far away and you never have to see us again."

There was a long silence. The wolven leaders looked to each other, unspoken words passing between them. Hasefi turned to her own companion. His eyes were wide, but his terror had become an apprehension that mirrored her own thoughts.

Finally, the Lady spoke.

"I cannot release him. Not while this Pack remains a threat," she added when Hasefi began to protest. "But with your word and his, I can only believe that his warning is true. He will remain alive."

"What about after the Pack is dealt with?" Hasefi asked.

"Then you may take him."

A rush of relief and joy swept through Hasefi, but it soon abated as dread flowed in.

"Is there something else?" Eilwyn asked, studying her closely.

"Yes," Hasefi replied hesitantly, looking to Salifen. "But I have terms."

"Tell me."

"I want free passage for us to return to the Tribe," she said and Eilwyn narrowed her eyes. "And I don't want our involvement to be known to the Tribe."

"A betrayer of her own kind," Morvak growled to Eilwyn. "Why should we trust her?"

"Because this isn't about your stupid hatred for each other," Hasefi snapped. "This is about fighting an evil that threatens both clan and tribe."

"You'd go against your own kind to help us?" Eilwyn asked.

"My kind are the dead lynxes that raised me and the wolf in your prison. I'm doing this for them. And—" Hasefi cut herself off.

"And what?"

"Will you adhere to my terms?"

Eilwyn's eyes flickered to Salifen. The novice healer shrunk beneath her blue gaze. "You have followed the High Heir here. Why?"

Hasefi thought Salifen would cower before the Lady's intense gaze, but he drew himself up despite his trembling body and spiked fur.

"Purpose," he replied. "Every gifted has a purpose determined by their ancestors. I believe mine is to help Hasefi." He met Hasefi's gaze. "And I trust her. All she wants is to help whether you're a lynx or not." He turned his gaze on the Lady. "For all her words, I believe she does care what happens to you and to the Tribe where I was raised. She's come for Kolahn, but she stays because of the Pack."

Hasefi ducked her head, astonished and embarrassed at how easily Salifen could see into her mind.

Eilwyn did not reply for a time, her gaze thoughtful as she studied Salifen, then Hasefi. Morvak continued to glare, but eventually, he turned his attention to the Lady, waiting for her word.

"Such a trust would not be bestowed on a betrayer," Eilwyn murmured.

"I was never loyal to them," Hasefi reminded her. "And Esafi knows that well."

"And yet you risk coming here for the well-being of her tribe, do you not?" Eilwyn asked.

Hasefi's ears half-flattened. "The Pack needs to be stopped. You know that as well as I do."

"Yes," Eilwyn sighed. "Every wolf does." With a glance at Morvak, she nodded to Hasefi. "My wolves will not reveal your involvement and both of you will be free to return to the Tribe."

Hasefi let out a small breath, but she was hardly relieved. It became difficult to speak.

"What is it, then?" Morvak demanded.

"On the night of the dark moon, Esafi wants to chase you from your home."

Eilwyn drew back and Morvak let out a furious bark.

"What?!" he snarled. "She dare think she could take our *home* from our paws?"

"This is very confidential information to be sharing with us," Eilwyn half-growled.

"Esafi has always been difficult, but to declare war for little reason seems unlikely," Morvak pointed out.

"You're right," Hasefi agreed. "Honestly, I have no idea why she wants this. She knows as much about the Pack from me as you do. But she just keeps saying that it's your fault they're out there in the first place." Hasefi decided not to mention the darker reasons Esafi thought chasing the wolves out would be beneficial.

"Perhaps she is right in that," Eilwyn replied.

"We cannot be held accountable for the actions of the Pack!" the Lord cried.

"Try telling Esafi that," Hasefi said.

"Your brothers," Eilwyn said. "Am I right in guessing the Pack was involved in their deaths?"

Hasefi nodded. "The Pack has no care for the lynxes. Like I said, my tribe was a training exercise. Even if I blamed you, I wouldn't think you deserved to lose your home."

"You're quick to think we'll lose," Morvak growled.

"I can't say I think things are in your favor," Hasefi said.

"Things rarely are," the white wolf sighed. "It seems we have a war to prepare for."

Hasefi shifted her paws. "I was hoping bloodshed could be avoided."

"You have said Esafi is immovable on this matter," the Lady said. "If she won't listen to her own kin, she will not listen to us. I'm afraid this is unavoidable." The white wolf stood. "You have risked much to aid us, even if all you seek is to free your friend. I will not forget that."

"If you fight, that puts you at risk against the Pack," Hasefi pointed out. "The only way we might fight them is to work together."

Eilwyn smiled, her expression sad. "You have lived outside the borders of the River. Hatred has long lived here, longer than any wolf or lynx alive now."

"I'm not a stranger to hatred," Hasefi growled.

"No. But you also learned love. There is little of that in these dark times." Her gaze flickered to Salifen before returning to Hasefi.

"I'll be fighting," Hasefi said flatly.

Eilwyn looked at her with surprise. "The Highchief would allow that?"

"Esafi said she'll free Kolahn, if they win. I have to make sure she doesn't kill him, instead." Hasefi's shoulders sagged as she met the white wolf's troubled gaze.

"But you are hardly more than a kit," Morvak protested.

"My experience against the Pack taught me a few things," Hasefi told him. "I'm not afraid to fight. Just to fight the wrong thing."

"Very well," Eilwyn said. She stood. "There is one thing I may offer you."

Hasefi's ears perked.

"I can have Kolahn brought here, if you'd like."

All of Hasefi's despair was forgotten. Desperate joy rushed through her and it took all of her will not to leap into the air.

Eilwyn's blue gaze turned warm at Hasefi's reaction and she nodded at Morvak. The Lord slunk out.

"Kolahn is not like the wolves of the Pack," Eilwyn murmured. Excitement made it difficult for Hasefi to pay attention, but she did her best to rein herself in so she could respond.

"He's not," Hasefi agreed. "Whatever force drives them, he fights it because he's terrified of becoming like them." She looked eagerly to the tunnel where Morvak had disappeared.

They waited in silence. Every heartbeat dragged on until it felt like moons were passing. Hasefi's claws scraped against the stone as she fought the urge to run outside and look for her friend. Then she heard their steps.

Morvak rounded the corner with Kolahn close beside him. Words flowed to Hasefi's mouth, but they were stopped short as her throat tightened with emotion.

Her friend's yellow gaze was blank and he walked as if numb. He hardly seemed aware of where he was and what was happening.

"Kolahn?" she squeaked.

His ear twitched and he lifted his head. A tiny light flickered in his gaze and it sharpened, focusing on her. He blinked and his eyes widened.

"Sefi?"

Hasefi launched herself at the wolf, wrapping her forelegs around his neck and burying her face in his fur.

"Oh, Kolahn, I missed you so much!" she whimpered. "I've been trying so hard to save you."

Kolahn said nothing, merely drawing her closer with a paw and pressing his face into her shoulder.

"I was so worried they were going to kill you," she whimpered. "But I didn't want to hurt them like the Pack. I'm so sorry."

"You shouldn't be worrying about me," he mumbled into her fur.

"Don't even start with that, you stupid furball."

Kolahn drew away gently, meeting her gaze. Then he looked past her to where Salifen was sitting. The novice healer's eyes were wide, but instead of watching her bulky dark-furred friend with terror, he was looking at Hasefi and his expression was filled with a mixture of joy and grief.

Eilwyn and Morvak were watching them, too, surprise on both their faces.

"You have found your home," Kolahn said, bringing her attention back to him. "You've found your kin."

"*You're* my home," Hasefi argued. "Or have you forgotten that?"

Kolahn shook his head. "This is where you belong, Sefi."

"No. I belong out there." She jerked her head in the general direction of the mountains beyond the River. "With you."

Kolahn blinked at her, looking both guilty and bewildered. "How can you still want me?"

Hasefi stared at him. "How can you ask me that?"

"I lied, Hasefi. I told you I didn't know of other lynxes. But I...I used to live here. I knew of the Tribe."

Hasefi shrugged. "You were scared I'd run to them and leave you behind. I don't blame you for that. I would have done the same, I'm sure."

"I don't think so," Kolahn said, a smile twitching his lips. "Maybe once. But you are different."

"Thanks to you, you silly furball."

Kolahn shook his head, but he said no more on the matter, giving Hasefi's ears an affectionate lick. Then he frowned, glancing at the Clan leaders. "How are you here?"

"Hasefi has confirmed your warning of the Pack," Eilwyn explained. "And I've agreed to let you go with her after they are dealt with."

Kolahn didn't look as pleased as Hasefi had thought he would.

"But we have another threat to face, first," Eilwyn admitted. Morvak looked at her sharply, but she returned it with a firm look of her own before continuing. "Hasefi has also warned us the Tribe intends to remove us from the River."

"They do?" Kolahn asked, glancing between Hasefi and Eilwyn. "Why?"

"My mother," Hasefi told him. "The Pack killed her kits and she blames the Clan for it."

Kolahn recoiled, his expression distraught. "You have siblings? Sefi, I'm sorry."

"Don't," Hasefi told him. "It's not your fault." She looked to Eilwyn and Morvak. "Is there nothing I can do to convince you to at least *try* talking to Esafi?"

"No," the white wolf replied, shaking her head. "It would risk your involvement and I cannot show any weakness to the Tribe or to the Pack." She closed her eyes for a heartbeat, then opened them, her face twisting with determination. "Once more, we must face this alone."

Hasefi looked to Kolahn, deflating. "Esafi said she'll claim you if they win," she explained to her friend.

The wolf tilted his head, eyes alight with sorrow. "You've risked a lot to come here, Sefi," he murmured. "I really appreciate it. But you've done all you can." He leaned in and pressed his nose to her cheek. "Whatever happens, I'll see you again."

Hasefi turned her head and gave his cheek a lick. Behind her, she heard Morvak rise and knew her time with Kolahn was ending. A desperate cry rose in her throat, but she was silent as her friend got to his paws and followed the Lord out of the cavern.

She blinked, staring at the tunnel entrance where his black tail had flicked out of sight.

"You will see him again," Eilwyn assured her. Hasefi turned to face the white wolf, not caring to hide the misery that had settled over her.

"We should return," Salifen said quietly. "The Tribe will know we were gone."

"Next time I see you," Hasefi said to the white wolf, "may be on the battlefield."

"So be it," Eilwyn replied, standing up. "I will have an escort ready to guide you back to the Fall." Her words were distant as if her thoughts were elsewhere as she spoke. "There is a warrior outside that will bring you to the ravine's mouth."

With no more words to say, Hasefi merely nodded and followed Eilwyn out of the cave. Sure enough, a warrior stood ready, their silver armor glittering beneath the moon. Their expression was unreadable as they jerked their head to Hasefi and Salifen before leading them through the ravine.

The fear that had gripped Salifen was all but gone and now he pressed his fur against Hasefi's armor to comfort her. She was grateful for it, but the touch was cold and all she could think about was Kolahn and the dullness of his eyes before he'd recognized her.

He can't stay here. But if the Clan is driven away, he won't leave until he knows they're safe. She stifled a sigh. *Maybe this will be enough to help them defend their home.* The thought offered little hope.

Before they reached the entrance of the ravine, an escort of two warriors and two rogues were already waiting for them, including the lead warrior that had brought them there. Suspicion glittered in his eyes just as it had before, but it was subdued by a flicker of curiosity. He said little, though, as he led her and Salifen out of the ravine along the dry streambed.

By the time they neared the waterfall, the moon was falling back to the ground. Faintly, Hasefi wondered how she and Salifen would get back to the Tribe without suspicion, but her despair was stronger than her fear and she would have walked right out to meet the lynxian patrol waiting on the other side if it weren't for her friend.

Salifen stopped her with a paw. His eyes glowed briefly before he took the lead and they slunk unseen past the two knights and keeper on watch. When they were far enough away, Hasefi recovered enough to talk.

"You've gotten quite good at that," she observed.

"I figured it'd be a good skill." He blinked sympathetically at her. "You'll see him again. Soon, all this will be over and you'll be right back where you belong, the River a distant memory."

Hasefi stopped and hung her head. "I didn't mean to sound like I didn't care," she said. "You were right. I care a lot more than I admit even to myself. You, Alarni, Ivanus, Nakilon, my father...it was so easy to get attached and I...I was so scared I'd forget about Kolahn."

Salifen sat before her, lowering his head so he could meet her gaze. "That would never happen. But only you know where your heart lies. With him, or with the Tribe, only you can decide. And don't worry about us," he added with a smile. "When this all turns for the good, we'll be glad we were able to help."

"Alarni might not be," Hasefi pointed out.

"She will be, if she isn't already. Alarni's always had a temper."

Hasefi shook her head. "This is more than that. I've put the Tribe in danger now. They have no idea the Clan is aware. I don't know what the wolves are capable of. Anything can happen."

Salifen leaned towards her, his gaze intense. "You did the right thing, Hasefi. The Lady was right—you didn't grow up with the kind of barriers that we did. You see past them."

Then why do I feel like I'm stumbling about blindly?

"It's been a long night," Salifen continued. "Tomorrow will be better."

The novice healer had just gotten to his paws when the brush around them shuddered. He jumped to Hasefi's side, eyes glowing, while Hasefi unsheathed her claws, imagining pack-wolves bursting from the foliage around them.

But the figure that came was Garfonis.

A keep appeared a heartbeat after and, when he took off his helmet, Hasefi realized it was Arsolin.

"Hasefi," Garfonis gasped, relief flooding his face. He turned his head to Arsolin. "Inform the Highchief that we've found her, then send your cousin back to me." Without a word, Arsolin put his helmet on again and raced off in the direction of the clearing.

"Garfonis," Hasefi said, her tone still flat with disappointment. She tried to appear cheerier, but knowing she would have to lie to him made it difficult and she merely hung her head.

"Where have you been?" her father asked, nosing her. He withdrew, his nose twitching. "You smell like flowers."

Hasefi jerked her head up in surprise, but Salifen spoke before she could.

"I brought Hasefi to a lavender bush," he explained. "She's been really stressed out about the war and lavender is often used to help treat anxiety." He blinked apologetically at her. "But I don't think I helped much."

Hasefi blinked gratefully at him, then returned her gaze to Garfonis.

"Is that where you've been all night?" he asked.

Hasefi nodded, still unable to bring herself to speak.

Sorrow darkened Garfonis's gaze and he touched his nose to Hasefi's ear. "I'm sorry," he told her. "I know how you feel about all this."

Hasefi drew away. "I'm tired," she said, slinking past him.

"Of course," he said and led the way back to the clearing.

Once there, Salifen murmured goodnight and retreated to the Healer's Cave. Garfonis brought her up to the Highcave. The lynxes they passed were quiet and, despite their usual curious glances, showed no signs of knowing that she'd been missing, which surprised Hasefi. But she didn't have the will to think of why.

She was further disheartened when Esafi was waiting for them in the sleeping chamber. Hasefi silently went to her hollow and curled up while Garfonis swiftly repeated what Salifen had said to him.

"Are you unable to explain for yourself?" Esafi said in Hasefi's direction.

"Let her rest," Garfonis said quietly. "She has a lot to face right now."

"We all do," Esafi replied, but no more was said to Hasefi and she was able to escape into the darkness of sleep.

Chapter Eighteen

It was the day of the waning half-moon. It had been almost a quarter moon since she and Salifen had returned from the Clan. Ever since, a pit of dread had formed in Hasefi's gut, growing bigger and bigger until she was nearly incapacitated by it.

Her tribe had tried to comfort her, but she couldn't face them, feeling too guilty, so she distanced herself from them.

Her training with Arsolin continued, and, inevitably, he'd noticed her change in mood, but she hardly spoke to him or anyone else about how she felt and he'd given up trying to ask.

She hadn't seen Salifen since, except in passing. Alarni was nowhere to be seen and, every now and then, she'd catch the sad gaze of Ivanus as he sat alone in their old spot.

All I've done is hurt these lynxes, she thought. *And most of them don't even know the extent of it.*

Despite the fact she and Salifen had successfully returned, she couldn't help but feel like every lynxes' gaze was on her, sharp and suspicious as the wolves in the Clan. She thought about what Esafi had said about her manner, and how Firalos and Alarni had called her wolfcat. The latter had tainted Kolahn's version of it, darkening the memory and making her feel like the betrayer Morvak had called her.

And I'll be fighting them, too, after all of this. Is there anyone I haven't hurt?

Movement behind her dragged her from her thoughts. She was settled on the edge of the Highledge, looking down on the clearing with unseeing eyes, her paws curled tightly beneath her chest. A black flicker in the corner of her eye told her that Arsolin had come up to join her.

She bowed her head, not wanting to talk, but he said nothing, simply putting aside his helmet and settling beside her.

After a while, Hasefi looked to her keeper. His gaze was on the lynxes below, a mixture of apprehension and sorrow in his expression.

"Are you okay?" she asked him.

He turned his gaze on her, a flicker of amusement chasing away some of the darkness there. "I've been trying not to ask you that."

Hasefi looked away, absently lifting a paw to touch the armor at her chest. She'd gotten the silver stone Salifen had given her attached to it and she ran her pad across its smooth surface, comforted by it.

"You haven't seen your friends," Arsolin continued softly.

"I don't want to see them."

"Perhaps you need to."

Hasefi lifted her gaze again to look at him questioningly.

"You're troubled," he continued. "I don't expect you to talk to me, but you don't have to keep this in."

"None of them want to talk to me," she insisted.

"Do you believe that?" her keeper asked with surprise.

Hasefi didn't reply.

"I think I know a particular novice knight that would like to see you."

She blinked in confusion. "Nakilon?"

Arsolin dipped his head. "Ever since your knight training was paused, he's been restless. But he won't come to you." The keeper angled his ears and, following the direction with her gaze, Hasefi noticed Nakilon pacing near the log where the novices often hung out. His head turned up to her, but when their gazes met, he quickly turned away.

Delight sparked in her chest, but it was quickly muffled. *I still haven't told him I'll be fighting,* she thought.

But he deserves to know, her own voice argued.

Despite her words, she looked to her keeper again. "Isn't there something else you'd rather be doing than checking up on me?"

He blinked warmly at her. "It's been tradition for seasons that, when a keeper is assigned to one of highblood, the keeper and their charge will remain inseparable until death or necessary cause. Even if it may not be welcome sometimes, I will care for you however I can."

Some of Hasefi's despair melted away and she let it out in a sigh. "You know I appreciate you, right?"

Arsolin purred, giving her shoulder a comforting nudge. "Of course I do. And you're allowed to be unhappy sometimes," he added seriously. "You are a strong young lynx, Hasefi, but everyone falls sometimes."

Hasefi slowly got to her paws, feeling a trickle of warmth return to the numbness that had claimed her. "Thanks, Arsolin," she said.

"Anytime." He looked to where Nakilon was kneading the earth, his gaze fixed on some unseen thing. "He'll tear up the clearing if you don't go to him soon."

A soft snort left Hasefi before she turned and padded down to the ground. She approached her friend unnoticed until she was practically beside him.

"Hasefi!" he blurted. "I'm sorry." He blinked, looking down at his dirt-stained paws.

"Everything alright?"

"Yes, of course. I just...." He lowered his head, his ears flat. Then he jerked up suddenly, his expression hard with determination. "I want to talk to you."

"What is it?" she asked, surprised and a little unnerved by the intensity of his gaze. The novice's mouth opened, but no sound came out.

Hasefi!

Hasefi nearly jumped from her pelt when Mersaka, her guardian under Kilarsa's command, spoke with a burst of excitement in her head.

Look there, at the entrance! Do you see the hunter that just came through?

The one with dark fur?

That is my father! Would—would you speak to him?

Of course.

"Can you hold onto that thought?" she asked Nakilon. "I have to do something."

The novice looked ready to protest, but Hasefi hurried away, feeling energized. She'd spoken to many of her tribe's relatives since she'd arrived, but she hadn't done so in a while, so she was pleased to be able to meet someone else kin to her tribe.

The hunter in question was with two others. They had just brought some prey back from a hunt and were now splitting off. Mersaka's father was a broad-shouldered lynx, his dark fur clad in tough brown armor. His had been modified with various fangs around his hood, making it look like an open maw around his face.

As she approached, his angled amber eyes narrowed before he sank into a bow.

"High Heir," he greeted, speaking slowly.

"Tydalok?" she asked at Mersaka's whispers.

"Aye," he responded, straightening.

Hasefi shifted her paws awkwardly before continuing. "If I am correct, your daughter was with me in my tribe."

The hunter said nothing.

"Well, I just wanted to say—"

"Say what, exactly?" he interrupted, rising to his paws so that he loomed over her. "You wanted to say how honorably she died for you, how grateful you are for her life like you've been telling all the other lynxes who lost someone in your tribe?"

"I—" Hasefi's words stuck in her throat, caught totally off-guard by Tydalok's reaction.

"Mersaka didn't deserve her fate," he hissed. "All because our ancestors decided you were special so everyone else had to die to keep you alive. Tell me, kitten, how is that fair?" Tydalok was barely a whisker-length from Hasefi, his nose almost touching hers. Hasefi merely stared at him with wide eyes, her despair returning in full force.

"Stop!" Then Arsolin was between Tydalok and Hasefi, shoving the hunter back a pace. "Speaking to the High Heir like this will not be tolerated!"

"She is not my High Heir!" Tydalok snapped. "I will not follow a leader whose tribe is dead because of her!"

Hasefi stumbled back as the hunter tried to push past Arsolin. Despite being smaller, the keeper was able to trip the bigger lynx and pin him with a paw to his throat.

"Fetch me a guardian!" Arsolin demanded to a nearby keeper and they hurried off. "Hasefi, are you alright?"

"Yeah," Hasefi gasped, finally finding her voice. "It's okay—I'm okay. What—what's going to happen to him?"

"The Highchief will decide."

Hasefi stared with wide eyes at the hunter who glared back with hate.

Hasefi, I'm so sorry, Mersaka told her. *I had no idea—*

It's fine, she told her tribemate, numb with shock. *It's not your fault.*

Nor is it yours, wee lass, Sefonis murmured, but Hasefi hardly heard him.

The keeper Arsolin had instructed returned with a guardian. The purple-clad lynx removed Tydalok's bracer, causing his armor to disappear. Their eyes began to glow green and they lowered their head, sending a stream of light towards the hunter's face until a smooth hard piece engulfed his muzzle, forcing his jaw shut. Tydalok was still pinned beneath Arsolin, but his glare didn't leave Hasefi.

Another keeper came soon after, this one with Esafi.

"What has he done?" the Highchief demanded of Arsolin.

"He spoke insultingly to the High Heir, then made a move to attack her," Arsolin reported, stepping off the hunter so the other two keepers could secure him.

"Take him to the prison-cave. I will speak to my daughter."

The two keepers and the guardian moved off towards the bottom of the Highledge where, to Hasefi's surprise, the gifted touched a paw to the stone and the wall moved until the lynxes could pass. Then the wall moved back into place.

"Come, daughter," Esafi commanded, jolting Hasefi from her shock. She glanced once towards her keeper before following the Highchief to their cave. Along the way, her pelt burned with the stares of the lynxes that had stopped their activities to watch the event.

This is worse than when I first came, she thought. *It's as if they all know what I've done.*

They couldn't, Sefonis assured her.

But it has been seasons since the prison-cave has opened, Gelinaf observed.

A shiver of dread moved through Hasefi as she ascended the path to the Highledge. She remembered talking about prisoners before and wondered if her interaction with Tydalok had just gotten him killed.

Esafi didn't stop until they had passed through the mainchamber and were alone in the sleeping chamber. Sifara had not been in the tunnels.

"Tell me what happened," Esafi demanded.

"I...just wanted to talk. Mersaka—his daughter was with me in the high mountains. I just wanted to...to apologize, I guess."

"Like you have been with the others?"

Hasefi's head jerked up in surprise. *Has she been watching me that closely?* she thought with alarm.

Your keeper likely reports on your activities per her request, Sefonis pointed out.

Then I've been beyond lucky if she doesn't suspect anything.

"I hope you have learned a lesson in today's experience," Esafi continued.

"About what?" Hasefi asked, coming out of her thoughts.

"It is unwise to remind others of what they've lost, especially when they blame you as the reason for it."

"But it wasn't up to me!" Hasefi protested. "You were the one who decided to send us away, weren't you?"

"The Wanderers gave us a prophecy," Esafi said sternly. "I would not be one to disobey them."

"Right, right...I was supposed to lead some destiny away from here. Can you tell me what that destiny was if I've just come straight back here?"

"I wasn't the one who led it," Esafi pointed out, her expression becoming strange. "But Myafos and I have already dicussed this with you."

Hasefi looked away, her ears flat.

"Do you remember what we said of the ancestors' will?"

"I don't understand the blind faith you have in them!" Hasefi snarled, raking her claws across the ground.

"Talk like that could get you thrown right in with that hunter," the Highchief growled.

"All I believe in is what I see and know to be," Hasefi hissed. "My tribe, Kolahn, trapped, the lynxes here who lost loved ones who deserve some sort of condolences, the Pack lurking within these very trees!" Hasefi paused, waiting for a response, but Esafi was silent. At length, she spoke.

"Do you think I don't care about the lynxes in my tribe?"

Hasefi didn't answer.

"What is it you think I do with my time?" Esafi continued. "I spend every heartbeat keeping my tribe happy, fed, and safe. I do everything in my power to eliminate anything that threatens them, to keep every lynx alive until they are called by the stars. And now I've been spending my days preparing for a war because the wolves dared cross our borders and kill my kits!"

"It wasn't them," Hasefi hissed. "When will you open your eyes and see that?"

"Whether it was a black wolf or a gray wolf, the Clan is at fault," the Highchief stated. "If they had gotten rid of the black wolves like they said, then they wouldn't have come back!"

"So, what, the only way is to kill them?" Hasefi scoffed.

"Yes!"

"If that had happened, then Kolahn wouldn't have been alive to save me and eventually lead me back here!"

"If the black wolves had been killed, your tribe never would have died!"

Hasefi bowed her head and silence fell between them.

"Hasefi," Esafi sighed. "You are so eager to face the Pack, yet you shun killing. What, then, do you expect to do to stop the Pack?"

"It's not the Pack I want to spare," Hasefi growled quietly. "But black wolves aren't what you and the Clan think they are. If they're treated like regular creatures and taught how to fight whatever darkness is in them, then we wouldn't have to fear them anymore."

"You have seen what they can do," Esafi said. "But you still do not know them. They can't be saved. Killing them would be a mercy."

Hasefi snorted. "Is that what's going to happen to Tydalok?"

"Is that the sentence you would wish upon him?"

"Obviously not!"

"Then he will not die. But he must be punished."

"For what?" Hasefi demanded. "Speaking his mind?"

"Speaking against the High Heir and attempting physical harm."

"He has a right to be angry," Hasefi said quietly. "I might even deserve his wrath."

Hasefi—

"If lynxes begin to think they can act against us, it will lead to rebellion," Esafi stated. "Has your keeper discussed the rebellions in our time?"

Hasefi shook her head.

"Perhaps you should ask for your next lesson." Esafi gave a dismissive jerk of her head.

"What about—?"

"He will spend the day in the dungeon," Esafi said sharply.

Too defeated to argue further, Hasefi got up and left the cave. She strode past Arsolin without a glance and moved across the clearing towards the ferns at the entrance.

"Hasefi!"

Hasefi looked up to see Nalikon trotting over. To her dismay, Arsolin stepped in front of her, barring the novice's way.

"Er, I mean, High Heir." Nakilon bowed, then sat up quickly.

"Let him pass," Hasefi told Arsolin and the keeper moved away.

"Is everything alright?" Nalikon asked her. "I mean, are you…okay? I saw what happened and—"

"I'm fine," Hasefi assured him. "If I let angry words get to me, I would have been dead moons ago."

The novice gave her a frightened look.

"Sorry. I'm okay. Really."

Nalikon held her gaze for a bit, before giving her a nod. "Okay. Well, if there's anything you need or you want someone to talk to, don't be afraid to ask."

Hasefi blinked gratefully at him. "Thank you." Being with him eased the despair she felt and she waited for him to offer an idea as to what they could spend the day doing, but Nakilon merely sank into a bow.

"Wait," Hasefi blurted, putting a paw on his flank when he started to move past her. "Wasn't there something you wanted to tell me?"

Nakilon was silent, his gaze intense. Then his eyes flickered to the ferns a few paces away. "What about that pool your other friends showed you?" he asked. "Did you want to show it to me?"

A purr rumbled softly in Hasefi's throat. "Of course."

They left the clearing together. A silence fell between them as they padded into the trees, thick with unspoken words. She knew Nakilon was thinking about whatever it was he wanted to say to her while she was wondering how she'd tell him she would be fighting against the Clan, leaving him here to worry about her and everyone else he cared about.

It wasn't until Hasefi had led him up a small rise to where Alarni and Salifen had showed her the pool in question that either of them spoke. Familiarity flickered in Nakilon's gaze as he looked down.

"You already knew this was here," she observed.

"Yeah," he admitted apologetically. "But it is pretty neat, isn't it?" He added, looking down again. Hasefi followed his gaze and had to agree.

The pool was at the bottom of a rocky pit about a lynx-height deep. Water trickled into it, coming from one of the streams that ran through the Tribe's territory. And when she jumped down to lap up some of the water, it tasted fresh and sent a pleasant, cool ripple through her.

She looked up from where she had tasted the water and saw Nakilon crouched at the other end. He lifted his head and met her gaze, a water droplet on his nose. Hasefi chuckled as he crossed his eyes to look at it.

"I've never seen a lynx look so goofy," she laughed as he licked the drop off his nose. Longing tightened her chest, causing her laugh to fall flat.

"Is everything alright?" Nakilon asked, his humor shifting to worry.

"Yeah, sorry."

He rounded the pool and sat beside her, pressing his fur against hers.

"I think what you're doing is really nice," he murmured and she gave him a confused look. "Talking to the lynxes who had someone in your tribe," he explained.

"You know about that?" she asked and he looked away, his ears twitching with embarrassment. "Were you watching me?" she said with an amused purr.

"I...may have been..." he admitted.

Hasefi chuckled again until she thought of how things had went with Tydalok. "Tydalok wouldn't agree with you."

"Not every lynx is going to be happy," Nakilon pointed out. "But some are." He lowered his head and touched her cheek with his nose. Warmth spread through her, sending a feeling she didn't quite understand through her. When Nakilon pulled away, his eyes were alight with affection and Hasefi felt a shyness take over, causing her to look towards the pool. She instinctively reached to her tribe, but they were far away.

"If I tell you there's something I want to say," Nakilon began slowly. "Can you promise nothing urgent will come up before I can say it?"

Hasefi snorted softly. "I can't really control that," she pointed out. "But I'm here," she added seriously. "It's just us."

Nakilon nodded, looking down at his paws. His tail was twitching nervously and his ears flicked, first the left, then the right, as if he were having some mental debate. Then he lifted his head, meeting her gaze.

"I know you haven't been here long and we haven't known each other for even a moon yet, but...Hasefi, I like you. I mean, I *really* like you. I—I get excited sometimes and, well, you're really cool and mysterious, so I thought maybe it was just that. But when I didn't see you in training anymore, I realized I really missed you and I wanted to spend time with you. As much as I possibly could. And...for some reason, I feel like that's not enough. Like something is going to happen and we won't be able to see each other again." His ears flattened and he ducked his head.

Hasefi blinked at him, utterly baffled. A strange mix of warmth and anguish filled her heart, splitting it open with such force she flinched.

"I'm sorry," he said, withdrawing. "I've upset you."

"No," she told him. "I...I...." she trailed off, having no idea what to say.

"I'm sorry," he said again. He got to his paws.

"I'm going to fight the Clan."

Nakilon turned his gaze on her again, alarm bright in his eyes. "What?"

"Nakilon...." Hasefi bowed her head, words pouring from her mouth like a stream overflowing with rainwater. "You were right, before, when you asked if I had someone. The Clan is holding my friend prisoner. I only came here to save him, but then I found my father and, when he brought me to Esafi, she wouldn't let me leave because of everything happening between the Tribe and the Clan." The truth about the Pack lay on the tip of her tongue, but she couldn't bring herself to let it out, knowing it would only make Nakilon's worry worse. "Esafi is taking this war to them and she means to free my friend if we win so I can leave with him."

It was unnervingly quiet when Hasefi stopped talking. If it weren't for her friend's golden paws on the stone where she was looking, she'd have thought he'd left. But she couldn't bring herself to look up and meet his gaze.

Finally, Nakilon spoke, his voice barely a whisper. "Leave?"

Hasefi crouched, trembling beneath the astonished stare she knew was aimed at her. "I'm so sorry, Nakilon."

"No," he whispered. "No it's okay. I, uh—" His voice cracked, causing Hasefi to look up. The novice's eyes glistened with anguish, rending a gouge through Hasefi that she'd never felt before. It was like losing everything again, but this time the only one to blame was her.

Why is this so hard?

"It's not your fault," Nakilon continued haltingly, getting to his paws. "Don't be upset. I just...I just need to be alone." Before Hasefi could protest, the novice scrambled out of the shallow pit and disappeared into the trees.

Hasefi stared after him, immobilized by the grief that had seized her. Her tribe was still far away and, for the first time, she felt utterly alone.

"Hasefi? Is everything alright?"

Hasefi looked up from where she had been staring at her helmet. She was in her sleeping hollow which she'd hardly left for nearly a quarter moon after she'd talked to Nakilon, except to train with Arsolin. But he, too, was getting busy with the war just around the corner, leaving Hasefi to wander aimlessly through her tangled thoughts.

But she was brought out of them when her father entered the sleeping chamber, his eyes alight with concern.

She said nothing, though, and lowered her gaze back down to her helmet.

Garfonis came over, placing his helmet with hers, then settling on the stone before her. They were silent for a time.

"What was it like?" Hasefi asked eventually. "When you fought against Resahn," she added when her father looked at her with confusion.

Garfonis' eyes darkened and glazed, watching something only he could see. "I'm not sure I know the right word for it. Hard? Difficult?"

"Impossible?" Hasefi offered.

Garfonis' expression softened before he lowered his gaze to their helmets. "We were flourishing more than we ever had before. The Highchief, your grandmother, kept us strong and healthy, much like your mother does now. We were so well off that we actually grew too big for the territory." Garfonis chuckled, but the sound was empty.

"We had stumbled upon a problem we'd never had. So we looked to the stars. And they told us to divide."

"The First Divide," Hasefi murmured and her father nodded.

"Seventy-seven lynxes."

Hasefi's eyes widened. "Seventy-seven—how could so many lynxes move at one time?"

"There had been a scouting party, much like yours," Garfonis explained. "When they found a new home, they sent for the others."

"My tribe was...a scouting party?" Hasefi asked in surprise.

"Of course. A tribe couldn't live on with only eleven lynxes."

Hasefi frowned. "If they were to find our home, why send a kit with the scouts? Why not wait until home was found?"

Garfonis hesitated. "The prophecy stated you would lead a destiny beyond the River. You were to guide the lynxes to their new home."

"Two moons old?"

Garfonis avoided her gaze.

This isn't right, she thought. *I'm not upset with him. Or with anyone but myself.*

"I'm sorry, Garfonis. I don't mean to attack you."

"I know," he told her with a warm flicker in his eyes. "I don't blame you."

Hasefi was surprised to see understanding in his gaze.

"When I was a novice, I watched lynxes around me die," he told her. "My mother. My father. Esafi's mother. My friends."

Hasefi's ears flattened and she looked to her paws.

"We've both suffered at the paws of Resahn's kind," she growled.

"I don't want this war," Garfonis continued and Hasefi met his gaze again. "As much as I pretend to hate the Clan and try to blame them.... I know deep down none of this was truly their fault. Even without your words."

"Then why fight?" Hasefi asked. "Why let Esafi go through with this?"

"You are not the only one who tried to talk her out of this, Hasefi," he said with a sad smile. "Most of the champions are opposed," he explained. "And the ones who aren't stand neutrally."

"Really? But if that's true, then why are you going to war?"

"Because the Highchief's word is final," he stated. "And we are loyal to her."

Hasefi opened her mouth to protest, but she thought about how her own tribe made no attempt to foil her plan to go to the Clan.

And you were right, she thought. *I'm sorry. I should have listened. I'm no better than Esafi. I'm just as blind.*

We understand, wee lass, Sefonis told her gently.

I won't let it happen again.

"Hasefi?"

Hasefi's head jerked up, her ears half-flat with embarrassment. "Sorry," she told him.

"Are you afraid to fight?" he asked.

"No."

"I am."

Hasefi shook her head. "I'm not scared of fighting. I'm scared of the consequences. Are we really going to try and push the Clan out of their home? Like Resahn tried with the Tribe?"

Garfonis was silent.

"Wasn't it Eilwyn who tried to stop it? And the Seer Alpha?"

"Esafi will not stop until the Clan is gone," Garfonis explained. "At least this way they'll have a chance to find a new home."

"Do you really believe that?" she asked. "The Pack will find the Clan and destroy what's left. What will happen then?"

"I don't know!" he snapped suddenly, surprising Hasefi enough that she half-rose in her hollow. "I'm just an Emperor of the Tribe. I can't be thinking about how the Clan will fare, too." He hung his head, slumping his shoulders. Hasefi could almost see the weight weighing him down and she stepped out of her hollow so she could press her flank to his.

Garfonis pushed his muzzle into her fur, burying his face. "I didn't want to let you go," he whispered.

"I know," Hasefi said.

"I'm selfish."

Hasefi pulled away, staring deep into his eyes. "Don't you think it'd be worse if you had no problem letting go?"

Garfonis flicked his ears and pressed his nose to her head. "I'm sorry for everything you've been through."

"Don't be," she told him. "I'm not. It's made me who I am."

Garfonis pulled away, studying her thoughtfully. Then he stood, equipping his helmet. "Come with me."

Hasefi picked up her helmet, too, and followed him from the sleeping chamber. On the Highledge, Hasefi was surprised to find Esafi and Myafos there. They both glanced at her and Garfonis, but nothing was said as she followed her father down to the ground.

There, Hasefi's surprise was strengthened. Lynxes were all about the clearing though, despite her presence, the Highchief hadn't called a meeting. No one was doing anything or, if they were, it was done absently. Gazes were turned to the sky, some alight with fear, others dark with memory, echoing what Hasefi felt inside.

Garfonis's gaze was dark, too, especially as he swept it over the restless lynxes milling about. While the deep orange of the sky was turning purple and the first stars were becoming visible, the moon had yet to rise. Even if it had, Hasefi knew it would not shine any light on them.

"When I was a young novice," Garfonis began, "we were preparing for war. Only we were on the other side of it—we were fighting for home. Lynxes had already been injured and killed and horror stories of the new beasts in the Clan had circulated. I was terrified. Novices weren't supposed to fight, but some of us were chosen to join. We had just divided. We were lacking troops. There was no choice."

Hasefi's tribemates stirred in her mind, especially Sefonis.

"Sefonis and I," her father continued. "We couldn't sleep that night. We were ordered to stay in our cave, but we couldn't. Our father found us in the Cavern of History—it was our favorite place to be. We thought he'd be angry, but instead, he brought us out into the clearing. It turned out we weren't the only ones afraid."

Hasefi gazed out at the lynxes again. Some of their gazes had flicked over to them in curiosity, but most were preoccupied with their own thoughts. Instinctively, she looked to the log at the edge of the clearing to her left. She couldn't spot any of her friends, but Firalos was there, alone, his head bowed and his eyes widening and shrinking as if he were watching something play before him.

He's nearly a full knight, she thought. *He'll be fighting.*

"Back then, war was not uncommon," Garfonis continued. "But what we were about to face was beyond anything we'd ever known. Most of us had no idea what to expect. Those that did were either too hurt to help or dead."

A blackness spread through Hasefi's chest and she saw once again the last moments of her tribe. But there were other bodies with them; her brothers, and lynxes she'd never seen, but somehow knew were those her father had spoken of. She thought of her nightmare and how everyone in that clearing had been the same.

All but one.

Hasefi looked up, but they were beneath the Highledge, so she couldn't see the Elder sitting above. Nonetheless, his eerie glowing eyes were present in her mind as if he were watching her through the stone.

"Hopelessness spread through the Tribe like a disease," Garfonis admitted. "We were sure that our last moments were playing out." He tilted his head up so he was looking into the sky above the forest. "But somehow, my father was able to return hope to all those around him, even though he himself did not have it."

Hasefi found herself looking into the sky, too, but instead of seeing the stars, she thought about the moon and wondered why it chose to hide sometimes.

A sound tickled the tufts of her ears and she jerked her gaze back to her father. His gaze was still on the darkening sky, but a hum had risen in his throat. Hasefi watched him, seeing memories flit through his starlit eyes. Then his mouth opened.

The night is always restless
And the air heavy with tension
When the coming of battle
Hangs on the edge of tomorrow.

Hasefi's attention wavered when some of the lynxes nearby stirred. Gazes flicked to them and they leaned towards Garfonis as he continued.

Tonight we sit together,
Hanging onto every moment,
Wavering 'neath fading light,
'Til darkness calls us from our home.

Lynxes had gathered now, forming a half-circle around Garfonis and Hasefi. The fear and darkness in their gazes had changed, glowing now with hope. A knight stepped out. Hasefi recognized Katrima, one of the mentors. She sat a pace away from Garfonis and added her voice with his while another knight in the crowd hit the ground in an even rhythm.

So we march, unsheathe our claws
We prepare to defend all that is dear.
We are shields, we are armor,
And we protect the ones that we hold near.

Hasefi's ears twitched as more lynxes joined, repeating the chorus and stomping the ground. More and more lynxes rose until the clearing thundered with voices and the very earth beneath Hasefi's paws shuddered as if tread by the marching steps of an army. The words, which had sounded forlorn before, became a defiant cry, weaving courage and strength into Hasefi's fur. It reminded her of when Eilwyn had howled and she'd felt as if a calming spell had been put upon her, but if there had been magic in that, there was none here, yet the song imbued the clearing with a fierce determination that chased even Hasefi's despair away.

Then, as if on some unspoken cue, the voices halted and the stomping ceased, and Garfonis continued alone.

This night we may be restless,

But we are the Tribe of the Lynx
And with the stars at our back
We will march and come home again.

Garfonis lowered his gaze after a few heartbeats of silence, resting it on Hasefi.

She looked around at the other lynxes, seeing their warm and hopeful and proud expressions. And, for a moment, she was overjoyed to be with them.

But unlike the calm that had lingered long after listening to the Clan, Hasefi's heartened mood wavered as she recalled her actions with the Clan.

Whatever happens tomorrow, whatever blood is spilled, is on my paws.

Chapter Nineteen

Hasefi's heart pounded in her chest like thunder. The clearing was dark below where she stood upon the Highledge. The dark moon was high above their heads, a black circle in the night.

Dozens of lynxes stood ready in the clearing. Though the fern entrance would allow no more than two side-by-side at a time, the Tribe was arranged in the positions they would march.

Knights were at the front, closest to the entrance, making three lines. Hunters made the last three and among them were dotted guardians and healers. Keepers were scattered about, with a single line of them between the knights and hunters.

The champions were on the ledge with Hasefi. All but Lisefi, the Huntmaster, would be going. She was in charge of the clearing and the lynxes staying behind to keep their home safe.

Those lynxes were out, too, along with others that couldn't join; novices, expecting mothers, the injured or sick, kits. Hasefi spotted Salifen and Alarni murmuring to a hunter before the latter moved off the join the ranks.

She looked again at the army assembled below. They had turned to the Highledge where she was, her father beside her. So many eyes were peering up, waiting.

"There's so many," Hasefi whispered.

"We have thrived these last few seasons," her father murmured. Hasefi shook her head.

"This is hardly a war," she said. "This will be a massacre."

"We don't fight to kill," Garfonis reminded her. "Not unless it's for defense." His words did little to comfort her. If things went well, the Clan would be homeless and easy targets for the Pack. If things didn't go well, the Tribe, if not both sides, would become vulnerable.

And that will be thanks to me, she thought. *And if the Tribe loses, I don't get Kolahn and any chance of the Clan and Tribe working together will be gone.*

There may be hope yet, Sefonis offered. *Perhaps Esafi's sight will clear once she's taken battle to the Clan. It is likely they have prepared for the attack. This will be made clear before long. It may startle her to reason.*

If she doesn't see it now, I don't think she'll ever see it. I don't know what else to do but wait and see what comes of this unnecessary battle.

Despite her words, she looked to her father, determined to try to the last heartbeat.

"What if they know?" she asked him.

"Know what? Who?" he replied, confused.

"What if the Clan knows we are coming?"

"They won't," he assured her, touched her ear with his nose. "They may suspect it, but we've given them little reason to expect retaliation."

"Not if they heeded your last words to them."

Garfonis flinched, his ears half-flat. "I thought they had killed my sons. I know the truth now, but it's likely they don't and to start war over lost prey...." he trailed off, uncertainty glittering in his gaze.

"This is wrong," Hasefi told him. "We're attacking them because of what the Pack did. It's not too late to stop this." Studying her father, she watched his uncertainty grow. But before either of them could say more, Esafi emerged from the Highcave and they were sent to the back of the ledge.

"I look upon all of you with pride this day," the Highchief began, standing tall on the edge of the Highledge. "I am confident that each of you will show the Clan the consequences of murder."

Eager shouts and cries came in response.

"The wolves have lived long in the land that was once our own. They have brought war and danger, not to speak of the dark times in which some of us still remember in our nightmares."

Unease was suddenly thick in the air, but Esafi continued before it could fester.

"They have overstayed their welcome. We will not stoop to their level and kill unless necessary. But we will no longer tolerate them by the River. Every wolf is to be chased outside the Great Forest. Those that refuse will be killed. Those that return will be killed. It is time for us to take back the land of our ancestors."

The crowd roared below, loud enough Hasefi was sure the Clan would be aware of what was happening without her own interference. But her heart dropped at the thundering cheers below. *Esafi doesn't care about whatever land the Tribe lost in some forgotten season. She's feeding them lies after starving them for information.*

They don't know better, Sefonis reminded her.

That's what I'm saying. For all we know, we could be facing the Pack on the other side of the River.

"Hasefi." Her head jerked up at the sound of Esafi's voice. The champions were filing off the ledge to join the army below that was leaving through the fern entrance. The Highchief stood before Hasefi. "You will join me in our march," Esafi told her.

They waited as the army filtered out of the clearing. Lisefi came, offering words to both Esafi and Hasefi, before retreating again to watch from afar. Hasefi caught the eyes of Salifen who offered a reassuring nod. Alarni was nowhere to be seen.

Just as she started to turn, she spotted a familiar golden pelt. Nakilon was hunched at the edge of the clearing near the fallen log. He was miserable; his fur was unkempt, and his head bowed. His eyes were dull when they met Hasefi's. She wanted to go to him, but Esafi urged her forward with a word and they passed out of the clearing and into the forest.

They joined the marching throng. Hasefi expected to join the knights near the front, but Esafi remained at the back with Sifara close by. Arsolin was with her.

"We aren't leading?" she asked Esafi.

"We cannot see the nature of the battle if we are in the thick of it. It is my duty to call and send orders to the champions or their chosen leaders to ensure they are safe while they perform their duties within the fight itself."

"Your duty," Hasefi echoed. "Mine is up there." Before Esafi could respond, Hasefi pushed herself through the ranks until she was up front with her father.

"Hasefi!" he blurted, flipping his helmet open without missing a step. "What are you doing? Is something wrong?"

"I'm a fighter. I'm not going to sit by and watch from the back."

"But it's dangerous for you to be up here."

"Not as dangerous as it will be for the wolves."

Garfonis looked ready to argue, but, instead, his mouth snapped closed and he said nothing more.

The lynxes behind her shuffled and Arsolin appeared at her side without a word. Together, the three of them led the marching lynxes directly towards the River.

It took much longer to reach than if she had been on her own. The dark moon had slipped from its peak, falling back to the earth. She realized, if the wolves had decided to wait in their home to defend, the Tribe wouldn't arrive until dawn.

The rushing of the River met her ears. Soon after, she could glimpse it through the trees. Curiosity piqued her as she thought about how they would get across if not through the path behind the Fall.

In answer, six guardians came to the forefront of the march as they stopped before the River. They stood together at the edge of the water, their eyes glowing and light scattering through the air to float across the ground and up into the trees like a wayward mist.

Amazement parted Hasefi's jaw when leaves lifted from the ground and fell from the trees, all floating in a wind made by the magical light that directed them towards the River. There, they lay above the water, creating a wide path for twelve lynxes to walk shoulder-to-shoulder with room to spare.

It took time for the leaves to reach all the way to the other side. If there was a wolven patrol about, they would undoubtedly notice the green and yellow light in the dark of night.

Esafi wants them to know, she thought. *She's confident in the outcome.*

The six guardians moved back, their eyes still alight, matching the glow of the leaf-bridge they'd made. Hasefi took a step forward so she could place a tentative paw on the bridge. To her surprise, the leaf-path held when she put weight on it.

Garfonis joined her, signalling for the troops to follow, but Kilarsa's voice ripped suddenly through Hasefi's head.

Wait!

The gifted's intensity sent the word out of Hasefi's mouth, causing Garfonis to hesitate and those behind to halt.

"Hasefi, we can't linger here," Garfonis whispered urgently.

"Roll a rock over the bridge," Kilarsa spoke through Hasefi.

Garfonis eyed her doubtfully, but he jerked his head to the keeper shadowing him who then scanned the ground until he found a pebble the size of his paw. The keeper scooped it up and tossed it a pace ahead onto the leaf-bridge.

As soon as the pebble hit, a spout of water erupted from below, tearing the leaves and making a lynx-sized hole.

"The River has been rigged," the keeper observed.

"They know we are coming," Garfonis murmured. His gaze lingered on Hasefi, but two lynxes came to the forefront.

"Spies," Esafi growled.

Sifara moved from her side to face the Highchief. "Perhaps it would be wise to call off the battle."

"No," Esafi snapped. "They cannot get away with what they've done. Where is Myafos?"

"Here, my Highchief." The Guardian Elder was with them, though Hasefi hadn't noticed him approach.

"Get your guardians to fix this. Sifara, send a scout through the waterfall path."

"What if it's rigged, too?" Hasefi pointed out.

Esafi's ears flattened, but she was silent. Frustration flickered through her eyes as they darted back and forth. Gazes flicked to the Highchief, becoming uncertain. As the silence stretched on, Hasefi realized Esafi had no idea what to do.

"What if we send a small group through, with gifted, to talk to the wolves?" Hasefi tried. "We might be able to avoid spilling blood."

"A parley would be wise," Garfonis agreed. "Especially if they have been able to prepare for our attack."

"They won't agree to an armistice and neither will I," Esafi growled. "Blood—*lynx* blood has already been spilled. We will wait until the River is clear, then we send ahead a scout."

"But their forest—"

"Silence! You are a kit, Hasefi. I am the one that commands these lynxes."

Hasefi bit down her words and waited as the guardians drew magic from the River, adding it to fix and reinforce the bridge they'd made. When it was deemed clear, an idea came to Hasefi and she turned to Myafos.

"Couldn't you send out a projection to scout ahead, instead? Like the ones used for training the older novices?"

"Don't be foolish, Hasefi!" Esafi snapped. "This isn't training!"

"It is a good idea," Myafos said to the Highchief. "It could save a life."

Esafi glared at him before giving a short nod. Myafos looked to a fellow guardian who sent out a projection of herself. It wasn't long before a distant cry sounded and the gifted's eyes stopped glowing.

"It was destroyed."

"They probably have magic against it," Esafi growled. "Now send an actual lynx."

Hasefi's mind raced as she thought desperately of some way to keep anyone from getting hurt. Getting hurt because of her.

"If there's magic against that, there will be magic against us," she blurted. "It might be best to have the guardians lead with the knights so they can detect any magic and have the keepers march from behind and on our flanks to avoid an ambush while they're focused."

Esafi let out a low growl, but her attention quickly moved to Myafos when he relayed Hasefi's words to his guardians.

"That was not my command," she snapped.

"We are breaching enemy territory, Highchief," the Elder replied, his tone even. "If you insist on moving forward with this war, then we need commands now, not when you decide to think up some."

Esafi growled again but jerked her head in a sharp nod to Sifara who then started ordering the keepers to keep a perimeter. Once positioned, the procession crossed the bridge with Myafos, Garfonis, Esafi, Hasefi, and their respective keepers, including Sifara, at the head.

The leaf-bridge held all the way to the end. Before any lynx crossed over, the guardians that had moved to the frontlines now stepped before the leaders, sending tendrils of light into the trees. Some of the tendrils writhed, accompanied sometimes by sound, sometimes shuddering with a burst of light. The guardians padded forward slowly, setting the pace for the procession. At this rate, the sun would rise long before they reached the ravine.

Where are they? Hasefi thought as they marched deeper into Clan territory. *We haven't seen a single patrol.*

Trees eventually gave way to an open field patched with stretches of rocky ground. The middle rose in a shallow hill, blocking their view as the procession climbed. *Surely they don't think magic is all they need?*

They probably didn't expect their traps to be set off, even with you fighting, Sefonis said.

But surely the gifted would notice after the bridge? There has to be something else.

"Wolves!"

Hasefi froze, sent back to the day of her tribe's death moons ago. Shadows appeared on the rise before them, snarls sounding over the marching pawsteps of the Tribe. A howl pierced the air and soon the hill was full of wolven silhouettes flowing down to meet them.

Hasefi, we're here. It's time to fight.

Hasefi snapped from her trance, realizing these wolves were much smaller than those she'd seen on that dreadful day and bore gray fur donned in various armors. Her father let out a piercing yowl in response to the wolves, joined by many others in the procession.

The gifted lynxes sent out a brief barrier of whirling debris as the Tribe sought to recover from the ambush. They were swift and, when the barrier fell, lynx met wolf.

Adrenaline coursed through Hasefi as she joined the charge, her gaze locked on a wolf in silver. Her tribe's strength filled her, but she silently commanded her tribe to wait until she said otherwise. Then she leaped at the warrior running down to her.

Her claws clanged against their armor, adding to the clamor that exploded around them which was deafening after the apprehensive silence. She was able to find a hold, latching onto the warrior's flank and seeking with her hind claws a weak spot.

The warrior writhed, twisting its neck to try and sink its fangs into her. But Hasefi let go, catching one of its back legs and causing it to stumble. Arsolin appeared, raking claws across the wolf's face.

Hasefi turned to a black-clad rogue that was facing a knight. The wolf had its jaw locked around the knight's foreleg and was jerking its head, trying to unbalance the lynx. Hasefi lunged forward, raking her claws across the wolf's ears.

The wolf ducked before the blow hit. It shoved the knight aside before snapping jaws at Hasefi. It would have met its mark in Hasefi's shoulder, but when it saw her, it hesitated, allowing Hasefi to claw its cheek.

The rogue recovered, opening its jaw in a snarl as it lunged again. Hasefi dodged, aiming a blow at its shoulder, but the rogue was quick, able to stay out of reach and dart between Hasefi and the knight who was limping on three legs.

There is damage at its left flank, Gelinaf spoke.

Hasefi looked to the spot in question, then rolled beneath the rogue's snapping jaws so she could hook her claws into the wolf's tough black armor. Using a bit of her tribe's strength, she tore through the material until she had a clear place to rake her claws deep into the wolf's flank.

An agonized howl left its jaws. It shook Hasefi off, then came to bury its teeth around the armor at her neck, but the knight returned, bowling the wolf over and pinning it to the ground.

Hasefi got up, looking for another opponent. A blow hit her hard in the shoulder, causing a jolt of pain to shoot through it and sending her tumbling down the hill.

She was able to recover at the bottom in time to face another rogue. It lunged. Hasefi avoided it, but the wolf anticipated her movement, swinging a paw to unbalance her. She fell and the wolf came close, locking its teeth around her throbbing shoulder.

Hasefi reached up, seeking to rip through the wolf's ears, but it jerked its head and the armor at Hasefi's shoulder crunched. She tried to wriggle free, but the wolf stepped on her and, adjusting its grip, sank its teeth into the flesh exposed by the bent armor.

An agonized and furious yowl left Hasefi's mouth. New strength burned through her, allowing her to twist beneath the wolf. She brought her hind legs up and, imbued with her tribe's strength, tore through the armor at the wolf's belly. It soon gave way, allowing her claws to meet flesh. Blood oozed from the gashes she made, seeping into her fur. The wolf let go of her with a yelp, stumbling off her.

Hasefi tripped it, then got to her paws. Before she could do anything else, however, the wolf cried out.

"I yield! I yield!"

Hasefi blinked in confusion as the wolf scrambled to its paws and fled back up and over the hill in the direction of the ravine.

These wolves are disciplined, but they aren't near as tough as the Pack, Hasefi thought with horror. *No wonder Kolahn wanted to warn them. They'd be slaughtered.*

These wolves don't fight to kill, nor do they fight for sport, Sefonis pointed out. *The Tribe is not much different.*

Hasefi turned and watched a knight hobble away, one of its legs crippled. Another knight was being dragged away by a pair of healers while a third sent a cloud of magic into the unconscious lynx.

Maybe it won't be so bad, then, as long as the Clan keeps their home. If the gifted can help both sides recover, we may yet be able to face the Pack.

Perhaps, Sefonis replied. *But despite the Clan's element of surprise, they do not seem to be faring well.*

Hasefi watched as wolf after wolf was sent fleeing into the trees. Some were injured, but others looked hardly touched.

Or they have another plan in mind, Hasefi thought. *They won't win with brute force and I don't doubt they know that.*

Something caught her eye to the right. Vines were slithering towards a group of knights and warriors that were struggling with each other. The vines moved past them, catching instead a keeper that had been on their way to help.

Seer, Sefonis observed.

Hasefi looked in the direction the vines came from, spotting a shadow within the trees at the edge of the clearing. There was no light about it.

It has masked its magic, Kilarsa spoke.

Hasefi broke into a run, weaving through battling lynxes and wolves until she reached the edge of the trees. A rogue came to meet her, blocking her path to the seer. Hasefi was ready for it and, with aid from her tribe, had it fleeing back into the trees with a warning yip.

The seer turned to Hasefi, alarm in its eyes. Then it turned and fled, its vines dissipating and the keeper released.

Hasefi, you are edging towards their side of the battle. Return to the champions. As Sefonis spoke, a pair of warriors appeared, baring their teeth at Hasefi. A rogue came from another direction. Hasefi charged, using the rogue's back to leap up and out of the way so she could retreat back to the center of the clearing where the height of the fighting continued.

Arsolin appeared and joined her, matching her pace.

"You are not easy to keep up with," he gasped beneath his helmet.

Hasefi threw him a grin. "Sorry. I'm not used to fighting with someone watching my back."

They said nothing more as they came upon a pair of wolves, a rogue and warrior. Together, they fought, sending first the warrior stumbling away, then leaving the rogue dazed on a stretch of rock.

Hasefi spotted her father amidst the battle. He was facing two silver-clad warriors with his keeper at his back. They were impressive on their own, but as a duo, the poor warriors stood no chance. The keeper flipped one over, despite being smaller, then turned to face the other while Garfonis pinned the fallen warrior and sank armored claws into cracks so they met flesh.

The wolf howled and scrambled to get away. Garfonis released it. A third wolf came to replace its defeated comrade, but, without turning, Garfonis kicked out with his hind legs, sending the wolf sprawling in the grass.

The keeper had managed to dislodge the remaining warrior's helmet. The wolf's left ear was torn to shreds and blood flowed over its armor. It tried to stumble away, but it fell. A seer appeared, hesitating before the two lynxes. They turned away, allowing the wolven gifted to drag its injured Clanmate to safety.

Hasefi joined her father, her keeper joining the other as a rogue came to fight.

"Hasefi!" Garfonis gasped, lifting his helmet. "I lost sight of you." His eyes flickered to her shoulder. "You're hurt."

Hasefi gave a lop-sided shrug. "It's nothing. How is everyone doing? It looks like we're winning."

"Our right flank holds, but our left side is wavering." Garfonis's head swiveled as he watched the battle around them. "I think one or more of their Alphas are over there. We'll need to take them out."

"But that's towards the waterfall," Hasefi pointed out. "Why put more strength there?"

"Cut us off from our retreat. Scatter us. We outnumber them, but if they cut us off, they can put us into a panic and pick us off easier."

"Is the Lady fighting?"

"Not that I've seen," he replied, "but if I'm correct, Lord Morvak is the one who usually leads battles."

"Could we get to him?"

"Unlikely, but we probably don't need to. If we can take out one of their Alphas, it may be enough for a retreat."

"And then what?" Hasefi asked. "They knew we were coming. Are we still planning to chase them from the River? Some of the wolves retreating seemed fine. Could they know what Esafi means to do? What if their main strength is waiting at the ravine and this is just to weaken us?"

Garfonis hesitated, but only for a heartbeat. "Our primary goal is to hold our line here. We need to keep the Tribe together and secure our retreat."

"Arsolin and I will look for one of their Alphas."

Garfonis started to argue, but Hasefi charged away, pelting around the base of the hill in the opposite direction she had come. Darkness darted nearby, showing her Arsolin was with her.

They stopped only to help those of the Tribe that were struggling or to face wolves blocking their path. Together, they sent wolves fleeing or left them where they were, but not without their own injuries. By the time they were nearing the trees on the left side of the rocky meadow, Arsolin was limping on three legs and Hasefi had blood coating the black and silver of her armor.

They paused to rest. Healers darting about had helped them where they could, but on the left flank of the battle, more wolves were present and healers had been pushed back while the fighting lynxes struggled to hold the line. Where Garfonis was, the lynxes had moved nearly to the top of the hill, but here, at its base, the wolves had pushed past it.

Arsolin stirred, meeting the charge of a warrior, but the wolf didn't stop, sending the keeper sprawling on the ground. Before he could recover, it wrapped its jaws around his neck.

Hasefi sprang forward, leaping up onto the wolf's back. She was unable to find a hold on its smooth silver armor and it shook her off. The fall jarred her, her armor clanking noisily on the patch of rock they were on, dazing her for a brief moment. Then, calling her tribe, she got to her paws and renewed her attack against the warrior.

The wolf twisted, putting Arsolin's writhing form between her and it, but Hasefi leaped easily over him, landing on the warrior's head and neck. Her claws pierced its armor with a terrible wrenching sound. The wolf let go of her keeper, stumbling back and trying to shake her off. Hasefi lifted her hind legs, tearing through the armor at the wolf's neck like it was made of leaves.

"I surrender!" the warrior yelped.

Hasefi let go, falling awkwardly to the ground. The wolf lingered long enough to cast a frightened look at Hasefi before it turned and fled.

"Arsolin," Hasefi gasped, dragging herself to her paws. The keeper was on his side, panting heavily. The black-plated armor around his neck was damaged and trickles of blood seeped out.

"I am okay," he panted, staggering to three paws.

"You need to find a healer," Hasefi told him.

"I can fight." He tried to straighten, but his body shuddered and he hunched.

"You can fight better with four legs," Hasefi pointed out. "Go to a healer. I'll be fine."

Arsolin started to argue, but a lynxian cry sounded nearby and Hasefi was off to help a guardian that had gotten cut off from their defenders.

A warrior was looming over the guardian, its teeth bared in a vicious snarl, dripping blood and saliva. The guardian didn't appear hurt, but they cowered before the wolf, ears flat.

However, when the warrior lunged, the guardian lashed out a paw in a forward thrust. The blow knocked the wolf back and it stumbled until it lost its balance and fell on its side. Hasefi reached the pair, finishing off the wolf and sending it fleeing up the hill.

"The Highchief has been pushed to the very edge of the battle," the guardian said evenly. Without a word, Hasefi followed the guardian until they were near the treeline. A cluster of lynxes were struggling to hold off a press of wolves. Lord Morvak was among them, the Warrior Alpha Kowvis with him.

I would like to sink my claws into that wolf, she thought.

Esafi, to the surprise of Hasefi, was at the forefront of the lynxes, fighting shoulder-to-shoulder alongside Sifara. The guardian with Hasefi ran ahead, sending forth a burst of magic that churned the earth beneath a wolf's paws, making it stumble heavily to the ground.

Before Hasefi could join the throng, a screech sounded nearby. A lynx flew past, followed by two rogues. Hasefi blocked the wolves' path, bracing herself to meet them.

She swiped at one, but another caught her hind legs and she fell. She managed to roll away before it could pin her down, but the other wolf was ready for her and bit down on her already injured leg.

Hasefi, Gelinaf said urgently. *Let me.*

Without hesitation, Hasefi let Gelinaf take over. Her head snapped forward and she tore a mouthful of the wolf's ear off. It howled and she was immediately on her paws. The second rogue darted to one side, but Hasefi followed and hooked her claws into its tail. The wolf tried to kick, but Hasefi rolled under its stomach and raked away with her claws. The wolf howled in agony before slumping to the ground. Hasefi rose, prepared to meet the other rogue, but it merely started at her with wide eyes.

Hasefi took back control. Something in the wolf's expression changed, like it was relieved, but it still made no move to attack, glancing apprehensively at its companion. Hasefi stepped back so the rogue could nudge them onto their paws. Then, passing her a final glance, the rogue helped its injured comrade off of the battlefield.

Thanks, she told Gelinaf and she felt his acknowledgment.

Hasefi looked again to where the Highchief and Sifara fought with their group of a dozen lynxes. More were scattered about, taking on lone wolves or getting split up; the line formation they'd had was all but gone.

A pair of seers moved forward in the wolven company. One had broad shoulders and used its magic to enhance its physical blows, crippling lynxes or sending them fleeing. The second kept the first healed, while also using its magic offensively to drive back any lynxes that sought to halt their advance. Rocks rolled to trip paws or darted through the air to hit a well-aimed mark.

Hasefi charged towards the fight, but others were faster. Hesilar appeared, pelting from behind Hasefi with magical speed. A guardian was with him. Together, they sent forth a light that mingled together, then flowed towards the battling lynxes until it wrapped itself around Esafi.

The Highchief reared up, then came crashing down, smashing the ground with her paws. The force sent a ripple through the earth that toppled some of the wolves, halting the fight for several heartbeats. Sifara leapt onto one of the staggered seers, immobilizing it was her claws and sinking her teeth through the soft golden robes and deep into its flesh. Esafi joined her, raking savage claws through the second seer.

Both gifted wolves fled.

Morvak and Kowvis fell back, too, while the remaining wolves fought until they, too, were fleeing back towards the hill in the center of the clearing.

Hasefi reached the lynxes just as Hesilar darted about, healing his tribemates or sending them home.

"Myafos is asking for assistance," the guardian that had come with Hesilar announced. "I will answer his call."

"Thank you for aiding me," Hesilar said to him. The guardian dipped his head, then dashed away in the general direction of the River with the guardian that Hasefi had followed and a third in tow.

Hesilar came over to Hasefi. Without a word, he lowered his nose and touched her shoulder. Barely a heartbeat passed and her pain vanished, leaving nothing but bloodstained fur where the wound had been.

"Thanks!" she gasped.

"We are trying to push towards their ravine, not away," Esafi growled, joining them, her glare on Hasefi. "Why have you come here?"

"Garfonis said we should focus on taking out one of their Alphas," Hasefi explained. "This side of the battle is failing; Garfonis thinks they mean to cut off our retreat. You've given us a bit of time, but I'm sure Morvak will be back. Kowvis is with him—maybe we could try to split them up."

"Their other leader isn't here," Esafi growled. "I want to take out her mate, then chase their tails all the way to the ravine."

"But the battle is here," Hasefi pointed out.

"Come!" Esafi called, ignoring her. "We go to their Lord!" Waiting for no response, she charged towards the middle of the battle. The lynxes in her company followed. Hasefi watched helplessly as they ran by her.

She's going to get lynxes killed unnecessarily, she thought.

You can't stop her, Sefonis agreed. *But you can help others.*

A flash of dark purple caught Hasefi's eye as a guardian ran past, away from the battle. There were no pursuers, but Hasefi spotted a rogue running from another direction, looking to cut off the gifted lynx's path.

Hasefi used a bit of her tribe's strength to lunge into a run. She met the wolf just as it leaped in the air, bowling into it so they both crashed to the ground.

The rogue recovered first, aiming its jaws at Hasefi's neck. But a flash of green light brought a flurry of leaves rushing between it and Hasefi, allowing Hasefi to recover and meet the wolf face-to-face.

The guardian that had been running joined her, aiming its own blows at the rogue. Before long, the wolf grew wise and fled towards the hill.

"Thanks," Hasefi gasped, doubling over as she fought to catch her breath.

"Nay, it is your eye I am grateful for. That rogue caught me by surprise." The guardian leaned forward, breathing softly over Hasefi's head. Light flickered around her and a strength entered her limbs, eliciting a relieved sigh from her jaw.

When she straightened, she realizing the guardian bore no injuries.

"You don't look hurt. Why are you running?"

"Myafos is summoning us. He requires aid."

"Then let's help him."

The guardian led her across the edge of the meadow until they were at the treeline. Myafos was there, his hood pulled back to reveal his gray and white face. His golden eyes shone brightly, piercing the dark air with their light.

He was surrounded by lynxes in purple, their eyes also glowing. One suddenly slumped to its paws and was immediately replaced by the guardian that had brought Hasefi.

"What's going on?" she asked.

"The Elder is facing the Clan's gifted Alpha," a healer explained, coming to treat the fallen guardian.

"But I don't even see him."

"A battle of the mind," a second healer explained, pawing something towards the first that dissipated into glowing mist before Hasefi could see what it was. "They are attempting to overcome the other. But Myafos is weakening. If the Seer Alpha wins, the war is lost."

"Any idea where he could be?" Hasefi asked.

All of a sudden, she was no longer standing at the edge of the clearing. She was atop the hill in the middle of the meadow, yet she had no paws on which to stand. Before her, a tall wolf stood, resplendent in golden robes with the black wolven print of an Alpha on his chest. He was mere paces away from the line where wolf and lynx met.

Garfonis was leading the lynxian charge, slowing pushing towards the Alpha. The wolf did nothing, letting those around him defend as he stood still, his eyes closed. As if she could see into his mind, she realized what the Clan meant to do.

It's not the retreat their trying to cut off! she thought, seeing a new surge of wolves come to defend the Alpha. *They're trying to cut our line in half!*

She had thought they could try and separate Lord Morvak and his Warrior Alpha, but the wolves had already done just that to the Tribe. With Esafi still trying to make her way back to the main battle, she was separated from her mate, the champion leading the battle.

Hasefi blinked and she was with the gifted lynxes again. Without volition, she looked to the Elder. His gaze was already on her.

Then he exploded.

Shrieks of agony and terror erupted around Hasefi as blood, flesh, and fragments of bone assailed them. Hasefi's armor and fur was splattered with gore. The nearest guardians were coated until their fur color was lost. Some of them fell to the ground as if dead. Others cowered and wailed wordlessly to the night sky. One of the healers recovered, rising on shaking paws, and called out in a grief-stricken voice.

"The Elder is dead!"

Shock rooted Hasefi's paws to the ground. Her tribe was similarly affected. But Sefonis was the first to recover and took control of Hasefi's body. He sent her charging back with unnatural speed towards the battle where her father had been.

The sky above was brightening with red as dawn approached, casting a blood-red glow over the battlefield. The rocks and grass were stained with the life of wolves and lynxes. Unmoving bodies from both sides lay about. But the true horror lay at the top of the hill.

The Seer Alpha was there, just as Hasefi had seen. Garfonis's charge had halted. Around the gifted wolf, chunks of earth and rock were being pulled from the ground, big enough to crush several lynxes at once. The Seer Alpha's eyes glowed madly in the red light, making her think of Vek and his red eyes.

"Fall back!" Garfonis yowled. "Fall back!" He shoved the nearest lynxes around him, jarring them from their shock so they could flee back down the hill. Sefonis had halted Hasefi and relinquished control, unwilling to bring her closer to danger.

Just as the fleeing lynxes reached the bottom of the hill, the Alpha sent the floating earth chunks down.

Hasefi ducked, though she was out of range. Horror raked through her as she watched the lynxes at the end of the retreat get lost beneath the massive chunks, killed in heartbeats. Terrified yowls and shrieks sounded. Even some of the wolves with the Alpha hesitated, not daring to move past the top of the hill.

"Hasefi!" Garfonis reached her, his eyes wide with the same terror as the lynxes around him. "You're—you're covered in—what happened?"

"There are lynxes still fighting!" Hasefi hissed, angling her ears towards the right side of the meadow. Lynxes were fleeing towards them from that direction now, but some of the wolves unbothered by the Alpha's destruction blocked their way as the gifted wolf pulled more earth from the ground. "We can't leave them!"

"We cannot fight their gifted Alpha," Garfonis pointed out, grief twisting his face. "We are defeated here. We must leave before—"

Hasefi forgot him, focusing inwards. *I need your help now.*

Strength surged into Hasefi's body, coursing through her limbs and hardening her pelt and her claws until she stood with the will of nine lynxes alongside her own. Her tribe's energy made her feel as if she could fly. Garfonis has stopped midsentence, his eyes wide as he stared at her, but she no longer saw him, focused only on the Alpha atop the hill.

He was looking at her, perhaps sensing the change. His expression held cruel amusement as he hovered earth and rock in the air about him, preparing his next blow.

We can't take a hit, Sefonis warned. *Not without some serious damage.*

Can we jump?

Absolutely.

Hasefi burst into a charge. The Alpha sent down his pillars. Some flew past Hasefi to the lynxes beyond, but one came directly for her. She glared at it, gathering her strength in her legs, fighting to reach the base of the hill. Then, she launched herself into the air.

Hasefi soared high over the lethal chunk, her momentum bringing her forward through the air so she cleared the hill in a single bound. She landed atop the Alpha, digging her claws and teeth into his armor. A strange shock passed through her. Faintly, she thought it might have been painful, but with her tribe's strength, it hardly affected her and she dug deeper into the Alpha's flesh. Blood oozed around her claws and into her mouth, staining her already blood-soaked fur.

A sudden blast tore her off the wolf's back. She landed heavily on her side, but she was on her paws in an instant. The Alpha did not attack her. He was staring at her with wide eyes but, unlike the other wolves, there was no terror in his expression. Something unsettling was in that stare, something that reached through Hasefi's enhanced state to put fright into her heart.

She braced herself to attack, but the Seer took a step back and lifted his head to release a surrendering howl. Another rose in answer, followed by more until the air was filled with the Clan's announced retreat.

Chapter Twenty

"They're retreating!" a lynxian voice called. "The Clan is retreating!"

Hasefi slumped to the ground in relief, watching wolves stream out of the meadow and into the trees towards the ravine. A rear-guard followed, eyeing the lynxes in case any decided to chase after them. But the Tribe was focused elsewhere.

With her own tribe's strength ebbing now that the battle was over, it took Hasefi a few moments before she could lift her head to look back down the hill. Her breath caught in her throat and her heart stopped.

The Seer Alpha's pillars had rent gouges into the ground where they hit, cutting through the earth until they stopped in a heap, no longer held together by magic. The crushed bodies of lynxes lay in the ruts, some struggling to claw their way out and others unmoving. Glints in the blood-red light of dawn showed Hasefi pieces of armor buried in the mounds.

This is what a gifted can do? she thought quietly.

Only powerful ones, Kilarsa replied, her tone just as hushed. *And now the Tribe's is dead.*

Rapid steps caught Hasefi's attention. She half got up to her paws, ready to face whatever straggling wolves might try and land a last blow. But the wolf that appeared was Morvak. He paused just two paces from Hasefi, farther along on the ridge of the hill. He hardly glanced at her, instead looking down at the carnage below. His jaw opened in shock. Then he looked to Hasefi, his expression unreadable, before turning and fleeing after his clan.

A wail tore through the air, a sound of anguish that ripped the hearts of any that heard it.

Hasefi jerked her head back to look down the hill again. She recognized the knight Katrima. She had been caught in the Alpha's attack, though she'd been lucky, suffering no more than a crippled back leg. The knight had dragged herself forward until she stopped by a crumpled pile of armor bearing the starry black patterns of the Knight Emperor.

Hasefi's blood ran cold.

"Father?"

The word barely left her jaws. She staggered down the hill, tumbling down the last bit. Of their own accord, her legs pushed her back up and pulled her numbly toward the crushed body and the whimpering knight bent over it.

She stared down, meeting blank green eyes.

"We need the Sage!" A keeper had appeared, his voice piercing through Hasefi like a set of razor talons. "*Now*! Someone bring the Sage!"

A guardian appeared. She knelt, slipping off the Emperor's bent and dented helmet. The head was in the same shape. The armor dissipated around the twisted body, showing the full extent of the Seer Alpha's destructive magic.

Hasefi, she heard faintly a voice in her head, but she didn't know whose it was. *He must have followed you. He must have tried to stop you.*

Another voice echoed in her head, her own, at first quiet, then growing louder until it drowned out the other.

It's your fault. You did this. This is your fault.

Someone shoved Hasefi aside. Hesilar was there, crouching before the unmoving form. He thrust his nose to the throat of the body, passing his paw over the warped flank. His eyes glowed, but the brightening of the day made his light dull. After several moon-long heartbeats, he withdrew.

"Tend to the wounded," Hesilar ordered the healers that had joined him. "Bring them home."

Hasefi was jolted from her shock with claw-sharp clarity.

"What?" she blurted. "Aren't you going to help him?"

Hesilar blinked sadly at her. "He's gone," he said quietly. "I'm sorry, Hasefi. The impact killed him immediately."

"No," Hasefi protested, shaking her head. "No, you can still help him. That's what you do, right? You're a healer aren't you? Heal him!"

Hesilar said nothing, grief alight in his eyes.

"Are you sunblind?" Hasefi snarled. "Don't just stand there! *Heal him!*"

"Hasefi, I can't," he said, his tone gentle. "I wish I could, but his spirit has already left."

Rage blinded Hasefi only to be consumed by anguish. A wail built up in her chest, but she could do no more than whimper when she collapsed beside her father.

"No," she pleaded. "Garfonis, please. You can't be dead. You can't be." She nosed his cheek. "Get up."

"This shouldn't have happened." The keeper that had called for Hesilar sat nearby. His helmet was off, revealing the flat stare he directed at Garfonis. "We were not prepared for an ambush."

His words sank cruel claws into Hasefi's chest, twisting the grief threatening to overwhelm her.

This shouldn't have happened. I did this. I *made this happen.*

Hesilar bent towards Hasefi with a healing light, but she jerked away with a snarl. Movement upon the hill caught her attention. Esafi was running over with Sifara close behind.

"The Clan retreats!" the Highchief was calling. "Now is our chance to—"

She stopped, her battle-hungry glare shattering into disbelief. Her head jerked back and forth as she took in the scarred and blood-choked earth and the bodies it held. Finally, her gaze landed on Hasefi.

"Highchief." The keeper hunched nearby got to his paws. "The Seer Alpha did not hold back his magic. I fear what this may mean for our Guardian Elder—"

"He's dead." The voice came from Hasefi's jaws, but it didn't sound like her. She didn't realize she had said it, either, until she'd gotten to her paws and stood, her eyes unseeing as they flicked from Garfonis to Esafi. "What's left of him is scattered on the pelts of those that were with him, including me."

Horror silenced the lynxes around her until all that could be heard were the moans of the injured and dying. Eyes bored into Hasefi before looking away. A hunter retched.

"The Clan must be punished." Esafi's voice was faint. She still stood rigid where she'd halted, her stare locked on Garfonis. "We must drive them out."

"The Clan has retreated," Hesilar said, moving away from a half-crushed knight that had ceased moving beneath his careful touch. "But we are defeated. It is time to go home."

Esafi's jaw opened and protest was clear on her face, but no words came out. She looked around, taking in once more the devasted clearing.

"Collect the fallen." Her voice came out flat. "Heal any you can. We return home." Esafi's head hung. Sifara murmured something in her ear before bounding away.

Hasefi watched the Tribe collect itself. Though the sun rose, the sky grew dark with clouds. But, like Hasefi, they couldn't seem to let out what they held, instead hovering as they grew darker and heavier.

At some point, Arsolin came to her. He might have said something, but Hasefi was deaf to everything and everyone, including her tribe. The one thing she could hear over and over again was the wail that had pierced the air announcing the death of the Emperor.

As she sat curled beside her father, lynxes struggled to move out of the clearing. Healers darted to and fro, helping who they could until the injured could use their paws, or summoning others to help carry those that may yet be able to say their goodbyes back home and those who would never be able to.

Katrima was still with Hasefi. If it weren't for the rasping breath coming from her parted jaws, Hasefi might have thought she, too, had perished. Only when a group of four made of knights and keepers came to collect the Emperor did she stir.

"Can you walk?" one of the knights asked Katrima.

Without a word, she got to her paws, her crippled hind leg hanging uselessly behind her. Whatever pain the knight was in, she showed no sign of it as she staggered away after the procession carrying Garfonis.

Hasefi watched them leave, moving across the clearing until they disappeared in the trees. She felt as if she were with them, but her paws rooted her to the spot.

"Hasefi." Arsolin nudged her shoulder gently. "It is time to go. We must return home."

"I have no home," she mumbled, but the shock keeping her still released its hold. However, eyes made her pelt itch. She looked around until she found the Highchief, hunched still where she'd stopped. Her glare was aimed at Hasefi and it was filled with a dark loathing she'd never seen from Esafi before. In different circumstances, it might have chilled her. But all she could feel right now was grief and her own loathing directed inwards.

She followed Arsolin into the trees, padding numbly beside him. Exhaustion and pain made her stumble, but she hardly noticed, unheedful of her keeper as he helped her along.

It wasn't until the sun had passed its peak and they were nearing the clearing did Hasefi's mind return. She didn't remember crossing behind the waterfall, nor did she remember when the remains of the Tribe's army had come together, trudging miserably back home as one.

Before they got to the clearing, lynxes were there to help. Healers had already arrived with wounded. Those that had remained behind to protect their home came to unburden those returning. Novices were with them, offering aid wherever they could. When Hasefi and Arsolin limped into the clearing, a familiar face appeared before Hasefi.

Salifen stopped before her, looking as distraught as she felt. No words left his open jaw as he merely stared, his bright green eyes darkened with abject misery.

"Hasefi!" Nakilon appeared beside the novice healer, his own eyes wide. "I—I saw the Emperor. I saw them carrying him in. I—"

"The High Heir needs rest," Arsolin told the novices. "And healing."

"It's my fault." Hasefi's voice was hoarse. "It's all my fault."

Despite Arsolin's words, Nakilon came to her, pressing his nose to her cheek. A whimper left Hasefi, sending a shudder through her body. The novice wrapped his forelegs around her, pulling her close, making no reaction to the blood and bits of gore staining his fur.

"I did this," Hasefi whispered into his neck. "I killed him."

"No," Nakilon told her. "Don't blame yourself. I'm sure you did everything you could. It's going to be okay, I promise."

Hasefi opened her eyes, looking over his shoulder. Salifen was still there, standing helplessly with anguish writhing in his eyes. Then a healer summoned him and he was gone.

Hasefi closed her eyes again, burying her face in Nakilon's fur.

I did this, she thought. *You warned me not to and I didn't listen. There's no one but me to blame. I'm just like the Pack; death follows me.*

You were trying to make things right, Kilarsa spoke, her tone gentle, though she could not hide her own grief from Hasefi. *You could not have known the consequences.*

But I knew there would be some. Even if you hadn't tried to stop me...even if my friends hadn't tried...I knew. And I still did it. It's just like my nightmare. Esafi was right.

We don't blame you, Kilarsa said.

Then why isn't Sefonis here?

His brother just died, Dahsefer spoke now. *He may be more upset than you.*

His words only served to deepen her guilt. *I can't stay here. I'm too dangerous. If the Tribe goes to face the Pack, their best chance is without me.*

Pain squeezed her chest and she wished more than she ever had before that Kolahn was with her, but when she thought of him, all she could see was the same expression he'd had when he'd seen the carnage she'd wrought once before to save him. *I can't go to him. I can't go to anyone. I need to be cast out for the safety of everyone. I need to leave forever.*

You need rest, Dahsefer told her. *We have drained you significantly and you aren't without hurt. See a healer and rest.*

I don't deserve to be healed.

A vigil will be set for your father and all those who fell, Gelinaf spoke up. *If you will leave, then at least say your goodbyes.*

The knight under Sefonis's command, Refarmi, spoke in place of her uncle. *Leaving will be difficult, even if you utilize our strength,* she pointed out. *Waiting at least until tomorrow's sunrise may offer you a better chance.*

You're not trying to stop me, Hasefi noticed. *You think I should leave.*

You are heartbroken, Hasefi, Tenarli added her voice. *As are we all. Minds cannot think straight while the heart suffers. All we can do is put one paw before the other until we can lift our heads once more and face the new day.*

Hasefi opened her eyes. Lynxes were moving all around the clearing, seeking to make space for the injured so they could be tended to. Others were hauling around prey or herbs; upon those that had fought their last, little bundles of blue-flowered rosemary were placed, filling the air with its strong, pine-like scent, and healers paid the bodies no more attention.

A keeper was helping a hunter to a pair of healers nearby. When the white-clad lynxes took the half-concious hunter, the keeper was left alone. At first, they appeared fine, then they swayed and collapsed to the ground.

"They need help," she whispered, pulling away from Nakilon. "We need to help."

Nakilon and Arsolin followed her. The novice darted off to fetch a healer while Hasefi pulled the helmet off the fallen keeper. Her eyes were closed, but her jaw was clenched, her breaths forced through her teeth in uneven hisses.

I believe this keeper has broken ribs, Dahsefer said. *But a gifted must verify once they'd removed her armor.*

Nakilon came with a healer. Hasefi repeated her Sage's words before moving off to aid another struggling lynx. Her companions did the same, saying nothing more than what was necessary to healers and to those needing comfort. One of the lynxes Hasefi came to breathed their last just as she spoke words of assurance. She moved on, floating through the clearing on numb paws.

Finally, Hasefi reached her physical limit and collapsed among the injured. Nakilon continued to help others at her bidding, but Arsolin refused to leave her side, especially after she rejected any healer that came to her. She lay on her side with her keeper curled close, his armor removed so he could press his flank to hers.

The day is almost over, she thought as the waning light stretched shadows across the clearing. The idea of night brought her comfort, though she couldn't explain why.

"High Heir."

Hasefi lifted her head with difficulty. Katrima was approaching, her armor removed, revealing the wounds she'd suffered. Her leg, however, had been healed, allowing her to sink into a bow with relative ease.

"I cannot express how sorry I am," the knight said, still bowed. "If I could, I would take his place."

Hasefi pushed herself so she was sitting upright. "No," she growled, causing the knight to jerk her gaze up in surprise. "Do you have kits, Katrima? Siblings?" she added when the knight shook her head.

"I have a brother."

"Go to him. Let him see you again so he can know you're safe."

Katrima blinked, puzzled.

"I wouldn't ever ask you or anyone to die so my kin could live. Your life is just as important as anyone else's."

Katrima bowed again. "If there's anything you need, I am at your command." She straightened and turned away, padding through the rows of injured lynxes.

Hasefi slumped to the ground again. She didn't want to fall asleep, knowing she'd be treated as soon as she did, but she was helpless to stop the wave of exhaustion that passed over her, sending her spiraling into deep darkness.

The next morning was black. The clouds had grown darker, desperately holding onto the rain within, so the cavelight was dull, mimicking the outside light. Hasefi's mood had only gotten worse. The reality of what had happened was the first thing to meet her, echoing the cruel dreams that had made her sleep restless.

She'd been moved to her sleeping hollow. Other than her, the chamber was empty. However, after a few heartbeats, Sifara entered. The Overlord removed her helmet and bowed before Hasefi.

"Esafi has asked me to retrieve you," she said. "She wishes to announce the events of the war to the Tribe, then hold vigil through the night for the fallen." Sifara's voice was steady, but her tone was dull.

Hasefi was prepared to curl up in her hollow again, but the urge to see her father one last time before she left the Tribe urged her to her paws. They were heavy with exhaustion, but her grogginess was pleasant compared to the grief raging inside her.

In silence, she followed Sifara out of the sleeping chamber, into the main one, and out onto the Highledge.

Lisefi and Hesilar were there, sitting at the back of the Ledge in their designated spots. Sifara went to hers. Hasefi hovered in her spot at the front of the Highcave, looking to where Esafi sat a pace away.

Her posture was stiff and straight. The black and silver of her armor was dulled by the gray light above. Hasefi couldn't see the Highchief's face, but she thought about the glare Esafi had given her back in the Clan's territory.

She blames me, she thought. *She must know something. Why else would she blame me?* She gave a mental shrug, dismissing the thought. *It doesn't matter anymore. None of it does.*

Esafi stirred. She rose and moved to the edge of the Highledge, peering down at the lynxes that had gathered below. Hasefi couldn't see the majority of them where she was, but she could sense the change in number from their last meeting. Some healers were still at work, too, darting in and out of the Healer's Cave to the left where the remaining injured had been moved.

"My tribe," Esafi began, her voice clear with a heavy note of grief. "Much of what I have to say I'm sure you've come to learn for yourself. There is little good news to share, so I will not delay the...bad." The last word fell flat. Esafi paused, lowering her head before raising it again and continuing.

"The Clan had been made known to our preparations. Traps were set, followed by an ambush led by Lord Morvak and two of their Alphas. Our gifted were able to disarm their traps, but the Clan...met us with great resistance.

"They sought to divide us. Myafos gave his life trying to stop their Seer Alpha and—and so did Garfonis. In the end, we prevailed, sending the Clan to retreat but...the cost was great. Too great," she added quietly.

"Highchief." A voice called from the crowd, making Hasefi and others perk up in surprise.

"We are in the middle of a meeting," Esafi growled.

"I understand and respect that," the voice said and Hasefi realized it was Katrima's. "But I believe we should show gratitude to the one who saved us."

"I just named the ones who saved us," the Highchief hissed, her fur bristling.

"I mean no disrespect, Highchief, but if it weren't for the High Heir, we would have been the ones to flee with many more losses. I saw her. She stopped the Seer Alpha. She saved us."

“It’s true.” Another lynx spoke. “I watched them fight. The Alpha was the first to howl retreat.”

“She flew like a bird!” another lynx called.

“Very well,” Esafi growled, silencing the muted chatter. She turned, bringing her gaze to Hasefi. It was hard, but whatever lay behind it was masked. The Highchief jerked her head, indicating Hasefi join her. She did, though she felt like an imposter standing above them.

“My daughter,” Esafi began. “It seems you played a big part in this battle.”

You have no idea.

“Hasefi!” a lynx called. Another did the same, then another, until the clearing was filled with lynxes chanting her name. Hasefi was jolted from her depression.

“Stop! Stop it!” she snarled.

The Tribe fell into surprised silence.

“I don’t deserve your cheer,” Hasefi growled. “Esafi’s right. You should be cheering Garfonis and Myafos and all the other lynxes who didn’t come home yesterday! *Not* me.” Hasefi turned and stalked back to the mouth of the Highcave. Hesilar tried to catch her attention, but she ignored him and hung her head.

“Grief weighs heavy on all of us,” Esafi said after several long heartbeats of silence. “But time moves ever on. Though we have yet to say farewell to our departed tribemates, I have chosen new champions to stand beside me. I fear we have taken the first steps into dark times and the need for strong leadership must be heeded if we are to make it through again to brighter days. Knight Katrima, please step forth.”

There was a moment of quiet, save for the shuffling of armor and paws.

“Despite your interruption, I have chosen to name you as my champion. Garfonis was an intelligent lynx with a mind for strategy and a skill for battle. He often complimented your abilities as a knight, making you his right paw. So, it is you I trust to lead my knights and to take on the title of Knight Emperor.”

The lynxes cheered the new Emperor as she came up the path to the Highledge. She sat in Garfonis's spot, her gaze darted everywhere but to Hasefi. Hasefi held no ill will towards the knight, but she couldn't bring herself to show it.

Esafi proceeded to name the next Elder—Silvera, the guardian that had created and modified Hasefi's armor. She, too, came to sit on the Ledge, but her expression was utterly blank, devoid of any emotion.

The meeting ended with Esafi laying out the vigil rituals and passing instruction to the Tribe on preparing for them. They were to begin at dusk and be carried throughout the night until dawn, when the guardians would take the essences of the fallen and turn them into soulstones.

Hasefi mumbled to no one in particular that she would return to her hollow for the day, hoping she wouldn't be forgotten for the night's vigil. Then she turned into the Highcave and spent the rest of the cloud-darkened day asleep.

Arsolin was the one to rouse her before dusk. Together they went out to the clearing and joined the rest of the Tribe as they prepared for the vigil of the fallen. The bodies had been fixed and arranged to look as if they were simply sleeping, their bundles of rosemary tucked between their forepaws. Each had their armor on.

Twenty-three lynxes. Twenty-three lynxes are dead because of me.

Garfonis was at the front, alongside an image that had been created of Myafos. Even though it was not truly the Elder, Hasefi felt like the image would lift its head at any moment to look at her. With what, she didn't know; blame, sympathy. But the image was still, just like the rest of the fallen.

Esafi began with a long speech, describing the overall bravery and dedication of those that lay before them. Then she spoke of each, naming them and identifying defining qualities and praising feats. Tydalok, Mersaka's father, was among the fallen, which only enforced Hasefi's belief that the hunter had been right to hate her.

Clouds still hung above, shielding any star and moonlight from reaching the lynxes beneath. The gifted around offered soft glows around each of the deceased, making Hasefi think of the starry pelts of her own tribe. A part of Hasefi wished her father could come to her like they had, but a part of her was relieved that he would be far from her now, safe, even if among the ancestors that had tried to kill her.

They must have known, she thought. *They knew how dangerous I was.*

Esafi finished and the Tribe was able to go forth to their friends and family. Some walked among them, offering words of their own. Others stayed, gazing grief-stricken or breaking down entirely beside the bodies of the lynxes they knew.

When the Highchief had named each of the lynxes, she had come forth and taken off their helmets, bracers, or collars to lay beside them. Hoods were pushed back, too, so the faces of each lynx could be seen in the gifteds' light.

Hasefi made herself walk among them, forcing her gaze to linger on the faces of each dead lynx until they were burned in her mind. When she came to the champions, she stopped before Myafos.

"Why didn't you say anything?" she whispered, her face close to the image of his. "Why did you let me do this? Did you know what would happen?"

She looked closely at his white and gray face, but it was still, offering her no answer.

Finally, Hasefi came to Garfonis. She curled up beside him. The strong scent of rosemary muffled most other scents, making it nearly impossible for her to breathe in his. But, when she pressed her nose to her father's cheek, she could pick up just the faintest hint of his smell, though it offered her little comfort.

I don't belong here. I hardly have the right to grieve. I knew you for a moon. All these other lynxes knew you most of their lives.

For the rest of the night, she stayed with him. She had no words, no thoughts. She didn't sleep, but she kept her eyes closed. At different points, she was aware of other lynxes joining her to add their grief to hers. Nakilon stayed with her for a time. So did Arsolin. But none spoke to her until, just before dawn, Salifen came.

"You didn't do this," he whispered into her ear.

"Yes, I did," she replied, not opening her eyes. "I should be lying here, not him."

"Healers are taught to be selfless," Salifen murmured. "But I will break that rule to tell you I'm glad you're not."

Hasefi lifted her head to look at him. He held her gaze steadily.

"I thought Alarni would tell Esafi what I meant to do," she told him. "I wish she did."

"She trusts you, Hasefi. And so do I." He blinked sadly at her. "If you blame yourself, then you have to blame me, too. I came with you, remember?"

"It was my idea," Hasefi protested. "And you still tried to stop me."

"We made a mistake," Salifen said. "That doesn't make you a bad lynx."

"Whether I'm good or bad doesn't change this," Hasefi pointed out, jerking her head towards the fallen behind her. "Death follows me, Salifen. This isn't the first time I've seen this. Or the second. I thought it was the Pack but...this time the Pack had nothing to do with it. *I* did this."

Before Salifen could respond, the Tribe shifted around them. Guardians had risen and were now coming to stand before some of the dead. As their light flowed from them to the pieces of armor beside the bodies, the clouds above finally released the rain they'd been clutching close.

The guardians' magic turned the armor into white light, which then flowed to the respective bodies. The deceased lynxes glowed brighter until their features were lost in light. Then each light floated up and shrank until all that was left were small, sparkling stones in place of the fallen and their bundles of rosemary.

The guardians moved among the remaining bodies until each of the twenty-three had been converted. Hasefi watched Garfonis disappear before her until his light, too, had faded.

The urge to reach out and touch her father's soulstone was great, but the guardian that had taken him used their magic to lift the stone into the air and followed after the other guardians and their floating stones into the caves of the cliff where they would descend into the Cavern of History and place the stones upon their respective walls.

Most of the Tribe followed. Some stayed in the clearing, despite the rain, alone or with the comfort of another. Hasefi turned towards the entrance.

"Hasefi," Salifen said, walking with her. "What are you going to do?"

"I'm leaving," she told him.

"Hasefi!" Arsolin's voice sounded and the keeper rushed over until he was between them and the clearing's entrance. He had no helmet, revealing his anguished and worried expression. "You should stay in the clearing. You haven't eaten since we returned and we could all do with some rest."

"She wants to clear her head," Salifen tried. "I offered to walk with her."

"Hasefi can speak for herself," Arsolin replied, not unkindly.

Hasefi snorted and muttered to no one in particular. "I shouldn't be able to speak for anyone."

"Please stay, Hasefi," Arsolin insisted. "There is no comfort to be found walking in this rain. It's safest at home."

"Didn't you hear me before?" Hasefi said sharply. "I have no home. I don't *deserve* a home."

"You are in pain," Arsolin told her. "And it's easy to direct that at oneself." He glanced at Salifen, then spoke with carefully chosen words. "I know there may be more to your pain than what has taken place these last two nights but trust me when I say there is nothing you have done to deserve any punishment."

A loud, bitter laugh burst from Hasefi's jaws, making both Arsolin and Salifen flinch. "This battle never should have happened," Hasefi hissed quietly. "But I don't blame Esafi, not anymore. The wolves knew we were coming because I told them. *I* told them Esafi wanted to drive them from the River. Everything that happened is because of me. I thought I could help save us from the Pack, but it turns out I'm just like them. So, if you want to keep your tribemates safe, Arsolin, let me go."

Arsolin stared at her with wide eyes, his jaw slightly open. The rain soaking the fur of his face and head made him look miserable in his shock. Hasefi went past him and a small, weak protest sounded from the keeper, but he did nothing else to stop her.

Hasefi pushed through the fern entrance. Rustling sounded and she braced herself to face one of the clearing's guards, but it was Salifen that joined her.

"What are you doing?" she asked.

"If this is the last time I see you, I want to say goodbye."

"Goodbye." Hasefi turned.

Salifen hurried to stop in front of her, blocking her path. She growled, but he paid no attention to it. "I don't want to stop you. I mean, I do, but I won't. I just…if there's anything I can do to help—"

"There's nothing." Hasefi went past him and, this time, he let her go. However, she'd hardly gone a few paces when the brush behind her rustled again.

"Salifen, I said there was nothing—"

"Hasefi."

Surprise made her turn. Nakilon was standing behind her, without his helmet, sorrow clear on his face.

"I thought you retired for the night," Hasefi admitted.

"Do you think I could just go to sleep knowing that you…?" he trailed off, pain alight in his eyes. "What are you doing out here in the rain?"

Hasefi's heart hardened. After her words to Arsolin, she saw no reason to spare anyone else's feelings. It was only a matter of time before they all hated her, and with good reason.

"I'm leaving. There's nothing for me here and all I've brought is pain and death," she told him. "I never should have come."

Nakilon blinked at her in confusion and hurt. "Nothing?"

"What?" Hasefi asked, kneading the muddy ground furiously.

"You said there's nothing for you here. What about—?"

"No, Nakilon, there's *nothing.*"

To her surprise, the novice knight stepped towards her, anger narrowing his eyes. "How can you believe that? All this time, helping lynxes—what about your other friends? I don't care if you couldn't think about me less, but those lynxes deserve more."

"You're right," Hasefi muttered. "They deserve more. Which is exactly why I'm leaving."

Nakilon said no more when she turned away. She left him behind and, this time, burst into a run, ignoring the pains and aches of her body which had been given little time to recover from the battle.

However, there were still those she couldn't run from. Kilarsa came forth in her mind.

Are you sure this is what you want, Hasefi?

What I want doesn't matter anymore. All I need to do is get as far away from here as possible.

What about Kolahn? Gelinaf asked.

Hasefi came to a stop, wrenching her claws with the suddenness of it to keep from slipping on the slick ground. She wanted to tell her Overlord that she had to leave him, too, for the same reason she left the Tribe. But her heart tugged her in the direction of the River.

He deserves better, too, Hasefi thought faintly. She turned, then began padding back in the direction of the waterfall. *But maybe, at least, I could say goodbye.*

The wolves will not allow you on their territory, Refarmi, Sefonis's knight, warned.

They'll have to kill me, then.

Hasefi pushed her tribe deep into the back of her mind, knowing that, if the wolves did try to kill her, she had no intention of stopping them.

www.ingramcontent.com/pod-product-compliance
Lightning Source LLC
Chambersburg PA
CBHW020605310726
48979CB00008B/1348/J

* 9 7 8 1 7 3 8 9 3 2 4 2 9 *